B R U T E

BRUTE

STORIES OF DARK DESIRE, MASCULINITY AND ROUGH TRADE

EDITED BY

STEVE BERMAN

LETHE PRESS

BRUTE

"Against the Grain" © 2023 by L.A. Fields, is original to this anthology / "Askesis" © 2023
by Lawrie Jackson, is original to this anthology / "The Boy Who Went Forth to Learn What Fear
Was" © 2023 by LC von Hessen, is original to this anthology / "Common Whipping" © 2018
by Naben Ruthnum, first appeared in *Granta Magazine* / "Cosi Fan Tutte" © 2017 by Doug
Weaver, first appeared in *Blunderbuss Magazine* / "Dance, Macabre" © 2021 by Phoenix Alexander,
first appeared in *The Dark* / "Dark, Firm & Dry" © 2022 by Rien Gray, is original to
this anthology / "Desire and the Black Masseur" © 1948 by Tennessee Williams, from *One
Arm* ©1977, 1979 by The University of the South. Reprinted by permission of New Directions
Publishing Corp. / "A Devilment" © 2023 by James Bennet, is original to this anthology /
"Dick Pig" © 2022 by Ian Muneshwar, first appeared in *Nightmare Magazine*, Issue 112 /
"I'll Make a Man of You Yet" © 2023 by Elton Skelter, is original to this anthology /
"In the Mouth" © 2021 by Edward M. Cohen, first appeared in *Angel Rust Magazine*, Issue 3 /
"Last Night at Manscape" © 2021 by Nick Mamatas, first appeared in *Bachelors*, Issue 1 /
"Needle" © 2014 by Peter Dubé, first appeared in *Beginning with the Mirror* (Lethe Press 2014) /
"Rituals" © 2011 by Joel Lane, first appeared in the chapbook *Do Not Pass Go* (Nine Arches Press)
/ "Stormed and Taken in Prague" © 1997 by Steve Berman, an older version first appeared
in *Black Elf's Dark Desires* / "Suitcase Sam" © 2005 by Tom Cardamone, first appeared in
Red Scream Magazine / "Swallow" © 2023 by Robin Robinson, is original to this anthology /
"The Window Inside" © 2019 by Drew Pisarra, first appeared in *Noctua Review XII*

Cover design by Ryan Vance
Interior design by Inkspiral Design

CONTENTS

INTRODUCTION
STEVE BERMAN

"It amused his warped ego to be what the queers called "rough trade."
C. Brossard, *Bold Saboteurs*

What happens when we go looking for trouble? Delights or dismay? Many horror stories and films begin with this premise, as do plenty of hook-ups. When you can't sleep and begin browsing Grindr or Scruff, why not invite the guy without a face pic who has been taunting you to come over? Dancing at the club? The fierce-looking man gesturing with a shake of his head to the back alley door seems promising. How about picking up a hitchhiker late at night on a lonely road?*

The allure of trouble is not only the forbidden fruit at the finale but the pleasure of abandoning good judgment for this win. And one of the more enticing pursuits for us sodomites is rough trade, those men, young and old, who could answer one wrong move on your part with violence.

In 1900, Oscar Wilde used "rough" as slang for the working class in a letter. *Alex [...] saw me with a beautiful boy in grey velvet – half rough, all Hylas.*

"Trade" has been used for sexual escapades since the sixteenth century, as well as for prostitution.

"Dirt" referred to heterosexual men who entice gay and bisexual men and then, before, sometimes after, would beat them. "Clip-queens" were street youth who merely robbed their victims.

In the modern era, "rough trade" referred to men who expected fellatio but would never return the favor. Total tops. As time passed, the slang's meaning changed further: aggressive men, threatening, perhaps some kink that left you messy and with a few bruises. Dangerous.

And now let's add the supernatural, the horror. Urban legends of gay men who walked home from the club and encountered someone, something, just as dangerous. We watch horror films and read ghost stories for that safe brush with death. Whenever the fear becomes too intense, we can look away or put down the book. But often, we don't want to be safe. We read to the last page. We answer the doorbell at 2 am. We submit.

The stories I have chosen for this anthology are scary and sensual, cruising haunted spaces and hitting upon other men whose masculinity is often not just toxic but also intoxicating. Rough trade demands one man dominate another, physically and/or emotionally. And while I applaud those who practice consensual BDSM, making it an exploration of limits and experiences, these stories are not safe.

But then, you could always look away. But I know you won't. Enjoy the brutes.

An admission: I did this numerous times in my 30s and 40s. Only as I grew older, more self-aware of my own mortality, did I realize how foolish it might be to invite into my car and then proposition a stranger. But I am thankful for one night of fogged windows and a terrifying knock on the glass. When I looked up at the rear-view mirror, I realized I had a chin covered with a nervous young man's semen.

RITUALS
JOEL LANE

THE FACTORY WAS UNDER A railway bridge, near the old post office in Digbeth. It had been disused for ten years or more. Beck had got the keys from one of his business contacts and dispatched his team there. It was a wretched night: heavy rain was dissolving the snow and ice of the previous week, leaving a wet grey blanket that reeked of car exhaust. There were four of them—plus Dalton, for whom it was a surprise party. They'd picked him up outside Bar Selona at midnight. He was in the back seat, wedged between Finlay and young Ross. The inside of the car smelt of aftershave and sweat. Finlay could feel their guest's tension increase as the car drove slowly through the Digbeth backstreets, past Victorian urinals and long-abandoned cars, in the weak light of the streetlamps. Nobody spoke.

Under the bridge, Colter parked the blue Metro next to a corrugated-iron wall and they got out. Ross linked arms with Dalton and Finlay walked behind them, glancing down the street as Colter unlocked the rain-blackened door. Something dark ran across the edge of the tunnel. The door swung open, releasing a sour wave of ammonia. Maxwell unzipped his black holdall, took out a small flashlight and shone it into the passage. The walls were spotted with mould, and the plaster had split. Finlay noticed a couple of footprints in the pale dust. No doubt Beck had used this place before.

When they reached the staircase, Dalton froze. Finlay punched him in the back irritably. He wanted to get home. Maxwell said: "If we're going to play silly buggers, we can be here all night. Nobody will hear anything. I'd recommend not." Dalton lowered his head and walked with the others up the metal stairs. Their feet stirred up flakes of rust and echoed from the hallway above them. Finlay wasn't entirely sure what Dalton had done. But what mattered was that he wouldn't do it again. Even through his boots, the building's cold was making his feet numb. But he could feel the solid weight in his jacket pocket—like a pacemaker, it gave his actions a steady rhythm that wouldn't fail.

On the landing they stopped at a double door. Colter pushed; it wasn't locked. They stepped through, and halted. An electric lamp on the floor lit up two men dressed only in leather jackets and boots. One standing with his back to a workbench. The other, a teenager, kneeling in front of him, sucking his cock. On either side of the circle of light were two men with camcorders. Around them were dust-coated machines on benches. Finlay heard the double doors swing shut.

"Fuck!" one of the cameramen said. It probably wasn't a direction. The standing performer opened his eyes and shuddered as if he'd received an electric shock. Finlay realised the intrusion had taken him to the scene's end-point. He reached in his jacket, took out the gun and said: "Get out of here now."

The boy rose to his feet and turned, wiping his mouth. He was dark-haired and very thin; his prick was erect. Embarrassed, Finlay looked to one side. So when the boy ran straight towards them, he was taken off balance and fired without thinking. Even as the shot echoed through the abandoned building, he thought: *He's just heading for the door*. The bullet tore through the boy's side and sprayed the electric lamp with blood. He fell and curled up, twitching.

The men around Finlay turned and rushed out through the doorway. He stared for a moment at the scene, then dropped the gun and ran after them. If there was any sound from the workshop, it didn't reach him. They were back in the street before it occurred to anyone that they still had business to attend to. Colter signalled to Finlay to use the gun. Finlay gestured that his hands were empty. Dalton was running away, through the tunnel to Fazeley Street and the city centre. Nobody went after him.

THREE DAYS LATER, FINLAY WAS drinking in the Black Eagle when some bloke said: "Did you hear about the shooting in Digbeth? Some benders were making a porn film in a derelict factory when a bunch of drug dealers walked in on them. They shot one of the 'actors'. The director was quite upset, but now he's selling the DVD for two hundred quid a copy." The group of drinkers laughed.

"The police made a statement," said another slurred voice. "They're keeping the body for examination, and there'll be another bulletin later." More laughter. Finlay wondered if the topic had been raised to test his reaction. Rumours spread fast.

Beck had refused to speak to him. The third time he'd tried to get through, an unfamiliar voice had warned him that 'Sorry' might not be good enough. He'd hoped to redeem himself by sorting out Dalton, but the problem had been found beaten to death in Walsall. Local boys never ran far enough.

Finlay raised the glass—neat vodka, his fourth or fifth—to his lips and shuddered as the cold spirit went down. The first guy was talking again: "… think they'd want to keep it quiet. But the night before the funeral, all the local queers are holding some kind of vigil in Digbeth High Street."

He was faintly surprised that there would be a funeral. It made him think of Sean, the boy at his secondary school who'd died in the third year. Leukaemia. The roses dropped into the grave, thudding like bullets.

THE BEDROOM WAS COLD. FINLAY had got home drunk and forgotten to put the heating on before crashing out. He was lying on his side, curled up under the duvet. His cock was painfully hard. For the third night in a row, he'd dreamt about the boy. Seen him kneeling on the dusty workshop floor, his lips around the barrel of a gun. Waking up as the gun fired. He glanced at the alarm clock. Half past three. What was wrong with him—was it desire or guilt? Either way, it made no sense.

Rain was scratching at the windows. As a child, he'd believed the outside world was only a city in daylight: after nightfall, it became a forest, impossible to find your way through. He'd found a story called 'Finlay the Hunter' in some book of traditional folk tales in the children's library in Yardley. It was about a hunter who'd been walking through a forest all day without catching anything and was tired and hungry. He knocked at the door of a cottage in the heart of the forest, and a very old woman answered. She invited him to come in but said there was nothing for him to eat. As they sat in the deepening gloom, he heard wolves howling close by. "My sons will be home for dinner soon," she said. He reminded her that she'd said there was no food in the house. "There is now," she said.

As he drifted back into sleep, the boy's pale figure crouched over him. The darkness in his mouth was tearing his face apart. Finlay lay on his back, drawing cold air into his lungs. He wanted to get another drink. He wanted to cry. He wanted to masturbate. All he could do was lie still. "Sorry," he whispered.

PURCHASED FROM THE CORNER SHOP, the *Sunday Mercury* comforted him with robberies and beatings until page six: a half-page story with the headline 'Seeds of a doomed life'. It speculated that the dead boy—named as Lee Winter—had been targeted by a 'gay Mafia' controlling the trade in drugs, rent boys and illegal porn. The director had apparently recruited his team from a backstreet nightclub that had no singers or disco, just dark rooms where no laws or barriers applied. There was a small photo of Lee, probably taken from a bus pass. His face was tilted, his mouth half open. There were streaks of light on his cheekbones. Finlay couldn't shake off the impression that the boy was looking past him, at something over his shoulder.

FINLAY SHIVERED. THE CLUB WAS hardly warmer than the street outside: a concrete floor with a few barrels for seats, a bar where drinks were passed through a chain-link fence. A bowl of foil-wrapped condoms stood on a low table. Set in the wall, a huge TV screen showed two men fucking silently. It looked like a punishment. Finlay bought a glass of vodka, though he'd already had too much to drink. He should have gone home. Couldn't they tell he didn't belong here? There was a risk he might even be recognised, and what would they do then? At least his leather jacket meant he wouldn't stand out. The unlit doorway beside the bar was curtained with black crêpe paper. He stepped through it.

A dark corridor led to another doorway, another passage. He glimpsed single men waiting in alcoves. There were mirrors in the walls, but nothing for them to reflect. A side door led to a flight of stairs, but the next floor was just the same: narrow passages that looped or twisted, leading nowhere. This was the forest. Just as he was losing all sense of direction, he stumbled into a clearing: faint overhead lights revealed a web of black fabric, pillars like tree-trunks. Men were standing in pairs, holding each other. It was like a still image of a dance-hall.

Finlay walked slowly through the artificial foliage. Techno music drowned all other sounds. A hand touched his arm. They exchanged glances, just enough to ensure they were strangers. The hands moved over his jacket, feeling the leather itself rather than the flesh beneath. Finlay dropped to his knees, reached up and cautiously touched the man's crotch. Fingers tightened in his hair. He closed his eyes and felt for the zip. Maybe after this, he'd be able to sleep.

As his mouth closed on the short penis, Finlay remembered the boy rising to his feet. He rocked slowly back and forth, as if praying. Rough fingers stroked his cheek. Then the rhythm broke: the man tensed and shuddered. Finlay's mouth was filled with a chalky fluid. Its scent was in his nostrils. He gagged, leaned back, swallowed. His eyes opened, but he saw only motionless trees and shadows. The man had gone.

It was raining when he left the club. There were no taxis in sight; he'd have to walk to New Street Station. The roadworks at the top of Hurst Street were covered with black tarpaulins. There was hardly anyone about. Veils of rain crumpled between the streetlamps. The unlit woman in the pane of glass above the porn cinema doorway was a shadow. He could see the rain turning to hail, but he was too drunk to feel the difference. Then he slipped and fell, jarring his knees. The wind whipped tiny hailstones into his face. He looked up, and the city's light shattered around him like a stained-glass window.

Confused, he rose to his feet and stumbled onward. The smell of vomit from a doorway made him retch. The pavement was marked with still ripples of hail. A taxi passed, the driver sounding his horn for no apparent reason. Finlay raised his finger at the disappearing vehicle. Coming back to the finite was so painful that at that moment, he could have killed just about anyone. Before he got to the taxi rank, he stooped and picked up a fistful of hailstones from the gutter. They took a while to melt, and left his hand clenched in a miser-like posture.

THEY WERE WAITING IN THE porch. Four young men, none of them known to him. Finlay went with them in the car. There was no point in resisting. Probably they weren't even aware why they were going to do it. They were just beginners, keen to belong, to uphold the rituals.

THE WINDOW INSIDE

DREW PISARRA

LITTLE THINGS HAVE ALWAYS BEEN the death of me. When I was in junior high, I won this Kelly green telescope from the Boy Scouts of America. It was a Model 53B, which—exactly as the catalogue had promised – was a sturdy, semi-collapsible, handheld device with adjustable focus and a carrying case in chocolate nylon that cinched shut with a short, black-cotton drawstring. The telescope itself was about the length of my forearm. Nothing fancy. More like the functional half of a slightly overlong pair of binoculars that had been smashed in two. It looked like a device for snooping, not exploring. I suppose it was the kind of toy I might've enjoyed had I been the type of kid who played at being a pirate. But I wasn't. I hated all forms of dress-up, be it costume parties, Halloween parades, or church. I wanted none of it. I was basically a loner who wanted to blend into the background for as long as I could for as long as I could remember. In short, I had moved outside my comfort zone big time when I hustled those 157 tickets to the Howard County Fair. And I wasn't about to admit defeat either when my third-place prize arrived in the mail with neither a tripod nor any serious powers of magnification. Bigger isn't always better, right?

So what did I do that first night? I pointed my spyglass up to the sky. So what did I discover? Not much. No stars. No comets. No Venus, no sir. No craters on the moon, even. At most, I discerned that the encasing, translucent shell of the corner streetlamp was ridged and dirty, its innards speckled with dead flies. Insert shrug here. In the span of ten minutes max, my world had gained a touch of irritable texture while the heavens above remained woefully out of reach. I guess I'd secretly wished for an experience that was only possible with something akin to the telescopic equipment at the Arecibo Observatory in Puerto Rico. I'd read all about that astronomical hub's sightings of neutron stars and the asteroid 4769 Castalia. I'd tracked down secondhand views online, which were impressive enough to make my newly acquired gadget appear totally useless. I didn't give a damn about the texture of industrial glass or the delicate veins in a thriving leaf. These were things that I could observe with my naked eye. So what's a boy to do? I became a Peeping Tom.

Understand it was summer. Which means it was hot. Which means I was lazy. Which means I stayed indoors. Which isn't that remarkable when you consider that I didn't have any playmates, real or imagined. Which is another way of saying that I really didn't like anyone and couldn't imagine I ever would. I was an only child whose father called him "perplexing" and whose mother dubbed him "artistic" in a way that sounded italicized. You could hear the curve of mockery when she complimented me in front of others. In truth, both of them considered me a lost cause. They had scientific proof to support such a claim.

You see, when I was very young, my mother had become alarmed when I showed little interest in guns, tools, and matchbox cars. My disinterest seemed unnatural to her, so she nagged my father to take me to a shrink. (My mother was a closet Freudian who held on tight to the idea that anatomy was destiny because she didn't want to work outside of some light domestic duties.) By some stroke of luck, the child psychologist my father consulted told him to come in without me for that first and only appointment, at which she instructed him to follow me around for a few months, to shadow me, so to speak, and see if I were happy. "If he's happy," she advised, "leave him alone." Evidently, I passed her test but not theirs. In their minds, my behavior remained abnormal, but without a doctor in their corner, they were at a loss. As a result, they didn't just leave me alone. They abandoned me. Different was too close to weird. A boy who liked dolls and crayons and reading was best to ignore. They'd been hoping for something traditional, someone on whom they could dump their own failed dreams. Since that was apparently not available, they fed me, clothed me then considered their parenting done.

I escaped this pervasive indifference by sneaking away to a crawlspace adjoining the master bedroom upstairs, a storage nook that smelled of fiberglass, dust, and pine. This may sound crazy, but I honestly found comfort in working myself into a state of heat exhaustion inside that unventilated hideaway. I didn't mind the occasional rash. The smell of asbestos made me light and free. In my haze, I eventually discovered that the dim light suffusing this paneled kid cave wasn't caused by cracks in the paneling or phosphorescent insulation. The ambient glow was simply diffused sunlight filtered by a dust-coated Catherine window located just below the eaves. Its position was strangely near the floor since it had been created strictly for the house's façade. As such, the small porthole looked as if it had been fashioned for a family of nocturnal dwarves who'd wisely vacated the premises.

I quickly realized that since the glass was slightly darkened with dirt, no one could see me from the outside, even if I brought my face to the pane. I spit-wiped a spot the size of a quarter semi-clear. The view felt God-like in an omniscient way. Sure, it was only the suburbs but even so, eavesdropping on the neighbors, the mailman, and Jehovah's witnesses was not without its seductive appeal. Perched on a splintery beam atop scratchy man-made clouds of a sort, I looked out on my domain and judged without mercy. Not much happened. People looked like case studies. Cars looked like weapons in wait. One day I saw my dad flirt with bulimic Mrs. Meyers. Another day, an obviously drunk Mr. Sova tripped while walking his Doberman, Duchess, down the steps. It was boring and not boring. But with my telescope, it was also intimate. Somehow life gets more interesting when viewed ten times larger and from a distance.

Eventually, one day, I tapped into the telescope's full potential. It was a Sunday. Morning services were over, but it was hot as hell, so the block was fairly clear. My crawlspace was like a dry sauna. There was only one thing moving: Victor Scathan, a classmate who lived across the street, was mowing his family's lawn with a queer-looking machine. This wasn't a gas-fueled one like ours. This was a strange, man-powered contraption, unlike anything I'd ever seen. It had a stubby wooden handle nailed to a long splintery rod that connected to an iron Y bolted to a shredder on rubber wheels. Where Victor had found this torturous object, I'd no idea. He was a collector of oddities, not so much an inventor as a tinkerer, a quiet kook whose very nature manifested itself in solitary projects involving the repair of broken relics, the restoration of antique junk, and the revival of anachronisms. Normally, I would've rolled my eyes at this latest throwback, but from my hidden vantage point, I felt compelled to stare instead.

The wood looked old. The four thick blades were slightly rusted and thick; the metal curved gently like reluctant DNA. A single, shiny bar in front acted as a kind of guardrail, while an open chute in the back directed all chopped grass off to the side. That is, whenever Victor could get enough muscle behind it. At those times, the blades would accelerate to a mesmerizing whirl that hacked off the top of the lawn like a robot-barber. The machine had none of the ease or accuracy of our gas-powered mower. If it made any noise, I couldn't hear it from my sequestered spot high above. As I zoomed in for a closer look, I spotted the brand inscribed on the main shaft: Folbate Rotary. As I scanned the lens upward, I noticed Victor soaked in sweat. When I held the telescope steadily, I could also see his triceps flex as he tried to power his machine down another row. I could even see his pecs bunch up beneath his T-shirt, so wet by now it had changed from white to gray. I could also see by how he was wiping his hands on his thighs that the wood handle was mean. He needed gloves. Instead, he blistered and bled.

Victor was strange. Stranger than me. Or strange in a different way. He was generally silent, which people interpreted as morose and attributed to his growing up with deaf parents as if there was something inherently wrong with such a setup. I knew all about quiet. Talking wasn't a habit in my house either. I'd actually first registered Victor as someone worth watching after one of my piano lessons with Peggy Orbison, the only music teacher in our neighborhood. Victor always had the time slot right before mine. Not to boast, but he wasn't as good as me when it came to dexterity or memorization. Yet, in his favor, he played with feeling, something I hadn't considered up until that point. I was all finger-work and speed. But as I watched his back arch into and away from the keyboard, it suddenly occurred to me that music was something that could be experienced internally and deeply so. That was a bit of a revelation. The fact that he was studying piano at all struck me as bizarre, given his situation. Perhaps his parents enjoyed the vibrations? Mine certainly didn't. They hated when I practiced at home and encouraged me to stay after school whenever I wanted to drill my Chopin or Debussy. The spinet in the living room was off-limits except when guests were visiting. Otherwise, I was encouraged to use a flat wooden keyboard when the time came for me to practice my scales. They told me that if I had any talent, I should be able to hear the music in my head. That it would make me a better listener. Perhaps it did. I could sort of do it, but I never felt it like Victor. Hearing and feeling aren't the same. He was a true piano player. I was more like a player piano.

I'll never forget his imperfect, impassioned attempt at that schmaltzy "Fur Elise" and how much the hunch of his shoulders entranced me. You could see Beethoven talking to his body, creating a muscle memory of the composition, channeling the notes through his fingertips as they touched the black and white keys as if they were all alive. I'd never done that. My body was a tool, an instrument, a thing to get things done, not a place to get feelings felt. At most, I was a storage space. So what was it about Victor's muscle movements, his vigorous push of the manual mower, that forced me to think of music, to feel a kind of music inside?

The veins on his arm popped out with each effort. Then he'd stop to pull a splinter from his hand and suck on his palm. I know for sure that's what he was doing. I zoomed in on his mouth through my telescope. I watched his tongue dart out without shame. I didn't miss a detail. When he'd pause to squint at the sun in the heat, I'd pull in close on his lashes, which were blonde, not red. He looked much better at those moments because his eyes were set too close.

I liked watching Victor. I liked this gawking in private, this longing unobserved. I liked how the sweat made a line down his back and then spread out like translucent wings. I laughed out loud when I saw how the seat of his pants had grown wet. And yet, I marveled at his perseverance. Our neighborhood was known for its big lawns. The Scathan's was perhaps the biggest of all. Of course, he'd sweat. I was sweating myself. Even so, when he pulled his shirt off, it came as a shock. Because seeing Victor's body made me realize how little I understood my own. Not just as I was right now, hunched like a gnome on an unfinished beam, perspiration periodically blinding my eyes. But my own body as a place of potential. Victor's body had evolved. Not that he looked old. What he looked was ready. What was he ready for? I had no idea.

I wasn't sure if I wanted to be him or touch him. Probably both. I kept watching him to figure it out. What I learned is this. That some men had breasts. That pecs came in shapes. That nipples could resemble buttons and candy and fruit all at the same time. That pale white skin could flush furious shades of pink and then turn gold even when glimpsed through dirty glass. That tan lines were erotic when they burned. That you could have a lot of bright orange hair on your head and your legs but little above your waist except in your armpits. That the drawings in my comic books, the sculptures in the church, the Big Jim, and G.I. Joe dolls were, in fact, based on real life, real people. That superheroes were real. That it all felt wrong or off-limits or out-of-bounds.

I wanted to be him for no reason other than to look in the mirror with pleasure. When he went inside, I went downstairs. I skulked down to the air-conditioned couch where my father was "reading" *Sports Illustrated*'s swimsuit issue. My mother was holding a tube for the vacuum cleaner, although I don't think the machine was in the room. "Good Lord," she said when I walked in. "What did you do, pee on yourself?" I said nothing but looked down at my pants. Midway down my right upper thigh was a round wet spot. I'd cum in my pants. I felt my ears redden with shame. My mother quickly surmised what was up, at least in part. She mock-screamed, then laughed, "Good lord, he's still hard."

What followed was violent and spontaneous.

Afterwards, outside, I found the kind of quiet that comes when your ears are overwhelmed by the sound of your own rushing blood. I felt free in a way that I hadn't thought possible. I had as little concern for the wreckage I'd left behind as I had for the welt I could feel rising on the back of my head. All of this would pass. I hadn't made this mess; I'd struck out at it. Now, I had no destination in mind except away. There was no one in sight. The heat continued unabated. The block was barren. There was no Mrs. Meyers, no Duchess, no Folbate Rotary machine. The lawn across the street looked shorn; our own looked scraggly. No matter. I walked towards the highway that defined my neighborhood's edge and hoped I'd never see either of these homes again. In one hand, I held the lens that had come dislodged from my weapon during the fight. Beneath the glass, I could see warped versions of my fate line and life line, side by side. I flipped the glass over. Everything shrank. I became small. I preferred it that way.

I wondered who would be there at the strip mall. Probably, no one. The place was a row of empties: an abandoned grocery, an out-of-business gift shop, an ATM with no associated bank, and a seedy bar called Tiney's. That was it. At the intersection, I stuck out my thumb. The sun was much lower yet the temperature held. I wasn't upset. I wasn't anything. A car pulled over. In the driver's seat was a man who glanced over at me with a sense of purpose that jarred me. At first, I wondered if he knew who I was, but no, that was highly unlikely. Even so, I got in, and within a block, he'd placed his hand on the back of my neck with a pressure that felt like ownership. I ignored the gesture, choosing instead to wedge the lone chipped lens in front of my left eye like a homemade monocle. The world grew mercifully blurry as we quickly pulled onto the freeway in a direction I didn't know. I felt a sharp bite on my cheek, so I squeezed my eye harder.

I turned to the driver and said, "Look at me!" When he did, he went pale. "You're bleeding," he said, turning his eyes back on the road. "I'm a pirate," I replied. "You're bleeding," he repeated. "No, I'm not," I replied. "I cry red." I wiped a crimson tear from my cheek, then held my finger out in front of his face so he couldn't miss it. "See?"

I kept my finger there until he took his hand off my neck and pulled over. I heard the door unlock. I didn't mind. I was used to rejection. Plus, the exit sign ahead looked unfamiliar, and that was good enough for me.

DARK, FIRM, & DRY

RIEN GRAY

ONE OF THE MOST IMPORTANT ingredients for making leather is piss.

Technically, it's ammonia, but the smell is identical even when poured out of a factory-sealed squeeze bottle. Our—*Definition:* me plus Samuel, my boyfriend by day and Daddy by night—basement in a concrete block ward of Chicago always carries the tang of a gas station bathroom, musk and sulfides coalescing into modern-day alchemy. There's no way to strip hair from hide without it, and everyone wants a smooth canvas for custom biker jackets and boots.

I pull fourteen-hour days when someone wants a complete set of clubwear for their next Hellfire Club hookup, but the money's good. Working with my hands feels good, too—scudding a fresh skin clean with the line of a dull blade; urging the slick pull of fat away in white, clinging threads; prepping the barrel with chromium salts for a nice tan that stops rot in its tracks. I've put on almost twenty pounds of muscle in six months between this job and finally going on testosterone.

The tanning's my favorite part, really. Everyone thinks of leather as black or brown, but when a hide comes out of the barrel. "Wet blue" they call it, before being dried and dyed into something that sells.

Samuel sources our hides from across the city. He's a big proponent of buying and selling local, even if that means driving two hours to some farmer who only slaughters half a dozen cows a year. I respect it; there's true pride in seeing the workline from start to finish, a silent brotherhood of industry passed between union men and blue-collar boys.

Except something's wrong with the hides Sam has been bringing lately. I know most breeds of steer by sight—soft brown Jersey cuts have a completely different weight and feel than the black double-layered coat of a Galloway, with enough curls on its chest to put any bear to shame—but these come in closer to kidskin after curing, soft and warm to the touch.

One of them has been sitting on the worktable for a week. Every time I go to unroll the package, my skin crawls. I've tanned half a dozen others like it, holding bile between my teeth until I can banish them to the barrel, but something keeps warding me off this time.

The whip and grind of steel break my focus as the top-floor service door rolls open; a booming voice carries down the stairs. "Joshua, where did you get to?"

He's home early.

"Down here!" I call back.

Sam descends with the heavy scuff of boots on concrete, surrounded by an aura of motorcycle exhaust and sweat. The latter gives his short salt-and-pepper hair—heavy on the salt—a sheen like good pomade, daring towards silver. I like dragging my nails through the matching streaks in his beard until he grips my wrist hard enough to bruise.

At fifty-two, Sam is precisely twice my age, but he was one of the first men to take a shine to me at the bar back when I was learning how to cruise. I shined him back, dropping to both knees to polish his solid black Chippewas. He enjoyed having a boy who knew leather around, and I enjoyed sucking Sam's cock after making his boots clean enough to reflect the beer taps. After a few hookups, I couldn't chalk up our chemistry to alkyl nitrite—it was real.

Under the half-light of the basement, Sam's shadow doubles in size, stretching the silhouette of his jacket into darkness. "Hope you're not getting into trouble down here, boy."

I welcome his tease with one of my own. "You know me, Daddy."

"Uh-huh." He taps his thigh, expectant. "Come here."

My hands are a mess of oils and dye, but he doesn't care. I close the distance between us and tilt my head to kiss Sam. His lips brush mine just so, making me work for it, the cool bristles under his mouth scraping the field of my five o'clock shadow. A calloused palm cups my ass, pressing hard through the denim to bring our hips together. Sam grunts when his bulge meets a gap between my thighs.

"Where's your dick?"

"Upstairs." Washed clean and on display like a Roman fascinus. "Chemicals down here will fuck with the silicone if it's exposed long enough. Want me to get it?"

Something warm and liquid soaks through my shirt, pressing against my ribs. I flinch, then realize it's coming from Sam's arm. "What is that?"

He pulls back, frowning. "Huh?"

The sleeve of his jacket is black, displacing all color, but the leather is unmistakably wet. I taste iron on the back of my tongue. "Take your jacket off."

Blue eyes narrow, but I hold Sam's gaze until he strips. Blood congeals through a slow drain into the bowl of his elbow, spilling lower down his forearm. Whatever cut him gouged right into the bicep and tore its way out with an uneven edge.

"Jesus Christ." I wouldn't have noticed if not for the stain; ammonia wipes out everything else down here, even this raw animal smell. "Sam, what happened?"

"Nothing." When I scoff, he shrugs. "Nothing that matters."

Samuel always pretends that nothing can hurt him, but I know the truth. So much pain is trapped in that broad chest that the world would split in half if it ever spilled out. All those decades of silence, decades of regret.

"I was helping one of the guys at Forte—" *Definition:* the bar where we met. "—take out a busted window some jackass put a rock through. He tried to pop the pieces out clean and made a whole mess of the glass."

Forte is six blocks away. "And you didn't use the first aid kit they keep under the counter?"

Another shrug, one shoulder this time. "Wanted to clean up at home."

Concern overrides the inescapable truth that Sam is a terrible liar. I take him upstairs to the kitchen, where my first aid kit is, and grab a few rags to mop up the worst of the blood. Once the wound comes to light, I do his stitches by hand, lacing together jagged edges of skin the same way I sew club patches onto beloved vests, so tight and neat the bond is almost invisible.

While I stew in worry, I cut the last stitch and set the scissors inside. "Do you want me to scrub your jacket? It'll crust."

"I'd appreciate it." His calloused finger catches my chin, forcing me to look up from the refuse of the table: weeping red sterile wipes, off-white surgical thread, a bandage's opaque backing. "But after that, how about I take care of you?"

My throat tightens. All I want to do is bury myself in Sam's chest and become half my size, lost in the vault of his body. "You're hurt."

"Doesn't mean I can't give my boy some attention." He smiles, soft and devastating.

I manage a smile back. "Okay."

It takes a teaspoon of meat tenderizer powder—any grocery-store brand will do—mixed with a spoonful of cold water to break up the proteins in drying blood. The paste has to sink in for an hour, so I hang Sam's jacket up, grab my dick from its perch off the counter, and go to where he's waiting in the bedroom.

My father was a butcher. His hands were the size of Sam's, although Dad never put them on me except to ruffle my hair. I was exiled to the cash register while my older brother learned the trade, chopping five hundred pounds of livestock a day into their disparate parts.

One day, he chopped the last joint off his pinky finger. I remember the gore, the shock, the disbelief—as if his cleaver became a living thing that betrayed him—but what I mostly remember is the inside of his finger looked exactly like the pig's feet we had out on display. Pale flesh, smooth bone, utterly disconnected. If you had cleaned up the mess and put them side by side, no one would have been able to tell the difference.

I know what it looks like when a blade breaks the skin. It's different from how glass cuts, a splinter pierces, or the hard crush-twist-tear of teeth.

Sam rolls me over onto my stomach, every movement taut with discipline even as two of his fingers gently work my hole open. I take him with ease, with relief, letting the rhythm blot out everything but the fact that when his body presses inside mine, I regret the nature of my own a little less. He whispers praise as prayer into my ear, and I feel like an altar underneath him, bearing the weight of a sacrificial bull, blood running hot.

Sam holds me when we're done, and the sharp sting of antiseptic pricking my nose is more substantial than our sweat and a day's faded cologne.

I've nearly fallen asleep when I remember he keeps a Ka-Bar knife in the top of the closet, its razor-sharp edge serrated in the very center.

SAM MAKES BREAKFAST, WHICH NEVER happens. Guilt hangs around him like smoke, stinging my eyes as I try to eat. I flinch when he gets close, fork slipping past grease and syrup, screeching against porcelain. Yet Sam is so deep in his own head that he doesn't notice—or is pretending not to.

I checked the closet earlier when he was in the bathroom trimming his beard. The knife wasn't there, but I can't be sure how long it's been gone. He could have sold it weeks ago, but I can't find the will to ask.

"How's your arm?" is what comes out instead.

He flexes it slowly, the velvet sleeve of his robe shimmering over muscle. "Better. You've got a good hand for stitches."

"Your jacket's clean too," I mutter and shove a too-big bite of pancake between my teeth. It sticks like wet cardboard in the back of my throat.

Blue eyes—loyal blue, wet blue—fall on me with inescapable weight. "What's wrong, Joshua?"

I swallow and almost choke. Despite our domestic spread, Sam wears his cop face. He was Chicago police for twenty years, living through the AIDS era on the down-low. I've heard too many stories about him finding the friends he saw at clubs over the weekend beaten bloody in lock-up the day after. Even those who escaped arrest often ended up in the hospital, sick and alone. I'm not sure how he could stand it; if Sam didn't use his pension to pay for the roof over our heads, I'd tell him to burn the money to ash.

But I still hate when he narrows in on me like a suspect, as if I've done anything to deserve that cold, panoptic ire. "What do you think is wrong?"

His shoulders straighten, drawing out the breadth of his chest. "Don't play games with me."

I'm not the one who came home covered in blood.

Maybe Sam got into a fight and came out on the losing side. Maybe he hurt himself on purpose, and pride will never let him admit it. Or perhaps he really was fixing a window, and I've spent so long breathing chemical fumes down in the basement that I'm forming monsters out of shadows, a kid scared of the dark.

There's only one way to find out.

"Where do the hides come from?" I ask.

Sam frowns, putting a deep crease along his jaw. "What do you mean?"

"The leather you've been bringing me isn't like anything I've ever seen before." The accusation sticks in my throat, too, lodged deep like a chunk of gristle and bone. I need space to breathe, for there to be a different answer. "Is it a new supplier? Are the boys up in Wauconda breeding fancy veal these days or something?"

He shrugs, but the movement stops at his shoulders; Sam's face is empty and still as stone. "Same as always."

Bullshit.

I'm up out of my seat before I can stop myself, ignoring the cold rasp of concrete against bare feet as I descend into the basement. The hide I wouldn't touch is still waiting on the table, curling up at the edges, brown and stiff. If I don't treat it soon, the whole thing will decompose.

Pushing past my disgust, I cut the band holding the bundle shut. I'm about to unroll the hide across the table when heavy arms come around me, squeezing tight. My body tenses, expecting pain, but Sam simply holds me, his embrace like an anchor, grounding. Musk and nitrogen clash with his aftershave, heavy with oakmoss and notes of decay. I can't breathe with broad hands pressed against my chest, sinking to the lungs.

I know who Sam is and what he's done. These same hands have held a baton, fired a gun, and twisted in a chokehold. What exactly am I afraid of? Is it that he's hurt people, or that I'm not the exception to the rule?

"It's okay, Josh." His voice is a baritone rumble against my back, vibrating down to the bone. "Breathe with me. In and out."

Panic eats holes at the edge of my vision until I obey, every slow rush of oxygen dulling the gnashing of teeth. The scent of death settles back into its familiar parts; I'm in a room full of skin and flesh, but I always have been. This is the house we stitched together from the detritus of hair and tallow, leather, and barrels of black dye.

Sam lets go of me, and it's like being unbuckled from a straitjacket.

I'm drenched in sweat, shaking but still standing. My hands grip the table, white-knuckled, an inch from the hide that's haunting me.

"I'm good," I lie, forcing my fingers to relax. "Sorry."

"I know I'm not in the house much," Sam says. "I don't spend as much time here as I should, helping you out. I'll do better."

He was never the kind to settle. Sam told me that early on, back when we were hooking up at the bar. Community was an impossible dream when he spent so long wearing the same boots that press down on queer necks, and even after retiring, plenty of guys at Forte gave Sam the side-eye. No arrests for indecent exposure or cruising are on *his* record, despite an equally storied career at bathhouses and leather clubs, cock loaded and ready to blow.

So he drifted, circling Chicago, on instinct to patrol. It wasn't until I brought him back, night after night, that Sam considered sticking around. When he volunteered to get us a place together, away from the suffocating silence of my family, I couldn't say no. He bought everything in this basement, from the studs to the soda ash.

"Thanks," I say as he takes a step back, velvet a soft, terrible temptation against my damp shirt. "I should get working. You mind doing the dishes?"

"Sure." He gets halfway up the stairs, then stops. "Let me know if you need anything, okay?"

I force a smile stretched out past my teeth. "Will do."

The second Sam is gone, I open the hide back up. The smell alone is brutal, but the subtle curves of ink at the very edge confirm my worst fears. There are plenty of reasons to tattoo cows—every purebred up for sale has a permanent ID—but it's always in the ear. Never along the cut and curve of the shoulder, right where a sleeve would begin. Never with blue and orange ink, a faint trail of flame snuffed out by a blade.

Only one species does that.

I shove the hide into my saltwater trough, pushing it down to the very bottom. The brine will cure everything. It did for all of the other hides Sam brought me, no matter how soft or smooth. If I treat this like any other piece of leather, who will know the difference?

Fuck.

THE NEXT NIGHT, SAM BRINGS me another.

This hide isn't clean. Meat and fat cling to the belly, and a net of curly black hair covers every inch of skin, too thin to be a Galloway. Sam isn't clean either; his hands are wet and red, leaving streaks behind as he drops the bundle on the table in front of me. I'm frozen in place as he washes up in the sink, scrubbing slow and methodical as a surgeon. The hilt of the Ka-Bar knife juts out from a sheath on his hip like a challenge, alarmingly clean. He must have done the rest of the work the old-fashioned way.

Blood drips onto the floor in soft little taps in contrast to my heartbeat, which crashes against the inside of my chest. When Sam finishes and dries off his hands, he looks at me, one gray brow raised in expectation.

"You going to take care of that?"

"You—" I gag on the truth. What do I say when he won't let me pretend? "Sam."

"I remember you telling me something your father said once. I liked it a lot." Sam is casual as if we're talking over a beer rather than what's left of a body. "That everyone should know where their dinner comes from. From start to finish, we become another link in the chain. So go on. Find out. Tell me where you stand."

The hide—the *skin*—is unmistakably human. I can't even take comfort in the notion that it might have come from a long-dead corpse; it's too wet and flexible with heat. The flesh along the inside is what butchers call DFD— *definition:* dark, firm, and dry, the state of meat when the animal experiences massive trauma before death, flooding the body with bitter hormones. One last defense mechanism, spoiling the presumed meal to come.

"Who is this?" I ask. "Who were they?"

They, as in plural. At least six—that I know of. Maybe it's only recently that I've started to notice.

"Doctors, mostly. A couple of journalists. One mortician." Sam leans back against the sink, and hooks his thumbs in the belt loops of his jeans, knife close at hand. "Murderers, every last one of them."

I blink. "So this is some fucked-up vigilante thing?"

He frowns. "They had decades to get right, Joshua. Thirty years, I watched them. I had their names from back in the day. Every one of these bastards was responsible for good men dying. The best men I know. Because they were sick with something the world refused to understand. They closed hospital doors. They turned out our dead. They wrote articles laughing about faggots getting their comeuppance. Back then, even the President laughed at us on a public mic."

Despite the bloody proof next to me, I understand the seed of his rage. "So you found them and skinned them alive?"

"*Thirty years*," Sam snaps. "Waiting for penance. Even as society changed, they weren't the least bit sorry. They didn't lose a single bit of sleep. So I took the pound of flesh they owed with interest."

I believe him, but it only feels like half the truth. "If you're so proud of it, why didn't you tell me? You had me doing your dirty work, hiding evidence. Sending pieces of your victims across the whole city as goddamn jackets."

"They're victims of fucking nothing. They're no better than cattle." Sam straightens up, shadow catching on the darkness near the staircase. "This is what men do, Joshua. When someone threatens your way of life, you draw blood."

There it is. Anger sparks in my gut, rising up to meet his fearsome fire. "If that makes you a man, what am I?"

He hesitates, just long enough. "Josh—"

"You made me complicit!" I slam a fist against the table. Blood splashes near my shoes, jostled by the movement. "But I'm not a man to you. Just playing at being a boy. Yes sir, no sir, I'll clean your leather, sir. Fuck you. You're a liar."

Sam takes a step closer to me, and I fight not to flinch. My largest blade, the shearing clever, is in the block just a few inches away. "I didn't want to lie to you. That's why I didn't tell you what I was doing."

"Not about the killing, Sam." I look him in the eyes—cop blue. "The who and the why."

He goes still, looking honestly confused, and that's more damning than anything else.

"You only went after the easy prey. Suits and t-shirts. But it's your police buddies that ruined us more than anything else. Where are they on your list, huh? Were you saving them for last? Are their lives worth more?"

One of his hands closes into a slow fist. "You don't understand. This goes back thousands of years. Since Jupiter fucked Ganymede. The Tyrannicides. Men who know when it's time to raise the blade."

"Dress it up however you like." My eyes narrow. "Are there *cops* on your list?"

Sam's fingers tighten, and his knuckles pop. Silence blankets the basement; even the blood has stopped dripping to listen. Then, very slowly, he shakes his head

"It's a different kind of brotherhood," he insists quietly.

"The brotherhood that still puts trans girls in lockup just for minding their own business on the street. One full of men who tell queer boys alone at the train station they'll get pushed onto the tracks just to watch them fry." Disgust sharpens my words, honing them to a fine point. "Not enough that you're a killer. You had to be a damn hypocrite too."

A sneer bares his teeth. "You've been with me this whole time. Didn't bother you a whit when I put you in new clothes and filled the fridge."

"Because I thought you changed." This is why the other leathermen at Forte weren't forgiving; surrendering the badge isn't redemption. "I thought you might have learned something after two decades wearing jackboots. But you just missed how they felt, didn't you? Went too long without a body to break and decided you were a big damn hero with the right to do it."

Disdain purples Sam's face. Towering over me like a titan, filling the entire room with his hate It's a total transformation, cheeks hollowing when his jaw pulls tight, blood rushing to his head, bruised ego brought to light.

He glances at the cleaver. Fear punches me in the gut, knuckles wedged in against my bladder.

"Sam, don't."

"And what if I do?" Our eyes meet again—his are empty, pits of annihilating flame. "Who would you turn to, except for the police? Who would save you except someone like me?"

Sam lunges—an old bull, seeing red. But I'm thirty years younger and just a breath faster. Fit for purpose, the fine ivory handle molds against my palm. The blade comes down in the middle of his chest. His sternum snaps, bone splitting, thunderous. I've cut through hides thicker than Sam's for years, and without his jacket on, nothing dulls the steel.

Oh, God.

"Sam—" Blood trickles from the gouge, pushed out with every beat of his heart. "Don't move. If I don't take it out, I can call—"

He interrupts me with a laugh, hissing at the end. A collapsing lung, drowning on dry land. "Well, look at that. A man after all."

Fuck, not like this. "Tell me what to do. Please——"

"Nothing." His voice is even, hypnotic and content. He looks happier than I've ever seen him before. "But that's okay. I killed my daddy too when I was about your age."

Shock stills me until Sam starts to sink, gravity taking him to his knees. I fall too, still gripping the cleaver, knuckles like marble. His head jerks then bows in silent surrender. I try to raise him up again, pressing our bodies together, but the steel sinks another brutal inch deeper. The hilt of his Ka-Bar brushes against my stomach, still sheathed.

When I kiss him, blood floods the inside of my mouth. His last heartbeat is a staggered statement of red, shaped like my name. Sam's eyes slowly turn to glass, empty and white, and I ease him down to the floor to rest on his back.

The silence lasts longer this time. An hour, maybe, of me watching his body and expecting him to move, to rise up and tell me this entire night was one cruel joke. The halo of sweat and blood around me dries, crystallizing to salt and rust.

He can't leave me. I won't let him.

Every frozen joint in my body screams as I get to my feet. I let instinct carry me, the clarity of adrenaline, back to the table and exchange the cleaver for my skinning knife. I inherited it after my father died, a fine six-inch curve with a drop-point tip. The wooden handle is ice cold against my sweat-laden palm as I kneel down next to Sam, searching for the center line on his stomach.

My opening cut catches by his belt buckle, a shaky crimson line. The next is cleaner, hand steadied by habit. I strip him the same way I would a royal elk, lengthwise slices curving out along the limbs until a loose length of hide drapes like a burial shroud down from Sam's neck. Ichor spirals slowly down the drain in the floor as I turn him over, drawing the knife up under broad ribs, flaying a cape from his spine.

It comes away in one solid piece, the perfect canvas for a long cure. My scraper whisks away black hairs and their silver siblings, leaving nothing but smooth skin behind. I layer the slick inside with salt, then fold the hide into a warm, familiar bundle. Then it goes into a barrel, sealed shut against the darkness. Tomorrow, I'll give the pelt a cold bath, washing away everything but the weight. There's enough for a jacket, maybe even a pair of gloves.

Leather lasts forever if you treat it right.

I'll wear Sam as a second skin for the rest of my life.

IN THE MOUTH

EDWARD M. COHEN

I

TASSELS SWAY FROM PILLOWS AND chairs are peaked with little gold balls. Plastic potted plants sit under hanging lamps with heavy golden chains. If I did not know better, I'd be convinced my periodontist was gay but he wears that wedding band like a badge. I figured as much anyway; football player's shoulders, trim waist, huge forearms. I know he plays tennis; so deft at the net there is no hint of the savagery in his hands.

I enter the waiting room to find him pressed close to the receptionist behind the desk. I am convinced he is banging her between patients. He calls out a happy hello and I feel my tongue stiffen. He skates to his examining room and I follow for my monthly scraping.

"I don't scrape," Dr. Gilford says. "A gynecologist scrapes."

He ties a blue bib around my neck and tilts me in the chair so I am sprawled before him. Piped music lullabies us and the examination light oozes ultraviolet sun tan rays. The walls are pink and the equipment, even the sink, is blue. Romantic paintings overhang instrument cabinets of teak. The leather on the chair is so soft, it caresses my ass deliciously.

"Open!"

2

I STRETCH MY MOUTH WIDE and he probes with a sharp hook, plunging into my tender gums, measuring the depth of new damage. He grinds across the surface of my teeth with an excruciating noise, loosening the dirt in tiny swipes, spearing rotten food particles, forcing his way into the clogged spaces—pushing, pulling, tearing.

"Jesus! How could you get so stained in a single month? Look at this, it's like a swamp in here. How do you expect me to get this all off?"

He looms over me so that I can stare up his nostrils. I see his bush of dark hairs dotted with wetness, the puffy pink skin filled with veins and the secret black holes leading into his body. When he criticizes me, my eyes fill with tears because I have such a crush on him.

"I see new pockets forming. They're going to get re-infected, just like before. You keep up the coffee and cigarettes, I'll have to cut away more gum."

"Oh, Dr. Gilford, no!"

I have undergone four savage operations in the last three years. He has torn apart my mouth, ripped away tender, infected skin, patched me back together again. Each operation has taken forty minutes with my jaw and eyes wide open, my tongue weighted with cotton to absorb the flow of blood. Through the anesthetic, I have felt the movement of his scissors, the tug of his pliers, the delicate pressure of his needle. He has made me stretch my mouth to the tearing point so he could shove his instruments into the back of my head. I could hear the skin being pulled free, feel the sudden spurt of blood, the angry pulsing of my body in rebellion against this rape.

3

EACH MONTH, I RETURN TO be scraped and, if I dare complain, he threatens me with more surgery. He has me at his command now. I am a rat being put through reflex training. And always, I come back for more.

"You're going to lose every one of these teeth. That's what will happen to you. By the time you're thirty-five. Because you don't take proper care of yourself!"

I have pyorrhea and my gums are decaying, shriveling away from my teeth. Hot tobacco smoke, liquor, caffeine, bits of food have eroded my gums and are gnawing into the bone. I have ground my teeth too often, chewed too much, sucked too hard. I am eating myself up alive. My secrets, my fears, my poisoned saliva have turned my teeth loose and brown. They rattle in my mouth.

"Have you been brushing?"

I nod.

"How many times a day do you brush?"

"Three," I lie.

"And flossing afterwards?"

"Of course."

"Oh yeah?" he attacks. "How do you explain the egg on your teeth from this morning's breakfast?"

All my secrets are exposed. Nobody knows me like he does.

4

WHEN I WAS THIRTEEN YEARS old, I got trench mouth from blowing Carmine Mazzelli on the roof of our building and my gums have never stopped bleeding. The dentist smeared me purple and it disappeared. My mother warned me to keep my mouth shut but I did not listen. He could be found every night, hanging around the drugstore on the corner and every time he motioned me to the roof, I went. Soon enough, the trench mouth returned and the doctor smeared me purple again but, by that time, I was hanging around the corner, waiting for him.

Dr. Gilford's hook has caused bleeding and I can feel the slimy ooze in my mouth, the creeping wetness that circles the roots of my teeth. He shoves cotton between my lip and my gum and I suck quickly on the grainy hide of his finger. He pretends not to notice. I pretend I didn't do it.

Carmine was short and stocky, compact and muscular, dark-haired, ugly, always squinting—perhaps he needed glasses. We were both poor. We lived in the projects. Glasses would have been a luxury to his parents just like, as my mother continually explained, my trench mouth was costing a fortune to mine.

His cock was like the rest of him, short but thick, always hard, red at the tip, ugly and tense. I tried not to look at it, or at him. I kept my eye closed. The sky was beautiful on the roof at night, so different from the ugly streets, from our depressing apartment, from the piss-stained stairwells. Still, every time I saw him on the corner and followed him into the building, up the stairs to the roof, out onto the tar, hot in the summer, icy in winter, under the stars, without a word, I sank to my knees and he pulled it out. I shut my eyes so I missed all the beauty.

5

DR. GILFORD IS DIGGING OUT one ancient curdle after another and, with each discovery, he waves his tool in triumphant disgust.

The quiet on the roof was amazing. From the time we got there till the time he came—absolute silence. Maybe the noise from the street travelled up that far but I never heard it. Never, once, did I hear a fire engine screech while I was blowing Carmine. The world stopped.

In bed afterward, trying to sleep, I heard everything: my mother complaining, my father shouting, the flushing, the snorting, the farting, the whines, people on the streets, music from open windows, police sirens, dogs. My father complained to my mother—probably about me. My mother shushed him. Eventually, they fell asleep but, even then, I heard every sound, running my tongue up and down the inside ridges of my teeth which produced its own grating noise.

I jabbed my tongue into the spaces between teeth, playing that the tongue was locked in and trying to get out. I created suction and drew little pieces of lip into the cracks between the teeth, holding them there till it hurt. Sucking on saliva, I could taste blood from my irritated gums. I tore at myself in tiny bites until my mouth was a burning hellhole and red drool dripped on the pillow. Moaning, clamping a hand over my jaw, I held my mouth open to let the cool air in. In the morning, the sheet was stained. How was I supposed to hide it from my mother?

Dr. G. has a machine that grinds away at the stain in rapid whirls and, as he brings it toward me, it quivers in his hand like the tail of a rattlesnake. I press my elbow into the hardness of his belly and search for the mound where his pubic hair might start. He smells grainy and dark like Carmine did and a knot of desire forms in my groin.

6

THERE ARE SECTIONS OF MY teeth that have been worn so thin that the nerves show blue below the surface and, as he scoots over them with his treacherous toy, it is hard not to yelp from my seat. The noise sends shivers up my spine. I close my eyes but the friction causes smoke and the machine continually squirts cool water and I cannot ignore the stench of burning garbage wafting from my mouth.

"Wanna take a break?' he asks. I am too paralyzed to answer. Despair blankets my vision. By my sob-like gasps for air, I express my gratitude for the reprieve.

"Wash out," he says. Too pained to express desire, I turn my head limply toward his crotch and wish I could gulp mouthwash from his cock.

SWALLOW
ROBIN ROBINSON

THE ASPHALT LICKED MY BARE back and the smell of first rain rose around me. Small black stones pushed into me, still warm from absent sunlight, still wet with rain. A groan escaped me, and even that small movement hurt. The spaces between my ribs were abused, raw.

My eyes stung when opened. Instead of stars, a ceiling of fog (or was it smoke?) caught the dim light of the nighttime and suspended a dull glow of gray above me.

Asphalt. I was on a road. I needed to move. I struggled to adjust my position, burning pain slowing even the light movement of my neck.

I looked down. My chest, wet with rain, was bare and flat. I was dreaming.

When I opened my eyes for the second time, the glowing grey became Ariel's room. A distant blinking charger cast shadows onto the ceiling. Ari was pushed into the crook of my shoulder, small, breathing softly. His head was heavy and hot, his dark hair a rat's nest covering his face. I pressed a kiss into his head, and he groaned, wriggling away from me.

"Sorry," I whispered, and closed my eyes. His eyes cracked open, and he murmured something inaudible. I stroked his hair a moment. It felt good to move— my arm was going numb from his weight.

It was difficult, in the darkness, to stop the looping negative thoughts. Usually, Ari's closeness was a cure enough, but his weight on my chest only pulled my thoughts back to the uncanny physicality of my dream, and that Grecian torso, marble in the low light, that was and wasn't mine. Oftentimes, when I noticed my body, and with it, the few remaining characteristics of my birth sex, there followed a low and constant mental hurt, as if needling radio static played continually, only for me. Tonight it pounded me from the inside out. Stiff, I sighed and stared into the popcorn ceiling above me, fuzzy with shadow.

Ari pulled me into him with an animal touch. His fingers pressed dents into my ribs. He was hard, or half-hard, on my thigh. Toothpaste-mint breath washed over my cheek like the surf. I kissed him, a familiar zap passing through my core when his lips slipped between mine.

I wanted to fuck him. The desire was painful, bigger than the skin containing it. I wanted to fuck him as a man, because I was a man and because he was pliant and masculine next to me. I kissed him hard, pushing until I could feel the imprint of teeth. His hands fell on my collarbones and I rolled on top of him. I pressed my tongue into his mouth.

A hand pushed my head underwater again. I gasped, taking in the water around me. The chlorine burned up my nose and down my throat. I pushed and kicked, I tugged at his fingers, knotted in my hair. The splashing was loud and frantic. The bright white of water and cement drowned me.

I pulled away from the kiss and blinked.

"Mattias?" Ari's voice came from below me.

"I'm sorry," I said, peeling myself away from him. "I don't know where that came from."

I lay next to him, and he swiveled towards me. "What happened?"

"Will Myers tried drowning me in the public pool after his older brother caught us kissing. It was the summer after sixth grade." I said. "I just remembered."

"Why?" In the dark, there was only our low voices.

"I don't know what made me think of it."

"No, why did he try to drown you?"

"Because his brother thought I was a boy."

He kissed me again, this time without any of the violence of lust. He rested his head again on my chest and yawned softly. "Sorry," I whispered again and closed my eyes. I laid still, listening to the distant drone of cars, the sudden creaks of the apartment, and eventually, his muted snores.

The asphalt's small black stones, wet and warm, licked my back like a cat's tongue. There was something very wrong with my ribs. With effort, I pushed my hands onto my chest. Their touch was rough and heavy on the soft flesh of my stomach. These were my hands— these were my stocky fingers and my familiar constellation of callouses, and yet I couldn't recognize the cuts or gnarled, fat knuckles. My biceps protested when I moved my hands above my face, into the light. They were grimed and tacky, smudged with black. My calluses were ripped— dead skin hung off me, craggy and serrated. I pushed those two hand-shaped things together, but the sensation of feeling was faint, distant, perhaps only imagined. I let them fall on my chest.

My hands landed, painfully, on my bare chest. I couldn't help but smile, though my chest ached and my cracked lips burned. My strange and weak fingers could feel so little, but I was certain the naked skin of my chest was flat, or near to it, and my nipples small and hard with cold, aggravated by my sandpaper palms.

Ariel was pressed against me. Gentle, stuttering breath on my neck.

The skin of my lips was torn as my hands were. My scabbed, brittle lips were huge with inflammation and my mouth was dry, a leather tongue tasting iron and salt. My top lip cracked with the motion of my smile. I laughed manically, or I tried to. Instead, the walls of my dry throat caught each other, and I coughed and kept coughing, the movement burning my intracostal muscles, and torching my weak lungs. Deep breaths were difficult, and the air seemed to crackle as it moved against the liquid left in my lungs. I hacked and hacked, but kept smiling. My body, which before was so heavy with pain, was light now, buzzing like a hive.

I turned my head. Two yellow lines of reflective paint ran aside me, stretching off into the dark. I was on a road. The black stone was pitted with potholes and streaking lines of tar.

I laid still for a moment and caught my breath. A warmth on my neck and a weight on my shoulder. Distantly, the slam of a car door. Was I in danger? I needed to move. No, that car wasn't here, it was there, with the breath. I knew, somehow, that there wouldn't be any cars on this road. I resolved to stand anyway, and I started by pushing myself up to sit.

As I sat, a trickle of cold liquid washed down my stomach onto my hips. My side burned. A gouge I hadn't discovered tore along the left side of my bottom-most ribs. It was a pit; the flesh hung, torn open, tender, and leaking something that wasn't blood, but a liquid much colder, smoother, less viscous. Water. I prodded the gap with my damaged fingers, water gently stroking my hand. Surprisingly, there was little pain from the wound itself. The meat of my chest, hanging loosely where there should have been a rib, bobbed with the stream. It was as if someone reached into me and simply took a bone.

I sat up further, and then, with difficulty, rose to my feet. The water gushed now, its flow white with motion, pushing dirt down my body and pressing my leg hair into little curls against my legs. I could walk, though with trouble. The muscles of my left side struggled to work with torn pieces, and my steps sloshed, feet and waterfall thumping wetly against the road.

I could see little through the fog. The road stretched away, with no lamps in sight. There was dusty earth to the sides of the road, and in it, scrubs and bundles of ferns. Above them, oaks knelt over the road. The sharp scent of eucalyptus hummed. Distantly, light hovered in the fog. I began to walk towards it, leaving a damp and dark trail on the street. Once my feet found a sloshing rhythm, I moved in a trance, wet and battered, towards the light.

I could hear the shushing of waves. Warm breath, and in it, a moan. A pungent ocean gust running over my wet, naked body, skin dried by salt. I stopped. The light was close, radiating from off a cliff to my right, turning the gray fog into a dull yellow. I stepped off the road, and into a thick brush of ice plant, stumbling while succulent stems cracked into slime under my soles. The breeze, growing stronger, carried flecks of salt water into my face. I flinched, squinting into the wind. It wasn't long until I'd reached the edge of the cliff.

The water wasn't much below the cliff, maybe only six feet or so. I knew that it was too high, that there should have been a sheer drop. Instead, the sea was at my toes. Splash from the gentle waves carried to my thighs. The water of my wound streamed down my leg, joining the sea.

The ocean was brilliant with light. Little pinpricks of incandescent color wobbled under the swells. Muted yellows in lines and patches bent, distorting.

Santa Cruz was under there, far away, but alive, with streetlights glowing still, and the mustard rectangles of home windows radiating comfortable light. Beside the alternating stoplights and glittering storefronts, long bands of seaweed arched upwards. Thick ropes of leaves, deep green and barely distinguishable, bent in the current. There were rows of them, some tangled, carrying their slimy leaves above the surface. Next to them, the rooftops of large stores crested. The colors of fast food joints shook under the waves, passing behind the bands of plants. Neon liquor shop signs were scribbles of reds and greens and blues. Far away—a Ferris wheel, turning next to the quivering contour of a rollercoaster. The circus lights of unrecognizable rides twisted. Lines of dark kelp carried into the far-away black of the sea.

Where was my house under there? Ari's? All the streets shook under the wake, water spraying white when hitting the blocky rooftops. I touched my wound, still wet and cold. I pushed my ripped hand inwards, against the current, into the vacancy. The world was so distant and distorted, so separate from this body. I felt empty with yearning, or, perhaps, so full of want that there was no room for even air. I looked up, searching for the moon behind the fog, but saw nothing.

There was something in my throat. I coughed, trying to clear it, but my weak muscles clenched. There was a thick stoppage inside me. I tried coughing again and this time tasted coins. I buckled over. The mass inside me was thick and solid. It moved up into the back of my mouth, expanding instead of releasing the pressure. The walls of my throat pulsed again. I forced my battered hand into my mouth, still wet with salt water, and tugged. As I pulled, the stretch of my neck burned, the thing pushing against me, its mucusy flaps tonguing my insides, stinging. My muscles continued to convulse while it came over my lips. Kelp? I kept pulling at the rope of plant, but there was still no relief in my throat.

I could breathe again. I gasped, and his ceiling was above me. The blink of my eyes felt like a creaking door. My breath slowed, and my pounding heart grew faint. A fan buzzed in the corner. The sheets were warm.

My arm was going numb again. I pulled away, gentle as I could manage, and sat up to look at the time. It was past 2:00 am.

"Mhm," He grunted under me. He shifted. I bent over him, and his eyelids flickered open. His big brown doe eyes were underlined with thick tired bands of blue. The whites of his eyes were like sparks in the dark bedroom. I kissed him, pushing my lips into his. His head dipped into the pillow as I pressed. I tugged at his hair and a small, deep moan passed from his mouth to mine. My t-dick stiffened, becoming a searing button of sensation against my boxers. Using his hair, I pulled his head aside. His unshaven cheek pricked my lips as began to kiss down his neck, opening my mouth to mark him, to bite him. I was hungry for a body like his—to have him, to be him, to hold him down and make him moan.

He wrapped his arms around the small of my back, clasping my tee shirt. I gripped his wrists and pushed them into the bed, all of my weight pinning his arms above his head. His breath was short, labored, and intense. I closed the gap between us and rushed my tongue into his mouth. He was tangy with iron and sleep. Little sounds leaked from him.

I worked my way down his chest, short hairs passing over my lips. I held his hands down with my left hand, and ran my other over his bare thigh, over the curves of his pelvis, pushing, groping at the warm flesh between my fingers. For a moment, it felt wrong that I could feel so much, that my hands were intact, calloused as they were. I took a moment to feel how his body bent around my touch. Then, gently at first, I felt for his penis. It was as hard as I knew it would be, thick and hot under his underwear, oozing, slightly, into the fabric. Ariel caught his breath. I pushed my hand against his dick and he writhed. My own genitals pulsed as he twitched under me. I let him go and peeled off his underwear, letting his dick slap against his stomach as it fell out the elastic. I grabbed it and worked him up and down, slowly at first, then quickly, carelessly. He grabbed at my thighs. I watched him, little movements and puffs quickening as he got closer, closer.

My lips formed a ring over the head. I drew my tongue along the ridge of his head and took him in further, the salt of sweat and precum filled me. His veins throbbed against my lips. I glided him to the back of my mouth and pumped methodically with my hands. He was in my throat now, and I couldn't help but moan. He placed his hand on my head, clutching my hair as I moved on top of him.

He twitched, muscles clenching and unclenching as his body was wracked with a jolting shudder. His semen spurted warm in my mouth. Salty and sticky dripped from my hard palate to my tongue. Breath escaped his mouth in a huff. I savored it when he shuddered again, pleasure rolling a wave through his head out his dick. His cum pushed into my mouth in bursts, once, twice, three times, sinking into the slits between my tongue and teeth and running a warm molasses trickle down the root of my tongue into my throat. I gagged.

Ariel didn't pull away, though it should've been over. He clenched, twitching again, and fluid came pouring out of him, frothing, salty and overwhelming, pumping into my cheeks. At first it seemed boiling, then frigid. I coughed, gagging again, while the liquid rushed, burning, down my throat. I reflexively jerked my head back, but his hand was stiff at the base of my neck, holding me in place. He pet my hair with his hand as he forced his cock further. The liquid tore a wildfire up my nasal cavity, as his grunts fell under the rushing flow and panic in my ears. I clawed at his thighs while the pressure inside me built— liquid poured over my mouth from the gap between his stiff dick and my lips. My skin and muscles screamed; my mandible felt as if it would tear from my skull. Frothing salt water poured down my chin and through the cotton of my shirt, hitting his legs in dribbling spats, soaking the bed. Water trickled out my nose, flaming, stinging, and was beginning to pool on his chest.

I choked, my throat and epiglottis protesting the strengthening flow, rioting in spasms inside me. My whole body shook and pulled while water crowded my lungs. I twisted, failing escape. I looked up at him with my watery, blurring eyes. His own eyes were closed, face scrunched in pleasure. His details were lost to me. I gasped for air that wasn't there, swallowing and over-filling with the stinging ocean of his cock. I tore into his naked thighs, though the pressure of his penis in my mouth and his hand on my back my head was still a vise. Soon, even his torso melted into watercolor as I lost the ability to focus. The water was pouring off the bed, splashing onto the carpet, and rising above my feet.

His hand clenched my matted hair and pushed the water further down my throat. My spasming body took him in. The splashing white water surrounded me, disorienting and brilliant. I was a child again, underwater and weak. A boy's silhouette was shimmering, velvet above me. The grip of his hand was the only real thing left in the world. Soon, he would let go, and I would cough up the liquid and its chemicals onto the concrete.

But there wasn't concrete for me to crawl onto, there was no pool, no release. The tide could never relent. I clutched my chest, tearing at the fabric of my shirt, my skin. I didn't have the strength to pull away, so I clawed to open myself up, to relieve the pressure. I fell forward, my face crashing into his pubic hair, water spraying out the thin slit between my mouth and his skin. Black spots overwhelmed the swirls of color in my vision until all that remained was the burning, the wetness, and the musk of sweat and the sea.

There was pain now, deep in my chest. The water tore through my organs, pushing through soft pink tissues and connective flesh. Bone twisted. Skin tore. I would have screamed if I could've. Instead, I convulsed in the dark, barely conscious, water and blood pouring through and out of my torso. Ari was warm below me. The water was surging, covering us both. My body felt light.

STORMED AND TAKEN IN PRAGUE
STEVE BERMAN

WOULD IT HELP TO TELL how haunted this city is? Walk the quiet, lonely streets and listen to soft sighs and sobs and whispers hidden in the sound of a footfall, the drip of rain, the rustle of cloth. Each building wears a patina created from smoke, acid rain, and simply too many years standing.

Most nights, I wander, taking the wrong alleyways from wherever to avoid my lonesome rented flat. I have been in Prague for three months, but doubt I'll ever leave. So many small streets call out and seem to breathe. I can find old bulletholes in walls, marks that threaten to add new carvings to the marble-like the crudest of chisels. Why is everything so haunted here?

Back in the States, I heard so many things about this city. Beer was so cheap that pocket change would last the whole night. Bottles of absinthe waiting to be downed. Clubs that pounded with trembling music and fevered bodies. Crowds of the eager, the young, looking to make their lives mean something, if only for a night. So I left the uncomfortable boredom that had held me so long and traveled across the Atlantic to claim something lurid for myself.

I had the funds to avoid the cramped rooms filled with bedrolls and blankets that other ex-patriots faced. I rented a small penthouse suite fallen on bad times. The building might once have been grand. Or else victim to an artist with no taste. Hard to tell with all the layers of soot and dismay covering the ornamentation along its sides. What most captivated my eye amid that grotesque current state was along the door. A figure reposing against the frame. Streaks of marble for hair. Or merely cracks in the stone. The turn of a thigh eaten away by pollution. I would return home, my mouth and head thick with the taste of vodka, and spend nearly an hour staring at the work. I could never reach past the grime and decay.

I DOUBT THAT THE CZECH scrawl over the club's old doors translated to Stormed and Taken; for all I knew, it could have meant Sweatshop Demands Blood. You don't need to understand any of the locals to survive here. Just have empathy for situations that might occur. It was my fellow ex-patriots that had dubbed the club. I commended their choice based on the decibel level leaking through the old brickwork.

The club's owner was a loathsome, middle-aged Frenchman who barely fit in his outfit of dark silk and metal clasps. Everyone had on their lips his years of suffering through the rigors of art school until he escaped to Eastern Europe, where his spirit could finally go unfettered by demands. Perhaps. A little learning in a Third World country could be stretched to become a recognized genius.

I barely glanced at the catwalks and the iron circular stairways. Hastily constructed frescos along the walls were fine. But trees fashioned from clay and bits of sticks, all set to rise from the scuffed floor and entangle the platforms?

But one did not go to the S&T to appreciate the trappings. What had kept it alive after four months was a raw and basic draw far better than loud music and cheap drink. It would have been raided back in the States, the owners and patrons lynched perhaps.

The Frenchman's one bit of creativity was to adorn the club with rented bodies. The most alluring locals, each a living bas-relief standing naked except for layers of plaster and porcelain masks. One to a niche, each still until you glance away and turn back to find yourself staring at their new pose and accompanying innuendo.

During an evening, a statue would sneak off its stand and waylay a dancer, bringing them back to their hole for the fuck of the evening. Though supposedly random, everyone knew that gratuity to the Frenchman could ensure that a hungry soul never exited the S&T. With flesh always in demand, the club never risked becoming passé.

On my first night, I dedicated myself to pure ego, wanting to be freely chosen as one of the lucky few to appreciate the local art up close.

If my sense of reality was any more skewed by what I drank that evening, Prague was kept inside those doors that night. The floorboards could be glimpsed only as a pause between footwork. The floor pounded with dancing feet, and the walls echoed the music.

Still, I barely glanced at anything other than the prizes in their niches. So much flesh and muscle and curves. All are slightly hidden under the finest of white coatings. I ached to touch and taste one.

Around me, youths dressed like dead poets and leather ghosts danced. The timid ones hung in clumps, looking about, never daring to embrace a serious sin. With every shot of vodka and sight, my eyes grew wet and wider.

The crowd around me began to part; a golem strode the dance floor. One of the statues on the prowl was a tall woman holding a paper-mache tree branch in her left hand. She idly swung the stick before her like a dowsing rod. My heart skipped out of whatever doleful beat the DJ played when I saw she was heading straight for me. I did not mind handling a woman tonight.

But before she could take me, a weasel rushed in to coil around her. One of the Frenchman's latest cronies, some little man from South America with an excessive appetite. I let myself imagine that the statue gave me a brief look of misery and lost joy while leading the weasel back to her niche. Some small comfort in knowing his trendy just-bought clothes would be ruined from the handling.

I kept to myself, bitter the rest of the night.

After drinking too much, I barely managed the walk back to my flat. Every step was a mixture of sway and lean and near-fall, as my hands touched the buildings along the streets, my feet stomping through dark puddles on the road. I realized I had found my way back home. I rested against the wall, my face against the cool stonework. One hand near my cheek, the fingers idly scratching at the loose mortar. Something began to give. Dust and bits of stone fell, and I looked up, shocked at what I had done.

I had torn loose some of the age from the doorway, revealing more of the old design. Something creamy and smooth. Perhaps a shoulder. My fingers dug around it, hoping to uncover more, but my nails only cracked and bled as the rest was too solid to move. Whatever form was in the cocoon would stay another night.

In Prague, the days are for exploring and a bit of drink with lunch. Those who spent the night in excess wander about like hollow shells, occasionally wincing at some unseen slight. Their bloodshot eyes dart about with concern. Battle fatigue, I suppose. I had physically recovered well enough, but my foul mood was still evident by the death of any taste all afternoon. Every bite and swallow was a chore of boredom. Tonight had to be when I sampled one of the statues from the S&T. The thought of waiting another week seemed too much to bear.

I was too eager to begin the night, showing up an hour before the crowd so that I might admire more of the decor. I avoid gawking like a circus mark, instead letting my eye fall on each bit of still flesh with an artisan's approval.

This time I ensured that no little vermin would get in the way. I made an effort to buy the obnoxious cronies of the Frenchman drinks. Only a few drops of the cheapest rat poison in each and every cup, an old trick I learned from my days as a bar-back in New Orleans. Not that they'd be dead, but it's enough to ensure stomach cramps and leave them dry heaving until the early morning hours. I walked away from the bar before the ill effects started.

A smell first alerted me. Almost musty but not unpleasant. I saw the faces of the crowd around me shift to masks of envy as they looked behind me. When I turned, I could only stare.

My eyes were held by the lines of muscle along a firm chest, down arms and legs wrapped in black ribbon and dusted with plaster. The young man had all his body hair shaved except for a long black mane slicked back. He lifted a hand for me to take. I did not hesitate.

The grip was rough and tight, leaving me hard in an instant, basking in the reaction of those around me as I was led off the dance floor and into an alcove no deeper than a yard.

The youth held me tight, my face pressed against his firm chest. Hearing his heartbeat disappointed me, for it betrayed the illusion of being fucked by something inhuman.

The smell of plaster mingled with the scents of sex, of semen and secretions, of sweat and sighs. I breathed it all in as rough hands tore my clothes off me.

My first taste of him was rich. The Frenchman must have made sure the plaster was flavored to not deter the lips and tongue. My hands and face traveled up and down the length of his body, never removing more than a fine layer of the plaster.

And then he took what he wanted. I was pushed up against the wall, cold against my naked front, my ass kneaded by his hands. I felt no breath against my neck though he was so close that my skin itched from where he touched me.

A moment later, I felt something heated and harsh impale me. I would have cried out, but a hand locked over my mouth, cutting off any gasp. A deep pain ran all through me, sending ripples through me. If I wasn't crushed against the stonework on every thrust as he fucked me hard, I would have collapsed. But thankfully, I could not move. Trapped, I let myself indulge in the raw intensity of living and surviving when all around me suffered.

I do not know how long he lasted. I had already sprayed cum all over the wall and myself. When finally released, I would have fallen had he suddenly not caught me in the most gentle of holds, licking the sweat off my cheek.

Wet trails went down my back and thighs. I looked down to see that some were bright red. My rear side must be marked with lines from sweet abrasion.

I weakly attempted to dress, often looking back up towards the object of my desire, who had become still once more. All the blood I had donated to provide lube was staining my shirt and jeans. I was a virgin to the Storm no longer.

The walk back to my flat was spent long remembering the act. I had finally discovered something overwhelming enough to capture my thoughts totally. I gave only a moment's regard to the stone of home. The blocks seemed in bad shape, the steps gave a little under my feet, and crumbs of mortar fell upon me as I opened the front door.

THE DAYS SEEMED FAR TOO long until the weekend, an imagined mental torment. I found myself walking past the slumbering S&T, seeing how its outside facade looked under daylight, wondering if the statues ever went home. . . and if I could walk them there. During this time, I also made a mental note to seek another place to live. The building looked more disheveled than ever, like an old person throwing off worn clothes. The only good that came from the decay was the unearthing of the sculpture framing the door. A figure with arms wrapped around itself, though not enough had crumbled away to reveal sex or design. But the whole lent a sad air of lost art to the place, a moving greeting to me whenever I entered.

I became a regular to the club, if not an all too willing sacrifice to any statue that would take me. They all came in so many stances and builds that saying I enjoyed them all was foolish. My emotions and my hormones reacted to stimuli with frightening speed.

Afterward, I would feel scared at how easily I lent myself to any of them. But the scene was too addicting, so I ignored the nightmares. I disregarded the scars on my body that were a mark of my patronage, my being taken.

On my last night at the S&T, I could barely rise from the floor after being pushed from an alcove. The Frenchman had the hired help gently escort me to a back room so that, with iodine and bandages, I could patch myself together to accept the graciously paid drinks he gave to a favored customer. I headed home, wondering if I'd collapse along the way.

The cool breeze that night rushed my scratched skin and made me feel delirious from the raw intensity. I think I began to cry, but at what, I could not tell. On the steps to my building, I raised a hand to wipe my eyes clear when a familiar touch took hold of my wrist: the rough texture, firm grip, no warmth. Had one of the statues from the S&T followed me home? Perhaps even the one I had been with that night. I stopped the tears and grinned at finally sharing my dim penthouse. But turning, I found the pale gray hand that held me led along a granite arm to the wall, where it met the caryatid. The face, still sexless under cover of ash and grime, turned to me, causing debris to fall at my feet. Then I was released, though I did not pull away; the shock of the sight still held my feet in place as I watched the figure's free hand rise to its head and begin to scrape out and free its features. I stumbled back, moving away from my home.

I spent almost a day curled in an alley nearby the club. I sought to convince myself that a monster did not lurk outside my apartment. Would the craftsman of old Prague adorn their homes with something horrid? What would I see when the stone sheets that wrapped my golem crumbled away? Perhaps something so startling in its beauty that I'd lose all my will and utterly succumb.

And now the end. The haunt is free. I am so weary of standing in the shadows and betraying my inner wants and desires. The doorway to my building has collapsed; the rubble before the entrance has been cleared away for me to come inside. Though my window is dark, I know something awaits me. And yet, I feel only a twinge of fear. Has my sin only been skirting the edge of the storm, never really braving the turbulent winds surrounding the eye? All sorts of thoughts make me stifle a mad laugh. An image intrudes upon my mind: would the lumpy mattress support us if I was taken to bed? And if that mass of stuffing and springs could not survive the embrace, how would I?

I'LL MAKE A MAN OF YOU YET
ELTON SKELTER

I HUM A TUNE IN line with the onomatopoeic singsong of the hand saw as it slices through Ryan's wrist. This isn't the intricate work I'm used to; this is crude and sloppy, and the saw is heavy and cumbersome, making my arm ache in protest as I rend the bone. I only need his hands, the only worthwhile parts of him.

It requires scissors to slice the last ragged scraps of nerve and sinew, and the other hand falls into my lap, as Ryan's arm smacks the bloody plastic sheet beneath him. The sound of traffic rings from beyond the woods, but nothing can take my attention away from the marvel of Ryan's hands, finally mine after all these years.

His touch, the way he stroked me, was like no other.

My own fingers thread his, our hands meeting in a lover's clasp. I smile at his wedding band, gleaming in the moonlight, a simple ring of white gold, probably nine karats. I imagine a twin on my own finger, and I whisper my vows into the night. "I do," I say with glee. "For better or…." I don't finish the sentence. It would be a lie. "Just for better."

His fingertips are still rough and calloused, thick with layers of dry skin, and the back of his hands ribbed with visible veins snaking down to the digits from the back of each beefy fist. As the ulna breaks beneath the bite of the blade, I imagine how those fists will look attached to the arms I keep in my workshop cooler. The thought of the fingers running smooth circles over the crest of Glenn's impressive pectorals, exploring their new home on this strange puzzle I'm creating.

It's all coming together, and the excitement crescendos like an aria. I nod, squeeze the disembodied appendage and place it in the ice box with its partner.

I fire up the flame of the blow torch. There was no way to save the others; my earliest efforts lacked finesse, and once you sever a major artery, there's little to be done to save a man. Of course, when you need parts like a torso... well, it's obvious I'm taking more than what my ex- will give.

A scent reminiscent of pork fills the night air, and my mouth betrays me by watering.

Hopefully, my quick growled words on a burner phone deliver the police. If Ryan died, it would be regrettable. He still has much to give someone else..

PABLO PICASSO SAID THAT "EVERY act of creation is first an act of destruction." The quote had lingered in my head since the first time I read it and had grown its wings, spread them wide, and flown.

I watched as Timothy gathered up his belongings and placed them in boxes. The silence any other time would have been stifling. At that moment, I was just glad the whole thing was ending.

From the start, I knew he wasn't the man for me. I was sitting at my desk, applying a fine sheen of cleanser to the pages of *De Humani Corporis Fabrica Libri Septem* by Andreas Vesalius, a first edition copy worth in excess of one hundred thousand dollars. Overall, the book was in good condition, but a part near the rear had started to come loose from its bindings, and the way it had been stored left the pages brittle and yellow. It was my job to restore it to as close to its former glory as its corrosion would allow and in doing so, maintain as much of its worth as I could. The pages would remain the same after they were cleansed and brightened, and aside from the addition of bookbinding thread, it would be completely original. It wasn't the typical Frankenstein matching job I was accustomed to; this was more like minor surgery on a patient with a grumbling appendix.

The images were delicate and hand-drawn, with detailed descriptions of their names and functions printed in the old-style woodblock pressing format that was standard of the era. I ignored the text in favor of the illustrations. I found myself transfixed by how the human body could be reduced to its individual parts, how there was a way to pull each section of the anatomy away from the other and still understand its workings and purpose. It got me thinking.

There was no single part of Timothy I cherished enough to study in such scientific depths as shown in the drawings on the page. He was just a passing fancy, a warm body to stave off the loneliness that seemed to pervade deeper and deeper into my soul the older I got. But there was never a single piece of Timothy that I would look back on with fond memories. His body was fine, better than my own, but I had seen better on the men I had been with before. I had seen better arms on Rhys and better legs on Alec. I'd held a finer torso in my arms from one lover and looked into deeper eyes in the kinder face of another. As I built a body in my mind, illustrated in the same way as the book I was working on, I realized Timothy would not fit into this puzzle.

So, I let him go, and when the door closed, I felt a pang of relief. He wasn't what I needed. No one was. But I could fashion what I did need from the parts of others.

Destroy, then create.

The daydream took on a life of its own, grew legs to walk, and arms to fight. It smiled, and with the honeyed tongue of a former love, it told me what I had to do.

MICHAEL HAD BEEN WHERE I'D known he'd be, after the due diligence I'd put into stalking these men, to finding where they would be and where they would go. Thanks to sedation, his limp couldn't deny the blade.

I transport the cooler, a plastic coffin, and transport the head to my workshop, placing it in the void of gathered pieces where the head should be. It doesn't make a perfect silhouette of a man, there is too much leg and torso, two sets of shoulders, and Rhys's muscular arms still come with his second-rate hands attached. I have to carve through more and more of this assembly of mediocrity to find the hidden treasure within. But this is my trade, and the thought of the task excites me. It's like taking the surviving parts of the same book and placing them all together to create one perfect volume. This is how art is made, how beauty comes into existence. The creation of something divine from the embers of the past.

I unpack Michael's head from its plastic and lay it in situ, where it eventually will crown this new and improved creation. His tongue lolls from his dead mouth, and it takes me back. Michael or Mike or Mikey (depending on the audience and the time of day) was a honey-tongued devil, and it was that mouth that made me stay. He kissed like he was licking the melting edges of a snow cone, long and luxurious laps that drove you wild wherever his tongue would find itself, inside or out. He could wow an audience into submission with words and lull a man to ecstasy when the lights were low, and there was no one else around, biting in the sheets to stop a scream from the waves of pleasure that would rock your body as he twitched and fiddled that long, smooth tongue of his into the deepest, most private parts of yourself.

The drapes block out the sun from the early morning sky outside in the workshop, and the primary source of light comes from two low free-standing lamps I have transported to highlight the workbench aerially. Gentle yellow light from wall sconces illuminates the walls where I have photographed and printed pages of *De Humani Corporis Fabrica*, tacked them up over old photographs and posters and pinned them to the thick fabric of the blackout drapes. Each page printed has been blown up to show detail, and every piece has been etched in red Sharpie, dotted lines bisecting where each part of man should end to allow adhesion to the next. I don't need to look at them, but they watch down, inspiring and encouraging what will happen next. Every image is etched in my memory, stored away like any other piece of knowledge that makes me the professional I have become.

I brew a pot of hot coffee as if this were any other workday, and ready my kit for the monumental task ahead, ensuring the handle of my awl is wrapped and ready to forge holes where the thread will snake beneath the skin to bring the parts into formation. This part, fixing what was broken, is my calling and I answer it willingly.

I have no idea how all these parts will look together, but separately they form a wonderful road map of my romantic history. I view them all individually through the lens of that old book, now restored to full glory in my workshop, now tacked to my walls as printouts of my dreams. And like the book, whole and complete, the body will soon be one.

HOURS PASS AS I WRESTLE with flesh in the humid workshop, buckets strategically placed around the table gradually filling with gore. Six buckets in all houses the cast off of slabs of fat and muscle from erroneous secondary thighs and biceps, a full pelvis removed from atop Alec's legs, ribs and bones that won't connect. Rhys's hands join his chest muscles in one bucket while strands of gore from around the socket joint of a femur or a humerus.

I use the tools I bought for the harvest to chisel out the forms I need, take kitchen knives and household items to help scrape back to the excess and reveal only the necessities.

As night falls, the final image of this creation of mine emerges from beneath the discard, joints that fit slot together with ease, the best parts of the men I have known all slide and lock into place on the workbench.

Everything afterward is second nature, the way the awl punctures the soft fabric of the skin, boring holes for my bookbinder's thread, the kind used on the oldest and most frail of volumes. I take thick, hooked binding needles and thread them with the familiar strands and let my mind do what I know it needs to, somewhere inside instinctively telling me what I need to offer to give life to this work of art.

As I run the stitch around each portion—careful not to snag the skin, careful not to break or rip the fragile edges of the parts—I focus solely on the memory I had in life with these men, remember with kindness and affection everything that made me love the parts of these men I committed these atrocities to acquire. And with the final stitch of each piece to its neighbor, the memory leaves my head for good and imbues the stitches with their living power. It's not enough to create the life I need, but it lays the foundations.

As I stitch the second hand to the end of the forearm, the memories have been swallowed.

The doorbell rings, and my stomach bottoms out.

There is no man without the central spark, and the man that has held my heart for decades is standing on the threshold of my house.

I feel bile rising in my throat as I take off my coveralls and dump them by the creature, remove the gloves, so my hands aren't thick with remnants of skin and coagulated blood.

I do not wish to answer the door, and I do not wish to see the man on the other side.

Austin has taken a part of me that I will never reclaim. I have spent my entire adult life trying to survive him, and his hold on my heart. Now, in the fading daylight, I open the door, and without looking at him, even a cursory glance, I take my gun and fire a single shot into the center of his head. No words could soften this blow, any second spent with him was just a caustic reminder of the way I felt the day he left me, my one love unreturned. The catharsis I feel is unparalleled, and I regret not doing this sooner.

The shot is still ringing in my ears as I drag him to the workshop, and much as he did to me, I rip his heart from his chest and hold it in my hands, the final piece that will bring the creation to life, the heart of my monster. When I stitch it into the chest of the creation, I do not provide my memory of Austin to seal the addition to the body. I keep that for myself, still too tender after all these years to unfurl from its hidden space at the back of my mind. Instead, I replace it with a new memory, one of the remains of his head as my bullet hit its target.

And then my creation is ready to be animated and brought to life, to live by me, a balm to fix the years of longing that were never met by any of these individual men.

I still don't understand how to make this work, but my instincts are keen, and my will is set.

It takes seven defibrillators and nearly thirty car batteries, all wired up to create a single throbbing current that will awaken the man on the worktop.

And when the time comes, and the electricity is flowing furiously, I lay the paddles on the center of its chest and let the power flow through it. I do this over and over and over.

But nothing happens.

The sun is rising for the last time since I set out to find my perfect man when I finally give in and let the failure wash over me.

I cry until I am sick, until I am bowled over in agony, mourning the loss of all that went into building this creation, everything I stole from the various men I had loved and everything in my head that had formed a comfort for all these years, memories so palpable they were like constant reminders of the possibility of togetherness, of perfect connectedness in a world that had proven cruel and underwhelming in matters of the heart.

It is all gone now, all my memories. I don't remember anything I once did about any of those men, simply that their memory had meant more to me than anything. I cry until my eyes dry out and grow heavy, and I let myself sleep, wrapped in this devastating failure with the void of my history, a ragged hole in my chest.

I'M AWOKEN BY FINGERS SOFTLY twirling fronds of my curls with deft fingers. In my daze, I groan in appreciation before I open my eyes.

I find my eyesight is blurry. As they adjust, a figure emerges in the half-light. My body aches, my limbs feel leaden and bile backs into my throat, but I can't taste anything other than the burn, and it stifles the scream I'm feeling.

My creation stands, is alive.

But nothing about him is recognizable. It was never meant to be a monster, never meant to be anything more than the sum of my love for all the men that had come before. But this creature is grotesque— thick, clumsy baseball stitches holding together blue body parts in varying stages of decay. The smell of rot and embalming fluid leaks off of it as it looks, somewhat vacantly, down at me.

"Wha—?" I try to say, but the words catch in my mouth. The monster continues to turn its fingers in my hair, fingers that were once dexterous, now clumsy.

I try to move away, to lift my arm and brush the hand from toying with my hair, but my limbs betray me. Everything feels like it's made of lead. The monster cocks its head, one pearlescent, rheumy eye dead, the other fixed on my face. I don't recognize the face at all; the memory all shifted to the monster in its creation. He looks hurt, rejected, and—despite his gruesome form, despite the unease I am feeling being in his presence—I gently reach out my hand and lay it on its arm.

The memory of Rhys comes flooding back on contact, the feel of his arms around me, the feel of his embrace. In shock, I pull back, and the memory subsides.

After a beat, I reach out again and lay my hand on its face. And Michael is with me once again, speaking in his golden tones, tasting my mouth, my body, with that devil's tongue. I run my fingers along the stitches of where its head meets its chest and feel the thrum of memory, alive, crackling like static electricity in the places where I have bound the parts together. It all came from my head, and now, it pulses through this monster.

When I let my hand fall away, the memory dissipates to dust. Much of the panic passes. I reason the memories must reside inside this monster, as if they were the spark that brought him to life rather than electricity. And now I know they can be accessed; I can bring them back if I keep this creature close to me.

I can't describe what it is; I feel it as I draw it close to me, lead its lumbering clumsy figure down onto the bed beside me, and press my body against it. But with the contact, I feel the call of nostalgia and want it to fill me, want to take it all back into me. The sacrifice of what I knew before seems less the closer I nestle into the arms of this hulking beast. And I give it a name, like a pet. I summon an apt name for the creation in my mind as I run my fingers over the thick bookbinder's stitch that holds his head in place.

"Gutenberg," I say aloud, realizing that is the first time the word has ever crossed my lips. It feels foreign on my tongue, but it suits the otherness of the creature in my arms.

I press my body against Gutenberg. The touch is not sexual, though I remember Glenn's thick cock and how he would use it to pleasure me. That same cock now hangs limp and bluish between us. To touch it, to handle it again, seems like spitting on the memory. This Gutenberg was never meant to be about sex, but companionship, something to stay by my side, something to be mine. Something I could own, just for myself. A possession that belonged only to me. Unintentionally, I sacrificed my past to create it, and all I wanted was to adore it. Adoration comes to me only when I touch it; its beautiful gruesomeness is tied intrinsically to the memories that made it.

I straddle its hips, pushing through the pain in my limbs as I lay my head flat on its heaving chest. I feel its breath pulse in and out, feel the beat of Austin's heart beneath its breast.

Pressed close to it like this, with its hands cupping my ass, with our skin-to-skin contact, I can remember everything, remember what it was I wanted when I started to build this monster. I am whole when pushed against the thick sturdiness of something that should not be able to exist but does; something created in the slipstream where science meets magic, crafted from my will and all the electricity I could muster in one go.

I lie, and though my body screams in aches and the start of a burning pain, I languish in the feeling of what was, the expectation of what might be.

I'm looking up into the monster's face when I notice the white orb where his eye had died has started to color, begun to grow golden in tone, and reignite in humanity. I see this as my sight falters again.

The pain in my body starts to scream, deep red welts emerging everywhere on my body where I forged stitches in the monster's only hours earlier. The pain grows and intensifies. I try to scream, but where its mouth is now slick with saliva, my tongue has dried, shriveled behind my jaws.

I try to push myself up and away from Gutenberg, but my arms fail and flail uselessly. My legs can't find purchase against the ropy muscles of his stolen thighs. I am swallowed in its embrace, the pain in my body not ceasing but growing with every second we are connected.

It sees my panic, and its borrowed face—Michael's face—folds into a look of concern.

"What's happening?" it asks me in Michael's voice.

I try to push it away, but I am too weak.

The sight in my right eye fades to nothing, my arms lose all strength, and my heart starts to slow, locking my breath somewhere in my chest.

Seeing my distress, Gutenberg pulls itself from beneath me and stands beside the bed.

In an instant, the pain starts to ebb, and I can breathe again, slow short breaths like ragged rasps as my mouth moistens with the first hints of saliva. Through my blind right eye, I start to see again.

As Gutenberg approaches, its arms outstretched as if to comfort me, to hold me once more, I buck away from it, move myself to the far side of the bed and raise an arm to stop it. "No," I shout, as loud as I can, through the dryness of my throat. "Don't come any closer."

The monster stops and looks at me, its right eye fading in color, its arms starting to go limp and rest against its sides again.

My mind races with the realization of what is happening when I am close to my creation.

It feeds from me by mere touch and takes all it needs to make itself whole. The closer it gets, the more I give.

I brought it to life with my past, and it feeds from my body to make it whole.

It was all for nothing, and for the first time since I lost my memories, I am glad they have left. "Get out of here," I yell and watch as its face folds into a look of rejection, tears gathering in the corners of its one good eye. "Leave!" I scream, and Gutenberg turns from me, grabs a sheet from the bed to wrap itself in, and walks to the door, stepping over Austin's corpse and out onto the street.

The further it gets from me, the more complete I feel.

The guilt comes first, a pit in my stomach that refuses to fade. Regret follows on its tail.

When I feel better, I know that it has gone far enough away to sever our connection as much as I need to get moving again. My memories are gone, but my body is regaining some of its function.

I look around the ruins of my workshop, at the cold dead body of my first love on the floor, at the defibrillators and batteries all twined and tied together at the foot of the workbench.

I will clean this mess up, and then I will rest.

And hope that the monster is lost in my memories soon enough.

In pain, aching, and reduced, I set to work as the dull throb of a gift I never meant to give moves slowly down my arms towards my hands.

IT TOOK HOURS TO CLEAN up the mess, the combination of the excess of gore and the pain in my limbs making the task more daunting than anything I had faced before. Even the harvesting of heavy limbs and the hauling of such dead weight was a cakewalk in comparison. The exertion caused my hands to seize and my arms to feel heavier than ever, and I wondered how much of this was due to the power I had unwittingly donated to Gutenberg.

The monster did not return that day, and into the night, I could no longer keep myself distracted. I turned to my work to fill the void created by what had been lost and grabbed some simple jobs from my pile of unfinished restorations. I choose a single restoration that requires little attention, simply a revitalization, minimal washing, some simple tape removal, and some color reapplication to some of the embossing on the cover. It will take an hour to complete, and muscle memory and attention to detail alone should be enough to complete the task.

I set everything out on the worktable, the same table where my greatest creation, my worst mistake, had been fashioned to live. I try to put it out of my mind as I set the book onto acidic-free paper coverings and open the front cover to assess any damage. Where the cover wraps around the book's spine, a large tear runs the length, with the first handful of pages detached and errant. I gently remove the pages from where they sit and set them into a hot water bath to start softening the glue as I take my book-repair knife and slide its rounded edge into the join between the cover and the spine. My hand shakes violently as I sweep; something that once came so naturally now seems so forced.

I flip to the back cover and repeat the process, but as I slide the sharp knife down the length of the book's spine, it snags, a deep crevasse forming in the brittle cardboard, marring a space where before I would not have to had to fix it. The cut is vast and ugly, and behind my eyes I see red.

This process once calmed me to sedation, now seems so daunting, so difficult. My fist tightens around the hilt of the knife, and in rage, I lift it and slam it down, missing the table and the book and embedding it into the meat of my lower arm.

And nothing.

Pressure but no pain. I stare at the blade as blood starts to pool where its shining silver tip has met the ashen hue of my skin, and tears prickle at my dry eyes, not from pain so much as sheer hopelessness.

Withdrawing the knife, the blood flows more freely, and I have to stand to keep the ebb away from the book and its aged pages. My fingers go numb, useless arthritic digits that refuse to comply as I set to clean and wrap the wound. When it is poorly swathed in a white bandage, only the tiniest pinprick of red marring the fabric, I set to remove the work from the table to dry out the moist sheets of paper, still clinging to the waxy stickiness of the glue strips. This will take more than I have to give, so I dry the papers and set them away, out of sunlight, to dry on their own. I pick up my tools, my awl, needle, a micro spatula, and a soft brush and throw them without care into my kit. And finally, I take up the knife. My hand cannot clutch its hilt any longer; there is no force in my grip.

And in that split second, it dawns on me that I have lost more than I ever intended to give. There is a wound in my arm that I cannot feel, and my hands are so useless that I can no longer work on my trade. The rage comes hand in hand with the grief, and I have nothing more to give the day. I sit on the sofa and try to sleep, but my body feels foreign and unwieldy, separate from myself.

I close my eyes and wish for what I have given back, but I know it will not return. Somewhere out there in the city, a monster that should not exist is running on the essence of my very being.

In the half light of my recessed home, I vow. I will take back what is mine.

The vow feels solid, like metal resolve, and it spurs me on. I sleep a deep sleep.

WEEKS PASS, DRIVING AROUND THE city, searching aimlessly for where Gutenberg might be hiding. At times, my body screams in pain, so I know I am getting close, but before a minute is over, the pain subsides, and the trail is cold once more. My rage builds inside like a campfire, every near miss kindling to the flame. I am burning alive with renewed fever with each useless pass of the areas where the pain was most intense, but I cannot find where the creature is living.

One morning, when exhaustion has ravaged my body, I wake in my bed, aroused, the thick swelling of my cock a refrain from the limp flaccidity of my normal state. Something has changed. Though my hands are useless claws, unable to flex or move with ease, I reach down and grab myself, hold the thick swelling in my fist and start to pump.

The orgasm sweeps my body quickly, and I spray myself with an epoch of backed-up semen. My body tenses and relaxes as I stop to assess the images in my mind that brought me there. Clear images of Glenn have flooded my mind; his sexual prowess and the gargantuan build of his perfect burly body returned to me. The change offers hope.

And gradually, more and more of my former self starts to return. First, the tiny trickle of feeling in the fingers of my left hand, then my entire left arm. With them, the blurry memories of Ryan and Rhys find their home, incomplete, shrouded in a new mystery, but the first sign of my becoming something more than what I had been reduced to since I gave myself to the creation of Gutenberg.

When finally, one of my eyes returns to full vision, I know how to end this for good. I regain a part of my memories of Michael, but with it, I regain memories I'd never seen before, sights and visions of the past weeks I could not possibly have been privy to. I see an old shack by the water, looking out over the bay. I remember feeling intense pain when I got near the Bay, and it finally made sense. I see sprawling tables with weapons and plastic sheets. I see needles and thread and blood spattering the flat surfaces. And I see, in the haze of this memory, pieces of the body I had given to Gutenberg, removed and discarded.

A different type of needle threads the skin of a foreign arm, and I feel Michael's longing for drugs. I am disappointed, mostly in myself for not seeing how it would all end back there, fighting tooth and nail for a borrowed high. It was what destroyed Michael, and it was taking Gutenberg down the same way.

With the vision, I can see what it sees.

I know how to find it.

WHEN I OPEN THE DOOR, Gutenberg is slumped down on the floor, a yellowed tube tying off the vein in his new arm, his eyes rolled back in his head. I could feel sorry for him if the rage wasn't so abundant. I gave him the ultimate gift of life, a part of myself I needed to survive, and he squandered it away. In my left hand, returned to full strength, I grip the hilt of the book-repair knife, with its sharp, rounded blade made perfectly for the cutting of ties.

The shack from my memories is dark, and the hollowness of the space amplifies the sound of the rain falling outside. I take a second to look around, in the full view of this house of horrors, the blood-coated benches, and the crude weapons that litter the space. A cold ripple shudders through my body. It is not a shack. It mirrors the room in which it was born, Gutenberg's version of a workshop.

I limp towards the workbench, fighting the bile rising in my throat as the scent of rot and death permeates the air. Discarded, abandoned on the table, one of Ryan's hands severed with no skill or care, joined by Rhys's arm. A single blue eye rolled away from the pair; Michael's vision is discarded and shriveling.

Gutenberg stirs as I limp towards it, opens its mismatched eyes, and looks up at me. I feel weaker than I ever have before, except in the places where my essence has returned. The creature smiles at me. "You found me," it says through the euphoria of its narcotic buzz. The voice is not Michael's. I remember Michael's voice, and whatever is speaking to me is not it.

"You've been busy," I spit accusingly and circle my good arm, clutching its blade at the worksurfaces, highlighting the horror that lays there.

"I needed improvements," a voice tone is bitter, twisted, and cruel, not the seductive lilt of a former love but something dark and twisted. The sound makes my skin crawl.

"Did I not give you enough?" I ask with tears threatening at my one functional eye.

The monster, my Gutenberg with strangers' parts, laughs, a lazy, immovable laugh, and meets my eyes with its mixed gaze. "You were never enough," it shouts with venom. "For any of these men. I have their memories, too, and all they wanted was to get away from you."

My body quivered as these words physically assaulted me.

The monster looks up, flicks his foreign tongue across Michael's lips, and carries on his attack. "Every one of these men hates you for everything you were, for everything they wanted you to be that you failed to be."

My rage is an incandescent inferno that blazes inside me. I kneel before Gutenberg, take its face in my hands, and pull it towards my own. I lean into the monster and press my lips against his. Instinctively he kisses me back, giving him the strength to rouse from the high. As it pushes its tongue into my mouth, wrapped in some smile of pity for me and the words he has spoken, I bite down with what little strength I have.

I grind until the tongue comes loose, let it fall to the floor, and shrivel, no longer a part of it, a part of us. Saliva floods my mouth, and I can speak again; I can taste the raw, coppery flavor of his thick blood.

The monster screams without a sound. Through my hazy vision, I watch his face contort into one of pain and shock. With my thumbs, I close its eyes and drive them deep into its skull, destroying the globes that give it half my vision. I wait for a beat and my sight returns to the other eye, so clear and rendered so completely that I have to stop and rub them clear, careful not to smear the blackened ichor of its punctured eyes on my face. I can see the monster clearly now, strung out on some drug, unable to fight, unable to scream, blind and defenseless. And with this clarity, this high-definition rendering of what I have created, I let lose my rage.

Lost in my own anger, I swing my blade down to the stitches that bind the mismatched hands to his odd arms and rip and tear at them, pulling them through and from the poorly matched limbs. As I do, my power returns to me, as does Ryan in full splendor. I hear his words in my head echoing, mocking me, using his hands to push me away.

I do not let up as Gutenberg flails with pain, and I use my teeth to sever the stitches that hold his arms in place, hook my fingers under them and rip with all my might and let the memory of Rhys come back to me, holding me away in disgust. The rejection stings, but I do not stop.

I reach my hand into his pants and sever the newly acquired cock from the beast, and feel some tingle of some stranger I never knew infuse me. I pull and scrape the sutures that hold Alec's legs in place and rip and tear until I'm reunited with his will to run from me. And it all hurts me and I can't seem to stop or seem to care. I am becoming whole again; I am regaining memory, but with it, I am regaining more; the other side of the coin, the things I worried I would hear but never did now, all yelling at me as I consume what is left of the men I once loved.

Gutenberg is nothing now. But I don't stop. I take my knife up and cut away the stitches holding his head onto his neck and let it fall and roll across the floor, immobile, dead for all intents and purposes. I watch it as it stills, and somehow, despite its empty eye sockets, despite not having a body to belong to, the head blinks its destroyed eyelids, and the empty mouth with its missing tongue groans.

Finally, as the torso slides down to the floor, I open up the stitches in its chest and remove its heart, and with the newfound strength in my powerful hands, I crush it, and the severed head on the floor ceases to make its noise.

I am covered in gore and blood, black rot dripping from my hands, my face, my mouth.

"Nothing wrong with being fucking crazy," a menacing voice whispers.

The sound startles me, and I turn around and around, but find I am alone.

But not alone.

"Don't be pathetic," it spits.

I realize this stranger's voice now rings in my head.

I scream and let the sound ricochet throughout the building, let it mingle with the sound of the rain outside before I climb to my feet and run out into the night, into the driving rain that I let cover and wash me, let it take the blood from my body and hands, let it absolve me.

"Now you've got what you always wanted." The voice taunts a thought he should not have been able to hear. "An end to the constant loneliness, the comfort of a man inside you, always."

I speak to the sound of the driving rain. "I didn't want this. I take it back."

New memories flood my synapses, forming in my mind as movie stills come to life. The man whose arm I severed was named Morgan, and he was a murderer and a thief. The eye came from a woman named Isabelle and the new hand from a mechanic named Avery. I know this all intrinsically. They were all bad people, the worst that mankind could offer.

Gutenberg hadn't been improving on what I had given it. It'd been replacing faulty parts with ones from people who chased death and inflicted pain. It sought to make itself into a monster.

"We will tell you are stories, we will seduce you with our thrills."

And the tongue, which had no name at all, and now only thinks of itself as Gutenberg, whispers all the terrible things it did in life. I am horrified at the stories told with gusto. My begging my screams to drown out the whispers do little good. And only then do I realize that this new Gutenberg's voice sounds frighteningly similar to my own.

DICK PIG
IAN MUNESHWAR

Ass o'clock in the morning and it's black out. *Black* black, the kind of black you only get in these miserable, middle-of-nowhere places. No, "middle-of-nowhere" is too generous; this is past that, right at the line where nowhere becomes miles of uncharted forest thick with months of snow and screaming with wolves and whatever other ungodly feral things make noise when everything decent in the world is asleep.

It's one of those animals that drags me awake, yowling from the forest's edge, shrieking at me like I owe it money or stepped on its child. I lurch out of bed but when my feet hit the floorboards there's no howling, no sound, nothing. Like it was never even there. Fuck this wolf. Fuck this whole entire place. The floor is freezing, just one long ice rink from here to the carpet in the hall. The house doesn't have central heating—of course, it doesn't—there's only a woodstove in the living room, and fuck if I know how to use a woodstove. I got it working with the logs I found out back but it choked and died twenty minutes later and by then I'd already cocooned myself in these quilts that still reek of mothballs.

As you may have surmised, I don't own this house. Strictly speaking, no one does. It belonged to my Aunt Norma, bless her, before she fell and broke her hip and the handyman found her weeks later, quite dead in her floral-print nightgown, frozen to the upstairs hallway. The hallway right outside this door.

I try not to think about that.

I pull my feet off the floor and tuck them back under Norma's smelly quilts. My phone's beside my pillow, half-charged, and there's a push notification on the otherwise darkened screen. I begin to swipe it away, but it's a Grindr message from someone called hungdaddy.

Well. It might be cold, and I might be tired, but who am I to reject the advances of a hung daddy? I tap on his faceless profile.

>*hey dick pig*

He's called me by my profile name. How personal. How touching.

As soon as I've read the greeting, a picture appears in the chat. It's a grainy, colorless photo of a naked man seated on a stool. His head is cropped out of the frame, but the rest of his mountainous body is visible, from the hairy shoulders down to his muscled legs, spread open. His cock hangs over the edge of the stool, halfway hard, lolling to one side with its own weight.

One of the man's hands rests on his thick, furred thigh. The other is raised and extends out of the picture, reaching for something just out of view. I double tap on the image, zoom in. The resolution is godawful—this pic could only have been taken on a flip phone—but even through the pixilation, the intensity of his grip is obvious. His muscles are knotted and his skin pulls so tight that the hollow of his elbow has become a deep, blurry pit. I don't know what's in that hand but, whatever it is, it's being crushed. Punished.

I am, predictably, quite hard now.

Hey, I type, one-handed, *what's up*.

>*I am always awake*

The reply appears immediately but I don't question the speed. I've slid back into bed and unbuttoned the jeans I went to sleep in.

Yeaj? I write, not really caring about spelling because, at this stage, we both know where this conversation is going. *What's got you up daddy*

Another image appears in the chat, instantly. It's actually not a different picture at all, I realize, but the same one taken from a different angle. This time, it's as if the photographer is sprawled on their back, lying between the man's feet. Most of his body is out of focus—his cock and balls are a blur, the coarse hair curling across his stomach reduced to shadow—but I don't really care because I'm halfway to coming and already feel the need for sleep eclipsing my horniness.

Fuuuuuck, I type, moving this interaction right along, *plz destry me with that dick*

There is, for the first time in the conversation, a pause. And then:

>*You crave destruction?*

I scroll back up to the first pic. I sure do.
Yessir. Wreck my hole.

>*You want to be destroyed. Wrecked. Annihilated.*

I stop jacking myself but keep my hand on my dick. hungdaddy's dirty talk needs some work, but I'll give him a pass. Twenty more seconds of this Dom Daddy shtick and I'll be cleaning myself up, ghosting him, and getting to sleep. The natural order of the gay universe.

Yeah, I type. I want you to pin me down and make me beg.

hungdaddy's last message comes through in one giant text block, like he's composed the whole thing already and has been waiting to send it:

>*I will destroy you. I will destroy every part of you. I will destroy until there is nothing left in you but your desire for nothingness and I will destroy even that. I will destroy you. I will destroy*

And it just fucking ends like that, mid-sentence. Jesus.

I back out of the chat and return to hungdaddy's profile. Before I block him, I take a screenshot of the profile image:

hungdaddy
online now
15 miles away

When I block him, his image disappears from the grid of nearby profiles. I shut off my phone.

That's quite enough Grindr for tonight, thanks.

The exposed skin between my thighs has gone clammy and I'm aware of how cold I am, how cold this whole damned house is at night. I pull my pants back up, tuck my erection away.

For a moment, the house is dead and it's just me and the sound of my own post-masturbatory breathing. I tell myself to ignore the phone screen right beside my pillow, to just close my eyes. There's so much left to do tomorrow, and I need to clear out of here before the realtor arrives in the afternoon. I need to sleep.

But then the howling starts up again. This time, it's not just one wolf but a pack of them seething through the forest, shrieking at the cold.

A goddamned symphony the whole night long.

In the morning I find myself at the kitchen table, drinking a finger of Scotch out of a coffee mug, staring absentmindedly at The Crack.

The Crack was the sole topic of Norma's correspondence with the rest of the family through the last years of her life. It's a jagged line that runs the height of the wall separating the kitchen from the dining room. It's so thin it looks like it's been drawn on with a pencil.

The Crack started worming its way into Norma's calls maybe three years ago; she would make the occasional reference to the house falling down around her, but then play this off as tongue-in-cheek melodrama. As her calls grew more frequent, though, the levity left her voice.

"You must do something about it," she would warble into the landline. "It hasn't stopped growing. Good Lord in Heaven, just look at it. It's like the Panama Canal. You wouldn't know this, since you never visit, but this wall—" she'd suck in her breath here, pause for effect—" is a *load-bearing wall*."

The monthly guilt trips became intolerable, so I paid a handyman in her vicinity to trek out to the house and assess the situation. He confirmed that there was no issue, that The Dreaded Crack was little more than the house shifting and resettling after an especially brutal winter.

That's when I started letting Norma's calls go to voicemail.

I know, I know—I'm making her sound petulant and demanding. It's unfair of me. We can't judge the dead only by the final, paranoid moments of their life. In truth, there were many things I admired about my aunt. She was a vintage eccentric. She spoke in an accent shared by no one else in my family, a half-baked homage to Katharine Hepburn that lapsed back toward her Gravesend roots more often than she probably realized. She was also the first adult in my family I came out to and goddamn if I don't remember the look that ignited in her eye as she pulled me close and said: "I always suspected that you were *so*, my dear. Let me tell you about cousin Alexander. He was the same way as you, and you wouldn't believe where he took me that summer we visited Berlin—"

Unfortunately, I was the only one who knew this side of my aunt. The rest of my family thought that Norma, in her dotage, was losing touch with reality. They made her perform the necessary rituals: go see this doctor, Auntie; go get these tests done; then go talk to this lawyer and you know, while you're at it, why don't you draw up a will?

That was what they really cared about—making sure her fortune made it into the right hands when she died. Their hands. Because that's my family for you. Vultures, the lot of them. Hungry fucking vultures bearing down on the old woman before she'd passed, trying to suffocate her with the weight of their lousy vulture bodies.

My family couldn't understand that Norma was never in touch with reality. She'd been fleeing it for decades, first by entombing herself in this remote Colonial, and then by filling it with curiosities and hidden secrets, building a labyrinth in which reality, that persistent bastard, could never find her.

It's morning but somehow still only half-light outside. As I hunch over the dining room table, considering my Scotch, my breath leaves my mouth in steamy wisps. They taunt me. I found a fur-collared coat and an old Cossack hat in Norma's bedroom, but no amount of animal fur seems to keep the chill away.

Norma used to say that when you're this far north winter tilts the land away from the sun and toward an in-between place. She told me this when I was very young, and I still remember the way she angled her teacup as she described the tilting world, how the brown liquid spilled from the brim and pooled in the saucer. I asked her what we were in between, and how we could get back, but she only brought the saucer to her lips, sucked it dry, and then ran her tongue around the bottom of the cup.

I was a little older when I realized she probably wasn't drinking tea.

I uncork the Lagavulin and splash a sensible pour into my emptied mug. Here's to you, Auntie Norma. Here's to your fully-stocked cabinet of mediocre whiskey. Here's to the secret you buried in this house.

My phone buzzes in my pocket, just once. I don't remember having turned it on after the Grindr conversation, but I must have at some point in the night. The cold kept me from really falling asleep; I was up in fits and starts, bleary and pissed-off.

There's a single notification on the screen. My mouth sours when I see the sender's name.

I open hungdaddy's latest message. He must have created a new account to find me again. This happens, sometimes, with guys who can't take a hint. It's annoying, but fixable: if you block and ignore them enough times they do, eventually, disappear.

>*where did you go*

What a fucking creep. I swipe back to hungdaddy's profile and am reaching my thumb toward the almighty block button when I notice that the profile has changed. The name and picture are the same, but his distance no longer reads fifteen miles. It's now one mile.

Aunt Norma doesn't have neighbors. In fact, I was a little surprised that there was someone on Grindr who was *only* fifteen miles away. The nearest city—and I use the word "city" quite loosely here—is a snowbound hamlet with a train station and a Kinko's some sixty miles south. Fifteen miles would put hungdaddy squarely in the middle of no-man's-land. One mile puts him within walking distance.

I click on the chat bubble out of habit, before I've considered whether or not I should. I move my thumb to close the app, but then I see what he's written. I stare at the screen long enough that it goes dark.

>*i can tell you where to look*

My eyes keep sliding over those words, again, again, again. And then it hits me like an ice cube sucked down my windpipe. I am being catfished. The only way hungdaddy could know that I am looking for something is if he knows there is something worth looking for. And the only way he could know *that* is if he was privy to Norma's will.

The opening of Norma's will was the closest my family has ever come to holding a reunion. The extended viper's nest of Caldwells shuffled into that lawyer's office, all of them dour and pale in their funereal getups, looking like characters in an Edward Gorey sketch. When the lawyer announced that Norma had left her entire estate to a nearby private school, most of them left in an entitled rage. But I stayed for the whole reading, for the line at the very end when Norma addressed me directly:

> *"To Edwin: I cherish all those childhood summers you spent in my house, all those marvelous secrets that passed between us. How I wish there was still one more to share. I would have left you the house but, alas, it is falling into ruin and would only have been a burden in its old age."*

To those unfamiliar with Norma, that might just seem like a slightly passive aggressive parting message. But I knew her too well not to see the references buried in those words. Norma worked in riddles; in her mind, it was almost gauche to say exactly what she meant. One line played itself over and over for me: "How I wish there was still one more to share." Between this and the references to the house, one thing became clear to me that afternoon: Norma left something in this house for me to find. Knowing her, it would be something so valued it couldn't be discussed openly.

Unfortunately, I wasn't the only one who stayed for the end of the reading. My siblings are relentless and hungry, and it seems one of them wants what Norma left me. This plan—trying to spook me out of the house using a hookup app—it's original, I'll give them that. It's probably my youngest brother, Barty. He's a twisted little shit. Or no—maybe it's Violet. Fucking Violet. She's the only one who would know my taste in men.

This realization is, in its own way, a comfort. hungdaddy now has a face, and it is the face of one of my ne'er-do-well relatives skulking in the forest, sending grainy dick pics and cryptic sexual advances. This is something I can deal with. I am, after all, well-practiced at enraging my family.

I throw back the dregs of the Lagavulin, set my cup down, and get up from the table. Norma's house key is with the realtor. But the spare key—the one she hid in the hollow of that dead oak out back—that one is safely in my pocket.

I inventory the downstairs, checking the locks on the windows and trying all the doorknobs. Most of the windows, blessedly, were painted shut years ago, but this house has so many goddamned doors—the front door, and the back porch's screen door; the basement door and the hatch on the root cellar; the small, warped door in the pantry that opens into the woodshed; and, finally, the door in the library's outside-facing wall that never opens. Since I spent yesterday creeping through every crawlspace, turning out every dresser, and peering under all of the carpets, I make an efficient survey of the house. The doors are locked up tight.

Breathless from all of this jogging, I settle into the library's ratty loveseat and take out my phone. hungdaddy—it feels perverse to refer to a family member this way, but they brought this on themselves—has not sent any additional messages. I type out a response, delete it, and start again:

You gonna tell me where to look? or would you rather come and show me. I know you're not used to the cold.

>you must open the door under the stairs

He's as prompt as ever. The house doesn't have all that many staircases—there are stairs in the front hall, leading to the second floor; there're the ones going to the cellar; and, if we're being pedantic about things, I suppose there's also the attic's pull-down ladder. In the past twenty-four hours, I have been up and down these staircases so many times I have the squeal of each tread memorized.

The staircases don't have doors, I reply.

At this point, the whole cat-and-mouse charade is starting to feel pretty fucking ridiculous. Whichever one of my grifting relatives is behind hungdaddy, they are cold and miserable outside, making themselves suffer just to frighten me. The whole thing is petty and obnoxious and—you know what? They should know better if they think I'm going to let them in when they decide to give up the ruse. They should know that no one in the family, not even Violet, is pettier than I am.

I'm drafting another pithy response when a third picture comes through. This was taken with the same camera as hungdaddy's others—it's all staticky, washed-out sepia—but it's not an image of a person. It's the inside of the house. The photographer took this standing in the front hall that extends into the dining room. The stairs to the second floor run up one of the walls in the entryway, and the photographer has focused on that bare, triangular piece of the wall underneath the stairs.

So, hungdaddy has been here before. This isn't surprising; most of Norma's relatives came here after the funeral for an afternoon of backbiting and store-bought crudité. There would have been ample time to take pictures. In fact, I'd be surprised if Barty hadn't slunk around, making an inventory of Auntie's valuables while the rest of us nibbled our baby carrots.

No, the surprise in this photo is that there *is* a door under the stairs. It's difficult to make out, at first. The wall is decorated with rectangular moldings, and the doorframe has been camouflaged to look like one of them. It's painted the same hideous taupe as every other wall in this house, and it doesn't seem to have a knob, but it's there alright. Clear as day. How could I have missed this?

As I haul myself up from the couch and debate how to shimmy this door open, one more detail in the photo catches me. I wouldn't have noticed it at all if I hadn't zoomed in a bit, and even now I'm not entirely sure what I'm looking at. The picture is taken at a slight angle, so it captures not only the wall but also the length of the narrow front hallway. A corner of the dining room is visible at the very end of the hall, and most of this corner is taken up by the lower half of Norma's farmhouse table. There's an object sitting at the edge of the table—a pixelated, shadowy thing.

I bring the phone's screen closer and closer to my face. It's just about touching my nose when I realize that I'm looking at the coffee cup sitting right where I left it twenty minutes ago.

I CLOSE GRINDR AND STAND very still. My heart's bolting against my chest like a hunted rabbit and all I can think is that if I stand very still whoever is in this house won't hear me, won't know where I am. This thought is so stupid it hurts—I have, after all, spent the morning slamming every door I could find—but I can't even think about moving right now. The clock ticking on the mantle across the room is so fucking loud. I want to tell it to shut up, to just shut up for one minute because it's covering the creaking sounds of the intruder crawling across the floorboards, the shuddering of the camera lens as it captures things I can't see until they're shown to me.

I allow myself a breath. It's unbearably loud, sucking all that air in, but I need to think this through. When I was a child, I used to keep a jewelry collection. Specifically, a collection of my mother's jewelry. I would sneak into her room while she napped and pilfer one earring from her nightstand. She would think she'd lost an earring, so she'd toss its now-worthless mate. After rifling through the trash, I would end up with both earrings and my mother was none the wiser. It was a perfect system, right up until Barty and Violet found my stash. My beloved siblings didn't go to our mother with the evidence of my crimes; that wouldn't have been cruel enough. Instead, over the course of the next four years, they slowly re-gifted all of the earrings back to my mother. Every Christmas, every birthday, every Mother's Day, I watched as my months of meticulously-planned larceny were slowly undone, and my siblings were praised for their discerning taste.

Our dear mother—so wealthy, so oblivious—never caught the grift.

I've had enough of Barty and Violet. We are not children anymore, and I won't play their goddamned games. I pull the Cossack hat tight around my ears and take a step forward. The squeak of my boot is a small rebellion.

First things first: I delete Grindr. After thirty-six hours my phone's battery is nearly gone, and it's not like I'm going to get any useful information out of hungdaddy.

I stride back through the dining room—telling myself with every boot-squeak that I'm in control here, that I'm *choosing* to let them know I'm not afraid—and I come to the front hall. This room connects all three floors and so, when I speak, I know that whoever is inside can hear me:

"I think we both know what's going on here," I call, hating how my voice cracks halfway through the sentence. "So come on out, and we can talk about this like adults."

Now, of course, the house goes entirely quiet. I can't even hear the clock in the living room anymore, and this makes me wonder about all of the other hidden noises I'm missing. Maybe hungdaddy is pacing the length of the attic, but it's too far away for me to hear the weight of his footfalls. Maybe he's hiding behind the brocade curtains in the drawing room, giggling to himself as he drafts another message. Or maybe he's—

My gaze snaps over to that horrible, taupe door under the stairs. There it is, as advertised. Even before I've stepped across the room, I see where the door's hinges disrupt the clean lines of the moldings; I see how the grain of the wood breaks from the wall's smooth plaster.

"What are you gonna do when I open this?"

I run my finger across the door's face, over the place where a handle should be. I don't know it for a fact until I say it out loud, but there it is, for everyone to know—I *am* going to open this door.

"You gonna lock me in and steal Norma's shit for yourself? What's the plan, friend? What do you want with me?"

A wind swells outside, kicking up pinpricks of ice that rasp against the windows. The house settles back to silence.

Now that I know I want to open this door, there's no turning back. The question is: how do I open it without playing into hungdaddy's chicanery?

Last night, when I went to the woodshed for kindling, I saw a mallet on the workbench out there. I jog through the pantry, brace myself against the bite of winter that greets me in the uninsulated shed, and carry that mallet back inside. Its wooden shaft is so fucking cold in my hands, but it's a good kind of cold—a frigid, heavy reminder that I am in control of what I do next.

I smack the butt of the mallet against the upper right-hand corner and the door judders in its frame. It opens more easily than it should, coming just far enough out from the wall that I can press my numb fingertips against its width and prize it open. The hinges squeal with disuse and I hate them for it. All of that unnecessary sound.

The space beneath the stairs is a closet. I almost laugh at the sheer mundanity of it—the line of hats and coats hanging from hooks; a collection of furs draped across the back wall, including a mink stole with little weasely feet and black marbles for eyes.

I turn my phone's flashlight into the dusty interior before I step over the threshold. It's a tiny closet, barely enough room to stand up in. I rifle through Aunt Norma's old coats, slipping my hands into their pockets. Everything smells, powerfully, of mothballs.

I don't know what hungdaddy expected I would find in here, but it's all pretty disappointing as far as secret rooms go. The coats are threadbare, their pockets empty; even the mink stole is too washed-out and mangy to be worth anything.

The phone vibrates in my hand and the movement is so unwelcome that it goes clattering to the ground. Even though it's frigid in here, my palms are sweaty. As I bend down and grope for my traitorous phone, bits of grainy refuse stick to my hands. I'm still crouched in the darkness when the screen lights up, right in front of me, and I see the push notification. My chest tightens.

I know—I *know*—I deleted that app not half an hour ago.

"This isn't funny anymore," I say through the open door to the empty hall. I consider, for a moment, tacking "Barty" or "Violet" onto the end of that sentence. I don't, though, because neither of them is in this house with me. I would feel a lot better if they were.

I open the app that shouldn't be there.

>*Above you*

It occurs to me, as I sit on the mouldering floorboards and stare out into the hall, that I don't have to look up. I can get up, right now, and walk out the front door. My car is still out there. The battery probably died during the night, but that's not what's keeping me here. I can walk if I have to. I've hitchhiked before. The only reasonable thing to do is to get off of this property and go south, back to a place where I understand how the world works.

But I don't. Here's the thing I haven't told you, but maybe you've known it all along: there's a want inside me I don't understand. Why does a child steal something as useless as an earring? I used to think it was for the thrill of theft itself, and for the pleasure of possessing something beautiful. But maybe I craved what would have come if my siblings hadn't interfered; maybe I wanted the retribution I would have faced when my mother learned that I had breached the trust between us. I don't know. I can't name that hunger; I only know that I turn my flashlight back on and shine it into the gloom over my head.

There's a latch built into the ceiling. An iron ring just big enough that I can slide two fingers through it and pull. At first it resists me, sealed into place by untold years of neglect, but I'm no longer interested in playing nice with the house. I'm in an act-now-regret-later sort of mood, so I just haul against the ring with everything I have, one foot braced against Norma's coats, pinning the dead weasel to the wall. The hatch in the ceiling comes unstuck and the musk of trapped air that gusts into my face is overwhelming.

I stare, for a long second, at the passage now opened above me. I am in a secret closet. The staircase is directly overhead. This passageway, and wherever it leads, cannot be here.

An unexpected emotion twists in my chest—if I didn't know myself any better, I might say it was yearning. I've spent the past day and a half in this empty house, sleeping in Norma's old quilts, drinking whiskey out of cups last touched by her lips, and this is now the closest I've felt to her. This impossible place could have only belonged to my aunt, and, of everyone in the family, it could only have been shared with me. I stand on my tiptoes and peer into the hole.

The passage is built into the slope of the ceiling, so I can turn my phone's flashlight down its long throat. As it turns out, though, I don't need to. There's already light at the far end. It's not daylight. It's the yellowed glow of an incandescent bulb.

It seems that I am expected.

I POCKET MY PHONE AND shimmy myself upward. Once I'm inside, flat on my stomach, I find that the passage isn't all that long. That dim, steady glow is coming from a room some ten feet ahead; from this angle, I can make out its oaken floorboards.

I start the crawl forward, my breaths coming shallow and quick. The hole absolutely reeks of mildew, so I turn my face into the coat's fur collar, huffing in the stale scent of Norma's interred wardrobe. The light in the room beyond doesn't seem to reach into the passage, but I don't need to see where I am to know where I'm going. I try not to focus on the bits of mold and fiberglass amassing under my fingernails; I'm so close to the impossible room, now; so close to what Norma has kept hidden from the vultures.

I shove myself out of the passage, twisting to get free of its narrow, grimy embrace, and push into the room beyond. As I catch my breath—clear my lungs of that fetid stench—I lay on my back and take stock. The room appears to be an attic, even though I know I'm nowhere near the roof. The walls, lined with exposed beams, slant toward one another as they might under one of the house's gables. From what I can see, the room has no windows; only bare bulbs strung between the beams, casting a dim, unwavering light.

I've been here before. This thought possesses me even though I know it can't be true. The passage to this room hasn't been opened in years—decades, probably—so why does it feel so familiar?

As I start to roll myself onto my stomach, following the lines of the beams from the ceiling down the floor, it comes to me. It's not that I've been here before. It's that I've *seen* this room before. In fact, I've seen it from this very angle. I hadn't really paid attention to that second pic hungdaddy had sent, mostly because the man's glorious dick was out of focus. But the wall behind him was in focus, and it's that wall opposite me now, framed by the two beams joined at the ceiling. I'm in the place where the photos were taken.

The phone buzzes, but this time I already have it in hand. I knew he would message me right at this moment. I may not understand what he is, or what he wants, but I'm starting to know the way he thinks, and this excites me more than I could have anticipated.

hungdaddy has sent two messages, and the app informs me that one of them is a photo.

The message comes first:

>*you must pass through the opening*

The picture that follows doesn't immediately clarify things. The photographer has foregrounded half of hungdaddy's face and, even though it's blurry, I can't help but study him. He's bald with a full, coarse beard, the kind of beard that leaves marks after it has made use of the softest parts of your body. He's staring directly into the camera, and I read him so clearly. He looks into the lens with a want so naked, so forceful, it might be mistaken for rage. But it's not anger, not exactly. I know how that intensity will translate through his touch; I know what his fingers will feel like around my throat; I know how his grip will tighten when he presses his girth through me and how my mouth will open not with the need to breathe, but with the need to taste the sweat raining from his face.

I've gotten so hard I can feel my pulse in my dick. I want to unbutton my pants and jerk off right here, in the cold, damp musk of this room as he watches me, but hungdaddy resends the message.

>*you must pass through the opening*

A small, useless whimper wells in my throat, the sound a dog makes when denied attention. I know what he wants me to do next, but I don't want to do it. I don't want to look at the rest of the picture.

I force myself to break his gaze, to study the part of the photo that's in focus. It's the wall again. The resolution isn't great, but even so, I can see the line running across its surface, top to bottom. It's unbroken and jagged, pencil-thin.

I look across the room. The deeper I go into this house, the more twisted its interiors become. Even though I'm not on the second floor, I'm looking at the roof's gables; and even though I'm nowhere near the kitchen's infamous, load-bearing wall, I'm looking at The Crack.

How can I possib—

I start this thought, but can't finish it. My fingers are so cold and the pressure of my erection against my jeans is a needy, unbearable thing. I delete the words and start again, but hungdaddy replies before I can hit send. He shows me what I already know:

>*you will do what you have to do, pig.*

I still don't know what he wants from me, but I don't have to. It is enough to feel the heft of his desire make a place for itself inside me.

I start to crawl.

At first, The Crack is so distant. Barely visible, a hairline shadow bisecting the wall. I put one hand forward and feel the room shift. No, not the room—something has changed within me. It's like hungdaddy has sewn balloons into all those minute spaces between my joints and when I move forward he purses his lips, sucks a breath into that hairy drum of his chest, and blows. This description isn't right because it sounds like I'm experiencing something painful. But this isn't pain the way you know it. The change is slow.

The room fisheyes as I move forward, the beams in the periphery of my vision bending into convexity. The far wall only grows nearer and nearer; it approaches even in those times when I am not moving my body. I do, at one point, hang my head to see if I am moving myself. I couldn't quite see my legs—they were so far away, still at the far end of the room—but I did see a dark stain on my crotch. I must have come.

When I reach The Crack, in the future, I see that it has changed. I was wrong this whole time, wrong about so many things. Auntie was telling the truth. This is like looking into the Panama Canal, like standing at the edge of some bottomless fissure splitting the earth. I am nothing in its presence, I am dwindling into meaninglessness.

As I stretch through the opening, I am so wracked with sensation that it is almost impossible to separate one feeling, one thought, from the rest of the flood. But, in that instant, before I am gone, I realize what the house has given me: the force of desire has razed all uncertainty from inside me. It leaves an emptiness, a newness, that never stops growing. I couldn't stop it even if I wanted to, even if I could want anything at all.

BETSY MORTIMER-SCOTT PULLS UP TO the house at half past four.

In her twenty-three years in real estate, Betsy has closed more sales than she can rightly recall. She's sold split-levels to newlyweds, tracts of land to wolf-eyed developers, and oceanfront monstrosities to the unimaginably wealthy. In all this time, Betsy has never, not once, told a prospective buyer that a house has "good bones." It is a morbid metaphor. The buyer should never think of the house as a living thing, waiting to be resuscitated by fresh drywall and a gallon of paint. No—a property is a starched canvas, a blank page. The right language is important in making the sale.

Betsy reminds herself of this as she steps out of the car, planting her booted feet in the undisturbed layer of snow. If there has ever been a half-living house, a house with bones awaiting reanimation, it is this one. The old Colonial sulks at the forest's edge, its siding the same color as the trees that surround it, its windows so lightless she can't properly tell if the glass is still there.

Betsy slings her purse over her shoulder and locks the car doors. As she walks toward the front porch, she corrects herself—she'll never sell this place if she lets such thoughts color her perspective. For the right buyer, this house will be charming. A storied New England gothic. Better yet: a secluded woodland fantasy. Woodstoves crackling through the winter. Mulled cider simmering in the kitchen, holly wreaths on every door. Betsy takes the porch stairs two at a time. The right framing is starting to come together. Somewhere in Boston, there's a middle-aged couple dying to move to the country and this place practically has their name stenciled on the mailbox.

Betsy pauses when she comes to the front door. It is open. Not wide open, but ajar. This is not unusual, given the circumstances: the last person to come here was probably a lawyer's lackey, someone too preoccupied to double check that they'd locked it behind themselves. Betsy has had only fleeting contact with the family, but even from those brief interactions, she knows that they're not the type to personally attend to the old woman's belongings. They had no real connection to her, no genuine interest in anything other than the will.

"Hello?" Betsy calls as she pulls the door open. "Is there anyone here?"

A spray of snow has swept inside. The house is so cold that the ice sticks to the welcome mat and the hardwood floor. Betsy brushes this away with her boots as she enters; the last thing an old house needs is excess moisture on the floorboards.

As Besty turns to close the door, she sees the lace curtains in the drawing room billow, touched by wind. The windows, she finds, are all open. Not just those in the drawing room, but the windows in the dining room and the kitchen and the living room. She could have sworn that the owner had painted these shut years ago, but she must be confusing this with another property.

"Hello?" Betsy repeats after she has closed all the windows and returned to the front hall. She doesn't know why she asks a second time. This house is empty. There is no one here and it feels, in this moment, like no one has ever been here. All those screenless windows and open doors. All those bannisters rimed with ice. This, perhaps, is what concerns her most about convincing someone to buy the place. It's this feeling that if she keeps standing in this hallway, she will become part of the house's vast absence.

Betsy hikes her purse up higher on her shoulder. Enough of this. She decides she will come back later in the week. The contractor is free on Thursday, and she could use his help in drying all the floors and getting the furnace working again. No point in working alone if she doesn't have to.

On her way out, Betsy closes the closet door under the stairs. She remembers to lock the front door as she goes.

"You do have good bones," she says out loud. It's silly to talk to a house, but there's reassurance in the weight of her own voice, in remembering that she is here and that there's work ahead. "I'll find a family to love you," she adds, "the way you ought to be loved."

Betsy Mortimer-Scott cranks the heat up in her car and wastes no time getting back on the road into town. The sun sets early this far north. As she drives, the bare trees lining the road cast shadows that reach across the pavement, a tunnel of interlocking fingers.

The sun falls away. Betsy flicks her headlights on. Every shadow is erased.

COMMON WHIPPING
NABEN RUTHNUM

'You've been here how long?'

'Two years ago. Christmas, '71. Quit my course in Scotland, came over. My family still doesn't know.'

'You never talk to them?'

'My old flatmate, Brian, he forwards me mum's mail. He even sends replies back for me. I put five or six letters in a big package, ship that to him, he takes them to the postbox once a week.' Brian had been Renga's first real lover, a resident in the psychology program who now lived with a fake girlfriend (herself a lesbian, a psychiatric nurse who was especially skilled in electroshock therapy treatments, as Renga himself had witnessed on a ward visit he'd made with an identification badge nicked from the Sikh resident who shared their Citroen).

'Two years.'

'Yes. And I still haven't played on a single track. I've written a lot, though.'

'Your Italian?'

'Mostly decent, but I run into trouble when I'm describing something a little abstract,' Renga tried to say in Italian. He could tell from the mingled confusion, pity and disdain on Massimo Troisi's face that he was butchering both language and accent. Renga crossed his legs to hide the dark stain he'd just seen near the left knee of his pants, and the physical movement smoothed his transition back into English. 'It's not good enough, is what I'm saying. Apparently not good enough.'

'Why didn't you go to India? Plenty going on there. You would have had more luck.' Massimo leaned back to allow the waiter to set down a platter of transparently thin cured meats. Renga took and gnawed, swishing liquor between his teeth to dislodge studs of pig gristle.

'No Morricone out there. And I don't speak Hindi.'

'So you're as useless there as you are here. And for money?'

Renga grinned and looked away. The waiter mistook his sidewards glance for another drink order, which was not a problem. Another glass of Fernet Branca arrived, bobbing with miniature semi-spheres of ice that would melt in seconds.

'I didn't think I was your only one. Just glad you're doing well,' said Massimo. This time he was the one to cross his legs, perhaps to cover a stirring under the expensive cream trousers. No one would have been able to see it. Like most of the cafes and bars Renga's clients favoured, Rubinetto was dark, underground. The stone walls were old, and the cement holding them together was no longer distinguishable from rock, the whole room tinted by decades of liquor stains and smoke.

Massimo poked Renga's knee with the tip of his shoe, something he'd been doing since they'd sat down. The origin of the stain. Massimo's constant touching was proprietary, his attempt at a physical claim on something he'd never encountered before. Renga was a rarity in the city, a place where most sexual options were anything but. Slender, more-or-less Indian, accommodating, with a pleasing accent. Passage-to-India rough trade.

'You enjoy this? Not with me, I mean. The job in general,' Massimo asked.

'I like the hours and some of the sex,' said Renga. 'Even some of the bad fucks you learn from. And anyone I go with is someone I know, or knows someone I know. Like you.'

'Right,' Massimo said. He didn't ask Renga which category of fuck he fell into.

'You like Cipriani? Stelvio?'

'Of course I do.' *Anonimo Veneziano* was currently the third-most rotated LP in Renga's collection.

'He just cancelled on a project. That's what the director says, but I think it was probably that he hoped Stelvio would do it and never got an agreement. They've got to get some kind of music on there. You got anything you can show the director? Mirazappa, a new guy.'

'I have a record.' He did. A pressing of one hundred vinyl discs, each with a cover that he'd screenprinted himself in a cheap shop in Mauritius, a red circle on a dark blue background.

'Is it classical sounding?'

'There's a variety of different sounds.'

'Hm. You might want to make something new, bring it in on tape. Mirazappa was very specific, says he wants something classical, chamber-sounding. Says Bach a lot, but I think Bach is the only composer he knows.'

'I can do that.' Renga would need to pay for six hours of studio time and a cellist, an engineer as well. And write something new, but that was never the problem.

'Why d'you like Morricone so much? I know why I like him, but you?'

'I hate voices, what they do in popular music. It's why I couldn't stand to go to India. You write for the movies there, you're a slave to the playback singer, the stupid melody they want. Morricone, he makes voices behave. Forces them to be music. There's a line, structure, something written on piano, a theme the flute will pick up when the voice can't reach. Either that or he just makes them yelp in the recording booth, at the right pitch, the right time. That I like. It's how voices should be used.'

'Right. For me it's the whistling. You know he laughs in all the wrong places if he's around when they edit? Really threw Sergio off the one time I was there, for *Buono Bruto*. Ennio's in his own world, takes a few things from the script, from discussions, then goes and does his themes.' Massimo gazed off as he said this, watching condensation form in one particular depression in the ceiling, which the waiter had already walked over to poke dry with a mop once that evening. Renga too was feigning an experienced carelessness, which worked well when he was selling his cock and mouth, and seemed to be effective currency in the movie world as well. Being present as Ennio saw his score matched to film for the first time was swoon-material, as the linen-draped manipulator across from him knew. The story was almost definitely a lie, or something Massimo had stolen at a party.

'I've heard that, yes. So when can I meet Mirazappa?'

'You meet him after you give me the music. I'll pay for half the recording and the musicians. We'll call it a little gamble. Fifteen per cent if Mirazappa likes it, and you give me a few free nights if he doesn't. He won't want to see you if he doesn't like the music. And he really prefers working with Italians. Didn't want to cast any Americans or Brits, but he did because he had to. You he doesn't have to use. So we have to make him want you. Got an Italian name for the credits?'

'Reinaldo Pazone.'

'You serious?'

'No,' said Renga, too happy to defend his carefully-arrived-at pseudonym. He gave Massimo his real address, something he rarely did with a client, and left the bar after promising to meet back there the next day—unless Massimo wanted him for another hour that night?

'I'm 52,' Massimo said. 'I'd just fall asleep.'

Massimo watched the departing boy, who'd reached for his wallet when the bill came with something approaching genuine grace. He walked that way as well, with the elegance of the unwatched. Renga didn't act like a whore. At least not like one who charged his extremely reasonable rates.

The need to shower overtook Renga as soon as he turned away from Massimo and headed up the stone steps into the afternoon. Under his light, stained shirt and cotton pants, Renga's flesh felt tacky, and the heat would soon turn this into viscous stickiness. It was an unpleasant, tactile part of a job he mostly enjoyed.

The apartment he occupied, on via Prospera Santacroce, was in cruel proximity to Titania a Roma, the studio he was supposed to be recording in by now—passing out charts of themes and careful indications, cueing violinists and guitarists, getting ready to scream at anyone who bucked his instructions. Aside from his keyboards, the flat was a couch, a mattress, two heaps of clothes, and thirty-seven unwashed teacups. There was a slight form on the mattress, a normal-sized head on the pillow, and a narrow comma under the sheet: Enzo, who had a key and often napped here after a night with a client. Renga didn't wake him, heading straight to the shower to wash Massimo's skin and fluids away.

He'd wake Enzo up by testing a theme that had occurred to him a few weeks ago, one that might fit Mirazappa's film. A massively heavy Fender Rhodes organ and a Roland Piano occupied the never-cooked-in kitchen, which was above the building's boiler room and the only place in the apartment where he could make sufficient noise to properly feel out his ideas. He'd even made some baffling walls out of egg cartons and Styrofoam, shutting the keyboards into a soft room-within-a-room that was tropically hot on summer days like this.

Renga enclosed himself in foam and took his place at the bench. He turned the Rhodes on, pressing the keys as the tubes warmed up. Enzo moaned from the other room, probably in pain from another night of feeding his body to sadists. Enzo only made sounds when he turned over in his sleep, which meant that he was facedown now. On his back, a river-map of junior lash-marks intercrossed with a few raised maroon scars that had been very expensive indeed for the man who had put them there.

The name 'Enzo' was arbitrary, a career pseudonym that had overtaken his birth name, 'Magnus'. A Swedish–Turkish mix, he was used to discussing his racial origins in the terms of a dog's pedigree, leaning toward purity and legacy for some clients, muddying his blood for others, even telling one client, a Catalan, that he was Renga's half-brother. This was the one who had left the marks.

Enzo had looked young that night, extremely young. All sorts of plays on fascist dominance had been acted out on the flesh that coated his bones like frost on grass. Many of his clients came straight from the old guard; Mussolini's closeted friends, former Futurists and politicians who had eventually washed up in the business and film worlds of Rome, either making regulations or doing their best to break them. The role Enzo had come up with, literal whipping boy to a fallen elite and its acolytes, justified the emaciated body he'd created long before he took on his name and career.

Renga wouldn't have been able to name Enzo's disorder even if he'd recognized it as sickness. The skinniness looked like a business strategy to his fellow hustlers, a committed shaping of his most essential resource to provide an experience that was unique in the city, and therefore highly valued. He could sew, too, and had effectively modified a number of formal jackets and surplus army garments into a variously-sized Nazi and Blackshirt collection.

He kept these in a dedicated wardrobe that stood locked in his own apartment, while his own costumes—rags, licked with blood in distressing areas—were stuffed into a suitcase under the living room couch. When Renga and Enzo went out together with clients, something they did often with new ones, to create a certain level of security, Renga ate off Enzo's plate. A few cherry tomatoes at the end of the meal usually sustained his friend and trainer.

Clients, including the Catalan, liked talking about general topics over meals, perhaps trying to make it seem as though they were taking out some foreign junior partners or courting actors for a production. Enzo had a different character at the table, wise, witty, presumably the opposite of the cowering pant-pisser he played in the client's room. More educated than Renga, as he was constantly reminding his colleague, he called this the geisha part of the job.

'Most physical beauty is an accident, but maintaining it is as hard as keeping two cars in perpetual collision,' he said, talking to Renga at their dinner with the Catalan. Another dark room, this one oddly empty, as though the Catalan had paid for several tables to be kept clear around them.

'That sounds wise and stupid at the same time,' Renga answered, deferring his conversational place to the third man at the table. Their tall North African waiter, idle since they'd been served their last bottle, had started to circle the edges of the room. He was using a long spoon to snuff every second candle, drawing the walls closer in.

'And how do you maintain your beauty?' asked the Catalan, who carried his own salt cellar and sprinkled each slice of steak before he ate it. The affectation made Renga quietly angry, distracting him from the taste of his own fish every time he saw the man drop a pinch from the engraved wooden box. He was about forty, but unhealthy, with skin the colour of an old rope in a gymnasium. The heartbreaking falseness of his wig made it clear that even great wealth couldn't cover everything.

'I maintain it the same way I developed it. I had to start the accident. My parents' shabby cells couldn't do the job. For my nose to make sense, for my cheekbones to counterbalance my jaw, I had to impose reductions elsewhere.'

Enzo took a photo wrapped in paper out of his wallet. He removed the picture from its folded sheath and pushed it over to the Catalan, who owned three garment factories.

The Catalan, who had lied and told them his name was Umbrosi, stared at the photo. The subject, a teenage boy, wasn't fat, but he was anonymous, a background actor who would never be called forward to deliver a line. Enzo described the process of unearthing himself from that accidental body.

Renga picked up the paper the photo had been folded in; it was a prescription, a few years old, for glasses. The doctor's name was Nordic-sounding.

'Is this your father's handwriting?' Renga asked. Enzo picked up the photo and the prescription and returned them to their folded clasp.

'No, he charged too much. I only go to doctors I can fuck for the bill.' Saying this in front of a client ran counter to Enzo's first tenet of the job: Never act like a whore. Whether he'd said it impulsively or with calculation, it worked. The Catalan laughed.

'Let's go to the house,' the Catalan said. It was eight miles from the restaurant, and they made the trip by cab. The Catalan never used his own car on nights when he was seeing a boy, Enzo said. His driver was an old friend, a scholarshipped classmate from secondary school who'd ruined his former career with drugs, and now clung to Catholicism and the job he'd been given. Umbrosi didn't like to make him uncomfortable by having him chauffeur Roman street meat.

Their cab took Grande Raccorde, a dull but effective route, circling towards the part of town where they needed to be before penetrating back through the concentric slices of the city. The house had all of its lights on: Umbrosi's theft deterrent and way of keeping his dogs comfortable.

They fell on Renga and Enzo when Umbrosi opened the door. Enormous, friendly, poorly-trained Irish wolfhounds, alien-bodied and unreal beasts that Renga had recognized from the inclusion of the breed in Powell and Pressburger's *I Know Where I'm Going*. They moved like new fawns in the constricted space of the hallway entrance, their legs sturdy but their bodies large enough to destabilize the tiny space they crowded into.

'They only live six, seven years. So I let them have their fun,' Umbrosi said. The larger of the two hounds had its paws on Enzo's shoulders and bore him back into the door, which closed beneath the boy's feathery weight. Umbrosi finally called the dogs when Enzo's knees started to wobble. They corralled themselves, backing single-file toward a pile of small Persian rugs in front of an empty fireplace.

Their heads bobbed as the immense curving backs receded, wheeling and trotting out of sight. Renga's former terror of dogs had been alleviated by the endless sequence of lap-bound near-invertebrates he'd encountered in clients' homes, small creatures with misaligned jaws and flat muzzles had no function or ability to threaten. Quite a few of these had bitten him, their soft teeth denting his skin and leaving sulky trails of mucous. Soon he was able to see kindness, deference, or indifference in the eyes of larger domestics. The scavenging wild dogs of Rome were quite easy to avoid, and were constantly being impounded or secretly executed by angry homeowners wielding guns left over from the war. The wolfhounds in this house had fewer aggressive instincts than their owner, who was watching his night's hire with a particularly charged lust that Renga didn't think he himself could ever feel or inspire.

Enzo straightened and brushed dog-hair epaulets off his blazer, which he then took off and hung from a hook by the door. His lucent thinness was exposed by his pearl-white shirt. The pants were narrow and tapered to pencil-thickness at the ankles, and a red leather belt was shelved on his hipbones.

Renga eyebrowed his friend. Enzo had told him that the Catalan's sessions always started with the dogs, but thankfully they weren't involved in any of the later portions of his evening's entertainment.

'Do you want to stay down in this room, Renga?' The name came out as Wray-Gah when Umbrosi said it, as though he were addressing some foe of Godzilla's. 'I can set you up in the screening room, if you'd like.'

'No, I'll stay here. The dogs are fine with me?'

'They're fine with everyone. I've never seen them hungry, perhaps that would change things.' Umbrosi was looking up the stairs, barely glancing at Renga as he spoke, touching himself through his right pocket. He'd prepared things for Enzo before meeting the boys for dinner, alluding to the 'scene being set' at least four times at the table. He wasn't like most clients, who kept their stuff in the basement.

'Most of these fetish dungeons they take me to, they're totally historically incoherent,' Enzo had once said after an appointment on Via Frattina. 'It's medieval as well as fascistic. Thomas More used to have people who read the Bible in English instead of Latin tortured, you know that? Maybe executed, I can't remember, but surely tortured first. This fat client today, takes tongs just to find his cock, he collects old implements. Devices. A flat piece of iron he paid thousands of lire for, with a handle at the back—he says he has its lineage, stolen from some museum when the Allies came. It's an abacinator. They'd heat it up white, hold it in front of your eyes, melt them right out. You cry them out, the sockets are left empty, the optic nerve seals up and shrivels. Terrible. I always worried he'd use it on me, get too worked up, but he's just a sweet dentist. And I never let him tie me up.'

Enzo had been silent since they'd come into the house, sinking into passivity, acting his way into the Catalan's fantasy. Renga watched them walk up the stairs to a second floor that had been imposed on the original structure, rooms slotted between the roof and the stone first floor, supported by grim, immense beams, which had likely been salvaged from some ancient barn. The wood throughout the house was the same greyed-brown as the hounds, a colour that Renga identified with Flemish paintings. Peasants copulating in the dirt by collapsing buildings.

Umbrosi needled Enzo in the back with a finger as they mounted the top stair. The boy stopped and let Umbrosi walk around him to open the bedroom door, which was just visible to Renga. The Catalan liked going through his sexual paces in his proper bedroom, the place where he slept and wanked and sometimes brought models and actresses for a night of puzzled slumber while he leaked a more salacious story by phone to a collection of trusted gossip columnists.

Renga took a post on the couch behind the curled enormity of the canines, with a copy of the only novel in English he could find on Umbrosi's shelves, *Double Indemnity*. The cushion next to him was stacked with copies of *L'Unita*, the communist paper. Umbrosi probably read it for research on the unions that he fought against to keep the shirts he made, but never wore, as cheap as possible.

He fell asleep a little after the dogs did, waking only when the negotiations upstairs passed from lash to bullwhip, and the yelps turned into three real screams, sounds that Renga had never heard from his friend, which rose and pitched into an androgynous then animal screech. One of the dogs moved its legs, dream running somewhere, following or fleeing a phantasmagoric parallel of the screams upstairs.

The theme that occurred to Renga as he was on that couch, starting with the screamed G that followed the first crack of the whip was a fairly plain nine-note run with an unexpected diminished seventh as the penultimate strike, a recurring pattern that would overlap successive bars to abolish any sense of certainty.

Enzo was driven to the home of a veterinarian after Umbrosi had finished ejaculating and started panicking. The Catholic chauffer had been summoned from the coach house, an explanation involving a fall on a stray rake left on the lawn conjured, and Enzo had been carted off, facedown, to be stitched up as well as possible. Umberto had left Renga with a huge roll of lire bound by an elastic band, the bounty for Enzo's flesh.

Renga forced that night's theme to return as he sat in his own kitchen two months later, with Enzo sleeping on his mattress in the next room. He struck them out on the Rhodes, playing them repeatedly, altering timing and emphasizing different notes while staring at the matte black plastic cover that concealed the strings and pickups. Eventually his eyes stopped working, filtering out the dull blackness, as a smell vanishes to a nose before it vanishes in a room. He corrected the theme, perfected it, then continued to play as a contrapuntal harmony line for xylophone unfurled in his mind. He placed the sound somewhere behind his right eyebrow, and auditioned a theremin accent behind his cheekbone before dismissing it. Cellos came in, and he put these behind his mandibles, two behind each back molar, keeping the arrangement sparse, manageable, bonding each note physically with a chew or a twitch, staring down into the keys and repeating until it was assembled. There was a counterpoint that almost had its shape, but kept shifting, like the features of a character in an amateur's novel, changing based on what they were doing, how they were acting.

'It's boring until it keeps happening. Then it's not exactly interesting, but you want it to continue, you know?' Enzo had swiveled open one of the soundproofing walls of Renga's practice chamber. He had his Wise Critical Judgment face on, which made it annoying to agree with him.

'That's about as good a description of a theme for variations as I could get to, I guess,' he said. Enzo pulled the practice room open all the way, signaling to Renga that it was time to pay attention to him, and walked over to the fridge. Slices of things, mostly: meat, cheese. Discs, tubes. Strings of uncooked pasta that would soon go bad; all brought by a client of Renga's.

Bottles of sparkling water, which both boys preferred to still, and which had become nearly the only thing Enzo consumed. As he drank the knot in his throat bobbed and wriggled like a caught fish, and the scars on his back moved when he turned. There was a light fuzz on the boy's skin that hadn't been there when Renga had first met him, the night they'd decided never to fuck just because they were supposed to.

'I got a project,' Renga said. 'An assignment.' He described Massimo Troisi's proposition to Enzo, who set the bottle down and drew his mouth over to one side.

'Do it right,' said Enzo, 'even if the john doesn't pay you enough. I'll give you anything extra you need. Don't give them some scratchy piano recording. Give them the whole thing, so they can't say no.'

'They can say no to anything. They've been saying no for years.'

'To you, not what you make. If you make that –' Enzo pointed to the air above the keyboard – 'they'll take it.'

'It's the Catalan, I think. The director of the movie is new, a beginner. I think it's him.'

'You think?'

'Massimo used his name. His real name.'

'That's a good clue,' said Enzo, stretching there in the kitchen, distracting his hands so they wouldn't reach for the scars on his back. His ribs expanded and the concavity of his stomach deepened, the brittle spine making a dusty cracking sound as he leaned backwards.

Two weeks later, Renga met with Massimo and the director on an enormous outdoor patio. It was the Catalan—false Umbrosi, real Mirazappa—and he stood and blanched when he saw Renga, the source of the music on the tape that he'd already decided to use. Renga had passed the chauffeur on his way to the terrazza, accepting and returning a nod.

'You understand my film without having seen it. I see it when – the, the violin strain, that's my heroine, the glove on her throat as she grips it and slips away, taking with her the leather but not his hand.'

'And the tension notes,' Renga said, leaning slightly across the table, ignoring Massimo's inquisitive brows and watching the Catalan. 'Those are the whips. From the title, you know.'

'Yes.'

Enzo didn't turn up for the premiere of *La frusta e il calice*, which came out stunningly fast, a month after the sound was finalized. He didn't reply to phone calls beforehand or afterwards. Renga thought he might find him at his own home, perhaps finally ready to have sex, now that only one of them was in the business of it. Enzo wasn't there, so Renga let himself into his flat an hour after the party had wrapped, walking over ankle-twisting cobblestones through a pre-dawn crowd of bakers, newspaper vendors and the drunken young.

Enzo's books, his fascist trousseau for clients, and his own clothes were still in the apartment. His wallet, with its paper-wrapped photo of the boy that might have been him, was gone. That, at least, suggested that he had left with some purpose. Renga looked for more missing objects in the apartment as the sun lay lengthening beams of heat across its uncurtained rooms, but found everything else his friend owned intact, present, abandoned.

THE BOY WHO WENT FORTH TO LEARN WHAT FEAR WAS

LC VON HESSEN

Hans takes his sweetheart Gretel, binds her to a rope, and guides her to the rack, upon which he ties her fast. Then Hans goes to his mother.

"That was stupid of you, Hans," says his mother. "Instead, you should have cast friendly eyes at her."

"Doesn't matter," says Hans. "I'll make it better."

Hans goes into the stable, cuts out the eyes of all the calves and sheep, and throws them in Gretel's face.

"CLEVER HANS," BROTHERS GRIMM,
KINDER- UND HAUSMÄRCHEN

THE SUN BEAT DOWN ON Connor's flesh, drawing sweat from his exposed neck and downward as an added punishment for inhabiting a body. For days, the temperature had hovered around 90 degrees: the repulsive New Normal of summer in New York. The flat of his hand still throbbed after he'd slammed his fist against the doorframe in a burst of rage. The rage hadn't left him even now.

This was all the fault of the United States Postal Service. The mail carrier fucked up and misdelivered his order. Online tracking claimed his package had been dropped off by his mailbox yesterday afternoon, but there was nothing beside said mailbox but a small Amazon parcel addressed to the next building over. The exasperated civil servant Connor spoke to on the phone today insisted his package must have been stolen by a neighbor, but nobody else in his building had ever given a shit about his mail, not in his eight years at that apartment.

The post office would admit to no wrongdoing: they weren't going to help him. He'd have to take matters into his own hands and look for the box himself. It had to be waiting at some nearby address.

Pretend it's a video game, he told himself. *You're going on a Package Quest.*

Exacerbating the issue was the fact that this package was rather *sensitive* and would lead to extreme awkwardness for all involved if it were mistakenly opened by anyone else. That hypothetical neighbor would unpack a man-sized leather body harness with extra snap hooks and D-rings for further restraint, a pair of leather horse blinders adapted for the human face, a Wartenberg pinwheel, a stainless steel butt plug, and a set of clover clamps with a longer connecting chain than Connor's current set of clover clamps. The box would probably jingle. The retailer's name was discreet—L. Sacher Products, Inc.—and there would be no outward indication of the cost, but the package's contents had set him back nearly 200 bucks: still relatively cheap for fetish gear since he'd taken advantage of a recent sale. He had no particular occasion in mind or partner to administer them: just more dainties for his hope chest. If only he'd ever had a man on a devoted and regular-enough basis to do what he *really* wanted. But no use dwelling on that now.

Connor felt oddly exposed walking in his own neighborhood outside of his normal rounds: a suspicious grim-faced man, peering through front doors and into front landings as if making a very obvious and clumsy attempt at casing them for burglary, even though he knew people dropped off promotional flyers in such places all the time. He'd just finished his own block, having seen no package of the dimensions approximate to his order, and was heading one block north in case the mail carrier had gotten the wrong street number.

This block was dominated by a typical row of old-school Brooklyn brownstones without alleys, all glommed onto one another in a tumorous growth of brick and mortar. Only one block away, and yet this specific assemblage of buildings was so novel and unfamiliar that he might have been visiting the entire neighborhood for the first time. If it wasn't en route to his regular bodega, laundromat, subway stop, and so forth, and there was nothing in the way of cheap takeout restaurants, he seldom ever traveled that way. Connor Egilssen was a creature of habit.

He glanced through entry doors' windows. He clenched and unclenched his fists. He grumbled under his breath.

And he cursed in astonishment. Between this particular stoop and its front gate was a stack of discarded paintings set out with the trash alongside the gaudy broken spider of a chandelier. The topmost frame caught his eye first, ornate black-and-gilt baroque surrounding a pastoral rococo scene. Closer inspection revealed the faint texture of brushstrokes: this was an actual painting, not a framed reproduction. It was unsigned, as far as he could see; likely the product of a talented amateur who had lived in that building, some elderly tenant who'd been here for decades and recently died, whose kids or landlord didn't share their aesthetic taste.

The rest of the stack consisted of Impressionist pastiches, all mediocre daubings of the same generic log cabin, all at the same angle and in far simpler frames, and all with the approximate color scheme of a slab of raw bacon. These held no interest to him.

He would absolutely take that landscape home. The existing decor in his studio apartment consisted of relics from college through his early twenties, unframed and thumbtacked to his walls: dog-eared horror film posters, prints of Surrealist paintings and Art Nouveau liquor ads, flyers from various goth DJ nights and extreme music shows featuring Holbein woodcuts and vintage porn collages. The painting would add a suitably adult touch. Connor Egilssen had failed today's Package Quest, but this was his consolation prize.

Back at home, having set the painting aside, Connor immediately shucked off his disposable mask, boots, shirt, and jeans. The cooling part of his AC unit was broken, and he wasn't enough of a handyman to fix it himself, so the cheapest option was to strip down to his undershirt and boxers with a rotary fan trained on his body whenever possible.

At the bathroom mirror, Connor splashed cool water on his head and slicked back his hair. He winced: the summer sweat had aged him a decade, shellacking all the crevices of his face. He noted the silver-grey streaks in his hair where the follicles just fucking gave up, so many more of them over only the past couple of years. Noted the blunted definition in his torso, like some sand-weathered ancient statue: he could appreciate softness and bulk on another man's body, but not his own. Good lord, the reality of encroaching middle age. Would he become a dashing silver fox or just some tragic old fuck? He never expected or wanted this, to be well into his thirties with no long-term partner, not now, not ever. Part of him secretly believed that, since certain aspects of his life had remained static thus far, it was only fair that his body's ageing process remain in that same limbo: that Time itself should slow until he could join the dance, his looks preserved in amber until some Major Life Change allowed a few wrinkles to creep in and a bit of hair at his temples to escape in the night.

Connor heated a frozen meal in the microwave for dinner because it was too hot to cook. He cracked open his laptop to continue his game of *Hastur's Meridian* and avoid checking his email. He would have to contact the retailer about his missing package ordeal and hope they didn't assume he was trying to scam them, but not now, not tonight. All his energy for interactions with other people had been drained for the day.

Before bed, he cleaned the painting's frame, wiping off encrusted grime and spiders' leavings, scrubbing away the sickly-sweet stench of German cockroaches. It must have been sitting around untouched for years.

He mounted the painting on his bedroom wall, hooked onto a screw left in the plaster by a previous tenant. There he could lie back and study it more comfortably.

The only man-made structure in the composition was a crooked, broken wooden gate in the foreground backing a small pond that curved out of sight at the bottom of the frame. To the right of the gate stood a single tall tree extending past the frame's topmost corner, and to the left was a dense copse of shorter trees. Behind the gate, a central gap in the foliage traced a faint dirt trail snaking through low rolling hills beyond, segueing into a mountain range visible in the far distance. And above the landscape was a pale, calm sky streaked with hazy cirrus clouds—though, to Connor's dismay, a few tiny spots of paint had flecked away here, revealing an angry orange-red contrast beneath, as if some earlier image had been painted over. Was the picture always like that, or did he accidentally damage it while cleaning? Christ, he already had too much bullshit to worry about.

Connor switched the rotary fan on his nightstand to the highest setting and stared into the painting as he fell asleep.

TIME OUT OF TIME, A wandering journeyman roams the countryside in search of a master. In the prime of life, he has neither apprentices below him nor guild above him and thus no encumbrances. He is young and free as a man of his station can be.

On these travels, the air was mild, but the road was long, and even this pleasant journey of a day's length has utterly exhausted him. His lungs rattle in their cage, and his toes and heels weep with blisters.

At the end of a dirt road through meadows and hills, he catches sight of a modest cabin beside a forest bordering the mountains and the huntsman who makes this cabin his home. Wiping sweat from his brow and stroking his beard, the huntsman studies this weary traveler; the journeyman, in turn, flushes under the strong, handsome huntsman's piercing gaze and sly smile, an axe slung over his shoulder and a hunting knife at his belt.

"Come, journeyman. I'll take good care of you." A wicked glint of his eye, a hand squeezing the hilt of his knife. "For a fair price."

"I have nary a coin in my purse."

The huntsman smiles. "No matter."

The journeyman is invited into the cabin. His host, the huntsman, offers him a basin of fire-warmed water from a nearby pond for washing off the perspiration of his travels. The huntsman fills his gurgling stomach with stew and a moist shank of meat. The huntsman removes his shoes and tends to his raw and bleeding wounds.

As the sun sinks, the journeyman spoons up the last of his supper while wrapped in a quilt by the fire. The bare toes of his bandaged feet settle into the rug before him, fashioned from the silver-grey pelt of a wolf. The huntsman sits quietly at his side, and he is contented.

After nightfall, the huntsman comes to collect his payment, and the journeyman is happy to give it. By unspoken agreement, the journeyman strips naked and crawls into the cabin's lone bed. The huntsman does not join him immediately but stands and observes him in silence for a time, hands on hips, backlit by the fire, only the gleam of his eyes and glimmer of his teeth visible in the glow of the moon, a long, living shadow—as the journeyman shivers in dread and pleasure.

The journeyman is tall and lean. The huntsman is taller with intimidating heft in his arms, chest, stomach, and thighs—and, as is soon revealed, between his legs, to the journeyman's gasp. The huntsman passes strong hands along his flesh, grasping and examining every part of him like prized livestock judged for slaughter, occasionally grunting with approval. The journeyman, in passive obedience, keeps his hands at his sides and waits for instruction until bidden to lie on his back. The heavy press of the huntsman's body sinks him into the mattress, which conforms to him like the slats of a pauper's coffin. A dollop of rendered fat from a glass jar by the bed is smeared between the journeyman's thighs to open him. A master of his art, the huntsman lives wholly off this land: he wastes nothing. Grasped firmly by hips and wrists, eyes seized in eyes, filled with masculine vigor, the journeyman is made the huntsman's own. The journeyman forgets himself and cries out with increasing ardor, nails digging into the huntsman's broad shoulders.

A strong hand covers his mouth as the huntsman pauses mid-thrust, flicking his eyes in warning, first at the moonlit window, then the pelt on the floor. A long, low howl echoes through the mountains and seeps into the journeyman's ears.

Wolves.

CONNOR DIDN'T WAKE UP UNTIL after noon the next day, a Saturday. The stress of yesterday's post office debacle must have taken it out of him, already pissing away several hours of his weekend. All the better that he didn't make music any more. He used to get the bulk of his lyric writing, mixing, and mastering done on weekend mornings alongside a strong coffee.

Nowadays he'd pivoted to writing reviews of other people's albums, moreso to keep his Con Egilssen byline out in the world rather than supplement his income since the pay was frankly shit. Returning from his regular coffee-and-bagel run at the corner bodega, he checked his mail—still no goddamn package, of course—and retrieved a squashed bubble mailer stuffed into his mailbox. Addressed to a "Conner Aggilson," it contained a cassette tape entitled *Dementius Lupus*, the debut noise release from a certain Rex Hart. This tape was hotly anticipated and he had been dreading this one.

Connor knew metal guitarist/frontman Rex Hart mainly by reputation, from the public persona he cultivated as a Thinking Man's extreme music bro and the predictably dour humorlessness that came along with it. He'd released a limited-edition chapbook, *Treatise on the Logos of Neo-Pessimist Persuasion*, available exclusively at the merch table during his live shows, where it quickly sold out. He was collaborating on a line of streetwear, *Hart x Hellmann*, with some trust-fund hipster occultist who used to run a bullshit art gallery on the Lower East Side before the pandemic and now hawked NFTs in LA. Even his egregiously macho monosyllabic name, redolent of a porn actor or pro wrestler, struck Connor as even dorkier for a black metal musician than naming oneself after a Tolkien character. And he had an improbably large following from the ranks of young people who'd constantly post talking-head videos about media they had consumed: a newfangled trend that made Connor feel fusty and old, and not just because it horned in on his side gig as a critic.

Of course, Hart's default promo pic remained studiously on-brand. Arms folded over a bulky leather jacket, Hart glowered at the camera in a Kubrick stare framed by long, lank, greasy hair. The hollows of his eyes were enhanced with dripping black grease paint over the blotchy white pancake coating his face. A big black frown had been crudely smeared over his mouth and much of his stubble-encrusted jawline: the effect was that of a tragicomic Depression-era hobo-themed clown. *Yessir, you sure are* brrrruuuu*tal!*

He knew none of these traits was *objectively* bad, per se, but taken altogether, Mr. Hart seemed engineered in a lab to personally annoy him. It's not like Hart was a cryptofascist or a rape apologist or whatever, at least as far as Connor knew; he just found Hart's persona to be obnoxious. A *ne plus ultra* of tryhards.

In a way, it made him perversely more interested in Hart's music, of which he'd had little exposure thus far: just the most recent LP from Hart's black metal band, which had compounded his conviction that Hart was overrated. Connor was simply not the type who Did Not Finish a subpar piece of media: a punishing curiosity forced him to press on and learn exactly *how bad* it was, right to the bitter, hubristic end. If nothing else, he could hate-listen to it during downtime at work.

He'd been working from home since the start of the pandemic and was thoroughly glad to ditch the hour-long commute to Midtown, the tourist-priced takeout that comprised the only office-adjacent lunch options, the cubicle chatter from his officemates regarding sports and superhero movies and whatever else a person of his broadest demographics was expected to care about. Recent anxiety-flaring inconveniences aside, he felt far more calm, relaxed, and even-tempered working from his couch, with a soundtrack of his choice on the stereo and a dress shirt on hand in the rare case he needed to video chat.

There was one massive drawback to his quasi-hermetic life: it had been an embarrassingly long time since he'd gotten any dick. These days Connor never met anyone new organically, nor did he expect any decent piece of ass from the internet to want to schlep all the way out to Bensonhurst to get laid, not for an almost-middle-aged ex-twink like him anyway.

He'd considered wading back into live events, but even that felt like a cursed endeavor. He was excited for an especially sick metal-and-hardcore lineup at a DIY venue up in Ridgewood until he'd spotted the name of a certain touring band since their frontman was a short-lived ex of his with whom things had ended on *very* bad terms. So bad, they were sure to end up in a shouting match or even come to blows if they were in the same room together. Pass.

And the local apps were clogged with tender softboy hipsters and bridge-and-tunnel meatheads who held no interest for him at all. Connor couldn't fuck a man he had too much contempt for, much less submit to or accept punishment from such a man. Physical qualities aside, he was turned on, above all else, by intensity. A scheming mind, honed diamond-sharp; a concealed threat that could rip him apart. One of his most treasured hookups was with a guy who'd done three years in prison and not on some bullshit charge like cannabis possession. These *just your average chill dude* types were cellophane to be torn away and discarded in order to reach the meat.

That evening, Connor forced himself to bang out that damned email to L. Sacher Products, Inc. It was a paragraph long and the most productive he'd been all day.

Gazing at the painting while he drifted off to sleep, he noticed, for the first time, the edge of a cabin barely visible in the cluster of trees.

COME THE DAWN, THE HUNTSMAN sets out into the forest by the mountainside with a crossbow strapped to his back to go hunting for the household. The journeyman stays behind, tending the fire and the vegetable patch. He steps through the little broken gate by the cabin to gather water from the pond.

Taking a rest from his toils, the journeyman rolls up his trouser legs and wades into the pond up to the knee. The surface ripples around him, and a series of bones tumbles from the watery depths up to the brief shore, loosely assembling into an incomplete human skeleton.

"Journeyman, hark!" says the dead youth in the sand. His fleshless jaw clicks and rattles. His joints and molars clack softly, muffled through strings of algae. "I was like you once. I was young, free, and beautiful until I came to live with the huntsman." He extends a skinless arm towards the pond. "This water is full of our bones, my brothers and I. Since you have known the huntsman, you will become my brother, too, and lie with us beneath the sand."

The journeyman lies on the shore, cradling the skull and loose bones of this poor dead boy who would never have a name again.

"I am so sorry this happened to you," says the journeyman. "Perhaps I could have loved you. Perhaps we could have loved each other." The little fingerbones reach up to stroke his cheek and wipe away a single tear. The bare jaw nuzzles his own. A blue flame flickers in the dead boy's gaping sockets.

"He took my thighbone for his knife. Beware!" The boy's remaining bones detach and roll back into the water.

A creeping unease fills the journeyman's heart for the rest of the day, his hand trembling when he spoons supper into his mouth or prods at the embers of the hearth. Tonight the huntsman wears a special knife in his belt, its hilt made from half of a human femur. The huntsman pats the mattress and nods for him to lie down, and the journeyman cannot disobey. In mere moments he has stripped and lain supine as the huntsman stands above.

By the flickering light of his lantern, the huntsman sinks his special knife down the length of the journeyman's torso. It ought to destroy the journeyman with pain, but he feels only an intense and curious pressure.

Discarding his heavy hunting gloves, the huntsman roots around in the gaping wound until he plucks out a dark, round, pulsing organ that fits easily within his large fist, severing its cord with the knife. The journeyman watches all this, unmoving; watches as the organ is tossed into a jar on the bedside table.

Curiously, the journeyman feels much calmer now. His wound is stitched up with heavy cord, like a leather purse; each pinprick makes him twitch, but the sensation is not unpleasant. The huntsman pats the sutured wound twice, gently. It hasn't closed completely and still seeps with nameless fluids.

Yet the ordeal is not over. The huntsman greases the knife's hilt and lifts the journeyman's legs before slowly, carefully driving the femur-handle inside him. It pains him greatly, too thick and stiff and oddly-shaped for such a purpose, but the journeyman knows this as a test to endure. He whimpers as tears trickle from his eyes, but he keeps himself from crying out. The huntsman thrusts by clutching the blade with his bare hands, which are now slashed open and bleeding; he grits his teeth, his focus only on the task before him, though he, too, shares in this pain.

The journeyman has, unexpectedly, stiffened: from sensation or duty, he cannot begin to say. The huntsman is merciful. He releases one hand, the blood of his palm slicking around the journeyman's member to relieve him. Before he spends, the journeyman considers that the bone inside him is only part of the kind, sad boy from the pond, after all.

He ought to be dead, but he awakens whole, encircled by the huntsman's loving arms. The dark organ is still in the jar, stoppered with a cork and resting on the mantel. His bare chest and stomach are marked with a long, faint scar. The huntsman's palms on his flesh are encrusted with dried blood.

CONNOR WOKE UP WITH A flat fog in his head and a painful twinge in his guts that soon turned into a bout of diarrhea. That's what he got for relying on frozen dinners.

Dementius Lupus mocked him. Released by a respected high-profile indie label, it was Rex Hart's debut venture into noise. Presumably, Connor thought, Hart wanted something more sonically *exxxtreme,* like many other metal-turned-noise-musicians. The man would probably get a strict undercut, found a retro synth project, and start DJing New Wave nights after he felt he couldn't go any harder. Lord, these guys could be so self-serious that Connor just couldn't take them seriously.

You can buy Cannibal Corpse and Mayhem shirts at Hot Topic these days, you know? Get over yourself.

Hart was enough of a critical darling now that he couldn't just send a link to a stream or download of his album like anyone else. Oh no: as a note alongside the tape clarified, any potential reviewer had to listen to *Dementius Lupus* in the proper physical format *only*. No FLAC, WAV, or mp3 allowed. Meaning without a decent stereo system—say, if Connor were to use the portable mono cassette player leftover from his '90s childhood—the tracks would be engulfed in a reverb of warm mush, like early black metal albums that sound as if they were recorded from a toilet bowl. At least Hart hadn't released it on 8-track or floppy disk.

This particular copy had a hairline crack running down the plastic cover where it had been roughly handled by the post office. The tracks were all untitled. The title itself was possibly bad Latin, but whatever, Connor had taken German in high school.

Yes, Connor had listened to the most recent album from Hart's band Oviposition, the release that had been their breakout success. Musically it was . . . fine? Not egregiously awful, but nothing to write home about? A little overproduced, maybe; a little too busy? Until a couple of songs in, when Hart's vocals slipped into an extended porcine squeal that made Connor crack up as he pictured a big tattooed hog teetering on its hind legs onstage with a microphone under its snout and a trotter clutching the fretboard.

That album's cover rendered the band's name in semi-legible lightning-static letters above a Satanic-themed Frazetta-style painting of a hulked-up guy in a loincloth and metal codpiece, with a bloody inverted pentagram carved into his pecs, raising a golden chalice over a dark, jagged chasm. At the bottom, all-caps Fraktur font spelled out the album's title, which was *Pissguzzler.*

Pfft. Bet he doesn't even guzzle piss. Piss-guzzling poseur.

Although perhaps he shouldn't assume Hart would be the one guzzling the piss. It was common to the point of cliché how many guys under the extreme-metal-and-noise umbrella presented themselves as total dom tops. Noise especially: shouting and growling through balaclavas in dank basements; using crowbars and chains as percussion; slapping faux-Xerox images of gagged and hogtied female porn models on the covers of their tapes. Though it was his own experience, and that of many women he knew in the scene, that most of these men were nowhere near as dominant in bed as they fronted.

Dementius Lupus's cover art continued that tradition, featuring a simple B&W photo of Rex Hart himself from the waist up, clad in a leather vest and one of those close-fitting zipper-mouthed sensory deprivation hoods that people who aren't involved in S/M call gimp masks. Inside the cover insert was another picture of Hart from the same photoshoot: sans hood, arms crossed, a pair of old-school studded leather gauntlets around his burly forearms. Connor grudgingly admitted that—having washed his hair, trimmed his scraggly beard, and wiped off that sub-Juggalo corpsepaint— Rex Hart was actually pretty hot: somewhere between Peter Steele and *British Steel*. He pushed away the image of himself lying prone in a wrestling chokehold, crushed by Hart's powerful biceps while an equally powerful bulge pressed against his asscrack. Did Hart listen to his own band's music while he fucked? *Probably.*

Predictably, many of Hart's, and Oviposition's, fans were straight out of high school and had never heard this sort of thing before: kids who were young enough that church burning was a silly old meme and the Satanic Panic was just Boomer kitsch. The numerous YouTube and TikTok takes led to glowing reviews by mainstream rock critics who were out of their wheelhouse and didn't quite know what the fuck they were talking about. Yet that didn't explain why renowned underground musicians were also starting to gush over him. Was Connor missing something? Was his taste *bad* now? He drummed his fingers on his knee in irritation.

Frankly, he'd rather get stuck reviewing more of the tryhard "transgressive" lit fic he was occasionally sent by his editor for the site's irregular book column. Perhaps yet another tired sexual history autofiction from yet another pseudo-nihilist edgelord who aspired to be the next Henry Miller or de Sade. Like that one 400-page brick entitled *Anatomy of a Body Count*, which, as he'd put it in his writeup, left him too bored to crank out the scathing review it so longed to deserve. If he just wanted to gawk at a bunch of anonymous cervixes, he'd go ask Dr. Tumblety.

See, Con, this is why you don't have friends. You're a cynical prick and you expect everyone to understand the obscure shit you're talking about.

Francis Tumblety, a homosexual medical quack from the 19th century, kept a collection of preserved uteri in jars to show off to his guests as dubious evidence supporting his outspoken misogyny. He was mainly known nowadays for being a Jack the Ripper suspect. The Ripper case had a peculiar import for Connor due to the early erotic imprint left on him by a true crime documentary that had briefly come on TV in his hotel room during a family vacation. His parents had turned it off at the earliest sight of gore, fearing it would scare him and his younger sister. But what little he'd caught led nine-year-old Connor to immediately fantasize about a fictionalized older version of himself held hostage in a locked, windowless room. His captor was a fourth-grader's loose conception of a Victorian Englishman: tall, handsome, quietly domineering in a dress shirt and suspenders, wielding a straight razor to unknown yet delicious ends.

Variations of this fantasy had haunted him ever since, the Ripper figure morphing from an idealized Disney prince of a dom into rougher-edged permutations: a leather-clad biker, a Prohibition mobster, a corrupt cop, a Commandant, a charming serial killer whose claws and fangs only came out after locking the bedroom door. And over the years, Connor's sexual fixation permeated his attempt at a music career—specifically, the noise project that combined experimental music with his dabblings in poetry, art, and acting— which culminated in his lone album, *How Some Children Played at Slaughter.*

His noise repertoire of sampler, looper pedal, and high school clarinet linked via contact mic to a pedal chain created the sinister, ambient backing to his aggressive spoken-word (and occasional shouted-word) performance of an original narrative prose poem. He'd released it as a C40 cassette tape with one continuous track repeated on both sides, and he'd released it under his own name, Con Egilssen. At the time, he'd thought using an obvious pseudonym for one's project was corny; nowadays, he didn't give a shit and rolled his eyes at his twentysomething pretension. He'd come to recognize that everyone under 30, his younger self included, was at least a little bit up their own ass. He recalled that Rex Hart was 29.

Slaughter's title and underlying theme were derived from a lesser-known Brothers Grimm tale. The gist of the story was this: two young boys decided to "play butcher" in imitation of the adults. One was the butcher, the other the hog, and preparing to "make sausages," the former slit the latter's throat. The little butcher was arrested and charged with murder, but the authorities were unsure whether to try him as an adult, his age bringing doubts about his capacity to fathom the seriousness of his crime. Thus a test of his innocence was devised: he was offered the choice of an expensive gold coin or a shiny new apple. The boy picked the apple and was set free, deemed not guilty by reason of his childhood ignorance as he was too young to understand the value of currency.

Connor had seized on the crux of this story and offered a twist. What if the test really proved the opposite conclusion: that the boy only grasped at what would fulfill his immediate animal needs, e.g., in this case, hunger? That he was fully aware of the seriousness of murder but killed solely because it felt good and right *in that instant*, societal expectations be damned—which was more akin to the psychology of real serial killers? And so the boy tricked the authorities by using their own logic against them. And he kept it up for years, well into adulthood. On this premise, Connor built a 20-minute track.

Slaughter was a failure. It didn't earn back the production costs from its now-shuttered noise microlabel and was mainly purchased by friends and acquaintances who, he assumed, just felt bad for him. He was shit at promotion: he just couldn't motivate himself. And *Slaughter* had been released when the noise scene was still overwhelmingly made up of cisgender heterosexual white guys: it was too introspective, experimental, and openly queer for the aggro dick-swinging posturing that could often result, but wasn't quirky or theoretical enough to be the art-school kind of noise, thus making it rather outré for its time. That alone had likely caused its doom—and led him to renounce music.

God, it was sweltering even under the fan. He didn't feel the heat very much, but his exposed skin had already sprouted a mildewy layer of dried sweat. Lightly scratching the back of his neck, his fingernails came away with crescents of dark grime. And he hadn't even gone out for groceries today like he normally did on Sundays. The supermarket was two blocks away, and in the fug of humidity it seemed a mountainous task. He'd be dripping like a shower head, his clothing soaked to the skin before he stepped through the sliding doors.

Not to mention that lost package. It still hadn't shown up, and surely it must have been found and opened by now, and some anonymous neighbor must be laughing at him behind brick and plaster. Someone he might well run into during his errands. Inspecting expiration dates on cuts of steak in the meat department while a stranger stage-whispers behind one raised hand: *Psst, there's our* pervert neighbor, *Con Egilssen, tee hee hee!* How he despised people who felt they were better than him for no real reason, who thought they had one over on him in some arbitrary power game.

Well, he wouldn't give them the pleasure. He'd stay home and skip grocery shopping today. He wouldn't even stop by the bodega.

But this meant he had no soda or seltzer at home. Oh, fuck it. Gin on the rocks with dinner.

A few hours later, a wild boar cavorted in secret through a thicket within the painting. It must, he thought, have been pareidolia seen in the brushstrokes. He may, just may, have been a bit drunk.

COME THE DAWN, THE HUNTSMAN once more departs for the woods with a crossbow strapped to his back. The journeyman stays behind and sweeps the cabin floor.

While sweeping before the hearth, a hollow noise and a chill draft emit from beneath the wolf pelt, which he rolls back to reveal a hidden trapdoor. He opens the latch and descends, lantern in hand.

At the foot of the ladder, the journeyman steps into a cellar. The room has been carved directly into the soil, support beams pressing into dark earth. A wooden shelf against one wall holds jars of glistening preserves, and the journeyman thinks of the organ on the mantel. Metal hooks hang from the ceiling on chains, and from these hooks dangle nameless four-limbed beasts, their torsos gutted, their skins flensed away, their headless necks dripping into buckets pushed into the dirt below.

The great gnarled roots of a juniper tree have worked their way through the corner of the cellar to grasp the dirt floor and coil around the scattered parts of dead men interred beneath. A wriggling in the soil catches the journeyman's eye, and slowly, from the waist up, a buried youth emerges. His skin is sallow as old bone, with great blackened gouges in his flesh. His lips and eyelids have withered back, and worms crawl in the empty sockets, yet the journeyman can tell he had been handsome once, before the rot.

"Journeyman . . ." the dead boy rasps. His voice has been worn to shreds by the suckling of roots and the trembling of maggots. "I was like you once. I knew the huntsman. He took a fancy to me. Listen: at night, he throws a wolfskin about his shoulders and rampages the countryside. He tore me apart with his teeth and claws."

"But at night, he lies with me now," says the journeyman.

The dead boy cocks his head. "But what of when you sleep?" He weakly waves a shriveled hand. "My brothers and I are buried here. Since you have known the huntsman, you will become my brother, too, and lie with us beneath the soil. It's men he hunts and ever will."

The journeyman reclines betwixt the roots and embraces him, stroking what remains of his hair, carefully clawing the maggots from his eyes. "I am so sorry this happened to you," whispers the journeyman. "Perhaps we could have loved each other." The boy's lank mouth twitches up into a small smile.

The wooden slats of the ladder creak under the huntsman's steps as the dead boy squirms back under the earth. The journeyman scrambles to his feet. The huntsman hauls a large bloodstained sack.

"I have shot a wild boar for us," says the huntsman. He looks the journeyman up and down with a smirk, for he knows what the journeyman has seen, and the journeyman knows that he knows. Still, the journeyman stands tall and does not cower.

The huntsman moves forward to caress him. Lifting the shirt from the journeyman's shoulders, he hoists the journeyman by the armpits to impale his back onto an empty hook. The metal pierces his skin and brushes the nodes of his spine. The huntsman loosens his belt and drops his trousers, intending to take him right there; but the journeyman's body sinks on the hook, a white flare of pain shoots through him as something wet starts to rip, and a swathe of skin is torn from his back as he topples into the dirt.

The huntsman, undeterred, pushes him onto his stomach and finishes stripping him. The journeyman stares at the large rag of his own flesh flapping on the hook until sufficiently distracted by the huntsman's tender ministrations. The huntsman fondles and massages his exposed muscle, bone, and tendons, preparing him, entering him. The dark loam is soft and warm under the huntsman's weight, and the journeyman's body sinks forward and downward at each hard thrust. The journeyman releases his seed into the soil with a cry as the earth fills his mouth and nostrils.

He ought to be dead, but he awakens whole, curled up in the huntsman's arms. He coughs, and a trickle of saliva from his lips is dotted with dark crumbs. In his sleep, the huntsman exhales and gently squeezes his waist with dirt-encrusted nails.

CONNOR'S MONDAY STARTED ON HIS knees before the toilet, retching up clear puke with half-digested grit inside. Fuck, at least he didn't have to commute through this. He'd just sit on the couch with his laptop and plenty of water, coffee, and aspirin at his side. He didn't even drink that much last night: age had clearly taken a slow pickaxe to his liver.

When sufficiently clear-minded during downtime at work, he started listening to the new Rex Hart tape. His critical notes quickly became a laundry list of flaws. Trite guitar noise. Basic-ass distortion pedals. Masturbatory knob-twiddling that felt like a sonic itch in his ear and made him wish for texture. What lyrics he could discern through the tremolo filtering Hart's vocals were full of florid words unnaturally crammed in together like . . . what was that stupid childhood game where one shoved as many marshmallows into one's mouth as possible and then tried to speak? It was like playing "chubby bunny" with a thesaurus.

By the end of Side A, it became apparent that *Dementius Lupus* was little more than a Whitman's Sampler of various noise subgenres Rex Hart had just learned about five minutes ago and decided to pastiche. Connor scoffed whenever he recognized each successive well-established artist Hart was transparently ripping off: The Rita, Merzbow, Brighter Death Now, early Whitehouse. It was awfully patronizing: *Hey kids, look how impressive my taste is!* Connor felt actively dumbed down by the experience.

Finishing this album was just prodding at a wound by this point, and not in his preferred style of masochism; but even if he weren't perversely curious to see just how much worse it could get, Connor was going to be paid for the task.

Frankly, the greatest torment was his humble opinion that he was a better noise artist than Rex Hart. Or had been, once. All the worse that he'd given up music after the piss-poor sales and minimal coverage of his lone album. Connor knew he could come off as abrasive—curmudgeonly if one wanted to be polite, an asshole if one didn't—but he had a thinner skin than most people assumed, and his pride could only be wounded so far. He knew the experience of playing an impassioned set for an audience of five people, four of whom were other acts on the bill, and not earn enough from the door to pay for the round-trip subway fare; he knew what it was like to be told "Sick set, man," after a show by some rando who'd proceed to shit-talk him online; and he certainly knew that the vast majority of music releases, let alone noise tapes, ended up quietly forgotten, but feeling so utterly diminished was too much for him. *Slaughter* had been the last straw. The world had cast its judgment of silence on Connor Egilssen; ergo, his talent was without worth. And since there was no specific person to punish him directly for his hubris, he had to do it himself.

And he'd done so by renouncing what had been his greatest and most productive psychological outlet. He'd sold all his gear a few years back, including his high school clarinet, and deleted the pirated copies of pricey audio editing software from his computer. Scorched earth.

As an added prong of the pitchfork, the old storytelling and performance urges had never fully left him. He tried to tamp them down and restrict them to highly embellished daydreams and sexual fantasies, never to emerge from his mouth. The words and phrases, the fictional figures. They mocked him, sometimes, for being trapped in his head.

After work, he went downstairs to check his mail. Still no package. Of course. It was funny, somehow: Connor had stood in that front landing countless times without giving it any thought. But now, suddenly, he felt caught in a tableau of some other place and time. The cracked and weathered Greek key-tile mosaic beneath his heels. The sun-faded ink at his buzzer and mailbox: EGILSSEN 3B. The metal front door, its window inset with a grille between glass like something from a prison. Or a madhouse. A distant sanitarium out in the mountains. *It's there to keep me in. It's there to keep them out.*

Heat pulsed through the front door. He considered that he should start budgeting for a delivery service so he wouldn't have to go out anymore.

At night a little man made of smoke with empty gaps for eyes wavered in the meadow of the painting. *Only a shadow, Con. Only a shadow.*

COME THE DAWN, THE HUNTSMAN departs to chop wood for the pile. The journeyman stays indoors and tends to the pot of stew. He casts a wary eye at the mantel, displaying the glass jar holding his organ and, now, a clump of dirt from the cellar in which his own seed has dried, wrapped in a drawstring pouch made from his own torn skin.

As he stirs the cauldron, a spatter of broth splashes out of the stew and lands on the floorboards beside him, as thick and red as blood. The droplets begin to speak in a chorus of the same sorrowful masculine voice.

"Oh! Journeyman!" Lumps of offal and bone burble up from the cauldron as if trying to re-form themselves.

"I was like you once," say the blood droplets. Their collective voice is full of slush, as though straining to speak through a barrel of wet gore. "My brothers and I were taken away and devoured by the huntsman. He carves our meat and rends our fat and grinds our bones. He lives purely on men and their leavings. This is what he hunts. He will not stop until he is dead, and he will never die. You will join us, my brothers and I. Since you have known the huntsman, you will become my brother, too. In the pot and in his belly." The smallest droplet pipes up most pitifully, its tone the crack and hiss of a burning ember.

The journeyman kneels before the fireplace and dips his fingers into the spilt blood. He rubs the blood over his lips and tongue as if to kiss the boy, to taste his copper one last time.

"I am so sorry," he mutters. "So sorry."

The huntsman enters the cabin with hatchet in hand. He sees the blood on the journeyman's lips and smiles. He stands by a wooden chair in front of the fireplace.

"Sit."

The journeyman sits. He removes his clothes without prompting, rests his hands on his knees, and awaits further instruction. The huntsman strokes his beard and nods.

He lashes a leather thong around the journeyman's wrists, tightening them together behind the chair, and ties two more around the journeyman's ankles, binding them to each front leg of the chair. He picks up a carving knife. He holds the hatchet in the other hand. He silently circles the chair, sometimes leaning forward to make slow, deliberate slices in the journeyman's flesh.

The journeyman looks down at the red lines covering his body. He realizes they demarcate butcher's cuts. Perhaps, he thinks, the huntsman will chop some of him off and toss it into the pot. At this, he nearly laughs, until the huntsman kneels on the wolf pelt between his legs.

The journeyman strains at his bonds with a thrill as the huntsman's mouth teases him, licking, nipping, tasting, before proceeding in earnest. The huntsman still holds both hatchet and carving knife: the journeyman cannot grow too comfortable. And yet, in time, he arches his back and releases down the huntsman's throat.

He is still in the throes as the huntsman sinks his teeth into the flesh and muscle of the journeyman's inner thigh, biting off a thick chunk with a sharp jerk of the neck. The huntsman straightens on his knees and bends forward, opening the journeyman's mouth. His teeth dangle the torn meat between the journeyman's own, waiting for him to bite off the end, to chew carefully, to swallow. Yellow fat seeps out from the inner edges of the wound like soft teeth grimacing.

The huntsman stands, loosening his fly before the journeyman's face and awaiting reciprocation: the meat was served unseasoned and now he would add salt. The journeyman's lips and tongue begin their work as the pool of blood from his wound spreads under his seat. He sits in a congealing puddle. He feels cold. His vision wavers and his jaw slackens as the huntsman presses a firm guiding hand to the back of his head.

He ought to be dead, but he awakens whole, cradled in the huntsman's arms. A dark bruise marks his thigh and a heady aftertaste rests on his tongue. The huntsman shifts and sighs happily, nuzzling the back of his neck.

CONNOR AWOKE HAVING SWEATED A cold, damp patch into his sheets. He had bitten his cheek in his sleep.

What the hell was he going to do about this album review? Word count aside, just how much forthright negativity could he pack in? Would he be dismissed as a bitter old bitch if he labeled Hart an overhyped dilettante? Would he be called pretentious if he called the tape pretentious? Anything resembling a niche scene or subculture was tight-knit to the point of being a tinderbox for drama. Rex Hart was both prominent and local enough to have numerous mutual friends and respected colleagues with Connor—and any more-than-mildly negative opinion was déclassé where everyone knew everyone. God, the irony of genres that prided themselves on being *dark* and *angry* and *pessimistic as fuck* having a low-key Good Vibes Only ethos.

Giving an honest review in such a case could be perceived as talking shit. It would involve starting beef. It would affect his assignment of any further albums to review. And the site he wrote for was small enough that he wouldn't get a guaranteed kill fee if they decided not to run it. He could write up some fluff, he knew; he could lie. But he would loathe himself for it. Especially considering the tape's ending.

During the final track of *Dementius Lupus*, the sound slowed into a dark ambient drone. A reverb-heavy, pitch-shifted woodwind pulsed eerily in the background. In crept samples of wolves howling, twigs snapping, ghostly moans, claws rending wet meat: a forest at night. It was by far the most interesting this tape had gotten yet. Then Hart broke in with a seductively evil growl: the listener was a weary traveler, invited to come inside, rest their feet, listen to a tale. *Have you ever heard*, he croaked, *the tale of* **how some children played at slaughter?**

And the storm coursed through Connor with that goddamn line. He'd immediately pressed the stop button, too pissed off to listen to the last few minutes. Would it even be an objective review, or would any legitimate criticism be tainted now? Was Hart aware of Connor's album; had he been plagiarized, and could he even prove it? Did the editor *know* about this and send *this specific tape* to *this specific person*, deliberately, to humiliate him? Should he just quit writing reviews, for that site, for anyone?

As he considered this, late in the afternoon, eyes glazing at his company laptop, he received a message in his work inbox from middle management: a breezy, chirpy message obliterating his current way of life.

We're going back to the office next month! went the mass email, with details about times and dates and lackadaisical safety measures. *It's time we got back to normal. Our clients expect us to be in 100% tip-top shape, and we're going to show them our best! We understand the end of WFH may cause some adjustment, but it was only ever an emergency measure, and we've got to get back to normal. We look forward to seeing you all back!*

The message set off a trip-wire response, shading his rage with despair. He didn't care what the company party line said: Connor was still afraid of the pandemic. Afraid of all the communicable, deadly diseases of close quarters. His isolated lifestyle had kept him safe thus far, but he knew it could doom him if he were ever infected, which was inevitable if he had to return to the rush-hour subway commute. His sister lived on the opposite coast and had her own family to look after, a young child and another on the way. His parents, including a mother with creeping dementia, lived in a retirement home in Wisconsin. He had few close friends and none living nearby, especially since people kept moving out of the city when work largely went remote during lockdown: he'd come here years ago expecting to work as a creative professional and had predictably failed entirely, like countless other transplants of his era. He could not afford to move, could not afford a bigger or better apartment unless he took on a roommate, and bristled at the idea of some stranger encroaching on his territory. So if he got sick, he'd be utterly fucked. There would be nobody to help take care of him through debility and pain. To advocate for him if he had to go to the hospital. To ensure he wouldn't get a cheap cremation or a nameless burial in a mass trench on Hart Island if he died. At least grant him a slab of something permanent with CONNOR EGILSSEN etched thereupon. *Please, god, let someone remember that I lived. Let me have* mattered.

He rose in silence and slammed his fist into the doorframe, biting his knuckle afterward to keep from screaming in fury. He stared at the whitewashed surface of his apartment door, that thin layer of wood keeping him in, keeping them out; imagined it covered entirely by clinging vines and thorns that some daring gallant must hack away to enter and save him. *I can't leave. You can't make me. I'll barricade myself in here. What can you do?* He could get out the gin. He could start drinking now. In fact, he would. He *would* drink on the clock.

And he hadn't heard any response to his email to L. Sacher Products, Inc., so he steeled himself to call them right after work. On top of everything else, he wasn't going to get fucking ripped off.

Tapping his fingers anxiously, Connor waited as the customer service line linked him to an actual human.

"Sometimes tracking says it was delivered before it actually is," said the woman at the help desk in a curious monotone. "You should give it some time."

"It was supposed to have been delivered almost a week ago."

"Have you tried waiting a little longer? Just a little bit longer."

"But the post office said it was delivered. They directly *said* it was." He was close to shouting now.

"Just a . . . little bit . . . longer. Justa . . . liddlebit . . . lon-ger." Her hypnotic cadence slowed in pitch, a machine running down. He could picture skin melting from a robot's metal skull like toasted cheese. He hung up on her.

Connor felt emptied. The mirror showed him a very sickly man. *All my blood is gone*, he thought, and it was almost funny. He curled up in his undershirt and boxers to attempt a stress nap.

Across the room, the painting was peeling away like a snake's molts.

AT DAWN, THE SKY IS red and mottled with evil, the texture of burnt skin. The journeyman studies the horizon as the huntsman stands behind him and squeezes his shoulder with a small, assured smile. He laces his fingers over the huntsman's own and smiles in turn.

A pair of ravens has landed on the fence posts.

"You were handsome once, my brother," says a raven.

"Ah, but not so much as you!" says the other, spreading one wing with a titter. "I spy the cabin where we first met so long ago."

"Yes, where that wicked huntsman captured us and killed us!"

"And was going to drop us into his stew until—"

"—Until—"

"We stole a raven's bone from the cinders, and joined hands, and enchanted ourselves—"

"And we flew up the chimney to escape!" The bird preens its dark feathers.

"Have you heard, my brother?" says the other raven. "A man is kept in the huntsman's cabin even now. He is trapped and ravaged nightly in the huntsman's bed and used for his meat, bones, and blood."

The journeyman has little patience for the mocking, gravelly croaks of the ravens, gossips all, and grating to the ear. He retrieves the broom from the cabin and chases the ravens until they fly high into the air.

"Fie, you birds! I am here of my own free will!"

He retreats to the cabin, to the secret work that has begun there. To the jarred organ and the pouch of seed-soil and the dried thigh-muscle, packed into a false body of the journeyman's height and breadth; a body crafted from human leather and scattered bones and blood-stew from the many dead boys, dressed in rags of the journeyman's old clothes and spread out on the wolf pelt. The journeyman kneels down to its open mouth and kisses a breath of life into him.

The awakened homunculus is sent forth into the wide world so the journeyman can stay here forever. He can be carved, stabbed, strangled, bitten, shot, tormented, and ravished, and each day he will wake up whole and alive in the huntsman's strong arms, without a care in the world but for their life together, out here in the cabin by the woods.

He devises transgressions, indulging in trysts and whispers with the boys in the pond and the cellar and the cooking pot and cackling in the sky, to instigate stern punishments, which the huntsman gladly and lovingly dispenses. He throws a wolfskin about his shoulders and prowls on his hands and knees at night as the huntsman laughs. He lets himself be hunted for sport, the huntsman weakening his limbs with arrow bolts, tackling him with a blade held to his pale throat. He straddles the huntsman's lap with a lustful and meaningful gaze before pressing a favored knife into his lover's hand. He does not fear. He will never fear, for a man with no true body cannot die. He does not venture beyond the broken gate, the little pond, and the trees at the edge of the mountains. He has no desire to do so.

And in another land, in another time, a boy's aging body falls back into bed. And in that bed, the homunculus of twig-bones and leather and rotting offal lies spotted with mold and dusted with mildew. The cockroaches hide in his crevices and the spiders weave silk between his angles.

And if he hasn't died, then he lives on today.

ASKESIS
LAWRIE JACKSON

"I USED TO BE SO fucking hot."

It must be the wine talking. It's not like him at all to talk so freely. Not just that, but he can feel the next words on the tip of his tongue: "As hot as you, even. Hotter, in fact." But with a little effort, Lawrence manages to restrain himself.

Across the table, the new flatmate's grin glints in the candlelight, and his wineglass flashes as he brings it to his mouth. Piano music streams, and a TV theme rises from the flat below in a blur. The faintest breeze comes in at the open window—why is it, any summer night, a little sigh of air always feels so sad?

He has never talked to anyone about that period in his life. This must be a new identity emerging with age, pure devil-take-the-hindmost. There ought to be some benefit, surely, to balance out the aches and pains. No pain, no gain – well, perhaps this is the gain: this boldness.

Yet he can feel the blush creeping over him. Invisibly, he hopes, in this light.

You've shown yourself up straight away, Lawrie.

The new flatmate gives a little laugh, but it's friendly. "I'm sure, mate."

Probably all he's hearing is typical gay male self-deprecation, adorned in the camp drag of arrogant wit. Or perhaps when Lawrence says *Hot*, Mark is thinking of Timothée Chalamet, or some other kind of physical fitness that was remarkable twenty years ago but fairly standard today.

The new flatmate's name is Mark. He's in his mid-twenties, and he's an estate agent. He had just been saying how his job keeps him fit, all that running around. That and his girlfriend—

she'd walk out on him if he started to lose his six-pack. But it's silly, really, and he knows it is, haha.

Haha, they had both been saying, and they both know it is absurd and that it is also as serious as the difference between rich and poor, man and woman.

That was the impulse, almost angry, that prompted Lawrence to say it, *I have had what you have now*, driving the words up out of some dark region of his chest. That pallid, delicate chest barely deep enough to contain his heart. A chest that once swelled like the bonnet of a car. He can feel his heart hammering in that small shadowy compartment even now, even as he longs to let it lie.

I'm telling you something real. I am a homosexual. I know about male beauty.

"No, sorry—I can't believe I'm showing you this, but …."

He grabs the phone from his pocket, moving almost instinctually. Must be the wine. His clumsy thumb skids over the screen, delving into the search terms. Only a few people's bodies exist in an alternate life out there, in that wide sargasso sea of online pictures: for the most part, they are bodies like Mark the Estate Agent's. Chris Evans. Chris Hemsworth. Zac Efron. Henry Cavill. Tom Holland. Tom Daley. Tom of Finland. Zane Philips. Pablo Perroni. Ben Theo Andrews. Michelangelo's David. The Westmacott Athlete.

This image. *The Picture.*

Mark laughs again, defensively this time, with the phone practically in his face. Then he really studies it. "Wow. This is really you? I mean, I have no experience in this area—no offence, haha. But that is—"

Yes, it is. Even at this point in history, though, he cannot say the words. If Lawrence were straight, there would be less of a problem. If Mark's girlfriend was here—Keeley or something—she might just be permitted to articulate it.

But then they would have to ask him—how did he get back to looking so *normal*?

Lawrence puts his phone back in his pocket. The hand holding it fumbles so that he inadvertently strokes his crotch, the unbidden hard-on there. Conspirator with a dark heart beating in his chest. He flexes the empty hand.

"My hands are weird lately. Think it's my shoulder." Haha. "I mean, I think the problem's in my shoulder."

"You want to get that checked out."

"Yeah, yeah...."

"Seriously. I injured myself once on the bench-press. Taking on too much, haha. I didn't want to admit it to anyone. Stupid, but...."

Again, they laugh at the absurdity of male insecurity as though it were not the force that spins the world.

"Anyway, I found a bloke in the end who sorted me out. Never told nobody but Keeley—well, and you now, mate."

"I get you."

"I can give you his number."

"Maybe."

"You're storing stuff up if you're not careful."

Lawrence doesn't want to say aloud that he can hardly store up very much more. Turning forty, everything in storage is already on display. There is no back of house.

Another mouthful of wine. He can only just feel the glass in his hand.

"Anyway, Mark. Tell me more about you."

"RIGHT, LAWRENCE. LET'S START WITH you popping your shirt off."

The tick of the air conditioner, the murmur of girls' voices passing, and then a peal of laughter that he instinctively hears as a response to his unprepossessing physique. The blinds, however, are drawn firmly down.

"Sorry—my, uh, trousers...?"

"Keep them on. But your belt—and anything in your pockets...."

"Oh, yes."

"And your watch."

It's a nice specimen, a birthday present to himself, quite new—he balances it delicately on the small occasional table, noting the time as if it is important to do so. They haven't spent as much time talking in preparation as he had imagined.

A sheet of tissue protects the bed; the headrest has a square of kitchen towel with a hole for his face.

"Breathe naturally. Don't even think about it."

In through the kitchen towel. Out through the kitchen towel. He thinks to himself: stop thinking. Stop thinking. Just let it happen.

The bedframe begins to creak in rhythm, and the tissue to ruck and rub.

"Tell me if something doesn't feel right."

"Haha …."

"Pardon?"

"Nothing, sorry." The air is pressed from his lungs as he utters the word, and it elongates like a cow's moo.

"Just give yourself up to me."

Disembodied footsteps cross the room above and back again.

"My daughter. She paces up and down when the news is on."

"Ah."

The physio hadn't looked old enough to have a daughter. Perhaps he is deceptively boyish. *Straight people just get on with life, no over-thinking. Particularly breeders.*

Somewhere, diagonally across the way from his feet, the expensive watch is slowly ticking away. *If this overruns, you'll have to tell Mark that you took his advice.* An admission of something. Weakness. You so rarely leave the house.

"You carry a lot of tension in your lower back."

"I suppose I should get up more. From my desk. Working from home, you know…."

"Oh, I'd hate that. Sitting down all day. That's not me."

Could one get immersed in physiotherapy? Lose oneself in caressing somebody's torso, trying to find the problem—iron it out? Then again, saying immersed, it sounds like being fascinated, but what it's really like is being afraid to turn away.

"And you said you'd been experiencing some workplace stress in the past year?"

"Something went wrong—oh!"

"Alright?"

"Yes, great!" His heart is drumming the mattress through the tissue: nowadays, all it takes is the word *workplace*. "Something went wrong with the email. In my organisation. Messages going to the wrong places, the wrong people."

"An office poltergeist, perhaps."

"Well, a ghost in the machine, haha." And at first it was funny. Then it got messy, and not just work-wise. Already, one colleague has vanished from the weekly Zoom meetings—with an absolute moratorium on the discussion about his behaviour *A popular guy, I always thought. Bit of a sexy dad type.*

"And you're fixing it?"

"Trying to. Ha \ha."

Forcing a laugh with no breath is hard enough, but through the kitchen towel, it feels even more eccentric, and whose benefit is it for anyway? He tries to imagine the physio is smiling. The voice is dispassionate, with occasional emphasis when he brings all his weight to bear on some muscle or other.

"Do you do anything to relax?"

"Watercolours. It's not really working, though. I don't think, at least."

"Right. Just a small adjustment now. Breathe in deep for me. Deeper, if you will."

"Sorry."

Somewhere in the small of the back, where the spine points to the bum.

"That's good. Now, very slowly out."

Shouldn't leave a book propped open because it will damage the spine. Then when it clicks, there's no going back, and curiously, your feeling of ownership over it increases.

CLICK

"And again, just one tiny adjustment, breathe in deeply. Now, let it out."

A movement you would normally freak out about. Pretend it's someone else.

CLICK

"Excellent. Ever used a gym?"

"I fell out of love with it. I mean, it's not really for me.

"I think you'll find exercise is for everyone."

He considers another *haha* but is afraid it'll be taken wrong.

"Right, go as limp as you can. Soft as a suit of clothes."

He sees his old work-suit, hung at the back of his wardrobe for six months now. Cheap plastic coat hanger. They break so easily. Should your neck really turn that far?

CLICK

"Do you live with anybody?"

"Flatmates. A new one just arrived. We seem to get on."

"I only ask because—family, romantic partners, they can lower your blood pressure."

"Not in my experience."

It's the physio's turn to fake a laugh.

"Or you could get a pet."

He makes a small ambiguous *hmm* sound.

"I'm concerned about this numbness you described. Can you feel—that?"

"… Sort of."

There should be other words for feel, like listen and hear, see and perceive. What happens if what you feel, feels wrong?

"I shouldn't worry myself if I were you, but… obviously, it's not quite as it should be."

He senses the physio leave his side. Should he take his head out of the kitchen towel? It's nice to be instructed to wait for direction. Ah, now the physio is back, and there is music playing. Time to relax.

He starts sifting through the train times from Wimbledon to Sydenham, albeit in a more relaxed way than earlier.

There's a new dull ache in the small of his back as he stoops to pull his socks on.

"Don't write off the gym entirely." The physio himself is trim, with cyclist's calves, and a squarish head set with friendly eyes. There could be a little grey in that stubble. Shouldn't stare. "It will help with your lumber support. You'll thank yourself."

It's just coming onto twilight, but the way to Wimbledon station is well-lit, and Lawrence finds himself striding purposefully as if his legs knew where they were taking him. The smells around him are all late summer. He finds himself worrying at the new ache. Not because it hurts—it's curiously satisfying—but is it a sign of good health? Is that what he went to a physio for? Is it a long-standing problem he's feeling for the first time?

In its blur of discomfort, he feels more aware than ever of the muscles working under his skin. He lengthens his stride, swings his hands. The fingertips itch restlessly.

"THAT BUNCH OF CUNTS AT the office are doing my head in. Funny lads, but not all day," Mark says. "Know what I'm talking about?"

Lawrence's heart races at the mention of work. He's been feeling good till now. Holding himself upright at the table so as not to aggravate that dull ache he feels almost makes him feel like a different person. Purposeful.

He stabs an asparagus spear with suppressed anxiety.

"Keeley's coming over this weekend. You free for dinner on Saturday night?"

"I can be."

"She's got me under her thumb, haha. Good day, mate?"

To avoid work chat, he describes the physio visit, downplaying the strangeness—why should it be strange? He doesn't mention the physio's calves, either.

Mark's face is a picture of vague concern until he hears about the gym advice. Now they're talking his language.

"Yes. Great idea, mate, do it."

"Maybe."

"I don't know where I'd be without it. It'll be great for your mental health. It doesn't have to be about, you know, building muscle."

"I'll think about it."

"Come on. You need something to put your mind to besides that shitty email stuff."

"I suppose so."

"And, I mean, you must know your way around a gym. That Picture...."

The ache, the holding himself upright, clenches as one.

"I should never have mentioned that, haha."

"You know there is such a thing as muscle memory, Lawrie."

For fuck's sake. We don't want to go digging up that body again, do you?

They wash up the dinner things. They half-watch TV, Mark texting his girlfriend. Lawrence does his watercolours. The brush sketches a cage. He hears Mark's light go off.

The flat becomes silent.

He goes to the bathroom and locks the door. He inspects his body in the bathroom mirror, then looks away. At least it's slender like a young person's—no body fat—so in theory, he should be able to pinpoint where he's gone wrong. Angling himself, tracing the shape of that constrictive feeling like a warning pressure on the back, it retains its mystery.

Habit dictates that Lawrence always prepares for sleep with a wank. He summons an image of the physio. Then Mark, who is, yes, undeniably hot, even at the age of the gym membership. Lawrence has seen him in the morning entering the bathroom in just his boxers.

Maybe you should paint his picture, Lawrie. Flip the roles around. Get out the fucking watercolours. Invite him to pose.

You're the old guy now. Not as senior as he was, and Mark's not as young as you were. It's the spirit of the thing. Age before beauty.

Except that's not quite how it was, is it?

He has moved to think of that beautiful body and how it was once venerated. Lawrence could walk about all day and feel it on him at all times, even in the middle of the night, like armour that went all the way down. And all the way out, too, if that's what he wanted. On a dark night in a strange town, he could project invulnerability. Shoulders out to here. Arms that bulged their shirt sleeves. In clubs, Lawrence could feel the body drawing looks.

No one now would think you had it in you.

What was it Mark said, muscle memory…? And perhaps something in his blood does remember, like stone tape theory.

The hand that frigs his hard cock is so numb it nearly grips too hard.

He dreams of the body.

ON WAKING, LAWRENCE FORGETS THE dream. Going through the business of the morning is almost like a waking dream itself, or like riding on the back of an animal that has been perfectly trained: brushing the teeth, showering and deodorizing the body, talcing the balls, shaving the jaw, moisturizing the face, eating up his porridge like a good boy.

He's lost his watch somewhere. Too distracted.

In the office chair, in the kitchen, Lawrence's hands work on the keyboard quickly and precisely, touch typing as if they know where to go: he doesn't have to think. His worrying transfers to the email problem. His body retreats in importance as if biding its time. Only at mid-morning does it assert itself, the ache in the back seems to knock and murmur, *Only me.*

Exercise is for everybody. You need something. You know your way around.

His online searching for a local gym—more expensive or less expensive, a short walk away or a pool onsite—shifts almost inevitably into searching for gym bodies, as if his hard-on were operating his typing fingers. Fitness models. Personal trainers. Short shorts, jumbo thighs, dumb expressions. Pecs. Abs. Biceps. Glutes. Gleaming. Swelling.

He doesn't call up the Picture itself, but he doesn't need to. He sees the body again onscreen suddenly, the body that was his, and the way they all wear it. Confident, diffident, cocky, or innocent (who, me?)—they all wear that body and wear it the same way. He can see it if he closes his eyes.

He lays a hand on the flat, hairless chest inside his shirt and pictures it—less flat.

Oh yes, this is what I dreamed of last night.

Quick wank. Then he heads out on a mission.

The nearest and cheapest gym is quite nice. It has an onsite pool and sauna. They take Lawrence's details and give him a card and a monogrammed towel. He reacquaints himself with the gym atmosphere. Shite dance music, metal chiming, instructors bellowing encouragement. His heart thuds in his chest. An employee in shorts and t-shirts, with plump biceps and pert little pectorals, looks at him sceptically.

"You need to have an induction, mate. You could do yourself an injury."

"No, no, don't worry, I remember how it all works."

"Oh—you've been to a gym before?"

Disbelief.

"Yes, ages ago. I used to love it."

That's a lie. Lawrence just wants to look a bit more in control. And yet, perhaps there was love involved way back when.

He treats himself to a swim as a reward for leaving the house.

The resounding of voices off the glass roof and the sound underwater which is surely the sound of his own head. Does everyone hear the same thing under here?

This is true immersion: not fascination or dedication, but being subsumed, removed from the ordinary world. Weightless, there's no clue as to what sort of physiology Lawrence has trailing behind him. Only when he actively attempts to swim the length of the pool does he feel the difference: a different ache, a hint of cramp.

The body remembers how to do it better than he does, the way you almost become another aspect of the pool, like light or sound: he just has to let it move. Nonetheless, it tests his stamina. Lungs gulp air. No need to think—in, out this time.

Even though he hasn't put it through an actual work-out, his body is exhausted, so much so it won't let him stay awake to read as usual; it doesn't even require a wank.

The body fills his dreams again, and this time he won't forget them, clings to them.

THE FIRST WEEK IS PARTICULARLY hard. Humiliation.

He walks around in the gym like a stranger. He learns, limb by limb, the limits of this body, the one Lawrence wants rid of. This new physique of his is even weaker than he assumed. Each time he selects a weight, it's too heavy, even when he thinks he has under-estimated himself.

He's ever conscious that injury is near—lifting something heavier than he can handle, lifting it in the wrong way, orienting himself in some way contrary to the exercise (no *CLICK*, this time, please). He sees other men glance at him in concern. He'll do himself a mischief.

He tells himself they are not looking. They do not care. That's in the past.

He knows very well that to change this body he must break this one apart. Smash it.

It all feels a bit silly.

But that's you all over, Lawrie. Go against your own character, and—hopefully—it will wear away.

You'll thank yourself.

The first month is an act of faith. In his own tenacity, his capacity for change, his muscle memory. He is following an old pattern, pursuing an old idea, older by far than him.

When he sits down to Lawrence's bloody watercolours, he finds he is sketching the body, the musculature beneath the skin, the proportions of antiquarian statues. They used to repeat it so often at college, the knowledge has been wired into him. Drilled into him by his Professor in first year. Perhaps it's the chief legacy of Lawrence's time at art school, that intrinsic understanding of masculine beauty.

Retrieved from the deep past, as an ancient statue dug from the dirt.

As the month drags on, the email system is just as much of a wrestling match, refusing to let him sort it out. Every day he logs on to flurries of misdirected messages, many of them about him, most of them blunt or aggressively rude: what's the wanker, the twat, the little poof doing at his desk at home, why hasn't he fixed it yet, where is he, what's his problem? One of the senders is David, his manager.

You'd think people would be more careful in the circumstances. You could bring this up at a tribunal if you were the sort of person who did that. Or perhaps it's intentional, Lawrie, meant for you to see.

His heart pounds as he replies to the email. "Sorry…."

David laughs it off. They make small talk by instant messenger. Fingers tap. "Think it'll be back to normal by Christmas?"

"Whatever normal is haha"

Mark is right. Lawrence deserves more than this cowering existence.

AT THE START OF SEPTEMBER, he starts training himself to get up and go for a run, first thing. He motivates himself with the beauty of the season. The smell of leaves, dirt, drizzle. The apricity of weak sunlight. The gaudiness of summer is beginning to wither and fall away.

Each day, however painful the run, there is a moment of transcendent beauty.

Then, without his noticing any change, the legs run as if it were their natural state to do so as if Lawrence were a runner who perversely spends much of the day sitting down.

By day, under his desk, they twitch and throb with longing for movement.

The lungs take longer to accept the situation, but one day they too are altered. More powerful. The scent of decay in the suburban street seems to become richer. He actually prefers being up and out to lying in his bed, restless and slow.

In the pool, his nocturnal swim is a pleasure once more. He reminds himself to push a little harder each time.

In the gym, he takes a certain pleasure in panting, gasping and sucking breath. He sometimes snarls with the exertion, then searches the room, smiling embarrassedly, for anyone caught staring. He quite likes the deepening tone, nonetheless.

After that transition, it doesn't matter what state the world is in heat, cold, pouring rain (increasingly, it is raining—this is England). The body is awake and wants to run. Lawrence finds himself frustrated at having to stop after an hour and walk about like a normal person, and he laughs.

You should be out every day, running across the hills. What were we thinking of, building these boxes of concrete and brick?

Were we trying to forget our true nature?

Then one evening, when he strips off after his workout, Lawrence sees it—out of the corner of his eye. In the mirror. When he steps closer and examines himself properly, of course, it's not quite the same at all. Nonetheless, a very strong resemblance.

Baby biceps. The faintest curve in the pecs. Shoulders open out like wings. Lawrence remembers this—and the biceps, the pecs, the shoulders seem to remember it too.

When he swims, the variety of aches is like a continuous ringing sound, like hearing a fire alarm somewhere but not knowing which building....

Mellow October darkness is deepening. It feels like everything is working its way toward something more honest.

He walks home in just his gym-wear, pumped and warmed by the exertion and by the blasting pool shower, and his sheer sense of growing ease, the bite of the cold air balancing with the ache of his body. The blood running in his veins seems to acknowledge the cold only to disregard it. Beads of sweat on his throat tremble like pearls. Stubble prickles his chin.

Lawrence feels satisfied, or perhaps, the body is satisfied with him – but it is capable of more.

Only when he sits down at the laptop next morning does the body behave differently: the raised pulse and the insensation. He finds himself thinking of the dream body again. He wants to see it—soon.

After this he makes a habit of going to the gym every night.

IN NOVEMBER, THE PAIR OF them grow moustaches for charity. Lawrence's springs up unexpectedly thick and dark. Must be the testosterone bubbling up in him. Funny to think how naff this would have looked in his days of art school. Now it's just this side of funny. Suits him.

If he didn't have so much momentum, this would be a good physique to settle for. But to some extent, it's not in his control.

Fuck that.

Mark insists on a selfie of the pair of them, throwing an arm around the older man's shoulder. Lawrence tries not to look at that arm in the photo. Instead, he notices what pale bumfluff his flat-mate has managed to sprout on his upper lip. He can see Mark regarding them both in the screen. His eyes meet his eyes.

"God, Lawrence …."

"Uh, sorry …?"

"Mate, I can't help noticing—I mean, it's really making a difference. You must be proud of yourself."

He is aware of his new body, of course, but mostly through the eyes of others. In the gym mirror or in the sauna, or walking to his morning work-out, stretching out that singlet that once hung loose on him. Mark's girlfriend, Keeley, when she visits. A nice woman, adores Mark, has been warned Lawrence is a poof—still, there's something in the way she looks at him when they're scootching around one another in the kitchen.

Lawrence shrugs it off, smiles. It wouldn't do to look like he cared. He could certainly never admit to looking out for a sight of the body—just once a week, now, on a Sunday. A careful inspection in the gym mirror for familiar shapes and signs. That would sound like vanity. Not that Mark himself lifts weights for the sake of his health.

Lawrence also chooses not to talk to Mark about the other men at the gym. They're a funny mixture, but now that his body is becoming like theirs, he feels a kinship. He's way behind some of them—the typical gym rats. They look like actual bodybuilders. There are other men to whom he can't help feeling a little superior—usually because they're carrying a bit of weight, something of which he has certainly never been accused. *Spidery.*

In the sauna, they all watch one another. Under the towel, his cock is achingly hard, but Lawrence feels he has learned some restraint over the past few years. He lets the body feel what it feels, wagging its tail like mad, but he doesn't let it off the leash.

And what does Mark look like under his clothes? How do you compare?

To deal with the frustration of impatience, he turns again to the fucking watercolours, but the delicacy required seems no longer accessible to him. He throws the lot in the bin in a momentary, snarling loss of control.

Mark comes rushing in, eyes wide, and listens to the explanation with sympathy.

"Maybe it ain't your thing any more, mate. Maybe you got it all out of your system in art school. Know what I mean?"

All Mark knows of that time is a glimpse of the Picture. A story he's imagined about how it came to exist. He imagines that's all in the past, and maybe it is. Could Lawrence ever imagine Mark in his old art college? The Great Man would have had a field day with that physique.

He certainly would have chosen Mark over Lawrence back in the day.

Some days, Lawrence imagines them together, doing what Lawrence did. First, unconscious display; then the posing, the sketching; then the real schooling. The Great Man could have taught Mark a thing or two, and the thought gets Lawrence hard.

But somehow, the fantasy never sustains for a whole wank. All can think about is getting that body back. Impatience grows. He gets a glimpse if he wakes at night and can take it by surprise. Heavy on him, hot and itchy and constricting as if he'd fallen asleep in his clothes.

There you are....

Then he slips back into unconsciousness, to permit the body to do its work undistracted. Rest is an integral part of the bodybuilder's routine—a ludicrous term, but he is a bodybuilder now, by definition at least, let's be honest – and everything he does in the day is simply preparation for the processes at night while the mind is elsewhere. The synthesis of chemicals, the nurturing of new growth, a little bigger and stronger to try and catch up with the activities of day-life. Hypertrophy.

Dreaming. Then the body wakes, well-trained, and starts moving before he has fully blinked himself awake. Out into the penetrating chill.

Lawrence knows he can at least rely on the body when he can't rely on himself.

WITH THE ARRIVAL OF DECEMBER, something else changes. The rogue emails stop. The problem is resolved. Now that Lawrence's manager, David, is off his back, he can return to the regular admin, system checks, and diagnostics. And resetting passwords when people unfailingly forget them. David praises him in an all-staff email. He congratulates him via messenger.

"Hope you can unwind a bit now. I know you couldn't get away in summer."

"Actually, I do have two weeks already booked: an Air B'n'B in Berlin."

"Nice one. Enjoy it. You've earned it."

Exchanging one city, one cage for another. Don't you know where you really belong?

Lawrence finds himself going online to cancel the whole thing. Click, click, click. He knows it's madness. He's been looking forward to it all year, but he doesn't want to disrupt his routine. If he breaks his habits now, it would just feel wrong, cataclysmic. In fact, the money he would have spent will come in handy for a personal trainer.

He waits for the dream body.

His trainer says to be careful. Lawrence is a testosterone factory.

It's a good season for eating more. Lawrence could ask for meat for Christmas, and it would sound so greedy, when of course it's only natural, the fuel he needs. The supplements he drinks are foul but then, taste is just a learned response. The lion doesn't complain about flavour.

When Sunday comes around, he can't quite bring himself to look: in case the body is there, and in case it's not. When he locks eyes with his own gaze in that mirror, he glances away, embarrassed. It's like being back at college and trying not to hope his crush would be in class today, trying not to hope he'll see you.

Sir. The Professor. The Great Man. He seemed old back then, but that only made him more magisterial. He was gay, from another era of masculine adoration. Physique Pictorial. Hellenic Statues. The silver screen. His love for the male body had been hard-fought.

There were complaints from Lawrence's fellow students: why do we only ever have male life models, why do we always go to the bloody British Museum to sketch the absurd old Greek gods. All this musculature, so naff…

In the end, there was an easy way to gain the Great Man's attention— and that was the first time he summoned the body.

Not for himself back then. Perhaps that's why it flitted away.

So you can't see it in the mirror yet – but close your eyes. Feel that throb at the base of the spine. The deeper breaths the lungs are taking. The stomach growls with a new appetite. It's here—or getting near.

One night, Lawrence is woken by something. He's utterly alert, like a beast at the cave mouth. Bump. Grunt. A high voice uttering no words. It's the sound of Mark and Keeley. Lawrence takes in the sound, detail by detail. Soon it's quiet once more.

No distractions from the sensation of feeling heavier, being more solid, more of *him*. A distant car sighs as it turns a bend somewhere. Surely there should be something more, some bass drone as the energies of his every fibre push themselves toward regeneration.

His cock is hard. Hearing flatmates fucking has always meant Lawrence needs a wank, but when he goes to touch himself, neither arm will move. Have they gone to sleep, trapped? He cannot lift a finger.

He cannot sit up. He feels a weight—not within but heavy *upon* his chest. Breathing slow and sure and deep. No sound of Lawrence's own breath. He's stronger than he's been in years, yet this force is immovable. He panics, and observes the heart beating regularly, unaltered by emotion.

Who's there?

There's nobody to measure how long it is before he falls asleep.

In the morning, when the body wakes smartly and takes Lawrence for a run, the memory of the night's events feel almost pleasurable. It's wild. Must be what happens when you deliberately steer your body closer to the brink. Sleep paralysis. Perfectly natural.

That evening's work-out is almost effortless. A pleasure. Afterwards, he looks in the mirror. And he sees it.

There you are.

"KEELEY, I NEED TO SHOW you something."

Champagne bubbles. Red meat. The tang of gunpowder after three crackers have been pulled. A paper crown like a headache. We three kings. Ho ho ho.

Christmas comes but once a year. Thank fuck.

"Is that you Lawrie? Swit swoo."

"Haha."

"Yes, but baby, the fucking crazy thing is—that was painted ages ago."

"Right."

"Some creepy old lech of an art teacher did it when Lawrie was, like, my age. Right?"

"He wasn't creepy."

"No, I mean, not creepy-creepy, but—it's just, like, it wouldn't happen now, right?"

"You know what it's like. You're guaranteed attention with a body like that." For a second, their eyes meet. "I enjoyed it. I suppose I wanted it."

"Someone would definitely paint a picture of Lawrie now, Mark baby."

"That's not my point, but—"

"I mean, he literally looks the same."

Mark has decided to eat instead of talking.

"Honestly, Mark, I liked him. A lot. He was a great man. A real artist."

"Did you keep in touch with him, Lawrie?"

Keeley has asked the question, ostensibly in all innocence but actually in defence of Mark. This generation knows what's what. Lawrence needs to see it from their perspective.

"He moved onto some other bimbo."

"Fuck him."

Mark laughs, if only because he's now vindicated.

"I'd rather fuck—someone else."

The hesitation was just a bit too long. Shit.

LAWRENCE'S PARENTS REACT TO THE body's return in different ways, but they both react. They both recognise it the minute they open the door to it. His Mum is delighted with it—he's "looking so well". His Dad raises his eyebrows and goes to get him a beer. Lawrence had half believed they would see it as proof of masculinity, but they saw through it all, he can tell. They know this hyper-manly body is more gay than ever. After all, they've just finished watching this year's *Strictly Come Dancing*.

His Mum is pleased she can feed him up. His Dad suggests he trim the beard.

He goes to bed, the same bed of Lawrence's teenage years, feeling lonely; as lonely as back then, and now even harder to get comfy in at this size, pushed up against the wall. At dawn, however, he wakes feeling sanguine and comfortable. The body is like Lawrence's companion in extremis, a close friend, the closest you can get. It wants to move, to play, to distract him.

So you did get a pet, after all.

To his surprise, he gets down to a work-out in his bedroom on Boxing Day morning, even before the sun is fully up.

You're getting like a monk, Lawrie. Only buff.

At breakfast, his parents look at him askance. It is "supposed to be a day of rest", they tell him. That's nonsense, of course, because there's his brother's family to go and visit today. He gives his nephews piggybacks all afternoon. He tells his brother about the email systems issue (because what else do you talk with close family about at Christmas). Midway through the conversation, he finds himself considering his brother's build through his Christmas jumper. There's a strange sort of pride in being so much bigger than your big brother.

What about this barman at the local pub? What about that lad poking at the fruit machine? What about the lad's mate? What about the passengers on the train? What's going on under their clothes, and how does he measure up? What are their girlfriends, wives, boyfriends, husbands thinking?

It's not lust. He's just drinking in that feeling of physical superiority.

He's been looking forward to meeting up with old schoolfriends but instead impulsively catches the train home, for a workout. Habit is hard to break, dangerous even. Besides, he has the place all to himself. It's a chance to look over his body in the mirror more closely.

You look yourself again. Exactly like the Picture.

A perfect copy. Only sadder—because you didn't know what was coming back then. The Great Man captured Lawrence on the Heath, just as the sun came up. Beautiful mark-making and use of colour. Pink on blue and green, burning on the canvas. A bright new day. He liked new things, as you were to discover.

Perhaps it's not a perfect copy after all—and not just for this sense of loss. Looking in the mirror, in overhead light, he can see it has taken on even more mass just in the last few days. The scale of it, turning and posing under Lawrence's control, looks familiar and also strange. It is potent with possibility. It is not, as Lawrence had imagined, complete. He's on the brink of surpassing himself. So big and strong now, yet not nearly big enough.

He's so hard. It must be the testosterone driving his bollocks wild.

He resists and then gives into a danger wank. Fortunately, there's nobody to walk in on him. Cleaning cum off the gym-floor tiles, he repents. Haha.

In the new year, the days pass unremarkably. He hardly notices the specificity of dates and events in the news so much as the notes he makes on his phone. The reps he attains or surpasses. The weight he lifts or fails to lift. The session always has to end in failure—if the target was attainable, he wouldn't be pushing his body. You have to break the body apart to rebuild it stronger. Progressive overload, innit?

VALENTINE'S DAY COMES BUT ONCE a year as well. An unknown gym rat slips his phone number into his locker. Mark cooks them a meal for himself and Lawrence. He's seeing Keeley this weekend, so this is fine, albeit right on the edge of comedy. Oysters. Asparagus. A fiery puttanesca with dark chocolate grated over it. Strawberries.

Lawrence thinks but does not say that he will need another meal later.

"I hope you're taking advantage of your hot new body, mate."

"Such as?"

"Well, I've got the ball and chain, but you shouldn't be free tonight, should you?"

"I don't mind. It's nice to catch up with you."

The mineral tang of the wine. The chilli making his pulse lift. The smile on Mark's face – so false, so unreal. He cannot stop talking about Lawrence's new body.

"What I'm saying is—well, I hope you're having fun as well as working so hard."

"It's not work."

Eat. Talk less. You sound so aggressive. He won't understand. It's the testosterone.

"What about dodging the 'New Year New You' newbie cunts? That's work, haha."

"That's easy. I go in the day."

"What, and do your work in the evening? That's what I call dedication—"

"I just skive a bit, Mark. It's not like David knows what I do all day anyway."

Mark is staring down at his wine as if the shape of the glass fascinates him.

"Well, say what you want to say, Mark."

"I'm not judging you. I'm just being your mate. I don't want you getting—unhealthy."

"I don't think this is what unhealthy looks like."

Surely not what unhealthy feels like. The heart begins to thud.

"Lawrie. Your body looks great. You look great. But skipping work—"

"Perhaps I shouldn't have told you about that."

"I was going to ask anyway, actually."

"Go on then, say it. Say it! I can see it written all over your face."

He stares back at Lawrence's angry eyes. Lawrence can feel the flush in his face, and see it in Mark's. It's like looking in the mirror, except for the bulk Lawrence feels around him, immersing him, buoying him up.

"Does that mean you *are* taking something, Lawrie?"

"Fuck's sake!"

He hears his fork hit the plate before he is conscious of it leaving his hand, his arm flicking like a whip crack. It's a shock, but he feels like it's coming from far away. As though he's watching this unfurl. He could pull back and prevent things from escalating. He's never raised his voice with a flatmate.

But Mark has never crossed the line like this before.

"The speed that you're changing—putting on gains—the body hair—

isn't natural."

"Faster than you, you mean?"

Mark's eyes are wide.

"You'd love this, wouldn't you?"

Lawrence doesn't intend to say this. Something might almost be speaking through him. His breath is coming in short snorts through his nostrils. Jaw clenched. Every inch of him bristles. Mark lays down his knife and fork. Stop this before he goes too far.

"Tell me you want this body, Mark."

"I don't know what you mean by that."

"Tell me you want it."

Mark pushes back his chair, gets up.

"Alright, mate."

"Say it, Mark."

"I want it."

Mark is reading something in his eyes that Lawrence doesn't know understand himself, but what is happening feels real, honest and just.

Unsmiling pleasure in one face mirrors the other. Anticipation of something more.

They are each the sort of man who always wants more. That's why they look as they do. That's why they are in this together right now.

"You want to touch it?"

Mark's jaw hangs over, and his breath becomes animal.

"I want to touch it."

"So beg."

"Please. Please, Sir. I want it."

Lawrence pushes his chair away from the table but does nothing more. It's for Mark to move now. To come, stand before him, and place a hot hand on Lawrence's body, tracing its shape through the t-shirt. The planetary orb of the shoulder. The arboreal reach of an arm. Trying to reach around the fore-arm and not succeeding.

Mark doesn't touch his hand to Lawrence's. That would be so gay.

"Can I take this off? I wanna see it."

He goes to lift the hem of the grey tee, and Lawrence bats the hand away. Laughs.

"Always takes me so long to wriggle out of it."

Momentarily, Lawrence's eyes are downcast, laughing at himself once again. Bringing himself down to Mark's level.

Then Lawrence grips the collar of the tee and rips it open in one impatient convulsion. Shrugs it off and sits back, half-naked, superior as an emperor once more.

"Fuck." It's one long breath.

The same hand of Mark's now traces the shape of Lawrence's pectoral, discerning the mass and weight through black fur. Grips the eagle wing of Lawrence's latissimus muscle.

"Mate, you're like a diamond."

"*Sir.*"

Mark's mouth is dry when he first tries to say it. He takes a big mouthful of wine.

"You're like a diamond, *Sir.*"

Lawrence rises now but expends no unnecessary energy. It is Mark's place to undo Lawrence's belt and undress him. Mark guesses it is for him to remain clothed and to kneel.

He opens his mouth to speak, to say this is getting too much, or to ask for directions. Lawrence knows that Mark knows what happens next. As a gentle encouragement, he pats Mark's cheek with the tenderness of a horse to a rider.

Mark takes Lawrence's hard-on into his mouth with the eagerness and trepidation of a first-timer, and with the usual mixed results. He must be trained to do better.

He's just like you were back in summer: he knows what he's capable of, and what he must discard of himself to attain it.

Little poof.

Lawrence drains his own wine while Mark learns to be a cocksucker.

Mark's eyes turn upward again. Lawrence is feeling good and he can tell his body has told Mark. The sound of Mark's heaving breath and the snicker of him licking Lawrence's precum off his lips.

"Good boy. Ready to go further?"

"You mean, you wanna suck me off too?"

"No."

"Then—what?"

Lawrence gestures for Mark to rise.

The sight of his nervous smile is even more arousing than having Mark take Lawrence's dick to the back of his throat.

Okay, that was nice too.

Peeling away the cashmere jumper, the smart shirt, the delicate neck-chain, he notes that Mark's body is not, in fact, significantly smaller or weaker than his own, after all; it's just that Mark has submitted. At that moment, he exults in his power to command. To rut. To make animals of them both.

If he had any of Lawrence's old self-doubt in his system, it sweats out of him in a single blush of excitement.

"Lie across the table."

"Be careful."

Lawrence doesn't respond to that.

"I'm being honest with you. Sir. This is new. I swear. Be careful. Please."

"Tell me you don't want it."

Mark's breath is more rapid, but he says nothing. He looks over his shoulder at Lawrence. He reaches back and parts his hairy arse cheeks.

There's olive oil on the table. That will do.

He grabs Mark's shoulder for purchase. He can feel Mark's heart racing. The beat goes right through Mark's body. It's almost like its pounding is what Mark really is. Lawrence applies his body to Mark's, adding one heartbeat to another through meat and fur.

Cock touches cunt for the first time.

"Oh, Jesus."

Crosses the threshold.

"Oh, god."

Now they're not quite they; the two of them combine into one larger *him*. The process thereafter is familiar from the phases of bodybuilder regime. At first, it's difficult. After that, it's easy. After that, it's just what the body needs. Progressive overload.

"Oh, Sir."

The noise as one and then the other climaxes is ear-ringing. They are inextricable.

Now they clean up. Laugh shyly. They eat chocolate mousse, at opposite ends of the sofa and watch *Beauty and the Beast. Tale as old as time....*

Mark goes for a shower. Jokes about the wine. Locks the bathroom door.

Lawrence goes out for his second dinner. After he's eaten, he calls the number from the gym and says he's coming round.

He's actually ready for sleep, but this is like a waking dream, so that's okay. The legs walk where they will. The body has a natural authority that directs the gym rat so that neither of them has to think. If anything, he's thinking with his appetite and the gym rat is keen to be prey.

And once he lets go of control, he doesn't feel any concern at all.

The night terror revisits him in the stranger's bed. No cuddling.

The body wakes before the alarm and goes for a run. Lawrence doesn't have to think about what he's doing, so he thinks about the events of the past twelve hours, but it feels like an empty exercise. He might just as well think about the events of *Beauty and the Beast*. Wondering what he might do next is like imagining what he might see in a movie sequel.

Walking home in the twilight, he smells the world returning from the grave.

That weekend, Mark goes to Keeley's instead of having her over to theirs.

At the gym, the body accepts the work and throbs with pleasure as well as exhaustion. There are glances from men there he knows are straight. He is exceeding expectations.

In the gym mirror, someone almost unrecognisable returns his gaze. Bigger than ever. Taller, somehow. The trainer says his hypertrophy ought to start plateauing soon, but if anything's accelerating. Speeding out of control.

Perhaps Mark's right—it's come a little sooner than is entirely natural. Like it was just waiting to be invited back. But there is plenty more work to do. This body is just raw material—it can be so much more, and you feel it wants to be. The Great Man was too easily satisfied, perhaps. The job was half-finished, all those years ago.

That's the part of it that really seems new. The look in his eyes. Blank like a trained animal's, awaiting its next command.

Time unfurls in a blur. The nights are unfailingly broken with several wakings to the night terror and the weight of the body. It's all part of the process. In the daytime, he runs, feeds, works out. Lawrence notices and enjoys the creak of the kitchen chair when he sits down to meals with Mark. He notices and enjoys a new animal smell filling the rooms they occupy. Then after a couple of days, he stopped noticing.

They don't watch TV together any more—in fact, they barely make conversation—but he starts fucking Mark regularly. Routinely; almost doctrinally. Lawrence can no longer quite interpret the expression in Mark's eyes, but their bodies fit perfectly together (with his unfailingly on top, that is).

Mark is not permitted to stay behind in Lawrence's bed to sleep beside him. Lawrence has to be free to go and eat or leave the house whenever he wants for other sex. He keeps his own company.

Sometimes he ponders whether this is right, even as his body is taking him out into the clear springish night air and moving around town, bed to bed, cruising ground to cruising ground. Sometimes he wonders if dating would be easier. Sometimes Lawrence notices he's exhausting himself all over again by wandering the city all night, but the compulsion is barely checked. In these instances, he sleeps during the day, anywhere he can. Sometimes the next day, he finds paper money has been slipped into his pockets. Tribute.

Muscle is rewriting him, just as the new regime is rearranging his life. He wonders if he should resist it, hold back, take stock, and then a laugh goes right through him like thunder in the middle of a gathering storm.

Just as the green fuse burns fiercely back out of the dark toward the light.

One day, Mark is gone from the flat more than a few nights. There is a brief text message promising to pay rent, even if he doesn't stay. He acknowledges the fact but is late to the gym.

He is missing his watch, so drops in unexpectedly on the Physio. The Physio doesn't want to let him in, won't believe he is the same guy.

He laughs. He's about to argue, but the tongue stills itself. The new body hangs on him like a disguise. Not only that – the trim little Dad has unmistakable intimidation in his eyes.

"I—"

Your body has taken over. You are a past trace of what this thing has become and what it can do. Even its voice has changed. Why shouldn't your words change with it?

"I want Lawrie's fucking watch. Do I need to fuck you up to get it, boy?"

He gets the watch. The strap no longer fits his wrist. He tosses it aside with a grin.

THE FOLLOWING WEEK HE IS called into the office. His inbox is full. Everybody's inbox is full. Messages on a thousand subjects. Projects. Budgets. Gossip. Flirtation. The email's gone wrong again. He feels an old twinge in the small of his back. Where the spine points toward the cunt. He rides the sensation, clenching his fists. They want to see him in the flesh.

He tries to fit into his suit. Each item either splits open in seconds or refuses to go on in the first place. *Shit shit shit. What have I done? I'm going to lose my job.*

I'll lose my income. How do I explain I have a responsibility now to feed this body? It eats like a tiger.

How did it come to this?

It's July. Sky's blazing. He can wear what he wants. Short shorts and a jumper that used to hang baggy on him and is now like a second skin. Lawrence needs to dress this body better, more appropriately, although in fact it would like to go entirely naked. It wants bare dirt under its feet and hands. Maybe he should move to the wilds, but what would he do when it wanted sex? On the Underground, he notices men and women looking at him a certain way. One guy surreptitiously takes a photo, and it makes him angry as well as horny. The body moves to follow the guy, but Lawrence knows he has to get to work. He has to maintain some control. He grits his teeth, holds the leash steady, and stays on until the correct station.

His fingerprint lets him in at the entrance. Funny. He moves through the halls smiling at people, but they look at him blankly. He is a stranger.

He knocks at David's door and waits to be called in. His heart begins to pound.

"Yes?"

"We have a meeting."

"I'm terribly sorry, sir. I have no idea who you are."

"Correct."

He steps toward the desk. David shrinks back, trying unsuccessfully to disguise the action. That's funny too. Lawrence picks up David's tablet and breaks it. He breaks the desk-top PC. He breaks the phone. He takes David's office apart. David is curled up in the corner.

He doesn't know what to do next but apparently the body does, because a fat wad of spit has just landed on David's face, a line of drool pointing back into his mouth.

He tugs on the leash. The body opens the door delicately, exits the room, stalks down the corridor, out past the security guy, out into the street.

The body is excited. It wants more. Violence would be good but it's also desperate to fuck.

Maybe both?

Lawrence could stop and consider the best option but the body doesn't stop moving. It dives into the crowd. On the lookout. All it requires now is connection. No words. The body is losing patience with words. It growled and barked its only utterance in the workplace. Now it's moving on.

It roams the city. He realises his feet are taking him down old haunts, like a beast on a chain dragging its owner. Or perhaps it is him who is being haunted. Certainly this corner of town, in all its familiarity, the cafes and bars and galleries, stir memories. He would like to go home to bed, but it would be more than he could manage to argue with the body once it gets excited.

It passes the British Museum. Perhaps it's looking for something remote from modern civilisation. That seems to be the mood it's in.

Now there's an idea in its head. Lawrence thinks it's a mad idea but that doesn't mean much now that it's been thought.

TURPENTINE. PAINTS. THE SWEATY BODIES of young people. His old art school smells exactly as it remembers it. The same London planes stand outside, motionless in the heat. Time seems to have slowed, crept backwards.

The security guard studiously looks the other way to avoid asking for his ID, and a smile comes to Lawrence's face. He feels at home. The heavy tread of his boots echoes on the same old lino. The same bland student artwork hangs in the corridors. He doesn't have to ask directions; even the memory doesn't seem to come from his head.

Lawrence was in love here. He used to venerate the stones of this place.

He slows, savouring the approach. It's the holidays, so only a remnant of the student body is still here. Their eyes follow him and widen, and again his smile beams.

He thinks of all the breakable things that will be in that office, but, out of some older habit, can't resist knocking on the door as softly as he can.

"Come."

He could smash the door off its lock—brute force—but he turns the handle delicately, the same handle turned by the same hand twenty years ago.

The Great Man is reading an email. He has glasses for that these days. The solid black bars of the frames accentuate his familiar strong, leonine features. He takes them off to greet the stranger, and a look of pleasure shines in his eyes. Desire and curiosity—but not recognition.

"Yes...?"

He is looking at your body. The body that once ignited the spark between you both. Drawn from the artworks you shared, a dream incarnated. The same body that drew him in, and which became his subject. The body that was the embodiment of their mutual secrecy. That body which he once studied so intently it filled him up and overflowed out of him onto the canvas.

"Sir?"

The word stumbles out of Lawrence's throat, which feels suddenly numb.

"Can I ... help you...?"

"I used to be your student."

This is the room where you met your teacher, and it is also where he dismissed you. Now he gazes upon the same man and reads none of their history in his body, seeing only this carapace of beast. Like something out of Greek myth, Lawrence has been transformed into something even more like himself, his wildest dreams. Now it is aflame, heart beating, perspiration dripping. Arms wide.

He moves into the hands of the beast.

"I'm sure I'd remember *you* ...."

Perhaps their history is combusting as they approach one another, flying off them in the heat in shimmering tatters, leaving them clean, purified and innocent as beasts.

Or perhaps the heat of close contact is baking that history into the flesh forever. Hardening that dream body into something more solid than muscle itself. The hands planting tenderly around the older man's throat. He can feel every pore there, every living detail. The wire brush of the beard against his throat, the beat of the older man's heart against his abdomen.

Take a deep breath in. Fill those lungs. Expand that infinitely expanded chest with nothingness. The scent of paints and paper and human sweat and pre-cum.

This will just be a small adjustment.

Half-focused eyes fall on a picture on the wall. A familiar Picture. That Picture.

Beautiful mark-making, blush pink on grass green and Yves Klein blue. Youthful strength glinting in the wider energy of wild, infinite possibility. A youth, quite sexy, looking toward the rising sun—looking away from the artist who is trying to capture him in that moment. Looking toward the open horizon.

Animals do not hesitate. But at that moment, Lawrence does.

TICK

The sound of a watch marking time, close to the ear. The eyes open and he wakes, realising suddenly that he has been dreaming, or at least, dreams were going through his head. He's not yet able to distinguish one image from another, the real from the dream.

The eyes search the room wildly for the Picture, but it is gone. No, not gone—he's not in the Professor's room any more. Somewhere else. He's in bed. And time is back.

TICK

The watch is on the wrist of a man who looks like Mark. Behind him is a window with a view of autumn leaves.

"He's awake. You're awake. Thank fuck."

"What happened? Did I—"

The words won't leave the darkness at the back of his head. Mark seems to hear them anyway, because understanding glimmers in his eyes. He's looking across at someone else, on the other side of the bed. Lawrence twists to look up at them.

It's Keeley. She smiles, and puts a hand on Lawrence's.

"No, Lawrie. You were interrupted. Firstly, by a bunch of security guards –"

"It took three of them to tackle you, big guy!"

"And then, by a heart attack."

"And you've been somewhere else ever since."

Lawrence just blinks, acknowledging it all. Listening and sensing out the full facts of the matter. The matter of his body.

The body is heavy, or maybe it is just weak. It has ebbed. It has been dedicating itself to long, perhaps to long overdue, deep sleep. It has been overloaded once too many times.

"Why are you here?"

Mark looks at Keeley again, blushing.

"The landlord had me as your closest contact."

He's embarrassed at the words. Keeley's tone is sharper.

"You don't have any friends, Lawrence. Your pals at the gym don't count. Your boss says he thought you were dead. As for what you did to Mark's physio, you should be glad he's got gonna press charges. And… I'm sorry … your parents didn't stay. They could barely look at you, to be honest: the state you'd got yourself in."

Lawrence knows it should be wounding, but there are no tears. Once again, his body has let him down.

Keeley pats his hand.

"Still, it's over. You can get back to normal and put all this craziness behind you."

She gets up, gives Mark a sharp look, and goes off to fetch a nurse with the good news. Mark leans in, holding a glass of water to Lawrence's mouth, like a boxing trainer with his fighter in the corner of the ring. Not a heavyweight any more, barely flyweight.

"Did you tell her…?"

"Mate—I didn't need to."

Mark brings his mouth close to Lawrence's ear. He forces the words out before they evaporate on his tongue. "What we did. That leaves its mark. You can't hide that."

"Right."

"Not just physically. I was on my knees. In every sense. Haha."

"Haha."

Mark's words are the faintest breeze in the ear. "You broke me."

Lawrence's words are the driest movement of the lips. "I'm sorry, Mark."

"No, Lawrence. No, no, *no*...."

Mark tips the cup to Lawrence's lips again. Suddenly there is something supplicatory about the gesture.

He doesn't need to hear what Mark says next. They share the knowledge already. Perhaps they always have done. Nonetheless, it's not about that. It's never just about the idea or the dream. You have to come out with it—and when Mark speaks again, it's a low utterance of pleasure.

"I told you before, Lawrence. I want you. I want you I want you I want you I want you I want you I want you *I want you.*"

Keeley and the nurse are coming in at the door. Mark smiles at them, the face of one who would never say such a thing.

He tells them he thinks Lawrence is feeling himself again.

What now? What next? It's in your hands.

On Lawrence's shoulder Mark's hand is resting. The sound of his watch drums like a heartbeat. The beat at the heart of the world.

Imperceptibly it starts to race.

TICK

DESIRE AND THE BLACK MASSEUR

TENNESSEE WILLIAMS

FROM HIS VERY BEGINNING THIS person, Anthony Burns, had betrayed an instinct for being included in things that swallowed him up. In his family there had been fifteen children and he the one given least notice, and when he went to work, after graduating from high school in the largest class on the records of that institution, he secured his job in the largest wholesale company of the city. Everything absorbed him and swallowed him up, and still he did not feel secure. He felt more secure at the movies than anywhere else. He loved to sit in the back rows of the movies where the darkness absorbed him gently so that he was like a particle of food dissolving in a big hot mouth. The cinema licked at his mind with a tender, flickering tongue that all but lulled him to sleep. Yes, a big motherly Nannie of a dog could not have licked him better or given him sweeter repose than the cinema did when he went there after work. His mouth would fall open at the movies and saliva would accumulate in it and dribble out the sides of it and all his being would relax so utterly that all the prickles and tightenings of a whole day's anxiety would be lifted away. He didn't follow the story on the screen but watched the figures. What they said or did was immaterial to him, he cared about only the figures who warmed him as if they were cuddled right next to him in the dark picture house and he loved every one of them but the ones with shrill voices.

The timidest kind of a person was Anthony Burns, always scuttling from one kind of protection to another but none of them ever being durable enough to suit him.

Now at the age of thirty, by virtue of so much protection, he still had in his face and body the unformed look of a child and he moved like a child in the presence of critical elders. In every move of his body and every inflection of speech and cast of expression there was a timid apology going out to the world for the little space that he had been somehow elected to occupy in it. His was not an inquiring type of mind. He only learned what he was required to learn and about himself he learned nothing. He had no idea of what his real desires were. Desire is something that is made to occupy a larger space than that which is afforded by the individual being, and this was especially true in the case of Anthony Burns. His desires, or rather his basic desire, was so much too big for him that it swallowed him up as a coat that should have been cut into ten smaller sizes, or rather there should have been that much more of Burns to make it fit him.

For the sins of the world are really only its partialities, its incompletions, and these are what sufferings must atone for. A wall that has been omitted from a house because the stones were exhausted, a room in a house left unfurnished because the householder's funds were not sufficient—these sorts of incompletions are usually covered up or glossed over by some kind of makeshift arrangement. The nature of man is full of such makeshift arrangements, devised by himself to cover his incompletion. He feels a part of himself to be like a missing wall or a room left unfurnished and he tries as well as he can to make up for it. The use of imagination, resorting to dreams or the loftier purpose of art, is a mask he devises to cover his incompletion. Or violence such as a war, between two men or among a number of nations, is also a blind and senseless compensation for that which is not yet formed in human nature. Then there is still another compensation. This one is found in the principle of atonement, the surrender of self to violent treatment by others with the idea of thereby clearing one's self of his guilt. This last way was the one that Anthony Burns unconsciously had elected.

Now at the age of thirty he was about to discover the instrument of his atonement. Like all other happenings in his life, it came about without intention or effort.

One afternoon, which was a Saturday afternoon in November, he went from his work in the huge wholesale corporation to a place with a red neon sign that said "Turkish Baths and Massage." He had been suffering lately from a vague sort of ache near the base of his spine and somebody else employed at the wholesale corporation had told him that he would be relieved by massage. You would suppose that the mere suggestion of such a thing would frighten him out of his wits, but when desire lives constantly with fear, and no partition between them, desire must become very tricky; it has to become as sly as the adversary, and this was one of those times when desire outwitted the enemy under the roof. At the very mention of the word "massage," the desire woke up and exuded a sort of anesthetizing vapor all through Burns' nerves, catching fear off guard and allowing Burns to slip by it. Almost without knowing that he was really going, he went to the baths that Saturday afternoon.

The baths were situated in the basement of a hotel, right at the center of the keyed-up mercantile nerves of the downtown section, and yet the baths were a tiny world of their own. Secrecy was the atmosphere of the place and seemed to be its purpose. The entrance door had an oval of milky glass through which you could only detect a glimmer of light. And even when a patron had been admitted, he found himself standing in labyrinths of partitions, of corridors and cubicles curtained off from each other, of chambers with opaque doors and milky globes over lights and sheathings of vapor. Everywhere were agencies of concealment. The bodies of patrons, divested of their clothing, were swatched in billowing tent-like sheets of white fabric. They trailed barefooted along the moist white tiles, as white and noiseless as ghosts except for their breathing, and their faces all wore a nearly vacant expression. They drifted as if they had no thought to conduct them.

But now and again, across the central hallway, would step a masseur. The masseurs were Negroes. They seemed very dark and positive against the loose white hangings of the baths. They wore no sheets, they had on loose cotton drawers, and they moved about with force and resolution. They alone seemed to have an authority here. Their voices rang out boldly, never whispering in the sort of apologetic way that the patrons had in asking directions of them. This was their own rightful province, and they swept the white hangings aside with great black palms that you felt might just as easily have seized bolts of lightning and thrown them back at the clouds.

Anthony Burns stood more uncertainly than most near the entrance of the bathhouse. Once he had gotten through the milky-paned door his fate was decided and no more action or will on his part was called for. He paid two-fifty, which was the price of a bath and massage, and from that moment forward had only to follow directions and submit to care. Within a few moments a Negro masseur came to Burns and propelled him onward and then around a corner where he was led into one of the curtained compartments.

Take off your clothes, said the Negro.

The Negro had already sensed an unusual something about his latest patron and so he did not go out of the canvas-draped cubicle but remained leaning against a wall while Burns obeyed and undressed. The white man turned his face to the wall away from the Negro and fumbled awkwardly with his dark winter clothes. It took him a long time to get the clothes off his body, not because he willfully lingered about it but because of a dream-like state in which he was deeply falling. A faraway feeling engulfed him and his hands and fingers did not seem to be his own, they were numb and hot as if they were caught in the clasp of someone standing behind him, manipulating their motions. But at last, he stood naked, and when he turned slowly about to face the Negro masseur, the black giant's eyes appeared not to see him at all, and yet they had a glitter not present before, a liquid brightness suggesting bits of wet coal.

Put this on, he directed and held out to Burns a white sheet.

Gratefully the little man enveloped himself in the enormous coarse fabric and, holding it delicately up from his small-boned, womanish feet, he followed the Negro masseur through another corridor of rustling white curtains to the entrance of an opaque glass enclosure which was the steam room. There his conductor left him. The blank walls heaved and sighed as steam issued from them. It swirled about Burns' naked figure, enveloping him in a heat and moisture such as the inside of a tremendous mouth, to be drugged and all but dissolved in this burning white vapor which hissed out of unseen walls.

After a time the black masseur returned. With a mumbled command, he led the trembling Burns back into the cubicle where he had left his clothes. A bare white table had been wheeled into the chamber during Burns' absence.

Lie on this, said the Negro.

Burns obeyed. The black masseur poured alcohol on Burns' body, first on his chest and then on his belly and thighs. It ran all over him, biting at him like insects. He gasped a little and crossed his legs over the wild complaint of his groin. Then without any warning the Negro raised up his black palm and brought it down with a terrific whack on the middle of Burns' soft belly. The little man's breath flew out of his mouth in a gasp and for two or three moments he couldn't inhale another.

Immediately after the passing of the first shock, a feeling of pleasure went through him. It swept as a liquid from either end of his body and into the tingling hollow of his groin. He dared not look, but he knew what the Negro must see. The black giant was grinning.

I hope I didn't hit you too hard, he murmured.

No, said Burns.

Turn over, said the Negro.

Burns tried vainly to move but the luxurious tiredness made him unable to. The Negro laughed and gripped the small of his waist and flopped him over as easily as he might have turned a pillow. Then he began to belabor his shoulders and buttocks with blows that increased in violence, and as the violence and the pain increased, the little man grew more and more fiercely hot with his first true satisfaction, until all at once a knot came loose in his loins and released a warm flow.

So by surprise is a man's desire discovered, and once discovered, the only need is surrender, to take what comes and ask no questions about it: and this was something that Burns was expressly made for.

Time and again the white-collar clerk went back to the Negro masseur. The knowledge grew quickly between them of what Burns wanted, that he was in search of atonement, and the black masseur was the natural instrument of it. He hated white-skinned bodies because they abused his pride. He loved to have their white skin prone beneath him, to bring his fist or the palm of his hand down hard on its passive surface. He had barely been able to hold this love in restraint, to control the wish that he felt to pound more fiercely and use the full of his power. But now at long last the suitable person had entered his orbit of passion. In the white-collar clerk he had located all that he longed for.

Those times when the black giant relaxed, when he sat at the rear of the baths and smoked cigarettes or devoured a bar of candy, the image of Burns would loom before his mind, a nude white body with angry red marks on it. The bar of chocolate would stop just short of his lips and the lips would slacken into a dreamy smile. The giant loved Burns, and Burns adored the giant.

Burns had become absent-minded about his work. Right in the middle of typing a factory order, he would lean back at his desk and the giant would swim in the atmosphere before him. Then he would smile and his work-stiffened fingers would loosen and flop on the desk. Sometimes the boss would stop near him and call his name crossly. Burns! Burns! What are you dreaming about?

Throughout the winter the violence of the massage increased by fairly reasonable degrees, but when March came it was suddenly stepped up.

Burns left the baths one day with two broken ribs.

Every morning he hobbled to work more slowly and painfully but the state of his body could still be explained by saying he had rheumatism.

One day his boss asked him what he was doing for it. He told his boss that he was taking massage.

It don't seem to do you any good, said the boss.

Oh, yes, said Burns, I am showing lots of improvement!

That evening came his last visit to the baths.

His right leg was fractured. The blow which had broken the limb was so terrific that Burns had been unable to stifle an outcry. The manager of the bath establishment heard it and came into the compartment.

Burns was vomiting over the edge of the table.

Christ, said the manager, what's been going on here?

The black giant shrugged.

He asked me to hit him harder.

The manager looked over Burns and discovered his many bruises.

What do you think this is? A jungle? he asked the masseur.

Again the black giant shrugged.

Get the hell out of my place! the manager shouted. Take this perverted little monster with you, and neither of you had better show up here again!

The black giant tenderly lifted his drowsy partner and bore him away to a room in the town's Negro section.

There for a week, the passion between them continued.

This interval was toward the end of the Lenten season. Across from the room where Burns and the Negro were staying there was a church whose open windows spilled out the mounting exhortations of a preacher. Each afternoon the fiery poem of death on the cross was repeated. The preacher was not fully conscious of what he wanted nor were the listeners, groaning and writhing before him. All of them were involved in a massive atonement.

Now and again some manifestation occurred, a woman stood up to expose a wound in her breast. Another had slashed an artery at her wrist.

Suffer, suffer, suffer! the preacher shouted. Our Lord was nailed on a cross for the sins of the world! They led him above the town to the place of the skull, they moistened his lips with vinegar on a sponge, they drove five nails through his body, and He was The Rose of the World as He bled on the cross!

The congregation could not remain in the building but tumbled out on the street in a crazed procession with clothes torn open.

The sins of the world are all forgiven! they shouted.

All during this celebration of human atonement, the Negro masseur was completing his purpose with Burns.

All the windows were open in the death chamber.

The curtains blew out like thirsty little white tongues to lick at the street which seemed to reek with an overpowering honey. A house had caught fire on the block in back of the church. The walls collapsed and the cinders floated about in the gold atmosphere. The scarlet engines, the ladders and powerful hoses were useless against the purity of the flame.

The Negro masseur leaned over his still-breathing victim.

Burns was whispering something.

The black giant nodded.

You know what you have to do now? the victim asked him. The black giant nodded.

He picked up the body, which barely held together, and placed it gently on a clean-swept table.

The giant began to devour the body of Burns.

It took him twenty-four hours to eat the splintered bones clean.

When he had finished, the sky was serenely blue, the passionate services at the church were finished, the ashes had settled, the scarlet engines had gone and the reek of honey was blown from the atmosphere.

Quiet had returned and there was an air of completion.

Those bare white bones, left over from Burns' atonement, were placed in a sack and borne to the end of a car line.

There the masseur walked out on a lonely pier and dropped his burden under the lake's quiet surface.

As the giant turned homeward, he mused on his satisfaction.

Yes, it is perfect, he thought, it is now completed!

Then in the sack, in which he had carried the bones, he dropped his belongings, a neat blue suit to conceal his dangerous body, some buttons of pearl and a picture of Anthony Burns as a child of seven.

He moved to another city, obtained employment once more as an expert masseur. And there in a white-curtained place, serenely conscious of fate bringing toward him another, to suffer atonement as it had been suffered by Burns, he stood impassively waiting inside a milky white door for the next to arrive.

And meantime, slowly, with barely a thought of so doing, the earth's whole population twisted and writhed beneath the manipulation of night's black fingers and the white ones of day with skeletons splintered and flesh reduced to pulp, as out of this unlikely problem, the answer, perfection, was slowly evolved through torture.

COSI FAN TUTTE
DOUG WEAVER

YOU KNOW HOW SOMETIMES YOU just randomly meet some guy and after a few hours of shooting meth, snorting "K" and performing most of the essential big city homosexual mating protocols you've perfected over the decades – which always have a component of showing whoever you're with that even though you're completely twacked out and would be hard pressed to maybe drive a tractor or fly an airplane, you still have the wherewithal to rig, in a matter of seconds, a series of mirrors that are not only at dildo level because, for whatever reason, we really like to see ourselves putting stuff up our butts, but they're also at TV level so you won't have to spoil the mood by sitting up to watch the gay porn that's always playing on the DVD. And you'd never admit it to anybody, but you're completely bored with gay porn because it's so fucking earnest – probably because if it weren't earnest, it would just be a bunch of queens fucking each other, and that's not exactly sexy, so the porn actors are always growling at each other and being earnest cops or coaches or convicts. You realize this greasy routine has somehow moved past the meaningless ritual stage and you're both actually having a pretty good time, probably because you become aware that this guy has quite a few qualities of the perfect man:

1.   He can negotiate the ins and outs of drug-induced paralysis.

2.   He can appreciate the indescribable weirdness of being stuck in a 'K'-hole without turning it into something "significant."

3.   He's okay with driving around with you in the morning to deliver dope, and he's totally not weirded out by the word "felony."

4.   And most important: He knows—like you do—that sex is about as important in the scheme of things as filing your state income taxes—that sex is only something you do to fill the spaces of time between doses.

So the sun comes up the next morning, you're still with this guy. And this is so uncommon that you feel like putting up a plaque commemorating the occasion: On such and such a date, you actually spent a complete 24-hour day with another human being without being locked up in a cell with him. And the second day starts with some casual cock sucking, or if you're really energetic, maybe sharing a complicated enema with a mixture of various drugs and booze, which is a great way to get to know somebody really quick, or you might drag the leather out of the closet and get dressed like cops or whatever where you strike a few poses and issue a few commands. And spending this much time with somebody carries with it certain circadian responsibilities, like eating and bathing and changing clothes. So in a grand gesture of hospitality, you pour out two bowls of Fruit Loops and serve your new friend breakfast in bed. Then you shower, get dressed, and head out in your truck to drop off various deliveries of meth to some of your straggling customers.

And during these little errands, you both kind of realize you're not in any big hurry, kind of like the andante section of a Schubert sonata, like you're both walking at a comfortable pace down the halls of an art exhibit, where you're not thirsty or hungry or bored or even particularly interested in looking at the pictures on the walls—or you're just on a really nice, really easy drive—like you're both just rolling down the road in a black Camaro and the windows are all open, and the wind is hot, and you know you look cool, and you know where all the switches are and everything. And you can take time—take time—the words seem so weird like they're from a third-world country or something, but it's still got some nice scenery here and there with trees and clouds and shit, but the important thing is there's no drama at all, and you realize that you're usually comforted by emergencies—you're addicted to them because you know how to act in an emergency, like when the cops are chasing you, or the Geisha went all psychotic in the check-out line at Home Depot, or what's-his-name turned blue in the bathroom because the heroin he shot is a bit potent.

And being with this guy gives you a little hope that things might be different for a while. It reminds you of a scene in a movie where two people are in love or something, like—I can't think of anybody right now, though, but it's like when two people like each other a lot like couples in movies or commercials, whatever, and there's usually like a slow motion scene with just the two of them in a meadow with millions of flowers or something, and that's like all there needs to be. And you're thinking that you and this guy might be—I can hardly breathe the word —compatible—that you've turned into a kind of unit; that you might actually have the potential to be like Dick and Tom, who're actually the perfect couple; who could actually be in the *Guinness Book of World Records* for shooting more meth over a seven-day period than anybody in history. They just seemed to fit together somehow. Even when they were homeless, which was most of the time, somebody from another country or another planet would look at them and there would be no doubt that Dick and Tom were perfectly matched, but instead of like a normal couple, they were perfectly matched kamikaze pilots, or maybe like twin Cadillacs from that book *Slaughterhouse 5*, but with suicide doors, where they just keep going full speed until there are no tires left and they don't even use roads anymore, and body parts fall off faster and faster, but they don't slow down until they just disintegrate into nothing. And they're so connected that there seemed to be a kind of force field around them that the police can't even penetrate, or maybe it just made the police blind to them, kind of like they were crystal meth Batman and Robin or something, which was pretty weird because, from the perspective of anybody who got loaded with them, they were anything but invisible. They were outrageous, which is really saying something from the point of view of another dope fiend, but it was true. Dick and Tom'd be up for a few days, and they had this habit of taking their appetites for twisted sex with other men right out in the daylight, like during rush hour on Franklin Avenue, and the sun is blazing away at like 7:30 or 8 in the morning, and they'd pour peanut oil all over their jeans so you could see the shapes of their cocks through their Levis really plainly, and they'd stand where there's a stop light at the intersection of Beachwood Drive and rub their bulging crotches like they were tweaked out fag fishermen in a boat out on Lake Homo trawling for nibbles from the schools of the elusive giant cockfish who are known to inhabit the area. This strategy probably worked eventually, but everybody who knew Dick and Tom thought it was really intensely outrageously stupid like you're just asking to be arrested because, in all those millions of cars packed onto Franklin Avenue all the time, there's usually a few black-and-whites. And even if any of those cops are homos, which I'm sure some were, what do you think's going to happen? Even if fate or the powers that be decided to pair two fag cops together as partners on patrol, which is about as likely as the people finally rising up and seizing power, do you really think they'd be driving down Franklin Avenue and look over and see these two saucer-eyed oily clowns on the street corner and say, "Gee, Marvin, let's take a few hours off so we can pick up these two studs and enjoy a few hours of crazy twacked out sex with them?" Anyway, that's Dick and Tom. Maybe somebody'll write a memoir about them some day.

So you and your new friend head back home, and you get high together and smoke some really potent weed, which makes you stupider than you'd like, but it's nothing you can't handle, mostly because you're a pro and have a kind of awareness of certain pitfalls, and, for the moment, you're okay with this guy has become part of your routine. But then, after a while, you realize that a considerable length of time has passed since this guy has said one word—has made one sound, or actually given you one signal that he's still on the same planet as you, which gets your attention a little because in normal circumstances this silence is a little bit of a red flag, and you try to remember exactly how long it's been since he's said anything. You think back to the previous hours, and you make concessions because of the compatibility thing, and you tell yourself that he might just be a quiet sort of guy, but you need a little assurance that things are cool, and you maybe conduct a little experiment by fixing yourself a dose in a spoon—and when you do it, you make sure that you squirt the water into the drug inside the spoon and stir it up in a really obvious way. And usually, doing this around another dope fiend is like cutting up a pork chop in front of your napping dog. They'll all of a sudden give you their undivided attention as if you're the center of the universe. But there's no reaction from this guy—he's just lying there on the bed like a raw piece of steak, and you say to yourself: Fuck! but maybe it's out loud, or maybe you just thought it, but it doesn't matter because you know he won't hear anything anyway because you've been fooled: this guy is totally tripped out, and his brain is busy busy busy constructing barricades and escape chutes and the most complicated contraptions that make perfect sense to the builder, but to anybody else who doesn't literally live inside his own head, they're completely fucking cuckoo.

And you maybe remember the first time you got fooled like this, which was shortly after receiving your journeyman meth dealer's merit badge, which was a couple of years ago. You're living this ultra-cool dealer's life, and you get a phone call from this guy – somebody you've seen around here and there, and he says he's a dealer too; that he's noticed what a nifty operation you're running, which should have been a sign that something was weird because calling your little business an "operation" is kind of a stretch. But being a pig for praise, you say something really bright like, "Oh, really? Golly, thanks!" He says he wants to meet with you to discuss a business proposition, so you're really honored at the moment. And you're kind of amazed that he sounds so businesslike like he has a briefcase with papers in it with graphs and stuff. He comes to visit, and sure enough, he's dressed clean and neat, and he's actually carrying a fucking briefcase, so you start to think you're going to have to concentrate on what this guy has to say. But you're just playing it by ear because you don't really have a clue about what's supposed to happen, and you both go into the bedroom, but you don't get high because, after all, this is strictly business. And he says he wants to join forces with you, to make a kind of alliance of meth dealers or something, and he begins to make his case to persuade you. And of course, he doesn't have a curriculum vitae or a business plan or anything for you to read, which is okay because you wouldn't have understood it anyway, but what he does instead to prove to you that he's a person of substance tells you all the steps he's recently had to take to trick the sheriff's department from focusing on him as a person of interest and a potential defendant. And then, as if he's the founder of the Meth Dealers' Peace Corps or something, he describes in the most self-aggrandizing and heroic terms how he's perfected a method that will confound law enforcement one-hundred percent of the time, which consists of erecting a series of 50-foot mirrors in the back of his apartment building, which, according to him, rendered him and all his business dealings, completely invisible to all the hundreds of sheriff's deputies and crime-fighting scientists who were out to get him. And before he gets five minutes into this pitch, you're trying to figure out how to get rid of him because it couldn't be more obvious that he's a guy who really needs to lay off his own product or turn himself in for a few sessions of ultra-high voltage Edison Medicine or maybe even submit to a little slicing and dicing of his amygdala.

It's kind of like that with this silent guy. You get pissed off at yourself because you've seen this before more times than you like to admit, and everything changes in a heartbeat from a budding love affair to babysitting duty, and your newfound ally has been transformed into just some potentially dangerous piece of luggage, and you try to remember the last time there was somebody tripped out like this who landed in a quiet land, because ideally, after a silent stretch, they'll start squawking about their impending death, like they're one hundred percent sure their pulse is out of control, and they can feel death beckoning and what's going to become of them? You just wish this guy on the bed with you would start spewing words—any kind of bullshit craziness, because words give you kind of a foothold, so you know where things stand—words make the situation more quantifiable. You begin to wonder how long it's going to be before this guy starts his ascent into sanity and you can safely send him on his way—or maybe drive him to where he lives or something, because experience has taught you that this condition has certain pitfalls: you turn them out too soon, and they have no more wits than a puppy, who finds himself out on the street in an unfamiliar part of town and is about as inconspicuous as naked Santa Claus roller skating in the middle of the street, carrying a surfboard under his arm and with a huge black dildo sticking out of his ass and maybe a propeller cap on his head and blood dripping from his arms where he's just slammed some meth. And just like a real puppy, this guy starts to panic because he's scared that he's been abandoned and will think nothing of walking up to a cop or maybe even into a police station and describing the place where he's been for the last day or so, and he wants to go back there, and this will create a real fucking nightmare, so you reconcile yourself to being stuck with this guy for as long as it takes as he lies on the bed for an hour, for two hours, and then three. And you start to wonder what's really going on with this guy, but you don't get drastic. You put your faith in your experience, believing that it's just going to take a little longer. And finally, after almost five hours, he gets up, walks into the bathroom, and pisses. And you feign goodwill and maybe say something innocuous like "How you doin'?" But after he flushes the toilet, he reclaims his spot on the bed and settles back into his silence, totally ignoring your query. You can just see the wheels inside his head spinning out unspeakable tapestries of paranoia. And you become a little more concerned because it's almost nighttime again and something's gotta give pretty quick, so you sit on the bed next to him and try to watch some television or something, and the phone starts ringing, and you know it's people calling for dope, but you don't answer because of this weirdo on the bed who started out being just a cool guy but is now a 100-percent liability and it's become obvious that this little mini-romance will start to affect your income if something doesn't happen soon. But with the patience of Job, you lie down next to him like there's nothing wrong, and you turn off the TV, and you're both just lying there. And for a few minutes, it's peaceful, like everything's okay. You take a wistful look at him—you admire his body and his handsome face and muscular arms—and you feel a certain amount of frustration because, in a perfect world, he'd actually be a real catch, and you maybe feel a little twinge of loneliness and self-pity because you've allowed your imagination to create something out of nothing ... one more time, and in a panic, you scramble to put these thoughts out of your head because acknowledgment of them creates a painful awareness that you're alone and you're not getting any younger; that your life is as arid as the moon; that you wish the last ten years of bad decisions and drug use and arrests and stretches in county jail and trying to avoid seeing your parents and brother and sister hasn't been real, but you feel so far away from where you need to be because there's usually a needle stuck in your arm and running amok has become normal. And you might say a tiny little prayer that will hopefully take the edge off these desperate thoughts, something maybe like please god ... please give me a sign of what to do ... I promise I'll ... but you stop yourself from adding any real substance to this prayer because you know it's foolish to pray, and you're glad no one has seen you in this moment of weakness. So you push all the bad thoughts out of your head, and because you can't think of anything else to do, you snuggle up close to this quiet guy, like spoons, and it feels good. You listen to his insides, and it's so quiet—kind of like the ocean at rest. There's a kind of deep, confident rhythm resonating deep inside him. And after twenty minutes or so, you sense a slight stirring. You hear his breathing change slightly like there's a tiny increase in frequency and a decrease in depth, but it's so slight you listen harder. There's a little catch in his lungs, and you can almost feel blood flooding into his dormant muscles. Then, in a kind of singular seamless, slightly magnificent motion, like an out-of-breath diver breaking through the surface of the ocean, he powers through your easy embrace, he sits up at once, looks around frantically like a cornered animal, then wildly—desperately screams to the world: "I …!" but the thought dies with the utterance of the pronoun, seemingly smothered by the paranoid imperatives of his overactive brain.

And your hopes, at least for the moment, are dashed with the reality that this guy is completely lost. And you wonder what it was he was going to say. I what? "I want to go home?" "I like you?" "I like puppies?" "I miss my mom?" Is it a truncated version of an expression containing the contraction "I'm," and he was going to say "I'm sick," "I'm the rightful king of France," or maybe even the plain, unadorned, "I'm horny." You consider for a moment the possibility that he may have been conjugating the future tense "I will," but stop before finishing your speculative thought. I will what? You know it could be anything, and you catch yourself before descending into your own puddle of paranoia by settling on the possibility that the only verb that makes sense in this context is kill: "I will kill you." And no matter how hard you try, you can't stop yourself from going there … from conjuring scenes of your awful, inevitable fate: murdered by an unbalanced trick who couldn't handle his dope. And all you can think of is how vulgar your death will have been. "I wasn't born to die this way," you think. "I haven't accomplished anything." And you think about how your parents will be so disappointed, along with your aunts and uncles and their kids, as they shake their heads in support of your parents' grief. "You're not to blame. We are sooo sorry …." And you want to call them and tell them you love them, and you'll come and visit soon, and you allow yourself to think about when you were a kid, and you were happy, and things were so much simpler, and your parents still trusted you. But you know that history has taught them not to put any weight at all on their promises anymore. And after you shake off these bullshit memories, you imagine yourself being resourceful, somebody with courage and a will, and you think that this could all be solved if you just killed this crazy motherfucker and deposited him in a dumpster somewhere.

This is crazy, you think. Maybe saying "I …" has nothing to do with the self-referential pronoun. It could be the truncated form of an expression of inner pain, like "Aiyyeeeeee!" or any combination of vowels strung together to give voice to the tortured soul; utterances that are so common in Italian opera or Mexican love songs: "Aiyyeeeee!—this is the only sound capable of conveying the profound pain I'm in"—a concept that is completely antithetical to the non-words so common in British songs, which stay as far away from any acknowledgment of inner pain—or even acknowledgment of an existence outside of lovely decoration – as possible, and which are instead cluttered with measure after measure of silliness like "Fa la la la la, la la la la," happy sounds which seem designed to deny the existence of any emotion at all: "Oh, let's not talk about that messy stuff, old man … have a spoonful of sugar and a jar of plum pudding and we'll all go a-caroling after the wind dies down." And being a human American citizen, you try to ally yourself—along with the rest of the population—with the hot-blooded Italian / Latin side because the British nonsense syllables seem so goddamned silly in comparison, so frivolous and superficial. "I have emotion," you might say to reassure yourself that there is absolutely no connection between you and the United Kingdom. And you don't know how long it takes— probably about 30 seconds or maybe just a fraction of a second—until you realize that no matter how fast you run or how many somersaults your brain does, no white guy from Southern California like you is going to be able to claim ownership of the authenticity so implicit in Italian opera. You've actually, over the years, mostly during the Christmas season, sung all those British nonsense sounds, the fa la la la, la la la la, more than once, and it felt good, it felt right, like you were full of nothing but goodwill, and were a contributing member to the brotherhood of man, and you wish you could reclaim those feelings like you're just so fucking tired of being some low-life who's always running into emergency rooms and away from the cops. You deserve to feel good, and you just want somebody to realize this fact, too, kind of like Bloody Mary from that Rogers and Hammerstein musical, *South Pacific*, that sounds so much like the music of Brahms with all that mature lyricism growing from thick foundations of rich, complex harmonies that are sometimes more like superficially cracked dishes of brown gravy than music, and you can just see corpulent, blossom-encrusted Bloody Mary with her brown skin and bare feet, standing on a promontory of that tiny south seas island describing her plight in song through the gossamer fog partially obscuring all that rich mountain top verdure, pouring her heart out in her pidgin English to all those millions of eyeballs and eardrums in all those darkened theaters, not only in San Diego but all over the fucking world: "Sweet and clear us can be too!" And her words embolden you until you're able to claim your share of legitimacy in this tiny instant of creation. And you might even make a pledge to yourself to remember to go caroling next Christmas so you can again sing: Fa la la la la la, la la la la! but the syllables still sound vapid, and you begin to feel self-conscious about how mindless they are, so you try to ennoble them, to elevate this silliness to a higher plane so you can own them. And what comes to mind right away is The Messiah by Handel, especially The Hallelujah Chorus, which seems to offer some substantive provenance to these nonsense filler syllables. That's it! George Frederick Handel and you to the fucking hubs! George and you, dude! You might be condemned for singing silly sounds, but they're actually heroic— heroic and brilliant—forged on the crucible of faith – sung by superior people that don't get bogged down in all that morass of self, the narcissism that invites injury and hurt feelings. Fucking self-absorbed Italians! Get on with it, man! Stiff upper lip and all that. Carry on!

And by now, your new friend has closed his eyes. He's just lying there— you can't tell if he's sleeping because you can see no evidence that he's even breathing. And you realize you're exhausted, so you close your eyes too, but your mind is still active, and you're thinking about what all this means. You want to go to sleep, but you wonder about what it might have meant if this guy had screamed another pronoun, like "You ...!" or "She ...!" or "They ...!" instead of that self-limiting and overly mysterious "I ...!" But you've been around a bit—you've read a few books—and you know a thing or two about human nature, and you know deep down that it doesn't matter how far any pronoun drifts away from the first person, the big personal signifier "I" … it's always going to ultimately return to some form of self-reflection. That's god's cosmic joke on all of us, you think, and you're struck by the futility of it all, that in all of human endeavor throughout all of history, and even before anything was ever written down, no matter how selfless or altruistic you've told yourself your motives are—you can never ever ever move past yourself; that everything you experience and everyone you meet will ultimately be mediated through the filter of you. And in what can only be considered an uncharacteristic flash of humanity, you look at this guy with a little compassion, and when you do, you see yourself, but more than that, you see mankind, flawed and fucked up and struggling and wanting—needing more than anything else to be part of something, to be safe—to be loved. So you turn off your phone, you take off your clothes, and lie down next to this guy because, in this instant, you've realized that we're all just clawing, climbing clinging microbes, hungry and striving for primacy, so maybe we can finally catch a lucky break and somehow squirm over the walls of this Petri dish. No one gets over on anybody else, and no one gets out of here with a gold star. You close your eyes and go to sleep.

AGAINST THE GRAIN
L.A. FIELDS

THE CARVER COULD MAKE ANYTHING out of wood. He could build a home, the furniture to fill it, utensils to eat with, and money by selling it. With that money, also made from paper and thus wood, he bought companionship. Men of flesh to overpower him, to possess and penetrate him. Men that would come, sometimes cum, and then go with money and a mien of distaste. They were unreliable, they were moody, and they were not always the beastly brutes he wanted. Instead, they were big with fat more than muscle, mean with stupidity not strength, and fucked with annoyance and contempt as opposed to the wicked zeal of an impaler.

The carver's taste in companionship was forged during his tutelage when he heard the other students talk of a blacksmith to whom the boys should never turn their backs. They spoke with fear and worry about this man, but when the carver finally saw the figure of their nightmares, he found he actually wanted the blacksmith's affections.

Silent and strong, with furrowed brow and iron-bending arms, other men practically melted around the blacksmith, made room for him, and deferred to him. As a fatherless boy, the carver loved the idea of a strong man like that at his back—a leader to guide him, a man so tough that he did not even flinch when hot sparks splashed his skin. A protector, a teacher, and in short: a man who would provide the dominance he craved. His apprenticeship with a mild-mannered furniture maker was a vast disappointment for him. The carver spent his formative years learning how to shape wood, and simultaneously yearning to be one of the striker boys getting their furnaces stoked by the poker of the legendary smith.

As an adult, the carver quickly found that real life could not match his fantasies. So one day, the carver decided he could hew a better man out of a bundle of boards than existed in the flesh. He gave his creation a dominating brow, a literally chiseled jaw, broad shoulders, sculpted muscles, and a thick, heavy cock that he carefully resined to avoid unpleasant splintering. He created a mechanism similar to a rowing machine so that when he pulled, the creation would thrust forward, whether he lay on his back atop his strong table, or prostrated himself belly-down.

The first performance was a success. This statue was dense, honey-golden, and sturdy. Though it was largely faceless, more mannequin than man, it was nevertheless able to get the job done.

With his hole and the member coated in cooking grease, the carver eased his brute forward. He let his vision blur so the man atop him would seem just like any other, frowning and forceful.

A fire in his hearth warmed the room. The movement of the machine caused the carver to sweat but also created small gusts of air to gently cool and caress him. The cock entered and filled him, and with one adjustment of his hips, the tip touched the right spot, and he started to swell, to rock, to rut.

The carver closed his eyes to a slit, and his wooden man appeared to come to life. He did not yet have arms, just shoulders, but that only sparked a fantasy. What if the man entering him had been in a terrible accident, his arms ripped off, his body mutilated? Wouldn't that make him angry, dangerous? He'd fuck you, he'd hate you, he'd want to take from you what was ripped from him? The carver wasn't a strong man, not as strong as the bull he'd created. Even without arms such a monster could trap him, kick him, bite him, and threaten to crush his hands—the hands he needed to work—unless he would submit himself to be sexually used.

The carver yielded. He felt his insides shift with the piston-like thrusts of a ruthless pounding. He regretted briefly that his hands were not free to pull himself off while he took inch after inch of warm wood, but he could find his pinnacle regardless. Being exposed as he was—wide open, naked, and pinned—the carver reached bliss.

As the world swam back, the carver thought (he could have sworn) that his brute lurched forward under its own power. But of course, that couldn't be true. It was only wishful thinking.

In the next few weeks, the carver outdid himself, truly impressed himself with his own skills. He created arms for the brute that he could hang on if he wanted to mount the thing's impressive cock. He sculpted a face for his new toy—a severe, stern face with an angry brow and a scar across his frown for character. He rigged a bellows he could operate with his foot, so the brute could thrust without occupying the carver's hands. They made it sound as if the brute could breathe.

The carver enjoyed himself for months. He created elaborate fantasies about the brute in his house: hiding to attack him, extorting sex for a debt, or being paid himself to reluctantly engage in intercourse with the pathetic body of the carver. Every position was had, and every scenario was thoroughly explored. When he found himself getting bored at long last, he added one last modification that made all the difference.

After enjoying the thrill of humiliation for so long, the carver became emboldened. He wanted to share other pleasures with the brute, wanted to violate this thing and befoul it with insemination. But first, he required a proper hole.

The carver found himself newly excited with the act of drilling a fresh cavity into the ass of his creation. He sealed the wood and oiled the hole, looking forward to violating it once the orifice cured. To make the squeeze tight, he cut a thin piece of tender meat and warmed it in a skillet before bending the brute over and stuffing him with tenderloin.

The carver entered the brute with a nasty zeal that surprised him. He wanted to pound his beloved creature, cause the table to scoot beneath them with the force of his fuck. He imagined the brute as a real man—big, strong, and muscled—being forced to bend over and spread his buttocks open to the air. He would have to submit to being examined, fingered, and penetrated. He would wince in pain and shame as the carver bucked against his backside, rearranged his guts with uncaring lust, and at last pumped him full of thick, slick, fluid spurts.

The carver collapsed on the back of his brute, panting and looking forward to the postcoital observation of semen dripping out of him like tree sap. His own breathing disguised the sound he knew so well but didn't realize was happening at the wrong time, all wrong.

The carver could hear the bellows puffing in, then out, but his foot wasn't on the pedal, wasn't moving them. The sound matched his own breath, but the carver wasn't moving. In a surreal moment of both surety and denial, he held his breath, but the sound of breathing continued. The brute creaked, but this time he was not settling. He was sitting up.

The brute had come alive.

AT FIRST, THE CARVER FELT blessed. He was either gifted by the gods, or he was himself a god with the power to create life. The brute was strong and helped him with his work, bending wood with his mitt-like hands. The brute could carry whole pallets of logs and stacks of stones. He helped repair the carver's roof, floors, and chimney. The brute labored all day for his reward each night, which was more of the carver's sap, his seed.

It was a beautiful idyll for several months, every day prosperous and purposeful, every night lustful and lewd. The carver had all he had ever wanted until he became too accustomed to it, and approached a baffling sort of boredom regarding his miracle.

The brute had no voice, but he communicated his opinions with a rudimentary sign language that grew more sophisticated as time passed. He had no desires beyond the seed that somehow nourished him. He was sentient enough to be satiated, but no more.

Conversely, the carver still had a need for curiosities. As a human being, he grew accustomed so quickly to whatever he could take for granted. He wanted newness, or rather a novelty. It became clear by the time the leaves changed that the brute would never develop any new fetishes or fantasies, would never be any more interested in him than the carver himself was interested in his standard morning porridge. He had to eat, and it was always there as a quick, warm meal in every season, but the carver knew that his sexual appetites would not long be satisfied by oatmeal.

The carver eventually lost his zeal for the brute. Each night he still fed his creation, but rather than toying with him, mounting him, enjoying him, the carver began to toss off his ejaculate like throwing scraps to a pet. Afterward, the brute would return to his seat at the table and rest unblinking until there were chores to do or the sun went down once again.

On the first night he declined to give the brute his evening meal, the carver discovered that there was at least one emotion in that blockhead: need. And under a frustrated need, there was anger.

The brute did not speak, and he did not have any facial expression but the arch look of a savage desert prince the carver had given him. But the wooden creature could move, and he could exude the same mood that animals had which even humans could understand. A beloved dog could communicate love with his wagging tail, and an affectionate cat could display her request with a rubbing entreaty. A bear could stand perfectly motionless and yet still stare with danger and menace. That is what the brute did the first night he was refused: he stood at the foot of the carver's bed all night rather than retreating to his corner. He seemed curious, then outraged, then glaringly angry. The carver was unsure if he would wake up at all, as the brute could easily murder him in his sleep with one powerful drop of his hand. He could likely wield a weapon as well—perhaps not one that required fine motor skills with his large hands, but certainly, he could lift a rock or a scalding kettle between both paws, or strangle the carver with bone-breaking pressure.

When morning arrived, the carver opened his eyes to find the brute's face right before him. No longer standing and staring, the brute had become confrontational. The carver yelped, then whimpered as he realized he was boxed into his corner bed. He had a very strong suspicion that if he tried to slide beneath the brute and move away, he would be harmed.

Instead, he relented. With trembling hands, he lifted his nightshirt and exposed his genitals and anus to his captor. One stiff nod of insistence from the brute, and the carver began to masturbate himself. His face felt bloodless and pale with fear, but because his desires were already so intertwined with fear, dread, and disgust, he could reach a turbid state and stroke himself boldly, to the brute's approval.

But the brute no longer had the patience of a pet. The creature knew enough to know that prodding his master in the rectum would send the seed flying, and so he delivered a rough jab, without teasing, greasing, or mercy. The carver cried out, his pain perhaps falling on deaf ears, or perhaps not, because the brute was changing in unseen ways the carver did not notice until it was too late. With two thick, wooden fingers inside of him, the carver did ejaculate onto the hateful face he'd so lovingly created. He also bled a little, and the colors of blood and semen mixed like cherries in cream as the brute slathered himself with both. Then the brute hesitated before returning to his corner as if he was disappointed with his meal.

The carver trembled, sure of only three things. First, he could no longer satiate the monster he had created; at his age, he did not have the capacity to regularly feed his beast's growing hunger. Second, he was solely responsible for either supplying food for this monster or destroying it, and both options seemed equally likely to get him killed. Third, he did not have long to decide on a course of action, because the brute had fingered him, and the brute had not been given fingers.

THE CARVER DECIDED TO ENTICE other men to his cottage to feed the brute. The first man he lured was curious and largely willing. The brute did not come to life around the stranger, at least not in perceptible ways. The carver put his creation in place, and told the other man to ride it, rub against it, rape it, and ensure that he finished upon the woodgrain. That was good fun for his guest while it occurred, though the man left in a considerable hurry when the magic of desire was gone, and what remained was something that seemed to stare through him—unnatural, unsettling, and inhuman.

The following two nights the carver returned unescorted. He had to feed his creature by masturbating himself. The glowering face of his creature held not the tantalizing imagined danger he once enjoyed, but instead a real threat that withered and chilled him.

On the final night, the carver chose poorly. The fellow he lured back was a young man of the street, a dirty-faced and thick-shouldered boyish ruffian that the carver would never have gone near before. Someone like this rude specimen would only prostitute himself under great financial duress. Someone like him would almost assuredly rob the fool who took him home alone.

As he led the youth back to the cottage, the carver could only hope the brute would defend his master—surely his creation would not bite the hand that fed, only the hand that withheld. The night would go one of two ways:

either the street trade would be honest and earn his money by expelling himself on the carver's overgrown toy, or he would be dishonest, and the brute would rob him of his seed instead.

The ruffian was at the carver's throat before the cottage door even closed behind them. He'd grabbed one of the carver's own knives to do it, the nasty boy, and under normal circumstances likely would have cut the carver's throat, and taken all his tools to sell or gift to other criminals.

But before he could finish his demands of "Give me all your money and jewels, you——," his voice was strangled.

The carver scurried rat-like to the corner behind his fireplace, with smoldering embers behind the grate. He watched in muted red light and shadows as the thief was bent over his table, eyes bulged in horror and pain as the brute's member punched right through his trousers and into his rectum. The carver witnessed the ruffian jolt with each thrust, and saw all his final thoughts cross his face — rage, fear, sadness, and at last acceptance. Then the ruffian's body went limp, his eyes dimmed but did not shut, and the brute released him like a hunting dog relinquished a fox's throat only after the life was gone out of it.

The carver was again alone with his creation, but his creation was no longer a material thing.

Just as seed had given the brute life, a glut of blood had made him flesh. He moved towards the fireplace because he felt cold for the first time. His joints no longer creaked and his footfalls no longer clopped. His expression had finally changed from the original fierce scowl to worriment and wonder.

The carver opened his mouth, almost reached for his new son, but first pointed at the bed to show his intention. "Blanket," he said, rubbing his shoulders to illustrate his meaning.

The brute only half understood. He brought the blanket but thought the carver wanted it for himself. The carver stood, accepted the blanket on his shoulders, but then shook his head and transferred it to the brute, to warm this newly naked man.

The corpse at his table was ignored as the carver stoked his fire, cooked some food, and inspected this new miracle. The brute had teeth and a heartbeat. The brute had fingernails and flecks of color in his eyes like the bark of a tree—beige, brown, yellow, and dots of green. The brute could eat, he could sneeze, and he could wiggle his toes by the fireside.

He was a sight to behold, but he would no longer consent to be held.

The carver embraced him when he was done eating, but the brute grasped his hands and put them back at the carver's side. He shook his head and made a guttural sound, the first hint of a voice. He did not want or need the carver's attentions anymore.

Instead, the brute dressed himself in the dead ruffian's clothes. Though the pants had a bloodied hole blown through the back of them, the winter coat hid it from view. His shoes fit, as they were overlarge working boots. The shirt did not, but again the coat hid the brute's shirtlessness from notice. The brute looked grand when dressed, but soon the carver would look upon him no more.

The brute took what he wanted for his departure. The knife the ruffian used would go with him, as well as the carver's winter hat with earflaps, and a leather belt to securely hold the ruffian's pants at his waist. The ruffian, thankfully, would also go with the brute. At first he hefted the nearly-naked body over his shoulders, but the carver retrieved a grain sack for the corpse, just for appearance's sake.

With his bundle, the brute nodded and headed for the door. Dawn was behind it, pale blue and frosty. The carver did not fret over what he was unleashing into the world—this was all magic beyond his ken and control— until the brute stopped on the threshold and reached for the axe notched into the firewood pile beside the door. In that moment of hesitation, even as the carver grew worried for his life, the old stirring in his loins returned. But the brute never looked back; he left the cottage and walked off into the woods, driven by some purpose that was solely his own.

The next day, the snow that held the brute's footprints melted, and the carver was left with a story he could never tell, even when the stains left by the ruffian's demise sprouted.

SUITCASE SAM
TOM CARDAMONE

EVERYONE CALLED HIM DIO. HE wasn't one to tell tales, though every old hustler has tales to tell. Not that anyone listens to the stories, to begin with. That's the first thing you learn in a Times Square hustler bar, of which there are a diminishing few: everyone's talking, but no one listens. The thing with Dio: he was different. He wasn't there to eke out a trick or scam drinks—he knew he was too old for that. He had too much dignity. Nor was he there to pay for it, either; the young Hispanic boys at the other end of the bar didn't interest him in the least. No, he was like me; he was here simply to drink or pretend to drink while getting discreetly loaded in the bathroom.

Dio and I sized each other up early on and got along well. We were about the same age and of the same disposition, except I wasn't like Dio: I was buying, not selling, so the pseudo-macho boys at the other end of the bar were an occasional interest. But not so much.

Like Dio, I liked to get loaded. I was brazen enough that if I wanted to fuck one of them, we could do it in the bathroom; I didn't need to pay extra for a hotel room. Dio would have still been cute if he hadn't turned so many tricks or so studiously flirted with heroin. He looked used up. His features were good, but his skin was drawn in some places while slightly loose in others. He looked like cheap hotel furniture, worn but ready, durable. We knew we could tell each other anything because we had done some bumps of smack in the bathroom stalls a few times. Anyone who snorts heroin instead of shooting thinks they're so fucking clever, beating the needle and all like you can't get hooked: the kind of lie that makes for a natural friendship. So one night, while we were particularly loaded, after many conversations, I confessed to Dio that I had once been married. Nonplussed, he asked me the question. "Have you ever seen a Suitcase Sam?"

I didn't understand the question. I was barely listening (we'd done some heavy bumps in the bathroom; everything glowed with that special, crinkly kind of yellow that shines through black and white movies as they age).

"No," I said.

His forehead was shiny, with yellow spots. I thought I could detect the hidden grid of a car headlight.

He smiled and relaxed into his drink. A game of chess was on, and he was in the lead. "That guy over there. He's a collector—that's what you call a guy who owns a Suitcase Sam. Most only own one. One's enough. But some guys, they've got to have everything."

I nodded, not knowing what he was talking about but agreeing with the sentiment. I looked over at the guy. Typical of the older men who frequented an establishment such as this: perpetually on edge, probably married, a wedding ring heavy below the silt of change and lint in their pants pocket. Nurse one drink, score with the right hustler, then off to a hotel that charges by the hour. "Funny thing about trade like that," Dio once told me, "all they want to do is suck cock. All this trade here, they're pussy bottoms, man." Except this guy who, ridiculously, wore sunglasses. He wasn't paying attention to the young men but conversed casually with the bartender.

Otherwise, he looked normal, a sad salesman with a wide suitcase by his side, a faded, pocked-plaid.

Dio said, "Don't stare." So I looked away.

"So what's a Suitcase Sam?"

Dio took a long pull from his drink, dropped the tumbler so ice crashed against the glass, lit a cigarette, and waited. I nodded to the bartender to fill his glass. As I had indicated earlier, he wasn't prone to histrionics or drama, so I figured this was worth my patience and money.

It was horrible what he said.

We were so stoned; I guess it loosened more than his tongue; it cracked the safe where anyone would store such things that no one should know, and if you were privy to something of such a nature, would naturally lock away. Some things were never meant to be shared.

And no one shares their Suitcase Sam.

First Dio asked me if I'd ever heard of the slave auctions in the Meatpacking district. One night, we laughed and confessed to having perused some of the more tawdry bars in that locale. S&M shit.

Though I had never been to such an auction, I knew of them. After all, it was no big deal–after all, they advertise in the *Village Voice*. "Well, that's kindergarten compared to a Suitcase Sam."

He measured me with a look that was disquieting, to say the least. And then the urge grew, just above my stomach. When I'm ready for another bump, it always feels like someone opened a window inside me, and the breeze blowing through might clean me out. I got up and went to the bathroom. Dio dutifully followed; as usual, I was holding, and he was not. Another bump. Then one for him, one for me. I collapsed lightly against the stall wall and slipped toward the floor, the porcelain bowl yawned slightly, and the shreds of toilet paper floating within coalesced into a white, scarred tongue. I thought I could live there, right there on the dirty floor. Why do human beings need more space than this? This was perfect.

"So these Sams," he slurs. "They want this. They want to be owned."

He paused, so I searched for something to say. I could hear an old man in the stall next to ours sucking a hustler's cock; I thought of animals gathering at a salt lick during the night near a cave: carnivore rubbing shoulders with deer. A spring bubbling nearby.

"Like a slave," I said.

Duo shook his head "no" for the longest time. I thought of how animal eyes captured in photographs taken at night have an added veneer; a blue florescent glow that erases the living pupil, creating saucers of cool pity.

"No, no, no," he said. "They want to be owned, but they need, they need...the element of escape to be removed. A pet doesn't even know its property; it's so fully owned." His eyes narrowed and focused on something over my shoulder, proud of his summation, as if it had only just occurred to him after years of searching. I looked at him, waiting for him to say more. I was comfortable leaning against the stall wall. The smack absorbed everything he had said.

The ancient cocksucker next door slowed his slurping, and the hustler, ready to burst, lit a cigarette. Smoke slowly poured over the partition. When you can hear someone giving head but can't see them, it sounds terribly like a child eating spaghetti. I wanted to share this stellar observation with Dio, but it seemed somewhat inappropriate, what with the topic at hand and all. I couldn't help smiling at my own thought, though, and he misinterpreted this as what, I don't know.

Dio got earnest. "See, they want to give up everything. If everything's gone, the only thing left of the world remains inside, and it can never get out." He shook his head as if overcome by a sadness that belied the effects of the smack I had generously just shared. Unexpectedly he pushed the stall door open and left.

Alone, I contemplated the sparkling toilet, mouth stretching in a massive "O"–as if about to draw breath. Next door, I could hear the old man's soul flap its heavy vermillion butterfly wings as the hustler shot a load down his throat.

I DIDN'T SEE DIO FOR a week after that.

Not that it bothered me. There are no expectations here. Scratch that. There is nothing but expectations, but a friendship just isn't one of them. Whenever Dio wasn't around, I refocused on the hustlers, ones I'd yet to sample. And I was patient. I wasn't interested in white poseurs flaunting ghetto chic; I like Hispanics, and I like them young. But every time I made a connection, I thought of that old cocksucker that night in the stall beside me and imagined him on his knees, growing useless insect wings, tattered membranes weakly unfolding as he nurtured the youthful, thick cock in his mouth. I could see the boy's mulatto face; a slight mustache, bored expression, no hint of ecstasy. Invariably he would yawn, and a mosquito's giant, gray proboscis would emerge to grease the old man's balding head.

So I was quietly relieved when Dio returned. And we did the dance, not greeting each other beyond a nod; I knew he was playing it cool. He didn't want to seem too eager to see if I was holding. As I said, Dio had class.

Later in the night, he saddled the stool next to mine and bought me a drink. Since he had last been in the bar, the old man with the suitcase and sunglasses had yet to return–he came in the mocking imprimatur of a famous Italian luggage design, suitcase at his side. I said nothing.

Another thing about Dio: He drank scotch straight, as did I. All these hustlers, trying to look huge in their sweatpants, new sweatshirts unzipped low to reveal fine, broad, hairless chests overlaid with gold chains. They all drank flamboyantly sweet drinks, sipping them noisily through the little stir straws.

Duo sighed and looked at me. He knew I remembered everything from our previous conversation and that I was too much of a gentleman to demand an explanation.

"See, what I was talking about the other night, should never be repeated." And he gave me a look that would crack tombstones.

I nodded. "Okay. Listen. This is it. This is like the end of knowledge and what people will do. Do to each other." I felt cold but was desperate for him to continue. "See, a Suitcase Sam wants it, but they don't know what it is they want. It just happens to them when they run out of options. No more 'safe words,' no more dungeons and leather masks. This is something that cannot be bought or sold because slavery, for some people, is the greatest of freedom, a release from everything." He pulled himself away from his drink, squaring his shoulders as if he were ready for something to approach.

I downed my drink and tried not to stare at the old man. The suitcase sat at his feet. It was the same worn one as last time. It looked heavy. Full. The window above my stomach began to open again. Forgoing another drink, I headed toward the bathroom. It was time for the first bump of the evening; Dio waited a few minutes before following me inside.

I tapped out a tiny brown pinch on my wrist in the stall and inhaled deeply. I saw too many of the luminescent larval cocoons spinning about the room. Only after remembering my guest did I tap out a graciously large bump onto his wrist. Dio inhaled, closed his eyes, and waited. I listened to the room; a languid faucet dripped honey, but no one else was there. So I grabbed onto my soul like a broomstick, aimed it a Dio, and spoke oh-so deliberately: "Tell me."

He blinked, eyes sparkling, then delivered. "It's amazing. They carve a person down until they are the perfect ... perfect receptacle."

He nodded affirmatively as the smack raced through his veins. "They carve people up until there is nothing left but the holes." He blinked.

His eyes rolled behind his lids just a bit; I'd purposefully given him an extra-large hit, wanting to get to this bottom.

Dio started a wet laugh. "See, cut off their arms and legs, blind them, pull out their teeth, and what do you got? Someone who lives in a suitcase, someone who aims to please because they can't aim at anything else."

Butterfly is all around, invisible, threatening. I laughed, too. Preposterous. I poured out another two bumps each.

A minute later, "So you want to see a Sam." He wasn't asking. He knew my intentions.

"Sure."

"I can arrange it, but you have to deliver. The old guy at the bar is hooked; he's been mainlining for over twenty years, and if he's coming in here, he's running on empty. Meaning he'll do anything for a fix, even break the taboo and show us his Suitcase Sam." Dio looked at me. His eyes were glassy yet dry like he hadn't cried in years.

THE NEXT NIGHT HE ARRANGED for us to see a Suitcase Sam.

And Dio was right: the old man was deep into his addiction and thus more prone to relax the strict code of secrecy among collectors. His apartment was nearby, in Hell's Kitchen. Ninth Avenue was a mess, a jumble of bars and dilapidated apartments, basically the spillover from Port Authority. We made our way up the dirty, uneven stairs of a five-floor walk-up, knocked on the door, and waited an inordinate time. The old man answered the door, agitated.

Fat and gray, wrapped in an even grayer bathrobe, he let us into an impossibly large apartment. An antique television broadcast indiscriminate images. I could see why he wore sunglasses at the bar; his eyes were fleshy, a pulpy maze of cataracts. He sat in the kitchen without saying a word, obviously waiting for a fix. Duo whispered to him assuredly while shooting me a rather serious look. I understood and produced a fresh bag of smack while Dio helped the old man secure his works. Grandpa was going to shoot his share of the dope, a procedure that always made me uncomfortable, so

I looked away. I studied as much of the place as I could in the dim light: a railroad apartment, every room tumbling into the other down scratched and dusty wooden floors; claw-like radiators gathered malevolently beneath each window. The old man got loaded, one arm tied off, and slack skin hung loose beneath rubber tubing. His spoon fell to the floor. He sat in his chair, crusted eyes rolling back in his head.

"Let's take a peek." Dio sounded like a kid, excited and nervous for the first time in our limited relationship. He led me to the front room, a dingy expanse overlooking Ninth, illuminated by the light of a long neon hotel sign.

Beside the bed sat a pregnant suitcase.

Dio used all of his strength to heft the bag onto the sagging bed. He popped both locks. I urged him onward with my eyes. I was ready for a fix, a drink, for anything, anything but what was in that bag. Dio flipped the lid.

A torso but…not. An odd, puppet-like thing. But living. It moved. It was pared down to the minimum of what you could call human.

Vomit rose in my throat.

No legs, no arms, face disfigured, smoothed, and limited. Sensing that its case had been opened, the thing roiled; all oiled hairless muscle; greasy ball-bearings of flesh. Open toothless mouth pouring out an indefinable pain. Eyes removed, lids sewn shut in a neat series of X's; ears soldered closed, everything shaved: the scalp and chest hairless. Arms clipped neatly at the shoulder, the legs taken as close to the pelvis as possible, all sealed with a thick scar of gristle.

I couldn't help but take a closer look.

This was a thing with two gruesome mouths; its anus distended from obvious, repetitious abuse, pummeled into a purple pout, greedy lips, sick mimic to the soundless pucker at the other end. Buttocks pulsating, cheeks almost clapping like a trained seal ready for a treat. Just then, it whinnied. The strange noise rattled from within its chest, guttural.

Its tongue had been sheared as well. It moved like a desperate snake, unable to shed a burning skin, frenzied from the attention. I saw how its genitals were gone, nothing but a mass of red scar.

Dio stood back, proud, responsible. "That's a Suitcase Sam.

"We might as well feed it." And he unzipped his pants and pulled out his cock, squat and limp but rising. The Suitcase Sam wagged in anticipation. He fed his thickening member into the redraw mouth.

It hummed with delight, gumming and slurping at Dio's dick while still in its luggage bassinette. I didn't want to see this, so I turned and took a desperate bump off my wrist.

BACK AT THE BAR, DIO was all talk. He was like a fountain, having finally found a confessor. Though I was more dazed than truly dedicated to such a travesty, I had to know.

"I found out about them from a guy I know who deals Ketamine; he gets it off a veterinarian who does the procedures. They're a tight group. Tighter than the snuff flicks crew but definitely a scene that likes to get together. These collectors, they show. Like fucking dog shows. And they take them with them everywhere. It's a whole culture."

He spilled the whole story. How they had been around for years.

They were the last stop in the sexual underground. Total domination means buying slaves from auctions and other masters and diminishing them, paring them down to base elemental attributes through surgical submission. Though fed cock and baby formula, they were clean-shaven to augment the fact that they were ornamental, not people. Most were smallish men, chosen for their thin, compact torsos. Apparently, their lifespan isn't terribly long. It's easy to forget to feed something habitually left in a suitcase—a real problem collector's lament.

Dio told a funny story about a collector who purposely carried his bag at the airport. When they scanned it, the baggage checkers naturally inquired. The collector coolly replied that he was transporting an anatomical dummy and nothing more. No one checked. I mean, why would they?

I felt uneasy that Dio was telling me so much at the very place where we had first seen a collector, at the other end of the bar, as if this place was theirs and our conversation a knowable violation. I wanted to go somewhere else but didn't want to interrupt his story since it was too unreal. I had just seen the world on a leash. Dio had inadvertently stumbled onto a secret that was the prelude to real danger. The pouch of smack in my breast pocket felt like bubblegum.

This bar, my thoughts, Dio's conversation, even my clothes, everything felt extremely claustrophobic. "Look. I've got to go." I pushed away from the bar and fled. I don't think Dio noticed I had left in a panic; we were too loaded to touch our drinks, but he was staring into the slope of ice and liquor in his half-lifted glass. Dio was frozen in the moment as if the wave building enough strength to crush him had also lifted him far enough aloft until he could see the ocean in its entirety.

I ENTERTAINED THE IDEA OF not going back to the bar, doing something else, maybe checking out one of the clubs in the Meat Packing District. But they didn't open until late. I didn't want to score, but I did. Restless, I got on the train and went downtown. At the bar, Dio was talking quietly to Randy, a young hustler new to the bar, new to the game. He had a quick smile, the largest, whitest teeth you had ever seen, and massive, black biceps highlighted by a new, white sleeveless t-shirt. No doubt Dio was dispensing tips of the trade, so I sat on the periphery. Then I noticed Dio had a suitcase tucked between his legs.

I froze and thought about getting up, but Randy was eyeing me, so I returned the smile. He must have been thirsty, hoping I would buy him a drink. I pulled out a twenty and told him to play a song in the jukebox. He got the hint and took off. The bartender brought me a drink, and I turned to Dio. "Taking a vacation?"

He laughed and patted me on the shoulder. "I'm going to take you for the ride of your life, my friend. Want to go to a convention?"

I eyed the bag at his feet. It lacked the radioactivity of the old man's luggage from the previous night. "What's up?"

"If you give the old man a gram, we're in. We just walk in with him, and no trouble. It just so happens that there's a convention in town tonight. This bag is just a cover. We won't go in until everyone else is there. No one will notice that we didn't open ours." He patted the bag at his feet.

The window above my stomach opened wide. I felt ready to dive in, so I got up and went to the bathroom. Dio waited a few minutes and then followed me in.

WE DID A WHOLE NIGHT'S worth back at the bar, so we had to go back to my apartment to re-supply and score for the old man. Dio appreciatively whistled as I opened the door. I explained to him that the place wasn't really mine. I rent it from an old college friend; it's been in his family for years, so it's rent-stabilized–meaning I pay a ridiculously low amount, which is probably what keeps me in drugs. All of the furniture is theirs. I own nothing but my clothes and a few unread books.

I called my guy. My dealer only makes house calls. That's how the best ones do it. Dio sat there nervously, rubbing his hands on his thighs while I eyed the suitcase. I gave it a lift: light as a feather.

I went out on the balcony and grabbed a loose brick from under a barren flower pot. I wrapped it in a towel and placed it in the suitcase.

Hefting the bag, Dio smiled as my door buzzer rang.

THE TRIP DOWNTOWN WAS A marvelous rollercoaster ride, skyscrapers bent like palm trees in our wake, the neon signs of Times Square celestial gates to somewhere delicious. The old man wouldn't get in the cab until he scored, so we went upstairs and waited for him to shoot. We did some bumps. He shot again then we were out. I noticed that his suitcase was identical to ours, resting side-by-side between him and Dio. I was paranoid that they would accidentally switch them. I couldn't stop imagining scenarios where this happened, costing us our precious lives: being caught and fed to a kiddy pool filled with Suitcase Sam's fitted with sharp silvery dentures, blindly snapping away. Or the old man, opening his suitcase and the brick and towel falling out, shrugging and pointing to the collectors and us standing impatiently as doors swing open and huge men in medical gowns and surgical masks lead Dio and me away. I recognize one of the men behind his mask. It's Randy from the bar. He flashes me a huge smile, stretching his mask until the cotton almost rips. My fear solidified when I realized we were driving over the Manhattan Bridge—I didn't know we were leaving the city.

DRIVING THROUGH BROOKLYN, I WAS mesmerized by the dark landscape, the low buildings and weak streetlights, shuttered storefronts and weedy vacant lots, and the occasional burning shopping cart.

We were back on an expressway, then off again, then idling in front of a nondescript hotel; a plane roared by overhead, and the sign over the building across the street was in Korean. We must have been near JFK.

We got out of the cab and followed the old man through the hotel lobby. No one was behind the desk. I renewed my fear of the switched suitcases and stared hard at both of them, then lit a cigarette.

The old man pushed through unguarded double doors and into a non-descript banquet hall. The tables had been pushed against the wall to ring the room with chairs, many vacant, others occupied by empty suitcases. I was glad I lit the cigarette; it gave me a focus, something to pull my attention, however briefly, away from the horror on the floor.

At first, the room looked filled with proud parents milling about as their babies frolicked on the floor. My initial thought was of infants, their floundering movements, and hairless heads. No, the heads were too large, and only the ones on their backs floundered about; any Suitcase Sam upright scrambled oddly fast, raised slightly on their nubs, sideways like a crab. One came at me quickly with a red, open mouth, a vacuum-like wound. A large, gregarious-looking man in a weathered cowboy hat broke away from his group and followed quickly behind the creature, scooping it up as I lifted my leg in revulsion. "Ups-a-daisy there, Beatrice! Sorry partner, she sure gets excited when she's around new people."

She. Dio said that all of the collectors referred to their Sam's as "she." The thing smacked its toothless jaws at me; strained movement behind the angry X's where eyes should be. The man asked me where I was from.

"The Upper Eastside." What's next? Is he going to ask me what I majored in at college?

"Great city you all got here. Hope to take in a show this trip." He placed Beatrice on the floor, faced it toward a pile of Suitcase Sam's bumping and nibbling on each other in the middle of the room, then sauntering away with a wave of his hand behind his head. Men clustered about the room. A few huge, bearish men in leather kept their Suitcase Sams on shiny leashes in matching miniature leather attire. Most were dressed casually and talked seriously, arms-crossed, about the care of their Suitcase Sam.

"Don't shave, hon, wax." "If I'm at work, I keep him in diapers—everyone but me has a Sam that can go on newspaper."

"This is my second Sam. I brought both to the San Diego Con, but they fight, so I only travel with one."

Sams scampered across the floor. Beatrice circled a yawning, pinkish Sam, a ball of taut muscle—as if removed limbs and curtailed senses had somehow refocused its energy into a glistening torso mad with veins and overly-accentuated arteries. The thing's shaved eyebrows had been replaced by long-healed symmetrical scars of meticulously placed cigarette burns. Human topiary. A bland woman with glasses and unnecessarily long, straight hair hefted her Sam in her arms like a massive infant while listening to whatever advice the twin leather daddies dispensed, their legs slowly entwined by their be-leashed pets.

Somehow I had failed to notice that Dio and the old man had crossed the room. I didn't think I could walk across such a minefield, a landscape of moving flesh and indifferent collectors. I could see smudged chalk outlines on the carpet. There must have been a race earlier. With prizes, I bet.

The old man was opening his suitcase. My heart, already sluggish from the smack, lurched into action. I remembered the possibility of switching bags. I wanted to cross the room, but my feet were heavy, and the carpet a muddy river, Suitcase Sams surfacing, faceless prehistoric turtles mad to gum my ankles. Well, if it's okay to smoke in here, maybe I could do a discreet bump; I needed something to help me cross that room. The old man hoisted his Sam from his case. As he held it above his head, it bleated in pleasure in a surprising show of strength and pride. Duo nodded and smiled and placed his unopened case down beside the old man's. Relieved, I walked slowly to the closest seat, sat down, and felt at the deflated bag in my shirt pocket. It was fl at, empty. We'd started too early and shared the last batch with the old man in its entirety. I thought about finding the bathroom and splitting the bag open; there had to be at least half a bump of dust in there. I would need to be in my apartment to call my dealer, and he wouldn't like coming up there twice in one night.

Dio sat down next to me.

"Interesting party." He patted my leg, removing his hand to reveal a fat bag of smack—more than a gram.

Surprised, I asked, "Where did you get this?"

Dio feigned a hurt look. "I owe you."

"Is it okay if I do a bump here?" I covered the bag with the small of my hand. The corners of the plastic bag cut into it like a budding diamond.

"Look around. You think anyone is going to call the cops?"

The old man had come to life in the middle of the banquet room, slapping backs and vigorously shaking hands. Dio rocked back in his chair.

I tapped out a bump of his stuff on my wrist and took a deep hit.

Looking at the bag, I noticed his shit was darker than what I usually score, grainer, too. And it hit me like a shotgun blast. Powder burns darkened the edges of my perception. Brown shadows expanded, seeping out from behind the vending machine in the corner, and the folded chairs by the door. And then everything got brighter.

A Suitcase Sam bumped my feet.

Beatrice again, beautiful. In my earlier panic, I hadn't noticed the skillful tattooing which adorned her flesh, the mocking imprimatur of a famous Italian luggage designer lightly covered with, replete with a floppy handle sewn into the small of her back. She sucked at the corner of my shoe as the shadows darkened. I looked longingly at the door. I saw the gray shape of the cowboy approaching, arms extended. Then I blacked out.

I WOKE UP WITH A start, violent enough to knock over the chair beside me. I had trouble opening my eyes, which instantly filled me with dread. I felt for my wallet, nearly hyperventilating, not knowing where I was. It was there. I noticed my shoes were off. Rubbing the sleep from my eyes, I looked around: I was still in the banquet hall.

The place was empty. Breathing deeply, the air stale from old cigarette smoke, I tried to stand, thought better of it, and sat back down.

The bellmen ignored me as I left the hotel. Likely I was an unwanted reminder of something they were paid triple to ignore.

I stumbled out into the parking lot. Receding daylight: I wasn't just asleep; I must have been unconscious. I didn't have enough money for a cab; the rocking assurance of the A train would help clear my head.

On the train, my mouth was dry. My head felt cleaved as if I'd been hit by an ax, the wound invisible.

At the Franklin Avenue stop, a gaggle of old women boarded the train, matching outfits and bowling bags, heading into the city for a night out. One old lady rested her white, withered hands across a pert, zipped bowling bag, gossiping close with her compatriot. I stared at the bag. Round, petulant, I heard it whisper. Velvety voices from within the other bags joined in. A barely perceptible chorus arose, masked by the machine hiss of a train making its track.

Next stop, Hoyt Street, I got off.

NEEDLE
PETER DUBÉ

IT ALWAYS HURTS. IT HURTS from the start, from the first touch. And it's always the same. The same pain every time, forever hinting at a difference that never shows itself; that never comes. A too-familiar pain.

A bare bulb hangs from the ceiling. It is directly above Drake as he lays there, legs splayed; sweat soaking into the bleach-stained denim he had tugged low on his hips. The same sweat varnishes his stomach and chest, pools in the slight depressions of his collarbone. That comfortable perspiration.

Drake opens his eyes, shuts them again, against the glare. Says, "Is there anything we can do about that light." The man working on his flesh grunts. But the overhead light dims, to be joined by a lamp on a nearby table.

Drake lifts his head to steal a look at the tattoo gun as it fires away at the taut expanse atop his ribs. A pattern of black boxes and blacker lines is taking shape. There are traces of indigo shadow along the edges of the openwork between boxes. He likes it already. He runs one hand over his belly as he lies back, wiping the sweat from his abdominal muscles, feeling them twitch with every jab. He brings the hand up to rub across the stubble on his scalp; he closes his eyes again, tracing the pain on his side as it moves a little higher. And he remembers Blue.

Blue, with his strong jaw and arced, sensual lips. He remembers the first time they met: a men's room ... jeezus. They were ashamed to be there, embarrassed by their desire—knowing the scene to be a cliché, but not knowing what to say; embarrassed by something they couldn't frame in language and too self-conscious to act the stale trope out, they said only "lame" and left the stalls to paw each other in the tunnels leading to a parking garage. Too horny to see the equivalence.

He can see those curving lips part again; take the head of his cock. Blue's eyes, the colour he was named for, looking up at him as he sucks away, greedy and needy and so fucking skilful. That spiky hair tickling his belly. Blue taking him down past the Adam's apple and still wanting more, his nose pressed hard against his pubic bone, the short brown hairs against that gifted mouth, that twice-broken nose. Nobody sucked cock like Blue. Nobody loved the power it gave him over a man more than Blue either. But Blue liked most kinds of power. Drake can feel his cock hardening again at that thought, despite (or in harmony with) the pain.

Blue fell to his knees, smooth as oil on glass and happy in his work. Ten minutes later a switch in his head flipped and he had Drake bent over a handrail, tearing him in half with a cock that was far bigger and no less crooked than that broken nose. And Drake can't remember a moment he felt more blissful.

There's nothing—nothing—like a good, solid fucking. There is nothing—nothing—like Blue. Or wasn't.

Now, the tattooist above him is intent. Jabbing minuscule fragments of pitch under his skin. Marking him forever; preparing him to return to the anonymous streets a new man. Drake feels his skin parting, burning, and calling to him. Reminding him.

When the fucking was over he had a beer with Blue. He almost never did this with one of his anonymous encounters, but Blue had left him sore and grinning ear to ear. Within days they were inseparable. Within a week or two they had stumbled all over each other avoiding any talk about what they were doing, shaking off almost all conversation because they were young, nervous, awkward with each other and—despite the dozens of nameless groping encounters in parks, and alleys, and movie houses they had both had, all of those were silent, unexpressed and inexpressive—they had no words for any of this. No language to name the time they spent together. And among what few words they could find, there was none like "love." That they could never speak. Guys like this never could. But they fucked. And fucked. And fucked. And fucked some more.

Drake lost himself in that sex. Forgot that the world turned, light waxed and waned, coloring the corona of clouds as nights ended, pitiless as a priest's gaze at mid-day. All he felt and tasted and smelled was Blue's cock, his tongue, his ass, the prominent knuckles on his hand, the soft skin behind his ears, the folds of his knees, and the mounds of his biceps. Their whole world was hunger, was need.

There were days they fucked at home in the dark, shades drawn, lights out, three violet candles burning at the foot of the bed, the slender empty hash pipe upturned in an ashtray on the nightstand. There were nights they fucked on the roof, so they could enjoy the naked splendour of the night sky as she enjoyed theirs. Long afternoons drenched in cum and contact and booze. Mornings they couldn't stand it anymore and pulled off the road to give each other hand jobs in the shadow of the on-ramp. Whole weekends they spent high, drunk, delirious in each other arms, heads spinning on chemical axes, faces buried in each other's intimate wet corners. Every fibre, every synapse, every single cell vibrating with its own mad, jittering pleasure. Drake still couldn't clear every memory of it from his mind, however much he lies there and let his flesh be mortified. Unbidden he recalled the night he tied a blindfold over Blue's eyes for the first time. The way he knotted it so carefully, to make sure it was tight, would stay in place but not pinch. How he went to his knees with care and took Blue's burgeoning dick nimbly into his mouth, never touching him, so the warm wet contact would be a shock, would come on him unexpectedly free of any visual or tactile cue, Blue would be all pure sensation. The way the big dick sprang to attention with surprise. Drake remembers every strange little trick of the tongue he pulled from his repertoire that night. He remembers that and the sheer salty taste. And the growing long silences.

Blue's blue eyes. Blue's cock. Blue's hoarse whisper that for all its clumsiness knew its way through his ear straight to the most twisted part of his brain. Blue's thrall.

The tattoo parlour's windows seem darker; the afternoon is fading. Drake has been lying there for five, six hours, or more. He looks down again, the ridges of his stomach flex. He sees the pattern on his side taking form. The butt of a pistol, its grip, filled in. The start of a barrel. His tattooist wipes at skin with a sterile pad; blood and sweat smear, and then clear away. The black ink and the indigo seem to glow.

The slow arc of the pistol's grip curves over his hip and frames part of his buttock. The chamber spreads across his ribs, and the barrel begins a deliberate climb up his side, pointed toward his armpit, through that to his neck. It's perfect; inked into his skin with pains-taking attention, each line discrete, precise, the patterning meticulous. The tiniest hint of a drop shadow lies underneath it. And, though not part of the design, Drake even loves the minuscule droplets of blood seeping out around the edges staining the negative space of his skin. Just the way they look, wet and red, means something.

Like the day Blue shaved his hair into a thick brushy Mohawk and they drank and wrestled all afternoon until they were too tired to bone each other, then fucked anyway: slowly, lazily with long, beer-soaked sloppy kisses that left their faces red with beard burn, their chins coated with drool. After, they'd gone out and gotten—more—high together, spent the night laughing and twitching.

At least, until they stopped laughing.

He remembers a quick pipe in the alley out back, then Blue shoving him. But he can't see the incident, hear the remark that provoked it. Something must have happened, though. The image of his lover's face bent with rage is fixed in his memory, and his imagination. Shortly afterwards, they went home and Blue started shouting at him. Shoved him again. Drake saw a red curtain fall over his eyes; drunk, stoned, furious—something snapped. He shoved back, slapped Blue. Blue's face dropped, stunned. Drake pushed him to the ground, ripped the baggy shorts he'd been wearing off him, hit him on the ass—hard. Through some distant window in his consciousness, he heard the yelp. He ignored it. He'll never know why, he tells himself, but his face burned as he spit in his hand, lubed his cock, and shoved it into Blue. That shout was clear. But Drake started pumping anyway. In. And. Out. Blue bucked a moment. Then froze rigid. Drake felt Blue tighten on him, then start to relax. A few seconds passed, some hard fucking too, Drake heard a different sound, Blue's low moaning, his grunts, the rasps of aspiration as he caught his breath. And Blue's ass starting to reach, rhythmically, back to him. To come in for the stroke, eager to greet its force. The push and pull and push again. The sweet gravity of it. The warm wet violence of summer rain, of summer storms, of panic, of heat and wet and flashes of lighting. In. And. Out. Of muck sucking at shoes. Of leaves hissing as the wind rises. Of tee shirts clinging. Stuttering talk stopped. Running. Run. In. And. Out. Of faces wet. The river's ineluctable rise. Floods. Floods. Still flooding.

But it was over as fast as it began. Drake collapsing into the dark pit of his too-quick coming. Falling onto Blue's back, sweaty and stinking of chemical smoke and beer and anger. Blue's back rigid, tense muscles not quite quivering. Then him shaking, tossing Drake from his back. And rolling atop, straddling the exhausted Drake and punching him once. Twice. Drake's eyes glazing in a mesh of thousands of points of light. The taste of blood in his mouth. Followed by the hot, salty taste of Blue's cock. Drake hearing the shout, "suck!" Drake sucking.

The jabbing of the tattoo gun has reached the top of his rib cage now. The anxious little flame dances harder for the invisible, angry mob in Drake's head. The man working says nothing, his silence intense and the tight-lipped expression on his face absolutely inscrutable. His eyes suggest fatigue, a hint of rheum and wetness. He's still so handsome, Drake thinks, as his hand rises unconsciously to stroke the deep red sunburst on his chest, placed there the last time he spent an afternoon prostrate in front of him, on this table. Though fully healed, Drake imagines a slight rise in his skin, a bump where the yellow and pink mark him, right above his nipple where the artificial sun shines in the gloom of this antiseptic studio. But Drake imagines a lot. And often. Sometimes it's a problem. Like when he confuses passion and love, intensity and truth.

He shuts his eyes.

It started to happen. Not often, but regularly ... the drinking and drugs, the violence and the angry fucking. A blurry rage of not-quite-rapes. Because neither of them had ever been good at talking, they shared their stories in this manner. A bruise took the place of confidence, a bloody nose or mouth became intimacy: it led them to each other's arms, the comfort and harbour of strong thighs, and broad backs. It let them touch each other—regularly, over and over—without explaining it. Let them touch each other as much as they needed. Too. Blue's smell. The stain of his blood on Drake's hand. Red. Beyond red. Drake sucks in his breath with the memory, and with the pain of a new line being drawn on his body now. The gun hurts so much in its passage.

They said nothing—they never did, Blue and he. For weeks they shared time and flesh, delight and pain, but they still had no shared language for any of it. They acted on each other, they touched and pinched, they sucked and came but never looked at the space they shared too closely, and both knew that what passed between them was too volatile to endure. It burst three nights ago. Hot. So very hot.

After weeks of spiraling, angry sex Blue finally went too far—a little—but too far still. They'd gotten high, gone out to shoot some pool and have some—more—drinks. The shelf behind the pool table was littered with their empty bottles; he can still hear the crash of one when it fell to the floor when Blue leapt into the air hooting at a particularly good shot and toppled it in his excitement. The sudden twist of the neck, the awkward look on his face. Drake grinning in response. But shortly afterwards, all of the accumulated empties were replaced by new bottles. They played on.

They went home.

They didn't switch the lights on.

The door clicked shut and Blue made a noise in his throat, a kind of growl, but with something metallic in it, a sharpness. Drake never saw the hand rise, never made out its approach in the gloom; he only felt it when the five-strong fingers closed on his neck. And he heard the hoarse voice whisper, "tonight I'm going to break you." Then that muttering mouth closed over his and a tongue pushed passed his teeth. For just a second. Until a stinging slap hit the right side of Drake's face. He pulled back, his spine stiffened and another whistling slap came. Blue's other hand went down the back of Drake's pants, grabbing his ass. Drake jumped back against the door pulling Blue into him, into a short hard punch in his gut. "Don't you fucking tell me that!" Drake shouted. He grabbed Blue by the shirt and felt his lover's erection as he pulled him close. Felt his stirring in return. "Fuck," Blue hissed the word. He pulled Drake off-balance and sent him to the ground. Fell atop him. Their thighs rubbed together, their muscled chests struck with a wet sound. Drake felts the hand fumbling with his fly, grabbing his cock. "No," he almost screamed. Blue spun round, forcing his crotch into Drake's face. Something in Drake snapped. Images of devastation crowded his head, herds racing towards black caves, abandoned buildings he's had sex in, a torn billboard with the traces of a golden arm alone remaining. Something snapped and Drake head-butts the groin above him—hard. All the angry pictures cleared, replaced by clouds of fire and sounds he will never know again. Shadows peeling off of concrete walls. Thing tearing. Things torn. Then he lifted his hand to strike a second time. Blue screaming. Rolled off of him, clutching his crotch.

Drake jumped to his feet. "Don't you fucking tell me you're going to break me. Don't ever say something like that. We do this shit together ... but we never talk about it. Don't you fucking understand anything." Blue just stared, half his face visible in the dark, tendrils of light creeping into the loft from under the door. Drake knew his lover's shoulders were bunching, his fists balling in the obscurity. He could hear the deep, ragged breaths being pulled in and released with an unequal rhythm. He kept waiting for the fight to come, but it didn't.

Blue said, "Get out."

Drake said nothing. He left and spent the rest of the night, the next day, the night again remembering. He remembered the stains on Blue's hands violet and red, overshadowing and tinting the yellow that was there too, the day they died his hair before a big night out: concerts and beers and friends falling over in an alley at the end of it all. He remembered the sound of thunder in the dark as he lay sleep-less, turning over and over and over in his bed eager for the morning so he and Blue could drive out to the country and get lost in the woods. The brilliant flash of lightning as crooked as the crack in the panes of glass that held the world out. He recalled the feel of his lover's hands and fingers, gripping him, probing at his body's openings, striking him and the purple colour again, of bruises this time. He sees images shake themselves out, sparks flying: the red rims of their eyes as they stared at each other as dawn broke over the city's roofs; the dust of beard as they kissed in elevators they'd stalled for time to do just that; the flights of angry angels, flaming wings spread and tails of scorpions in hand like scourges he had imagined the night some bonehead called them faggots at a show; the broken tooth he'd given to the man; the rage and sorrow like a torrent of bulls blinded and heading for open water; and always, always the things he'd wanted to say to Blue and never could... the words that failed him, the soft phrases he was too blunt to say, the anger he should have shared and couldn't and the fear. Always, of course, the unspoken, unspeakable uncertainties that clawed at his guts and the poor rags of his hope. The day after all that, he booked an appointment for the tattoo. Got here on time. Explained what he wanted and shrugged off the shocked expression he got in reply.

The inked handgun covers his left side now, a still-empty banner winds around it, waiting. Waiting for words to come at last, though they can't be spoken they can take shape here, in flesh and time and torment. The skin is raw and secretes lymph and blood and bad memories. There is room. At last, there is room. But the tattoo gun is switched off. With wet blue eyes, the man holding it stares at him. Looks as if he is about to speak.

"Just do it. Put the fucking words in." Drake bites his bottom lip.

The man turns his head from Drake.

"Do, it Blue. I'm paying you for this, and I want every fucking word. I want it to say exactly what I told you—'My worst mistake was you.' Make it say that."

Drake closes his eyes. His teeth are tight against each other. There will never be nights again. There will never be enough time, or armies of the spirits of light with arms in hand, or without. And though there have never been enough, there will be no words ahead. Drake wants to cry. Wants to explain why he cannot. But he says nothing more.

Blue sets his chin. With gun in hand, he leans in, and the pain comes back.

Drake knows the pain and the need for it.

It is familiar, and it makes him sweat.

LAST NIGHT AT MANSCAPE

NICK MAMATAS

THE COPS IN THE 1950S could do nothing about it, thanks to a few well-positioned lieutenants who were regulars. The hippies in the 1960s were way too straight for the scene, but they had their own things going on. The NIMBYs of the 1970s, the Yuppies of the 1980s, the recession of the 1990s, and the boom and dot.com bust of the 2000s just made the Manscape sleazier and then much cleaner by turns.

2010s though. The techbros, overgrown babies looking to get married, they ruined everything. The Manscape was half a square block of adjoining basements under factory buildings. The sliding doors and dogleg corners hadn't been built by queers—maybe it had been the Syndicate, or had to do with water tables and tiny fault lines under the city. But the labyrinth of corners and alcoves and a few long halls, all exposed brick, made from an amazing club for men. Now women were coming, and track lighting, and LED monitors on the walls, and bathrooms made of materials determined to stay white and unscratched, and a goddamn underground oyster bar, and elevators to the street.

Theo wasn't a techie, he was just a tech, a guy who worked with his hands to lay cable. At the hiring hall, the Manscape gig went unstaffed for three weeks. Even in San Francisco, a lot of guys don't want to be associated with faggots, especially not the kind into anonymous sex deep underground. When Adrienne, the office manager, called Theo in and told him of the third-shift job, she did so without a smile.

"This is the job for you," she said plainly. "You're the right man for the job." Adrienne was a heavy, older woman, all flannel and baseball caps, but she wore blue eyeshadow and hipster glasses too.

"How did you know?" Theo asked.

"You're just like your father," she said.

Theo thought about that as he descended the shaft, huge coils of cable hanging from his shoulders, several of the same waiting for him at the bottom. Theo's father had laid copper wire for the phone company for years. He was the best. And when he left Theo's mother, it was for another man.

Theo was just like his father. He knew the Manscape like the back of his hand. The regulars liked the calluses on his palms; they could tell it was him in the Dark JO Room. "A little harder, Theo," one older man always prodded him. Theo never even saw his face, but he could smell him, could feel a bushy mustache when they kissed in the dark. Another man, a twink who hung around the urinals, liked having his balls squeezed, and liked complaining about the firm proletarian grip of Theo's hands. The first time it happened, Theo apologized and tried to withdraw, but two reedy hands clamped around his forearm. "No, no," keep going the guy whispered. He must have weighed a hundred pounds, but he had strong fingers like tree roots. "I just like to whine a bit. Please don't leave me."

Now the Manscape was like any other set of basements, any other mile of hallway wrapping and coiling in on itself. There were going to be drop ceilings, and Theo's job was to run cables for the servers, the LED screens. It wasn't a one-person job, but there was only one person available to do it, and Theo had all night.

It was hard work and required constantly moving back to the starting point of some splice or connection to recheck, untangle, or push a cable through a hole. He had to move the stepladder with him, or kick it down the hallways for the company of noise and clatter.

Soon enough, despite the map on his smartphone, and despite his own experience prowling the halls of Manscape for warm mouths and tight asshole and smooth hands, Theo found himself lost. Lost enough, anyway, in alcoves unfamiliar and halls that seemed to lead the wrong way, though of course, every hallway in the world is necessarily a two-way route.

And then there was the smell. Manscape had been limned with plenty of smells; the umami cleanliness of spilled semen, the musk of sweat, wisps of commercial deodorant and cologne, occasional darker odors … but this was different. It smelled hot, and animalistic, and ancient. Theo wasn't paid enough to follow his nose to whatever soil stack had burst, even if the smell was strangely mixed with bubblegum scent, so he gave it a wide berth.

Then he saw a man. A young fellow, in a white sleeveless t-shirt and khakis. With greased hair and the tanned arms of someone who works outside. Something about him didn't look quite right; he carried himself with a posture, a swagger, Theo only knew from old movies.

"Hey!" Theo called out. "What are you doing here? This place is off-limits." The greaser turned the corner and his footfalls stopped. Theo trotted after him and found an empty alcove. No way out. And a miasma of that odor again.

Theo tried to make a call, but he had no service. He was there to make sure that the future establishment would at least have WiFi, after all. And he was in no mood to confront some homeless guy, or anyone confused enough to think the Manscape was still open for business, though a brief fantasy of an uncut cock dangling from those khakis kept Theo from being too frightened.

Footsteps sounded just occasionally enough that it couldn't be a coincidence. Theo wasn't alone, and it wasn't just the greaser wandering the area either. There were too many—just a handful, but more than one set. And low voices too, some cooing and others sharp.

The boots were loud. Theo spun and saw the Top striding toward him, his sub at his heel. Old Guard leather guys with mustaches people didn't even wear for comical effect in movies anymore. The Top glared at Theo; the sub kept his gaze on his master's boots.

"Get down off that ladder, son," the Top barked at Theo. "I ain't seen you around before, and there's no way you're ready for breathplay." He squinted as he approached. "Is that … plastic rope?" The sub glanced up, but Top sensed it, and shot him a look.

"You guys don't belong here anymore," Theo said. He almost added You might get hurt but who knew how they'd take it—as a threat or a promise? "Manscape is closed. It's going to be…" what did it say on the stupid prospectus "iMind. A physical exploration of the Freudian structures of the human mind. With Wifi and touchscreens and oxygen bars and a library and a petting zoo."

Top turned to the sub. "This one is all hopped up on something. Let's go." They walked past Theo, their bodies warm, their smells human and alive. He wanted to touch them, not to see if they were real, but because he knew they were.

There was no reason not to finish the work. And Theo was sure he'd see someone else if he kept moving. And he did. An elder with an overcoat and dress shoes and wrinkled albino prunes for balls. Two young guys, corn-fed wrestlers or rugby players who seemed to have come directly from the Greyhound bus terminal, who stopped to ask Theo what that smell was. A short queen, skin tawny, who waved jauntily and said "You be safe up there with all them important things, hoo-kay?"

It was nearly dawn, Theo guessed, though there was no way for even a single photon of sunlight to enter the Manscape, and he was nearly done. Maybe it was the tiredness or the stench, but he was sure the man to walk by him, brush past his shoulder, was his father. His father, ten-years dead, but the shoulder and shirtsleeve felt real. Theo followed, not the man, who of course had turned another corner and vanished, but the smell.

Manscape was no less confusing for it being gutted, but the smell was easy to follow. Like an armpit. And noise too, getting louder. Slapping, groaning, giggles, the occasional yawp and shout. And then he entered a space he'd never seen before, one that he was sure wasn't on a map, wasn't even possible.

The bull, and that was a good name for him, was huge. Not huge like a bodybuilder, though there was plenty of muscle. Just like an animal, with huge limbs and a torso the size of a twin bed's mattress. His cock was just as huge as it should be, but the ballsac was nearly comically outsized. The bull had propped up a few play mats into an ersatz lounge chair and sat, disinterestedly stroking himself.

Everyone else was gone, though Theo could still hear their activities reverberating throughout the chamber, thanks to the trio of other entrances.

"Who the hell are you?" Theo said as he opened his mouth, immediately regretting it. The bull's biceps were the size of Theo's head.

"I'm the host," the bull said. "You're my guest." His voice was casual, much smaller than his frame suggested.

"I'm not staying. You can't either. The new owners have plans for this place."

The bull scratched his balls. It was like watching someone manipulate a pair of honeydews in a laundry sack. "They didn't run their plans by me."

"It's going to be called iMind," Theo started. "A Freudian experience ..." The bull's glare killed the words in Theo's throat.

"Get over here and worship me a while, kid," the bull said, gesturing toward his cock. "That's why they sent you."

Theo ... well, maybe under other circumstances. Why not? he thought. It would be something he could tell his grandchildren about in the unbelievable future age when all social barriers to sexual conversations had collapsed. The future, it was going to be something. It already wiped out Manscape, the fucking future.

"Uh ... how long is a while?"

The bull shrugged expansively. "You know. Forever."

"They didn't run their plans by me," Theo said, sounding braver than he wanted to.

The bull snorted and reached behind his pile of mats for an enormous club. It was a huge carved cock, one that fit with the bull's balls. "Have it your way." He was up and halfway across the chamber. The sickening smell of the bull's snort pushed the clean air from Theo's lungs, but he held down a wretch and turned and ran.

"Fine!" cried the bull. "Tire yourself out!" Theo flew from hall to hall, doubling back, shifting from left foot to right at forks before blindly tumbling one way or another. The bull, that smell, was right behind him somehow, though the giant footsteps echoed off the walls at a leisurely pace.

Theo hit one dead end, then turned back and hit another. From the corner of his eye he caught a glint of something and squeezed his eyes shut, ready for a killing blow. When none landed, he laughed aloud and threw open his eyes. The bull sounded in the distance. Theo cringed at that, but knew he had a chance. The stepladder was just a few feet away. And where the ladder was, the cable ended.

"I heard that giggle, friend!" shouted the bull. He was close. Theo ran, keeping an eye on the ceilings where he had run cable all night long. Left, right, long, then short, and he was at the shaft. The bull was ten yards behind him. Theo climbed the ladder, and didn't look back over his shoulder, didn't want to feel a hand clasping around his ankle, or the thud of the club hitting his spine.

"Hey!" the bull shouted from the bottom of the elevator shaft when Theo was halfway up. "You think I ain't gonna follow you up there?" He dropped the cock-club and took to the ladder, clearing four rungs at a time.

Theo had his key out, inserted it, turned it. "C'mon! Follow me! I want you to!" Theo spilled out into the damp and hazy dawn, the monster right behind him, nudging him to the ground.

"This is what you want," Theo said, craning his neck to look up at the bull. "Here's the fucking city. Take it. Fucking take it back." The bull peered up at the high-rises, half-built, and then down the long expanse of Market Street.

"Don't mind if I do," the bull said, and walked into the fog.

DANCE, MACABRE

PHOENIX ALEXANDER

HERE IT IS, YOUR FATHER says as he pulls up to the club, the car headlights making bright meat of the young people queuing outside. The eater of my youth, he says, so many good nights here, proper good, lad, you have no idea. He licks his lips and says a name that could be 'Elysian' or 'Elysium' but you're hustling out that car so fast you don't quite catch it.

Hey!

He calls your name. You turn, smoothing your hair, hoping no one pays too much attention. But they are looking, oh yes they are. Just remember son, your father says. Beckoning you to come closer. You duck your head back in the car, smelling the beer on his breath and his Brut deodorant. He tells you that if you see a girl you like and want to go for a kiss, just try and think about how you're showing her how much you like her through your lips and you move them like this ....

You turn away in horror and all but run to the bouncer-guarded gold gates of the club, cringing at the image of your father with his eyes closed, moving his lips horribly independently of each other, like small fish, in the car interior.

You are eighteen years old.

The club is everything you thought it would be, and more: all of life between its vaulted walls. The stonework—you can't tell if its real masonry or just effect—is audacious, grandiose, demanding respect as loudly as the music that seems to come from everywhere, nowhere. The sound is the greatest you've ever heard. Inchoate vocals, bass like a God's heartbeat. It brings you in, somehow; it doesn't hammer you down. Though you're embarrassed of your lanky frame and pimples and a thousand other weaknesses you immediately feel alright, here. And that's before a drink.

And you go to the bar and you get a drink, nestling in between the warm bodies of girls, their tan shoulders perforated by the straps of their tops. The loose striped shirts of men nuzzle your flesh; you feel the breath of someone taller, pressed behind you, exhaling on your scalp. The small hairs on your neck tingle.

This is life!

You order a blue drink, because a girl next to you is drinking it. And because it looks fun. Sugar fizzes against your lips and you throw your head back and chug. Drunk-fast, let's go! Drink up! Chin chin!

You're buzzing by the time you reach your friends on the far table of the dance floor: Jeff and Natalia and Samira. A quadruple, perhaps, except Jeff goes red at the mention of making a move on Natalia, and you don't find Samira attractive. You're not sure if you find any girl attractive but you will, your mother tells you, you will, and then the image of your dad's lips moving in the dark car comes back and you chug more of the blue fizz.

I love this song! Samira shouts.

What? You shout back.

I love this song!

Hand-grabbed, you are dragged onto the dance floor. The four of you dump your coats and bags on the booze-gummed floor and begin to dance.

Elysian, or Elysium, soars around you; a building weirdly bigger on the inside, gaudy in its columned facade but expansive here. Cathedrals aren't this holy, surely. The ceiling seems miles above you. No reaching that airy expanse up there, above the punching hands and whirling arms; that is the lights' domain.

And oh, there are lights.

Projectors like turning sentries swing beams of blue and neon green overhead. The colors glow and you drink more, bumping into someone behind you (sorry, sorry! It's all good, you both laugh, keep dancing).

Happy birthday! Your friends scream.

Happy birthday! Screams the blue booze in your blood.

Happy Birthday!

Louder; euphoria makes your limbs light and someone behind (the bumped-into) screams Happy birthday! And the cry is taken up by his group and they scream it too, alcohol splashes on your feet and the music slams and it's alright, but what's not alright is, horribly, as your eyes whirl up above the clubbers the ceiling of the club moves, membrane sliding over membrane like a lung after a breath is drawn. Just once.

What's the matter? Your mate asks. You're too disoriented to see which one.

I'll be right back, you say, trying not to vomit.

You. The bathroom. Muted-but-still-mighty club music finds you here, vibrating the walls.

Your feet stick to the floor.

An animated toilet attendant yells in a thick Jamaican accent: No splash, no gash! Cologne bottles revel in myriad colors behind him on the countertop, making you ill to look at them. You mutter something you hope is funny as you fumble at your fly and pop out your dick to piss. The word 'gash' makes you uneasy. It brings to mind long clean red wounds rather than anything you'd want to be inside.

You finish. Stumble over to the sink and slap water around your hands from a tap that rocks in its installation. You look into the mirror. A crimson-faced horror looks back. Rabid-eyed, cheeks bright with rosacea. You have aged a decade, you're sure of it. You look at your watch to break the fright. It's only 12.24 am. No longer your birthday—but palpitating hours to go before you sleep.

You drink too much. Predictably. It's the club, it's the people. The fucking music. That's the lifeblood, you realize; THAT is life, strong and pulsing and unceasing even as the clubbers are, as the night unfolds, brought low. The DJ is a marionette twitching with unnatural energy.

You stop having fun.

We won't talk about what you did in the line for the taxi rank in the dead hours of the morning. The way you fell into the man with the beautiful facial hair and thick body, remembering, only after everything else in your mind had been blitzed, your dad's advice on how to kiss. A resilient thing, that repulsion. You are etched with it. How your lips protruded and moved, like little fish themselves, against the fragrant bristle of the man's neck. The laughing it off. The embarrassed rejoining with your friends.

But that's not what keeps you up at night. It is the taxi driver's words when your friends scream out that yes, it was your birthday and yes, it was your first time at this club.

Welcome to 'El! The driver guffaws.

Elysian. Elysium. 'El. So witty!

You rock, drunk out of your skull in bed. You shake with mirth. Ha! It's hilarious, the funniest thing.

And then it isn't.

You go to university. Samira and Natalia and Jeff do, too. You all promise to stay in touch but after a few months, you don't.

Studying doesn't interest you. So you don't do that either.

Your nights are spent in sweaty rooms, pumping your fists to music, arms raised for a ceiling that is not El, with its vault high as heaven and stonework that moves like a membrane. There are no visions in the mirrors of these clubs. Student dives, more like. Impoverished things. The three years pass like scenery beyond a car window.

You speak to your dad often.

Kissed any pretty girls? He asks at the end of every call.

I have kissed some pretty things, yes, you reply.

You got the degree in the end: booze-soaked though it turned out to be, a sodden thing, figuratively speaking, interesting but not interesting enough to make a career of.

So you take a job in your home town.

You go back home.

To the Elysian.

You finally learn its name and, as you step through its arched doors that first night back you feel breathed in by it, and exhale yourself, offering your respect.

I didn't know you back then, you said. I was a youth.

A rumble shifts the dimensions, minutely, just for you. The club has heard. The club appreciates.

Music riots. Lights glaze the air; the music lifts.

Then slams.

You dance.

You wake up on the morning of your thirtieth year and, vivid as lust, you see the years of your life standing in a row like bottles, but the bottles are opaque, and you can't see inside. How was that time spent?

Who can answer that?

The job is dull. Eight-nine-ten daily segments of time sat with a headset helping ungrateful callers manipulate the tiny machinery of the devices that structure their lives. A highlight is when someone in your team (battery hens sat upright in black-backed chairs that fuck your lower spine after ten minutes) says the infamous words: *Have you tried turning it on and off again?*

A snatch of song from a passing car radio on your fag break: 'I can't wait/for the weekend to begin!' And it's true, you can't! The cigarette suddenly tastes like nectar. Honeyed smoke pours down your throat.

It is Thursday. Only a day to slaughter and then the lights, the vaulted ceiling, the music.

The belonging feeling that comes from becoming a breath drawn deep.

No boyfriend for you yet (let's not even say that word) but you do like to invite men, boys really, to your apartment and piss on them, among other things. Sometimes unexpectedly.

Sometimes it gets ugly.

(You have bad days, who doesn't?)

One encounter struck you in the mouth, called you a monster, left.

That was fun to explain to the guys in the office.

Trouble with the missus, one laughs. Not quite amused.

Yes, you say.

The few women of the office avoid your gaze.

You go to the Elysian.

Dance, rise, slam. Fucking perfect as it always is. Deep air, is what you are. Deep air inside of a living thing so much bigger than you.

Gasping breaths and gasped-in drinks later you go to the bathroom to piss (you naughty boy, that's what got you into trouble in the first place) and a reflection greets you in the mirrors: your own, yes, and a slender youth standing behind you whose skin shines like polished bronze.

Shh, he mouths, undulating. Don't turn around.

You don't. But your erection pushes painfully against the sink's porcelain edge.

You are so beautiful, he says. The purple bruise on your chin fades before your eyes. You are made pristine. Tears overwhelm you (ignore the boisterous laughs of fellow pissers, the way the attendant tugs at your arm to go get some water, go get hydrated).

How can I thank you? You ask the bronze boy.

You know how. He says. Promise you'll always come here. For your whole life. Promise you'll always come back.

I will, you sob. I promise. God damn! I promise.

One more thing, he says. His skin shifts over his bones; the mirage melts into one word, one feeling, one impulse:

Dance.

You are forty-five years old.

Went quick, didn't it?

Everyone else in the office left and you are the survivor of Information Technology services: the bitumen that rises to the top. You are a manager now! Congratulations.

Buildings were built and felled around the drab tower in which your office, one of many, hides quietly, tumorlike inside something vast. It's a comforting thing. It is a tomb of days.

And Friday night at five pm … oh boy. Talk about the Resurrection of Christ.

You calm down, sexually, try to get a partner. Younger than you, sure, much younger, but still respectable to society. Not embarrassing enough to take to a work function.

Or the Elysian.

That was the one time you disappointed it.

Way after midnight, in the hours when the music hit wyrdest, you see the bronze-skinned youth in the bathroom mirror again, and he hooks fingers at the edges of your mouth, forcing a grin out of you, showing your teeth.

Don't turn around, he says. Don't turn around.

Your cock flaps half-in your jeans, sprinkling piss on the urinal. You're a good-time gal, the youth says, you're a party-lad, a free spirit, you don't wanna be tied down, hmm?

You try to answer but can only gurn, spitting, against his manicured nails.

Because you'll get tired one day, he raves, tired in your happiness, distracted by cooking or monthly budgets or joint bank accounts or a fucking wedding and what kind of biscuits to get with your morning tea and you'll get soft, did I mention tired, complacent in what you think is happiness and one day you won't come back to me.

I will, you bray. As best you can.

Prove it! The youth shouts, throwing you forward, unhooking his fingers. Your face hits the mirror and the red-faced freak is back again: your reflection, flashing old, flashing young the next moment.

The club's promise.

You end it with your fella the next day, hungover and looking resolutely down at eggs-growing-cold that he made you for breakfast. It is harder outside of the Elysian: where there is no music, and where daylight is unkinder than any strobe.

I hope you find what you're looking for, he says, sobbing, leaving your place.

Joke's on him: you've already found it.

DEPRESSION CONGEALS IN YOU AT the thought that it is Sunday, and work tomorrow—but the world of your mind turns to focus on a brighter hemisphere, in that it will be Friday again in five days—and then you'll know where to go. You'll know what to do.

Slaughter the days, lad. Slaughter the days.

Ten years later.

Your father passed away in the night.

When I die, put me ashes in the El' and have a fucking party around them, he said, the last time you saw him. You say you're not sure if they'll agree to that, panicking that you'll disappoint your father on his deathbed, but also panicked by the thought you'll make him a promise you can't keep. I'll call, you say.

And you do.

Do you think the management of the Elysian agreed to host a party around a dead man's ashes?

You should know by now.

Anything for you.

It's getting painful to walk these days but you still make it to the club. You still keep your promise.

The Elysian has inhaled you and when you are outside its walls you don't know how old you are anymore; in the mirrors that are not *its* mirrors you have lost your hair and your skin is marked with unyoung pigments, strange shapes, folds.

But inside … you stand and sway under the lights, gulped up to the ceiling. Slammed by beating music on all sides you stand upright. You do not hear the **C'mon, Granpa!** yelled, not horridly, at you by younger revelers.

In the bathroom the gold youth gyrates between the walls of an empty cubicle, putting on a show for you. You have been so good.

When you stagger out in the daylight hours you see the battlefield of the city: lost shoes, lost clothes, broken glass making nebulae across the cobblestones. It's the crepuscular world that has to be made right before the city wakes. To see it clean, healed, is a wonderful thing.

A drunk woman slumps on the ground, clutching a fire hydrant like a life buoy. Her heels and party dress are miraculously intact, like it is the night's beginning.

Wanna go t'viscerum, she mumbles as you pass.

You chuckle.

Alissa … Lissen ….

Elysian, you smile. It's mine.

Saliva laddering her neck, the woman bleats happiness.

Your childhood friend Jeff died. There is a lovely obituary to him on the news site. He leaves behind a wife, no kids.

Poor Jeff.

His portrait looks perfectly pleasant. You are sure he led a perfectly pleasant life.

Unfortunately, you haven't been feeling great, recently. Well, it's a bit worse than that actually. You fill the bowl with blood when you go to the toilet, and shitting is agony.

The colonoscopy appointment is inevitable. As is the outcome, really. The doctor's face says it all.

There is not long left, she says, mournful.

So it is.

You know you should feel devastated, broken, a living tragedy. And you do, for a moment—but you can't help but hear a snatch of song from the reception area outside, and your mind smiles at the thought of the lights, the music, the ceiling like a lung.

I can't wait! For the weekend! To! Begin!

You bump into Samira, quite by accident, in the supermarket. Two young women flank her, their features sullen but hers, undoubtedly, shifted a few degrees. Her children.

Oh, it's **you**! She smiles, lunging forward into an embrace. Gosh, you're a bag of bones! How have you been?

You tell her.

Shit. She turns to the girls. Take the groceries home, she tells them. This is an old friend. They agree, leaving. I look at the strength of their limbs: the muscles taught as they bear the shopping bags.

Coffee? Samira says, taking your arm.

A pint, you counter.

Her eyes flicker downward.

Sure.

You drink too much and tell her everything, everything. You watch her go from hand-clutching warmth, leaning in to you, to a coiling inward, a physical change in her body. By the end of your monologue you have disgusted her.

I can't believe that place is still open, she says finally. Meaning the Elysian.

We had some good nights there, remember? You say. The booze's glint in your eyes, in your voice. You can hear it.

We had some nights, she replies.

She tells you about her life. About Natalia's; how she's a successful poet, and taught creative writing at college her whole life. About her own career as a social worker.

There is judgement in the recounting of these lives, clear as spirit. You zone out after a while. You get the message. Your mind goes there—where you will be in just as soon as you're done with her. There are no days to kill anymore. Work is finished; there is nothing left between you and the Elysian.

Jeff, Samira, Natalia .... Your own father, who got out, never returning to the club again after raising his family .... Who's to say they lived better? Who can measure that? It is a rare thing to belong to someone completely in this life, you think.

You were good. You were rewarded. And you were so grateful.

The Elysian raises its walls, right then and there, around you.

You died, Samira tells you. Perhaps she has been saying something important but you didn't hear it. She is crying. You died in life! Leaning forward again, seizing your hands. The funniest thing.

Oh no, you correct, tapping your feet on the gummy floor as a fan made of neon green bars of light radiates across the entire, glorious, fucking place, and the bass hits, and the drop comes, as it always does, forever more, Amen.

"I lived."

A
DEVILMENT
JAMES BENNETT

ESSEX, 1645

WHAT, PRAY TELL, IS THE opposite of 'exorcism'?

Ephraim Tempest asks this of the dark as the cottage door creaks wide and he catches the scent of the dead. Fruity, yet not fresh. *Windfall apples,* he thinks, *worm gnawed and brown.* Sulphur sours the air or something akin to it. There is a pressure that aches in his skull, in the bones of his crooked leg. A Royalist musket ball became lodged in his knee at Powick Bridge two years ago—sadly, thirty-five was not old enough to escape conscription—and while the war turned him into a man of the cloth, lately a parson of Coggeshall, the wound still aches like buggery whenever maleficium is near. Roused, he strokes his swallow-tail beard and employs his cane to further prod open the portal.

Aye, brimstone travels on the wind.

It is as familiar to him as the fog that hangs over Moonewick, yet another ramshackle, mulligrub village hugging the marshland coast of the Tendring Hundred. Out there, past the skeletal masts and abandoned oyster buckets, stretches the grey expanse of the sea. Water reigns here, winding in creeks, sedge and the nigh on sweet mud until the land itself becomes a low chain of islands, hazy with insects, ghostly under a defeated sun. Ephraim is up to his shins in Essex. The sea lies so languid and flat that one might pull up one's boots and walk to Holland, and to Hell with the whole accursed business, the calamity in the cottage.

At liberty he is not when Hell is already at his door. Ephraim senses he's close now, closer than he's been in any of the reeking fishing dens east of Colchester that he and his prentice have traipsed through. He guessed it when the Widow Hocket—a pickthank if ever there was one—accosted him on the Frinton road, babbling of 'daemonologie and strange effects' from the saddle of her scrawny pony and pointed him with puffing cheeks and trembling finger to the midden heap he presently stands in. It took a brief inquiry to confirm her claims, ascertain that the deviltry described fit his quarry, for every swill-belly and arseworm from here to Norwich saw witches and imps in their backyards these days, the consequence of a panicked world. Even in London rational gentlemen boasted to others of 'great black dogges' seen off in the mist and sea monsters in the Thames. Hopkins, the self-styled 'Witchfinder General,' had left the rabble mad for it, hungry to see their loathsome neighbours put to the test and even better to swing. It was the English way.

Screams, there were. Sparks flying out of the chimney, the Widow said. Imaginative for a backwater fussock. *A foul eggy pall over all ....*

This last had turned their horses for Moonewick, Creedence John Caul and he. Oh, Ephraim pays no mind to witches. Goodwives at best, he thinks them, bored and tinkering by the hearth with old books and customs, folklore and the like, and he suspects that the famed gallows-hound who's gone before him holds more interest in shillings and defenceless quim than ridding the kingdom of evil. In his capotain hat, buckled tunic and muddy black cloak, Ephraim Tempest—a 'pricker' as the yokels hereabouts would have it—has been chasing the Devil Himself.

An old hand, a Puritan stood on the doorstep, he knows better than to reach for his psalter, although he dearly wants to. His prentice, John, flashes silver under his chin, his crucifix gripped between white knuckles.

"Jesus," John says to the shadows, trembling like the novice he is.

The other smell in the cottage is sweat and it wafts not from Ephraim.

John is golden where his master is ash, streaks of white at his temples. The civil war, still raging around them, has gifted Ephraim more years than his due while the younger man's eyes are not yet dulled by the many grim and righteous tasks ahead of him. Exorcisms, prickings, duckings aplenty. Pull off enough fingernails—one never gets used to the sound—and strong shoulders are known to slump, smooth skin weather. Bright gazes go out.

My John.

He should not think about John in the way that he does. His prentice is pure in a way that troubles him, a finger in the ribs of his sin, the secret he keeps. If he were a better man, he'd use the riding crop again, flog himself for his debauchery—and yet the crop, he'd discovered, makes him hard too, his plums fit to burst. *Lord have mercy!* In the cellar of his Coggeshall parsonage, with all the shutters closed, Ephraim has punished himself to conclusion, and punished himself again, roaring his outrage at godless temptation as his seed speckled the floor.

Thoughts like that will not do.

"Jesus looks not at this place," Ephraim replies, pushing past John into the hovel, the bundle of sticks, stones and damp thatch that passes for a Moonewick home. It is heresy, his statement, and along with his wicked dreams about his prentice (the way his rump moves under his breeches, how he might smell at night when disrobed... *Lord, desist, I beg you!*)—he imagines his own cross at his neck burning at the slight.

He knows the truth of it though. Knows it like the creature he hunts. Jesus has left them to it. Determined as the crows wheeling above, he's chased the thing across the Essex marshes, seen its deprivations in six villages and more, and has a reasonable grasp of its needs.

'Tis an incubus. A fugitive from Hell.

Ephraim can sympathise with the lad. Even he is shuddering under his cloak and he has several exorcisms behind him. This will be the sixty-sixth. Yet before the incident in Coggeshall, the shadowy face in the cellar, he has only ministered to marsh folk, seen the odd hag jig at the end of a rope.

It is my first devil.

Thinking this, he steps into the cottage and limping, locates a lantern. When he bends to light it, the little room coughs up the goods.

There are six of them when there should be seven. That is the first thing he observes. An empty chair around the table, kicked over like a missing tooth. Seven is a number sacred to the church. God rested on the seventh day. Jesus spoke seven times as he bled out on the cross. Seven daemons were driven out of Mary Magdalene. Traditionally, seven are required to summon the dead. In this case, it seems these men and women attempted to make contact with the fiend that was plaguing them, the teeth in the dark that fed off their cattle and soured their milk, shat on the altar and swived the odd farmhand as he slept. Had they hoped to appease it?

Ephraim has heard all the rumours, examined the evidence. In Eight Ash Green, an infant was born with two heads, each one bawling to bring down the sky. In Wivenhoe, the wooden cross in the town square was struck by lightning, charred and cloven in two. In St Osyth, an elderly nun had cut off her breasts and left the scraps in the font as an offering. And always, the same old tale of the shadow with the tourmaline eyes, oft burning from a familiar face, that of a brother, a lover, a friend, who soon enough turned out to be a corpse, left in the muck behind a barn, down a well. The devil has a taste for young men, it seems, failing to discriminate between labourer or lord. It wore its victims like doublet and hose, dancing them like puppets for as long as it pleased it, discarding each before prancing on into the Essex peculiar, leaving ruination in its wake. Ephraim can only guess at the fiend's purpose. Experience, and the ache in his leg, tells him it is nothing kind.

He looks at the six men and women around the table. To all intents and purposes, the séance looks like any other. The chamber dark, fragranced by wax and ... *that damnable stench, the odour of the pit* .... The symbols etched in the wood are unknown to him, crescents and sigils to daemon kings. He has seen similar elsewhere. The glass in the middle of the table to snare and amplify the spirits. The villagers, huddled and afraid in the Moonewick inn, have every reason to believe that Judgement has come.

"Good Chri—" John struggles to get the words out, call upon his saviour.

When the devil got in, the glass shattering, it sucked the lot of them dry. Smith, baker, weaver, tranter, mason and tailor—the Widow Hocket gave Ephraim their names; it suits him to think in terms of their occupations, a distance between himself and the heretics that he cannot establish with his cane. The creature sucked at them so hard they crumpled inward like paper dolls, their cheeks gaunt against the surface of the table, their eyeballs sunken like coals in snow. The hollows send him their withered regard. *You come too late. Too late.* Wisps of hair, white as cobwebs, flutter in the draught from the door, the feeblest of summoned ghosts. All six are still holding hands, faith-cum-cadaverous stiffness. A circle of bones with a gap.

Damnation.

"Grk!" His prentice, poor, winsome Creedence John Caul, cannot voice a prayer because he is retching, a steaming slop upon the floor, a piquancy under the foulness. The young man bends over by the wall, completely unmanned by this hinterland tomb. *Fool.* Ephraim spies an opportunity, a path he could forge to his prentice, embrace him, perhaps, brush back his fine, fair locks ....

Enough! He pushes the tip of his cane against his boot, hard enough for his leg to gripe with renewed fire, the blood in his groin to abate. The incubus, the escapee, has left its own spice on the air. There is a tang, Ephraim thinks, of desperation.

Invitation. It comes to him then through the murk. He breathes in old smoke and brings out his psalter. *Surely, the opposite of an exorcism is an invitation.*

One of the circle is missing. The cobbler.

John drags himself out of the cottage.

"Five shillings." Ephraim spoons tepid soup into his mouth; the Hare & Sickle offers the best in all England according to the maidservant and the parson is too ravenous to differ. "Far from the premier rate for a casting out, my lad, but it'll have to do. Even these lodgings are costly."

He squints at the timber walls resting upon the rough quarried stone, the panels a mess of dried dung and horse hair. If Grimsditch, the innkeeper, saw his expression, he would know precisely what he thinks of it. Fog, the same colour as this morning and the one before, presses against the leaded glass, eager to enter. Soon, the farmhands will return from the fields, the fishermen from the creek, and the peace will be broken. Ephraim has work for them. Work they will not like.

Creedence John Caul, a touch of colour returned to his cheeks, grunts on the opposite side of the table.

"A night's rest, then we'll push on," Ephraim continues. "The thing never tarries where it kills, no doubt to preserve anonymity. Come morn, we'll head west along the coast to Point Clear and Brightlingsea, then on to Maldon on the Blackwater Estuary. It is leading us quite the dance, eh?"

This direction has not been chosen on a whim. The Widow Hocket, ever the volunteer, informed him that the missing cobbler, one Godsgyfte Laverocke, has family out that way.

Is it wise to presume that blood calls to blood, he wonders?

On the road, they'll be asking every wretch and rapscallion they meet along the way whether they have seen the man, a tall young gent with an Irish lilt, a birthmark high on one cheek and infernal, tourmaline eyes...

John Caul says nothing. Ephraim sets down his spoon, gently so it does not clang. The line of his prentice's shoulders, ox-thick under his shirt, looks as stiff as the cane by his chair.

"John, you must compose yourself," he tells him. "There will be worse sights ahead."

"Of course, master. I shall wake at cockcrow. Ready our horses."

"I bid you naught. You remember in Coggeshall I gave you the choice? You could've stayed and assisted the curate, collected the tithe at mass."

"What with your leg 'n all, Sir?" John peeps at him through his fringe, a bright, damp curtain. "Who was going to help you into the saddle?"

For a lad nearing his twenty-first year, John has yet to harden with the blows of life, both penury and heartache. The convent that raised him has sheltered him, true; Ephraim fears he has not fared much better. Those eyes though, cornflowers in dew, invite all kinds of concessions.

"Pish. Do not turn this on me." The pastor steals a breath, sprinkles sugar onto his voice. "Oh, John. Do you think you're here solely to feed the horses? Tell me what ails you. Please."

"'Tis them, master. In the cottage." A nod, a sigh, both so heavy. Ephraim knows the weight of it for he bears it himself. How one copes is simply a matter of experience. "They say God is merciful and watches over us. Yet the scholar in Aldham. The fiddler in Fordham Heath. Both as hale as I am and I've barely filched a honeyed almond. Why did the fiend choose—?"

"God moves in mysterious ways, John Caul." Ephraim thinks that the six men and women around the table, their ill-advised attempt at a binding, will be with him for as long as he lives. Unsure what to tell his prentice, how to calm him, he can only stew in his own hypothesis. The daemon, the shadow, has a penchant for youth, of that there can be no mistake. Perhaps it is the reason why Ephraim himself has escaped devourment, with his frosted locks, his crooked leg, though he suspects the notion is a comfort rather than the truth. And he is not about to relate this to John when his ward appears so rattled. "It is not our place to question Him. Be at peace, lad. Should you wish to return to the parsonage and seek sanctuary there, I shall think no ill of you."

Though it quietly stunned him, Ephraim tried his best not to show it when his prentice reached across the table and took his hand in his own.

"Perish the thought, Master Tempest." John managed a smile. "You know well enough the bond between us. I would follow you into Hell."

There is a moment then, a long moment, when the world appears to stop spinning. The Hare & Sickle is far from warm, the hearth burning low, and yet Ephraim fears he is going to faint. Following this, the knife of remorse, the insufferable frustration. Can John Caul see into his heart?

A little too swiftly, the parson retracts his hand.

"Very good. Then, if it please you, the horses shan't ready themselves."

HE COMES TO HIM THAT night, his prentice. Of course, Ephraim thinks it a dream.

Well, he is weary. No one in the inn was inclined to carry the corpses from the cottage and a quarrel broke out over whether the dead should be buried in the cemetery at all, sorcerers as they were. "Holy ground is precious," Culpopes, the old bibliopole said over his ale, "especially in these here times." Murmured assent and grumbles about the war and apocalypse greeted this. Like any nowhere place, Moonewick is as bound to its memories as to the land. A crooked tree where a robber once hanged, a pool where a child drowned, all of these places held sacred and the villagers in suspicious regard of any outsider who meant to meddle, trespass on the customs of the past. In the end, they said, avoiding each other's eyes, all of them were going into the soil of the Chapel of St Sythe and most would prefer not to share it with the damned. Ephraim, a clergyman and a stranger, was not one to say otherwise.

This led to talk of a messenger, some mud-faced urchin or other being dispatched to the nearby town of Clacton-on-Sea to fetch the bishop in order to make a ruling on the matter, which in turn caused consternation as Reepe, the bishop in question, was likely to demur thanks to the Rebellion and Cromwell. Arch under the brim of his hat, Ephraim rapped his cane for silence and learnt from the throng how Parliamentarian soldiers had stolen a bell from the Parish Church of St James that very spring, along with organ pipes and the lead from coffins to melt down into ammunition. Reepe, it appeared, was a pious man; even should he deign to come consecrate the site, a tithe was certain and the burgess had already paid Master Tempest for his exorcistical services, or rather for setting foot in the cottage. Besides, blessing or no, local gossip would be bound to mark the village as accursed, so perhaps it was best to avoid diocesan intervention, after all. Men had oysters to sell. Instead, the good and faithful folk of Moonewick agreed to set to torch the cottage with all of their poor dead neighbours inside.

Ephraim can still smell the sweet smouldering thatch when he lies back on his pillow in the inn, yawning and blinking at his psalter, and trying to expunge the trials of the day, the memory of those white, emaciated faces. He's thinking of the journey ahead, one he has no appetite for, and wonders whether his leg or his spirit will give out first on his merry way from here to hellfire.

As it happens, the night effaces the need. The parson lies reviewing a passage on witchcraft when he hears his chamber door creak open, the candles fluttering, and sees Creedence John Caul creep in in his nightshirt. To spare them their shillings and modesty (and his own peace of mind), Ephraim furnished the innkeeper with enough coins for two rooms, so to see his prentice at this hour disturbs him greatly.

Has there been a sighting of Godsgyfte? Please Lord, no further slaughter!

The question dies on his lips as he watches John, the lad unspeaking, draw closer to the bed, tugging on the laces at his breast. In the dim light, Ephraim makes out his golden fuzz, the firm muscles of his chest underneath, and a serpent winds around his throat.

Despite himself, he sits up and waves his little book, an ancient, reliable ward.

"Young John Caul. Are ye raddled? What by the saints are you about?"

In response to this hallowed enquiry, John puts a finger to his lips, then slips off his nightshirt over his head. *Christ forgive me.* Ephraim cannot avoid spying the way the worn cotton slides over the young man's maypole, thickened and bobbing between his legs. Then, whilst he all but expires against the bedstead, Ephraim takes in the naked aspect of his prentice, his pale, sinewy legs, the darker patch between them, his rod. His eyes trace the ladder of hair from his navel, over the pan of his abdomen, his nipples, his neck, his -

"God's wounds, boy! What—?"

John Caul is upon him, a smooth wing of flesh sweeping him under, his lips pressing hot against his own. Ephraim protests, every catechism, every excoriation he has ever heard from a pulpit flooding his mind, screaming of abomination. Yet words hold no power over his blood, as he's discovered prior in his cellar, and he is already rock-hard in his drawers, throbbing against the younger man's thigh as he presses himself against him. He does not push John away.

Oh, he smells of the horses, the oats and the straw all thrown up to heaven, his sweat like angelic tears!

Cursing, Ephraim is mounting his own assault, his tongue screwing into John's mouth, tasting wine, eels and perdition. His hands, ringed by Saint Christopher, travel southward, seeking to grip the veined, rigid shaft of John's arousal, pull his desire even closer. John Caul will have none of it. With a grunt he shoves his master back on the bed, his other hand tearing at cotton, releasing his Cyprian sceptre to the air.

"No," Ephraim manages, or perhaps only thinks it as he parts his legs regardless and watches that gilded mop of curls plunge towards his groin, the forge there. He groans, hands twisting the sheets, John's lips closing upon him. Unscoured palms stroke his thighs, his stomach, his plums – the first time a man has ever done so – while John performs his impromptu worship, his mouth, a gate to inferno, sliding deliciously to-and-fro. A finger, greased by spittle, slips into his ballinocack, prompting further lamentation. *Oh!* He releases the molten orb between his legs to pull at his buttocks, by turns thrusting himself and opening his cheeks, a virgin-cum-whore at his prentice's touch.

How long, how much, has he yearned for this? *Burned.* In every glance that he berates himself for, every glare that meets the lad's smile, Ephraim has buried his secret, an ember hissing deep inside. It is no good, he knows this, and not only his passion will go up in flames. Tomorrow, he will turn to the riding crop again, strip himself before the glass and lash at himself till he bleeds, until his tool can no longer draw on his poor pounding heart and the corruption that gnaws him inside. Tomorrow—

God!

Spine arching, undone, Ephraim scales to climax, his seed shooting from the depths of him. Tenacious, John gags, his palms fast against his master's hips, swallowing the salt of him. It is over. The sin committed. For a moment they lie there, priest and disciple, wrapped in the sheets, empty of thought and glowing. Before Ephraim can muster a word—what in all likelihood will be a denial, followed by a call for prayer – there comes a heavy banging at the door.

"Master Tempest, awaken!" It is the innkeeper, Grimsditch; he recognises the man's nasal whine. "'Tis the cobbler, Godsgyfte, Sir. E's been found dead on the common."

Ephraim, tugged by shock and the knowledge that indeed this is no dream at all and he only told himself so, is sitting upright in bed, his legs swinging for the floor. He pushes his prentice away from him now, signalling for him to keep quiet. John Caul is merely John Caul again.

"Ah …. Of course. At once, Sir. Grant me a minute to enrobe."

Except … John is *not* John, is he? How long has he spent with the horses? Did something befall him out there? Some …. Even as the cold, clammy hand of Judgement settles upon Ephraim's shoulder, he looks up from the bed and observes his prentice grinning at him. Their efforts glisten on his lips, his skin, yet it is nothing compared to the gleam in his eyes. Lung-punched again, the parson climbs to his feet, reaching for his cane and crucifix. He realises three things all of a sudden, thudding like musket balls into his leg, his old wound screaming in the gloom, which grows dense with a certain, unwholesome quality. Firstly, there shall be no journey tomorrow. Its purpose has been annulled. Secondly, that if Godsgyfte has fallen, then his quarry must be elsewhere, the incubus abroad. And thirdly, that the man before him is likely possessed, occupied by that self-same daemonic force. Possessed and preying upon him, feeding on his darkest desires…

"Thou son of Lilith!" Ephraim leaps for the table, the silver glinting there. His psalter, his drawers go flying. "Get thee behind me, Satan! Out, foul spirit! You *dare—?*"

Creedence John Caul throws back his head in a sonorous laugh, his amusement shaking the walls. Nay, he is no longer the lad John Caul! His steady gaze is the bluish-black shade of tourmaline, tinged by the erubescence of Hell.

"Out! Out, deceiver!"

Like the gates of Heaven slamming shut, the window shutters fly open, wrenched by the shadow of the fiend. There comes a furious wind, the candles snuffing out, and a billow of foul smelling smoke. *Brimstone.* Then, sinking to the floor clutching his cross, Ephraim is left with the sound of Grimsditch thumping on the door, the echoes of devilish laughter and the sting of his own mortal shame.

"WHAT DOES IT WANT OF US, your devil?"

Your devil. Ephraim notes that, sitting round the table in the hall. Once Gideon Rooksbill, a former quartermaster of the 'New Model Army' had broken his fast and declared himself at liberty, the Moonewick elders agreed to meet to discuss their predicament. It was a question of discretion. When the parson first emerged, pale and unkempt from lack of sleep in the main room of the inn, Culpopes, the bibliopole, had counselled him to remove the matter to a privier place lest the farmers, fishermen and goodwives should panic. The wheat would go unthreshed, the fish uncaught, the sewing and spinning undone, he said—his vision of a doom-struck world. The Widow Hocket added to this, insisting that no bantling within thirty miles must learn of it, the business in the cottage and the haunting upstairs, employing her wisdom to lever her, alongside the parson, the burgess, the bibliopole, and the grand old soldier into the village hall. If she sat silent enough, the others appeared to suffer her.

"Would that I could tell you for certain." Ephraim folds his hands upon his bible, the pages open before him. He has led them all in the Lord's Prayer and naturally, fallen short of telling the whole of it, particularly the fact of his seduction. Creedence John Caul, possessed by Lucifer, had attacked him in his room during the night. "What does any creature of the pit want, corporal? To tempt the faithful into sin. To destroy the works of God."

"Indeed."

Rooksbill, his moustache overgrown, his eye querulous, looks up at the cobwebbed rafters and the leaning grey walls as if to imply he sees no such works at hand. Ephraim has met his ilk before. The way he's dressed for the muster, his leather tunic, knee-high boots and orange sash, marks him out as Ironside's man and not one for spiritual abstraction, let alone talk of the occult. Regrettably, he brought his sword and pistol with him, and while it may gladden the pastor to inform him that such weapons will prove of no use against a daemon, it is apparent that Rooksbill was born to the fray and what he cannot stab or shoot he despises. It is also clear that the corporal is quietly thrilled by Ephraim's arrival, and by the evil at large, presumably welcoming the interruption in his retirement, his daily tedium of shooting foxes and rabbits in his garden and recalling old battles in the inn. Catching the man's glare, it occurs to him that Rooksbill likely laments finding himself lawfully restrained from shooting a parson too, and he softens his tone somewhat as he continues.

"Forgive me," says Ephraim. "One only has tomes to go on, grimoires and the like. A devil like this is known as an 'incubus', Sir, a spirit that feeds on the darkest desires of men. While one sleeps, the creature – which may take womanly guise also—creeps into one's chamber and upon embracing one, sucks out the essence of one's soul. Sufficient… congress and the creature is able to climb inside a person entire, invading their body and assuming their visage. Having chased the thing from Coggeshall whence it first assailed me, I can tell you that the incubus favours young and able-bodied men. All its…" he searched for the word again, "*hosts* have been such, in any case. Such is the case with my prentice, John Caul."

"Saints preserve us," says the burgess.

"Condolences, Father," whispers the Widow. "You must mourn him."

And he does, it is true. There is simply no time.

"The end times have come." This from Culpopes, loosening his neckband like a noose. "The astrologer Lilly said as much. The year thick with skirmishes and bloodshed. Folk corrupted by the spheres, rendering us rapacious and cruel. Daemons walk among us."

Everyone crosses themselves. Everyone but the quartermaster who guffaws, coughs behind his hand and tells the old bibliopole that he is quite safe, considering what the parson has told them. The 'daemon', he says, favours the young. Then he peers at Ephraim, who is not quite old either, his eyes becoming slits.

"Whence did it hail from, your imp?" he asks. "Why come to Moonewick? There's a city of wayward souls down west of us and only we faithful round here."

It is Culpopes' turn to cough, yet Ephraim answers as well as he can.

"According to old Hebraic texts, the *lilim*—succubae and incubi—spring from the womb of Lilith, Adam's first wife. Disobedient, unruly, she was expelled from the Garden of Eden and said to consort with the fallen angels, breeding our family of fiends. The grimoires describe them, shadowy figures with jewellike eyes, able to assume physical form, purloin human flesh. Each one preys upon the living, the weak and the unwary, craving to escape their infernal dungeon, claw their way out of Hell. A man, you see, can become a bridge, if the sin is great enough. The temptation too sweet. I trust, Sir, that satisfies you."

No one in the draughty hall looks satisfied, least of all Rooksbill.

"Fascinating, Father. Yet that is not what I meant. I meant why has this creature fastened itself to you?"

As if sitting over the pit he has spoken of, Ephraim feels heat climb from his cravat, up into his whiskery cheeks. He can hardly tell the man about his cellar in the parsonage, his nightly exertions haunted by sin, the image of a naked John Caul circling like a vulture in his mind, making a mockery of his sermons. Nor of the crop, his futile scourge. This, he believes, provided the lure in question, a stench of lust rising from him that sailed across worlds, into the abyss to the snout of the fiend. What, he has pondered these past few weeks, could be more appealing to such a creature than a devout yet struggling soul?

He cannot tell Rooksbill that. He will not. And he certainly shan't tell him about the strange and terrible wonder that greeted him in the mirror this morn, the march of silver at his temples receded, replaced by a lustrous black. Devil be damned, it seems to him that the thing's touch, the fever it stirred in him, has conjured a rare kind of magic, black and foul nonetheless. Their exchange in his bedchamber, sweat, kisses and *sperma universalis*, appears to have undone a degree of his age. While he knows not the reason, he cannot share the trickery of this, the enticement, and so under the table he places the tip of his thumb in the wound in his thigh and he presses, hard enough to straighten his spine and clench his jaw, fling fire up his nerves to his lips.

"'And I will cut off witchcrafts out of thine hand; and thou shalt have no more soothsayers.'" For added effect, Ephraim raps his cane on the floor, those around the table startled to alertness, their eyes wide in the echoes. "'Thy graven images also will I cut off, and thy standing images out of the midst of thee; and thou shalt no more worship the work of thine hands. And I will pluck up thy groves out of the midst of thee: so will I destroy thy cities. And I will execute vengeance in anger and fury upon the heathen, such as they have not heard.'" He offers them an admonitory look, the visiting parson once more. "Micah. Chapter five. Verses twelve through fifteen."

Rooksbill is shaking his head, but his time he does not laugh.

"So you mean to arm us with crosses and words, send us out into the fog?"

"Nay, gentlemen." Ephraim spreads his hands, appealing to their judgement, a skill he has learnt so well. "All of us here have heard precisely what the fiend wants. Sirs, I mean to lay a trap."

With a spring in his step that was not present yesterday, Ephraim Tempest leads them back to the Hare & Sickle, the burgess, Culpopes, Rooksbill, and the Widow Hocket, all of them—himself included—thirsty for a mid-morning ale. Fired by purpose, the autumn chill creeps into the pastor's bones regardless for he knows that all of his action is a house of straw, founded upon concupiscence and vice. Oh, he is well aware of his transgression; 'tis improbable that John would've come to him thus of his own volition, hardened by ardour and ungodly want, so he grasps the grave liberty he's taken, the spot reserved for him in Hell. The weakness of which he's spoken is his own and he must utilise his cohorts swiftly and wisely, however reluctant they may be, if he hopes to repent of his sin.

An invitation, aye, he thinks, limping hobbledygee through the mud. *The stink of brimstone is mine own now…*

Fog wreathes the village, a frightful veil in which anything could lurk, yet conceals the ruins of the burnt cottage, a boil on the face of his faith. Crows bark, revelling. The sea reeks of salt and death. Moonewick is small and news has spread, an impression evinced by every closed shutter, every barred door. Today, the wheat will indeed go unthreshed, the fish uncaught, the sewing and spinning undone. The quartermaster's question scratches at Ephraim like the stark trees, the blasted ground that pulls at his boots and smears the hem of his cloak. Why indeed? Why chase the devil across the Tendring Hundred like some pudding-head when he could've been sat by his fire in Coggeshall with a warm caudle in his hands and all the horrors of the Holy Book locked firmly between its covers? For all that, he thanks the Lord that Rooksbill hasn't pressed the matter, or inspected it too closely, steering him to enquire why the fiend as described should appear to a priest in *manly* guise, instead of some beauteous, buxom doxy.

If only his answer was faith; he has followed the thing because it has witnessed his failing, the flaw in him.

Forsooth, it is his devil. And he would put out its tourmaline eyes.

"… CHOPPED OFF THE ARCHBISHOP'S HEAD only last January," Rooksbill, the quartermaster, is saying, drawing Ephraim back to the here and now, the crowded belly of the inn. "If Old Laud wasn't safe in the Tower, how can any man be? King, Cromwell or no, these are dark times, my friends, and no heartfelt prayer will avert it."

This last is for his benefit, Ephraim surmises, confirmed by the man's raising of his tankard to where he stands watch by the window along with his pointed wink.

No friend of mine, Ephraim thinks. *The old dog likely links my appearance to the murder of Godsgyfte and waits to applaud my own. Then he'll paint himself the hero.*

It is dusk and half of them are drunk, fettle for the task at hand. Grimsditch is making a fortune from the preternatural threat, the villagers tired and thirsty. All afternoon, the six of them have laboured – or rather, directed any farmhand they could bribe with shillings to stack the logs and roll the barrels around the Chapel of St Sythe. The parson has been praying that the fog won't lift, reveal the rude workings of his plan, so there is at least some comfort in the settling gloom. He's impatient, afeared. The past two hours have been taken up with hymns and booze, and several of Rookbill's war stories.

Ephraim is conjuring a retort, something veiled about living by the sword, when he hears the Widow Hocket shriek and she flings her cup away from her, startled, she claims—once the burgess has shaken some sense into her—by the sight of an imp reflected in her drink.

"'Twas Beelzebub his'self, I swear!" Her bosom heaves like a grounded river barge. "Knife bearded and ember eyed! The devil looking in!"

On another day, Ephraim has no doubt that the room would've erupted in thigh slaps, fleer and heckle at the confession of the lady sop. On this, every villager falls still. The devil *is* looking in. Forsooth, he has come to Moonewick and is rapping 'pon the door. The pastor knows this before the echoes fade, his leg in anguish, his throat dry.

Knock. Knock.

"Who in the name—?"

"Hush!" Ephraim presses a finger to his lips, urging Rooksbill to hold his tongue.

The sun, thin as it is, has only slipped into the marshes when Culpopes, the bibliopole, gives a tut and hobbles to the window, daring to look out. It's too late for Ephraim to warn him (for he has read of such things and one does not go a-peeping at pandemonium) and the next moment Culpopes is wailing, his hands clapped to his face. At once, the parson spins from the leaded glass and presses his back against the wall, clutching his crucifix and cane, sinking into the drapes. *Jehovah!* Culpopes tumbles to the floor, the throng crowding around him, clucking. Through the forest of their legs, Ephraim can spy the blood, bright and trickling between the old man's fingers. The daemon outside has blinded him.

"Oh, Ephraim, my master, my heart's gleam." The terrible singsong winds through the timber frame of the inn, and the dirty glass, coming from the hellion outside. Yet it is the voice of his prentice he hears, a pin in the poisoned organ. It is black rock and lava too, the sound of them grinding together. "Come, my love. Let me fondle and kiss you, stroke you to boiling point."

"Begone, Deceiver!"

This is my sixty-sixth exorcism, he reminds himself. *Reepe could do no better than I.* The man outside is no longer his prentice, his body (golden, strong, smelling of the—*enough!*) intruded by the creature he stalks, and he fumbles for the psalter in his tunic, kissing its cover for strength. "Release John Caul, I command it. Return thy vile self to the pit!"

Had we summoned the bishop it would have served us none, the pastor tells himself. *The struggle is between myself and the devil.* He alone is left to this travail.

"Aw," says John Caul in the same mocking tone. He stands so close, the parson can sense it. He stands on the opposite side of the wall, his lips all but pressed to the wood. "You were not so unwilling last night."

"Blasphemy and lies!" Ephraim cries, his blessed book shaking.

The colour climbs again to his cheeks and his rebuttal is not merely for the benefit of the daemon. Yet he is fortunate that every face in the inn, all the villagers crowded against the rear wall, is fixed on the window and heedless to the vituperation—its cruel verity—coming from the darkening street. A shadow falls across the room and not all of it belongs to the dusk.

Gideon Rooksbill has heard enough. Sweeping back his cloak, the old quartermaster draws his flintlock, long handled, cocked and aimed at the window.

"No!"

Hands to his ears, Ephraim braces for the blast, the shattering of glass. Instead, he hears a click and a dismal sound—*phshh*—snapping his gaze back to Rooksbill who stands, red faced and trembling, gawping at the weapon in his fist. The gun, doubtless disused since his retirement, is rusty or poorly knapped; it barely made a spark. The stench in the room, sulphur and smoke, comes not from the corporal's pistol.

"Jupiter's balls! Damp powder!"

Mortified, this would be Fairfax, Rooksbill begins fiddling with the weapon, fumbling in his pocket, presumably for flint, serpentine and ball.

Ephraim shakes his cane.

"Curse you, you bacon-faced fool. You'll not thwart the daemon with that relic."

"What good hast thou scripture done, Sir?" Rooksbill fires back, employing the declined English to skewer him all the deeper. "Is it not thee who's drawn this unearthly evil down upon -?"

His prosecution goes unfinished. The quartermaster, the blood high in his cheeks, utters a wheeze, followed by a choking sound. While the villagers sit breathless, huddling in shadow, Ephraim feels ripe to laugh, stamp his foot at the timely interruption. Then he sees the way the soldier's eyes bulge from his face, the spittle bubbling from his lips. The next moment, Rooksbill drops his gun, goes stumbling to his buckled knees.

"Good God, man. Fetch water! Water!"

No one moves to obey the pastor; a devil is at the door. Cursing, Ephraim hastens forth, shoving his psalter under his arm to better assist his persecutor. He halts, tripping over his cane, when Rooksbill vents a thunderous belch and disgorges his guts on the floor. *Hurk!* An object, fat, speckled and green, glistens between the man's spread hands. It is only at the sound of a second belch, more resonant than the first, that Ephraim realises what he is looking at.

It is a toad. Rooksbill has coughed up a toad.

"How——?"

He scarcely has time to absorb the marvel, astonishing as it is, for that is when the Widow Hocket releases her second shriek of the evening, turning all heads towards her. Slack jawed, the pastor takes in the latest gapeseed, the impossible sight before him. Something, some unspeakable force, has taken hold of the poor woman and plucked her into the air. Shrieking, the Widow goes bumping and rolling over the beams, her skirts and petticoats aflutter, her arms and legs flailing. One of her shoes comes off, a muddy, tatty thing, bouncing off the table below her like the fruit from some blasted tree, rotten and discarded.

"Come out, come out to play, my sweeting," sings Creedence John Caul.

Zounds.

With a crash, the daemon wrenches the struggling Widow through the window of the inn.

OUTSIDE, IT IS RAINING TOADS. They thump on Ephraim's psalter, its poor protection held over his head. Each corpulent, slimy drop of amphibia falls from the heavens and thumps to the earth, the things oscillating songs in the mud, hopping this way and that. Some meet the toes of his boots, spinning out of his way. Others squelch underfoot. He does not wish to look at them, accept the loathsome miracle, the maleficium at work. The fog and the dark churn around him, coiling from creek and bog, and he prays he can make it to the chapel in time, snatch up the lantern there. October hushes through leafless trees. The sea slops and the houses creak, Moonewick holding its breath. Even the crows have fled. His blood pounds.

John Caul cackles. "Will ye not look at my face, master?"

Nay. Ephraim plunges on through the brume. In his panic, he has forgotten his cane in the inn and yet only now marks it, wondering at his firm, untroubled strides even as his wound throbs and stings. The vigour of fear or an evil touch? Should he pray for release or kneel in thanks? Bewilderment swirls in his skull. With an ache in his breast, he knows he mustn't confront his prentice either, lest he be turned into stone.

He is not *John.*

Instead, he looks up at the Widow Hocket, kicking in the air a little way ahead of him, several yards off the ground. She flies upside down, the Widow, her woollen skirts muffling her shrilling. Her drawers are like sails, billowing towards some monstrous misfortune.

Despite his peril, the daemon close by, pity stabs at his heart.

"Unhand her, brute! Your business is with me."

This is true, he imagines. He knows not why John has refrained from attacking him—perhaps it is the crucifix, perhaps not—but the young man merely keeps pace with him a short distance away on his left. Nevertheless, he can guess at it. He touched upon the truth of it in the hall, fumbling in the dark, his suspicions forming. Before, he conjectured that the incubus, this son of an ancient Hebraic goddess, does as it pleases, seducing men and thus stealing their flesh, exploiting each one until it grows weary, or simply hungers for another, its appetite boundless and cruel. Now he lights on a different reason, yet hardly dares think it, cradling the feeble flame of his hope as he strides for the true one in the porch of the chapel. Precarious as it is, it would not have been wise to grab a lantern from the inn, walk this path of cinders, a stretch of no more than fifty steps that feels like the long road from Hell.

To his surprise, the daemon obliges him.

"Very well, master. Anything for you."

From the corner of his eye, Ephraim observes the shadow in the shape of John Caul shrug and raise an arm. In time with it, the Widow Hocket tumbles through the air, the trajectory of her scream descending into a nearby pigsty. There comes a splash, the squeal of hogs. When an obscenity colours the night, Ephraim allows himself a shuddering sigh. He cannot speak for the quartermaster in the inn, and Culpopes may never again pore over his books, yet he will court no more deaths on his watch. The loss of his prentice is enough. And yet—

"What do you want of me, daemon?" Toads thudding on his shoulders, his head, the parson mutters from the corner of his mouth. "Have you not seen the sin in my heart? Already, you have torn him from me."

With its utterance, he is a bottomless pit, empty with the knowledge. Why take another step? Why risk it? Wicked, futile as it was, his passion for John Caul had been a lamp in his loneliness. Without it, he has no reason to go on.

"Can you name it, this sin? Can you, Fear-Not Ephraim Tempest?"

The parson closes his eyes at his grace name. It has been many years and those who once used it are long in their graves. Regardless, his pace does not falter, the Chapel of St Sythe clear in his mind, no more than ten steps ahead. There are words he could summon, oh yes, words from Leviticus or the tale of Sodom, which he's read a thousand times in his own Coggeshall pulpit, moralising to his flock. Then there are lawful terms like 'buggery' or backstreet vulgarities such as 'riding below the crupper'. Ephraim knows them all. Yet when he thinks of Creedence John Caul, the object of his lust and the days of his craving, he accepts that he is in transit to purgatory in any case and none of them strike him as just.

"I cannot."

On the nape of his neck, the daemon's breath, the brim of his hat crisping.

"Have you ever considered that perhaps it is no sin?"

EPHRAIM IS AT THE CHURCH now, mud giving way to stone. Sheltered from the toads, there is scant time to think, to consider the question, and in his heart he already knows the answer, has pondered it across the Tendring Hundred. It amounts to the hypocrisy, the self-defeating nature of his faith. To deny the spirit, to stifle the flesh, the honest, innocuous desires – why, it is to shut the fruits of God in a closet, grouse when the scent turns sour.

This sin, he thinks, *is but the vinegar.*

And guilt its aftertaste, bitter and futile. Drinking its poison, monsters are born. What does it matter? There is only him left to heed his sermon. He is preaching to the perverted. Lost....

Such will be the key to his deliverance. On holy ground, the daemon faltering, the parson turns to face his tormentor.

"Are ye in there, John Caul? Do you know me?"

The creature halts on the doorstep, bedevilled and smirking. In every way, from his pale forearms to his sturdy shoulders to his curly gold hair, he is Creedence John Caul, born of Skye Green and given to a convent, later employed by the parson of Coggeshall. His eyes, however, tourmaline, crimson, say otherwise. Yet the twist of his lips, the tic of one cheek, the sheen of sweat on his brow—all these things that Ephraim has seen have furnished him with an inkling. Even as the incubus hisses, spurning his words, the daemon has given to itself the lie.

"Nameless fiend, you are not so unbound," Ephraim tells it. "Nor are you free of the pit. Pray tell, do I have the right of it? Godsgyfte the cobbler, however many farmhands have fallen to your wiles, you cannot hold them fast. Your leave-taking is not of your doing. Do they fight you, daemon? Do their spirits evict you? And in return you leave them all dead."

"What do you know of the *lilim*, priest?" It slaps a toad out of the air. "You prattle at the hour of your doom."

Ephraim takes a step backward, his leg no longer singing. He turns to one side, reaching for the lantern on the wall placed there earlier. With quivering fingers, he picks up the flint and lights the candle, a thick stub greased with oil. Gently, dancing in time with the pale flame, he straightens and lifts the lantern, shadows dancing a gavotte through the porch.

"I know you require an invitation, Sir, to set one foot in this church."

"Fire, Sir? Forsooth? You mean to controvert me with fire?"

John Caul bats at the lantern. He ventures not over the threshold. Can it smell the serpentine over its own stench? What has a nightmare to fear?

"A bargain then, Sir. Release John Caul. Unscathed, alive. Then I shall give you what you want."

The daemon does not ask him to explain. There is no need to. With the silver receded at Ephraim's temples, his leg straightened, his pain gone, the fiend has been preparing him, his vessel, grooming him like a Suffolk Punch ready to pull a plough, raking up the earth. It is apparent in its gaze as the parson tips his hat and walks into the chapel. Shadows leap to the rafters, the mice scurrying.

Aye, it has been apparent since I went down to my cellar all those days ago, in search of my riding crop.

He recalls the strange clenching in his guts, the tongue that flicked from the eye of his spicket, the anguish clutching his plums. How he howled and fell to his hands and knees, the thought of John Caul a-whirl in his mind. How, like vomit, like a toad, the black shadow had climbed out of him, clawing its way from his throat. It had leapt to the window at once, the incubus, the fiend, and went dancing its way over the green, laughing into the marshes. Free.

Reaching the altar, Ephraim slips off his cloak.

"Come," he speaks softly over his shoulder, placing his hat and the lantern next to the bible on the cold stone surface before him. "Come, if my terms suit."

The pastor is tugging his shirt over his head when he hears the soft thump, the sound of flesh hitting the earth, an echoing groan through the nave. The heat up his spine, the whispering wind, tells him a shadow has entered, discarding John Caul in its wake. Here lies a greater prize, the original flesh, succumbing to its hellish defector. Kicking off his boots, undoing his belt, Ephraim can sense the creature's impressions, its delight, its triumph at its conquest. Together, anchored by the parson's willing form, how it will go a-striding, out over the midge-stirred ponds, out over the lands beyond, out into the waiting world. Oh, what pleasures it will reap, what guileless flesh, what sweet, delicious murder! And when the body rots, when Ephraim is done, on and on the daemon will go, learning of places, people and politics, climbing its way to the throne. A score of years it gives itself, Ephraim reckons, until the empires of the earth rest under its boot.

Glancing skyward, the pastor steps out of his breeches, naked as the night, and bends himself over the altar. Face pressed to the pristine cloth, palms to his buttocks, he parts himself, offering the shadow his portal.

This is the opposite, he thinks. *My invitation.*

It is the 'oculus infame' of the witches. Or something akin to it.

Come, give me your kiss of shame. Come, enter. Come.

There is pain then, a thickness inside of him, hotter, deeper than he has dreamed. His spine concaves, his muscles taut, greater to welcome the daemon, the darkness flooding in. Tourmaline eyed, Ephraim looks up at Jesus on the wall, his own tribulation flying from his throat. Before oblivion claims him, before all the lights go out, he thrusts out his arm, sweeping the lantern to the floor.

Get thee behind me, Satan.

A crash, a spark. The trails of gunpowder lain down that noon—courtesy of a grumbling Rooksbill—go up with a crackle and a flash. Brimstone sours the air, the dust itself igniting, as flames creep across the chapel floor, steady as scarlet penitents, heading for the open door. Beyond, stacked timber surrounds the shrine, piled in the shape of a five-pointed star, a tangled symbol of wood, oil and salt. It is another wonder that Ephraim has read about, a sign to bind the daemons of the air, the spirits of fire, the ghosts of the earth. The villagers have built the circle high enough to lick at the thatch of the church.

As it should be, as he told them, to grant him time to lure the fiend inside where, trapped by holy stones and the symbol, Ephraim would send the bastard back to Hell. *Fear not,* he said to their mired and troubled faces. *The Lord our God shall lead me from the flames, return me safely to your side.* It is to be his final sin, his final falsehood. Perhaps they only half-believed it—Christ knows they've seen wonders this night—but the lot of them want the evil gone and there is no one here who will mourn him.

There is only one way. One last temptation....

Inside him, the daemon is roaring. It rages of treachery, destruction, and threatens carnage, but Ephraim holds it fast. He does not know how long he has. Smoke stings his eyes, sucks at his lungs. The pain is divine. He knows that the creature, pledged to him, cannot simply take flight. His body, a cage, will not withstand the flames. The bible beside him blisters. Jesus ripples on the wall. Together, sinner and summoned, parson and devil, will go down to the Major Infernum.

Clinging to the altar, his seduction, he prays that John Caul will escape.

Will any of them? He can pray.

"Master!"

Coughing, rolling himself along the altar, the stone cool no longer, Ephraim turns to see a figure in the flames, familiar to him as his own buried heart. The organ, thumping, aches regardless to see him. A broad-shouldered mirage, surely—the oaf will fare no better in the furnace, his gold melting in moments. Yet John is here, wonder of wonders! He has wrapped a tapestry around him, torn the Sermon on the Mount from the wall, an act of desperate sacrilege. A beam falls, sparkling, and his prentice skips to one side to avoid it, near tumbling into the blazing pews.

The daemon is howling in Ephraim's head, its fury rattling his bones, but he cannot voice his own objection. The smoke is too thick, his eyes too raw, and although he beats at John's chest when he reaches him—*you fool! You fool!*—he shares not his prentice's strength. He cannot persuade him to unhand him. Grunting, Creedence John Caul slings his master over his shoulder and carries him from that place.

Outside, the villagers gather, clustered behind the pyre, the pentagram. The timber pops, crumbling to charcoal, the wood damp and burning low. The fog rolls on, but the toads have gone, praise Jehovah. The Widow Hocket hops from foot to foot, mud-smeared yet breathing. The tale she will have to tell. Rooksbill comes hobbling from the inn, sword waving in hand. He will tell travellers that he ran the thing through, and for the glory of Cromwell. The others—Grimsditch, the burgess, the maidservant and the farmhands—all stand gawping down at their smouldering saviour, Ephraim bundled upon the ground. John Caul has dragged him from the chapel and brought water from the well, which eagerly the parson drank, the pail dousing coals in his breast. The Widow steps forward with thanks or a prayer, tears carving streaks down her cheeks. Ephraim shakes his head, holds out a hand.

"Come no closer, I beg you." His voice cracks off the stars, Orion shrouded by smoke. The Chapel of St Sythe is ablaze. "Step not inside the circle."

The woman needs no further warning. Forsooth, she needs no words. All she has to do is look at him, the tourmaline gleam of his eyes, to realise the business is not through.

John Caul is weeping. His prentice cradles him, an awkward nurse, and tears hiss off Ephraim's brow, his lips, sweeter than autumn rain. Ephraim does not know how long he has, if the symbol will hold. The shadow in his heart, ever churning, tells him that the matter has shifted. To what degree he cannot gauge. Not here. Not yet. The daemon, the incubus, is within him. In some way he senses its doubt. A contract binds them, flesh to fire. This is not the fate he had planned.

When Ephraim stands, he calls not for his cane. His leg remains renewed, firm as the days when he raced the other novices at Emmanuel College, long before battles and brimstone. Ah, but the night seems so boundless and bright! There should be pain, scalding and the like. All he feels is enlivened. The knowledge prompts a groan.

"Master, what ails you? Tell me. Please."

Gently, Ephraim pushes John away.

"I shall require boots," he says half to himself, mustering a smile. The tapestry is rough, scratching at his skin; he no longer need fret at the cold either. In his skull, the daemon writhes, untouched by the earthly season. "Perhaps I can find some on the way. My lad, I am afraid this is farewell."

Creedence John Caul wipes at his eyes, straightens himself out of manners. He asks not where the pastor will go. It isn't a question of pride. The matter is clear and it would not be wise, would not be safe for the parson to stay. Besides, there is no world that will spare them their secret.

He nods, laden.

"Mysterious ways. Aye."

My John.

Because a man can bleed without visible wounds, Ephraim Tempest turns away. As he walks down the sward, heading for the river and the marsh road beside it, the shadow inside him stirs, whispering of futures unknown, dark paths where no mortal has walked, pleasures no mortal has known.

Ephraim thinks in more practical terms.

He must learn to live with his sins.

THE AUTHORS

PHOENIX ALEXANDER is a queer, Greek-Cypriot writer of science fiction, fantasy, and horror. His stories have appeared in *F&SF*, *Beneath Ceaseless Skies*, and *Black Static*, among others. Links to all of his work may be found at phoenixalexanderauthor.com, and you can follow him on Twitter @dracopoullos.

JAMES BENNETT is a British writer raised in Sussex and South Africa. His travels have furnished him with an abiding love of diverse cultures, history, and mythology. His short fiction has appeared internationally, and his debut novel *Chasing Embers* was shortlisted for Best Newcomer at the British Fantasy Awards 2017. His latest fiction can be found in the well-received *The Book of Queer Saints*, *BFS Horizons*, and *The Dark*. Novella *The Dust of the Red Rose Knight* came out in March 2023 and a short story collection *Preaching to the Perverted* is set to follow next year from esteemed publisher Lethe Press. James lives in the South of Spain where he's currently working on a new novel.

TOM CARDAMONE is the editor of *Crashing Cathedrals: Edmund White by the Book*, and the author of the Lambda Literary Award-winning speculative novella *Green Thumb* as well as the erotic fantasy *The Lurid Sea* and other works of fiction, including two short story collections. Additionally, he has edited *The Lost Library: Gay Fiction Rediscovered* and co-edited *Fever Spores: The Queer Reclamation of William S. Burroughs*.

EDWARD M. COHEN's story collection *Before Stonewall* was published by Awst Press; his novel, *$250,000*, by G.P. Putnam's Sons; his novella, "A Visit to my Father with my Son," by Running Wild Press; his chapbook, "Grim Gay Tales," by Fjords Review.

PETER DUBÉ is a multi-genre writer and translator, and the author, co-author or editor of a dozen books of fiction, non-fiction and poetry. His novella, *Subtle Bodies*, an imagined life of French surrealist René Crevel, was a finalist for the Shirley Jackson Award and his most recent work, a novel in prose poems entitled *The Headless Man*, was shortlisted for both the A. M. Klein Prize and the ReLit award. In addition to his creative work, Dubé is co-editor of *The Philosophical Egg*, an organ of living surrealism and is a member of the editorial committee for the contemporary art magazine, *Espace Art Actuel*. He lives and writes in his hometown of Montreal.

L.A. FIELDS is the award-winning author of literary, historical, and LGBT fiction. She has an MFA, a day job, and a calico cat.

RIEN GRAY is a queer, nonbinary writer of horror, erotica, and romance. Their work has been previously published in Cipher Press' Unreal Sex and Cursed Morsels' Shredded, and they have an ongoing series starring a nonbinary assassin, starting with Love Kills Twice. You can find them on Twitter @riengray. They live in Chicago.

LAWRIE JACKSON has been writing erotica for a few years now, including Misadventure in Space and Time and Muscle Worshippers. His alter-ego has sold stories to other Lethe Press anthologies.

JOEL LANE was the author of two novels, *From Blue to Black* and *The Blue Mask*; several short story collections, *The Earth Wire, The Lost District, The Terrible Changes, Do Not Pass Go, Where Furnaces Burn, The Anniversary of Never* and *Scar City*; a novella, *The Witnesses Are Gone*; and four volumes of poetry, *The Edge of the Screen, Trouble in the Heartland, The Autumn Myth* and *Instinct*. He edited three anthologies of short stories, *Birmingham Noir* (with Steve Bishop), *Beneath the Ground* and *Never Again* (with Allyson Bird). He won an Eric Gregory Award, two British Fantasy Awards and a World Fantasy Award. Born in Exeter in 1963, he lived most of his life in Birmingham, where he died in 2013. Much of his fiction is in the process of being reissued by Influx Press.

NICK MAMATAS is the author of several novels, including *The Second Shooter* and *I Am Providence*. His short fiction has appeared in *Best American Mystery Stories, Tor.com, Weird Tales, Asimov's Science Fiction* and many other venues. Nick is also an anthologist; his most recent title is *Wonder and Glory Forever: Awe-Inspiring Lovecraftian Fiction*. Nick's fiction and editorial work have variously been nominated for the Hugo, Bram Stoker, Shirley Jackson, Locus, and World Fantasy awards.

IAN MUNESHWAR is a Boston-based writer and teacher. His short fiction has sold to venues such as *Clarkesworld, Strange Horizons*, and *Black Static*, and has been selected for *Year's Best Weird Fiction* and *The Year's Best Dark Fantasy & Horror*. He has taught writing in the Transitional Year Program at Brandeis University, in the Experimental College at Tufts University, and in Clarion West's online workshops. You can find out more about his work at ianmineshwar.com.

DREW PISARRA is the author of two poetry collections, Periodic Boyfriends and Infinity Standing Up, as well as two short story collections You're Pretty Gay and Publick Spanking. His first radio play, The Strange Case of Nick M. was commissioned by Imago Theatre and debuted on K-BOO FM. A literary grantee of Café Royal Cultural Foundation and Curious Elixirs: Curious Creators, he was also a participating poet in A Gathering of the Tribes, a two-day reading marathon at The Whitney Bienniel 2022: Quiet As Its Kept.

An emerging writer, ROBIN ROBINSON is a bisexual transgender man, and much of this story is abstracted from my own experience. Robin has published a poem *The Mandarin Literary Magazine* and was a semi-finalist in The Blank Theater's Young Playwright's Festival in 2019. They are pursuing a degree in Literature, with a concentration in Fiction Writing, at the University of California, Santa Cruz.

NABEN RUTHNUM is the author of *Helpmeet, A Hero of Our Time* and other books. He lives in Toronto.

ELTON SKELTER is a queer horror author from the South West of England, where he lives a quiet life as a part-time customer services rep to finance his writing ambitions. He has short stories from Dark Ink Matter in the Bram Stoker Award and Splatterpunk Award nominated *Human Monsters Anthology* and a story in the *ABCs of Terror Volume 4*. His debut novel, *Life Support*, was released in June 2023.

DOUG WEAVER holds degrees in music, journalism, and creative writing, all from California State University Northridge. His debut novel *Be Safe*, about a group of HIV-positive gay men in Los Angeles, was published in 2017. Earlier in his career, having *nearly* perfected the use and commodification of various illegal drugs, Weaver found himself the recipient of generous amounts of hospitality courtesy of Men's Central Jail in Downtown L.A. He lives in Long Beach, California with a certain cairn terrier named Duffy, and he currently he teaches English at a liberal arts university in Los Angeles. He enjoys playing Bach at the piano.

TENNESSEE WILLIAMS (Thomas Lanier Williams III) is he is considered among the three foremost playwrights of 20th-century American drama. Think the Southern Gothic: *A Streetcar Named Desire* or *Cat on a Hot Tin Roof*. He also wrote short stories, poetry, essays, as well as memoirs. Gay men should read his collection, *One Arm and Other Stories*.

LC VON HESSEN (they/them) is a writer of horror, weird fiction, and various unpleasantness. Their work has appeared in such publications as Bound in Flesh, Stories of the Eye, The Pinworm Factory, The Book of Queer Saints, Your Body is Not Your Body, It Was All a Dream, Neo-Decadence Evangelion, and multiple volumes of Nightscript and Vastarien. Their debut short story collection will be released in 2024 through Grimscribe Press. An ex-Midwesterner, von Hessen lives in Brooklyn with a talkative orange cat.

THE EDITOR

STEVE BERMAN is a Lambda Literary Award-winning editor of forty anthologies, almost all queer and/or speculative fiction. Many years ago: One night in bed, he turned to the teenager beside him, a chatty and bratty boy, and covered his mouth with one hand. The boy grew silent, grew still—Steve thought at the time, the boy relaxed, but the truth was the boy tensed, stirring only on the inside, skull and spine, crotch and crossed toes. Steve never knew. How could he when they broke apart? Then, years later, the boy, now a chatty (perhaps bratty) man, messaged Steve after seeing his name on a book and remembering that night especially, messaged Steve, and told him that the moment shared in bed instilled in him a fetish to be asphyxiated during sex. Steve resides in Western Massachusetts.

Printed in the USA
CPSIA information can be obtained
at www.ICGtesting.com
JSHW022053121023
50071JS00004B/135